STRANGE

ROBBY

SELINA ROSEN

Meisha Merlin Publishing, Inc.
Atlanta, GA

STRANGE ROBBY Copyright © 2006 by Selina Rosen

This book is printed on an acid-free and buffered paper that meets the NISO standard ANSI/NISO Z39.48-1992, Permanence of Paper for Publications and Documents in Libraries and Archives.

Strange Robby

Published by Meisha Merlin Publishing, Inc.
PO Box 7
Decatur, GA 30031

Editing by Stephen Pagel
Copyediting Beverly Hale
Interior layout by Lynn Swetz
Cover art by Hoang Nguyn
Cover design by Kevin Murphy

ISBN: Hard Cover 1-59222-046-0
ISBN: Soft Cover 1-59222-047-9

http://www.MeishaMerlin.com
First MM Publishing edition: July 2006

Printed in Canada
0 9 8 7 6 5 4 3 2 1

For Joy Hatcher, my one true fan,
for always keeping the faith.

STRANGE

ROBBY

SELINA ROSEN

CHAPTER ONE

"And how does the wise man die? Just like the fool.
Therefore I hated my life; because the work that is
done under the sun was grievous to me: for all is
vanity and a striving after wind." Ecclesiastes 2:16-17

ROBBY PICKED UP the old TV and put it in the truck with the other items. It had been a long day, and he was tired. He took the money the woman handed him, thanked her as he stuffed it into his pocket, and then he started down the alley glad that had been his last pick up for the day. Now he could go home. It wasn't that there was no work waiting for him there, just that he didn't feel as rushed when he was working at home.

He felt it first. He wanted to ignore it, tried, but he couldn't. He looked up the alley and saw him—saw *it*, a black mark dancing across the face of the planet. He stared at that darkness, and as he did he saw what was in the man's mind; the sins of his past, the crimes he had committed and those he longed to commit. Robby saw the evil blackness of the man's soul, and though he wanted to, he couldn't just walk away.

SPIDER WEBB LOOKED down at the corpse then at her partner, Tommy Chan.

"Looks dead ta me," she said.

Tommy nodded and laughed. "Crying shame, that."

"How about a little respect here, detectives. The man *is* dead. He's been murdered." Lieutenant Toby looked at the body and made a face. "Or something. This is the sixth one like this in three months. I don't think *that's* any laughing matter. Don't you guys have any leads yet?"

Spider started to say exactly what she was thinking, but Tommy elbowed her in the ribs and answered the lieutenant, "Give us a break, Lieutenant. We aren't the only ones on this case. The FBI is just as clueless as we are. This guy is sharp; he leaves no evidence. Even forensics can't figure out how he's doing it. Believe me, we are doing the best we can with what little we've got."

"The captain's giving birth to monkeys over this shit. The mayor keeps promising the public we'll catch him any day, and we don't have a fucking clue."

"The two beat cops said they saw a man run away from the scene. They got a pretty good description of him." Tommy held up his comlink communicator. "Call up suspect F6," he ordered. A three dimensional holographic image of a weasel-faced white guy appeared over his comlink. "Spider and I are going to see if we can't track him down."

"Good idea. This shit here is more or less up to forensics now." He looked at the face of the corpse and grimaced. "Poor fucker died screaming…"

Spider started to say something, but Tommy took hold of her arm and dragged her away.

"Could you at least *pretend* to be concerned?" Tommy whispered angrily as they walked away.

Spider only shrugged. "Not about that."

CARRIE LONG WATCHED the two veteran detectives as they walked away from the crime scene, more because she found Spider Webb incredibly intriguing then anything else. The woman was almost six feet tall and slender, with short, black hair and blue-gray eyes that seemed to dance when she was amused—which she seemed to be most of the time. Her skin was uncommonly fair but not in a sickly way. Carrie thought she was stunning. As assistant district attorney it was her job to look for clues that might eventually lead to a conviction if they actually caught the killer, but she was far more interested in where Detective Webb and her partner were going than the crime scene.

She watched them walk away thinking that you most probably couldn't find two more different people. Tommy Chan was Asian, probably topped out at around five foot six and was built like a small tank. He wore his long hair in a ponytail that reached to the middle of his back and looked serious even when he was joking.

Carrie tried to think of some good reason to follow them, but the only good one was the one that she didn't want to admit even to herself. Those two knew more than they were saying; she was sure of it.

For the thousandth time she found herself wondering why she only seemed to be attracted to the kind of women who were nothing but trouble.

"Ms Long."

Carrie's head snapped up, and she must have looked as startled as she felt, because the young officer looked concerned as he asked. "You all right Ms. Long?"

"Ah...gruesome scene." She shrugged. "What was it you wanted?"

"The lieutenant wanted to show you something." He nodded towards the body with a sympathetic look on his face.

Carrie nodded silently and walked over. Bodies, no matter how badly disfigured, didn't bother her nearly so badly as someone catching her with her guard down.

TOMMY AND SPIDER walked up to the bar, and Tommy showed the holograph of the "suspect" to the bartender.

"You see this guy around, Tony?"

Tony shrugged. "He doesn't look familiar."

Tommy turned off the image and put his comlink away. "In that case, bring us a couple of beers."

The bartender handed them their drinks and they walked over to a corner booth and sat down. Tommy took his comlink out of his pocket and purposely dropped it onto the surface of the table.

"Oh shit." He picked it up and showed it to Spider. "Would you look at that? It erased the composite drawing of the suspect. Wouldn't you know it? I didn't take the three seconds it takes to save it on the main frame."

Spider shook her head, a look of mock horror on her face. "How very careless of you! Especially after the Lieutenant gave us all that huge briefing addressing that very subject just this morning...Speaking of ole needle butt, what was all that bull shit back at the crime scene about?"

"Gee, I don't know, maybe it had something to do with you walking up on the murder scene and dancing a jig around the corpse," Tommy said. "I can't imagine why the lieutenant might think that maybe we weren't putting our best efforts into this case."

"That 'poor fucker' was a child molester with six convictions. Jails get overcrowded, some bleeding-heart dove starts screaming that it's 'uncivilized' to keep people locked up under those conditions, and so they let...how many of them go this month?"

"Six hundred and fifty two. Mostly first offenders..."

"That's not the fucking point. We catch them, and the system lets them go on what ever the technicality of the month is. If someone's willing to come along and kill 'em, I say we give 'em a fucking reward and a goddamn medal instead of trying to catch him and lock him up."

"We're not going to catch him if we don't try." Tommy took a long sip of his beer and looked around to make sure no one was watching, although it was hard to say whether it was because he was drinking or because of what he'd just said.

"Well, we're going to have to at least start going through the motions, or someone is going to catch on," Spider said, lowering her voice still further.

Tommy nodded. "Well, it doesn't help that you keep having an orgasm every time we find a stiff."

"I'm louder when I'm having orgasm, but you're right. I'll try to cool it. It's just hard for me to get too worked up when the so-called 'victim' is a fucking psychopath in his own right. It's poetic justice if you ask me."

"Nobody's asking you, so just keep your big mouth shut for a change. You don't have to act grief stricken, but you don't need to rent a hall and throw a kegger, either."

Spider nodded her understanding.

"Aren't you going to drink your beer?"

"We're on duty, Tommy," Spider said.

Tommy looked at her in disbelief. "Tampering with evidence is okay, but drinking a fucking beer..."

"Okay, all right." She laughed, wrapped her hand around the bottle and raised it to her lips.

Tommy found himself staring at her hands again. He tried not to, but they fascinated him. Her fingers were abnormally long— freakish even. On a six-foot seven-inch basketball player they would have been proportional, but not a five-foot eleven-inch woman. He looked too long, and she caught him—again.

"Don't start with my fucking hands again," she hissed at him across the table.

He laughed and shook his head. They had been partners too long. He sighed and looked at his beer bottle. "Remember when we first started? Green kids right out of the academy…"

"I wasn't exactly a green kid, but yeah, I remember. We thought we were going to change the world—or at least the city," Spider said, a far away look in her eye.

"Now we're in our late thirties. I was almost killed once. You've been shot twice. I'm on my second marriage. You have no fucking life to speak of, and what the hell for? So that we can lock them up and the fucking lawyers can let them go. We haven't changed a goddamn thing."

"Speak for yourself. I change my underwear every day." Spider shrugged at the pained look he gave her. "And I don't have a life for a very good reason. I haven't figured out what it is yet, but I'll let you know as soon as I do."

They both laughed.

"Maybe we never should have gotten our fucking shields. We should have just gotten some big, bad-assed guns and started blowing shit heads away," Tommy said, only half kidding.

"I've thought about that, but the pay and bennies are nonexistent for street vigilantes."

They laughed again, then looked at each other, all hint of amusement gone.

"So…" Spider took a drink of her beer. "What now, pard, huh? Could we really do anything else? What else do we know? We've become those people we used to hate. We don't care about the job anymore. We're just here for the good insurance program and so we can collect our pensions. We're pathetic."

Tommy nodded. "It's a sad statement to make that the only good I feel I've done is the three perps I killed in the line of duty, and the fact that we are now running interference for a serial killer."

"Sadder still, I'd gladly lose my job, my benefits and my pension to protect him. After all, he's living my dream," Spider added.

"Hard to believe that in our old age when we look back at our lives our finest moment will be when we helped keep a killer *on* the streets."

SPIDER FIXED HIS pillows and then sat down beside his bed.

"You're looking good today, Henry. The weather outside is brutal—cold and windy. Weather man says it might snow."

She sighed, looking into his face for any sign. Any sign at all that he heard her.

"Any way, the Fry Guy—that's what the news people call him—anyway, he got another one today. This one was a child molester. A guy the system decided was rehabilitated on six different occasions.

"I hope they never catch this guy, Henry. Tommy and I were talking today. This guy is kind of doing our job for us. Doing the job the way it ought to be done. Get these guys off the streets and keep them off in a way that means they'll never be a threat again, and in a way that they don't cost us any money. We're supposed to catch this guy—bring *him* to so-called justice. But how can I justify doing that?" She turned her head and looked out the window. "You know what's ironic? If we caught this guy he'd probably get life in prison without parole—or the chair. And for what? For doing what should have been done in the first place, except that our namby-pamby government doesn't have the stomach for it. You kill a violent criminal, and they don't hurt anyone ever again.

"They're painting a picture of this guy as some kind of psychotic with a God complex, but I think this guy is someone just like you and me, Henry. A man who's sick to death of watching the guilty run free while the rest of us live in self-made prisons to keep them from raping or killing us. I thought at first that it was a cop, maybe retired, who had access to these guys' records. Problem with that theory is that with the new comlink system any one in law enforcement on any level can call up any case file, so it doesn't really narrow the list."

She looked back at Henry. "I don't think it's a cop anymore, anyway. I think—stop me if this sounds too crazy. I think this guy is…well, different. Not like you and me. Well, not like you, anyway. You know how he's killing them? Their eyes are burned out. It's like their brains were cooked in their heads. The guys in forensics say it's like microwaves or something, but they don't have a clue as to how or why. They think maybe he got hold of some kind of new military weapon, but if it is, the military isn't claiming it.

"I think this guy has something else, though. Some kind of telepathic power—pyrokinesis or some damn thing. Of course I'm not going to tell anyone but you that—they'd have me locked up."

"Is SHE THE guy's wife?" The nurse was new on the floor.

The head nurse looked where the woman was pointing and sighed. "No. The guy doesn't have any family. That woman is a police officer."

"She's trying to find out who did this to him?"

"They caught the men who did this to him. It's really a very sad story. A young man was attacked by a gang of thugs. That man, a total stranger, ran in to try and save him, and the attackers shot him four times and killed the other man any way. The man he tried to save was that woman's brother. She comes here every day and sits and talks to him for fifteen minutes to an hour. She's paying to keep him here, otherwise he'd be sent to some state run facility. It costs her a small fortune. I guess she feels responsible for him because of what he tried to do for her brother." She shrugged. "I can't say that I get it."

"How long has he been in a coma?"

"Sixteen years."

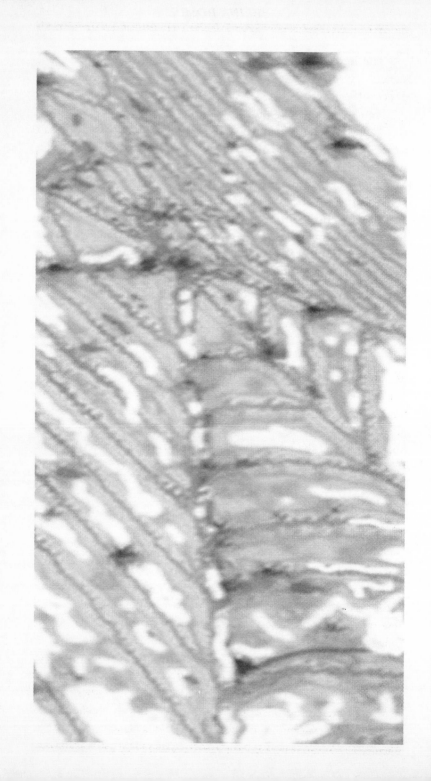

CHAPTER TWO

*"For there is a man whose labor is with wisdom and
with knowledge, and with skill; yet he must leave
it for a portion to a man who has not labored in it.
This also is a vanity and a great evil."* Ecclesiastes 2:21

ROBBY PULLED UP into the driveway and was greeted by his two youngest siblings—Duane, four, and Elvita, three. His grandmother waved to him from the window, and he smiled and waved back. She was too old to keep up with the kids for long, but she did her best until he could get home.

He was tired; he never got much sleep. He had a lucrative business picking up the trash the garbage men wouldn't—the big stuff too bulky to go into the compactors or trash bags.

He got up and went to work picking up people's trash at five in the morning. He got home at noon, and then he went to work turning one person's trash into another person's treasure. When his other five siblings got home from school he tried to help them with their homework. He cooked their meals and made sure they kept themselves and the house clean. He tried to teach them values and give them love and discipline. He also tried to give them what he never had—a childhood.

Robby's life had never been normal. Born Robert Strange, he hadn't been in school long when the other kids had started calling him Strange Robby.

His white father had been killed during a mugging when he was only two. His mother hadn't taken his death well, and she had moved from Shea City to LA where she apparently tried to sleep her way through the phone book. There was a long string of men, only a few that Robby really remembered, and all of those he wished he didn't. Mostly he remembered being cold, hungry, and lonely.

When Robby was five, his mom came up pregnant and married the first man who showed up with a paycheck. Janice was born, and eleven months later Evan was born. *Their* father decided it was too much responsibility, and he ran off with a coke whore. Or at least that's what his mother screamed when she was mad. She ended up in the arms of a grade A, number one creep named Jimmy Brown. Brown had been a drug user for years, and it wasn't long until he had their mother hooked on crack cocaine. He would drop in long enough to father a baby and take all their money, and then he would be gone again.

His mother became less and less responsible. She would leave and be gone for weeks at a time. So when Robby was ten, he started taking care of the house and caring for his brothers and sisters. That was the year Donna was born. Then Jimmy came back and Mama had Colistia, then he came back again and she had Devan. At the ripe old age of twelve, Robby was caring for five children including three babies who had to be changed, fed, and bathed regularly. Needless to say, Robby had to quit school, but he made sure the other school-aged kids went. Not only did it mean that they got an education, but it meant that they got to eat two square meals a day. By helping them with their homework over the years, he'd managed to get the rest of his education, even if it wasn't official.

His mother had often been gone as much as she was home. She spent all their—her's and Robby's—Social Security death benefits on dope and Jimmy Brown, so Robby went to work at a local pizza restaurant. He would sweep the sidewalks and the building, and the owner would give him a large pizza and a big salad every day. Eventually, the man was so impressed with Robby's work that he let him clean the bathrooms and threw in a large soda and ten dollars. The money helped Robby get the kids some of the things they needed.

One day when Jimmy walked in with his mama they were both high, and Robby saw the blackness for the first time. He saw what the man did, and what he wanted to do. The evil in the man's soul was clear, and Robby felt the power inside himself—the power to stop the blackness from creeping into anyone else's life ever again.

That night Jimmy ate all the pizza, and the kids went to bed hungry. Then he beat up their mama, stole the last of her money and went off—no doubt to buy more drugs.

Robby followed Jimmy, pulled along by the darkness that was suddenly as tangible to him as any rope. Jimmy hadn't seen him—hadn't heard him. It was as if Robby couldn't be seen at all. As if for a little while he was hidden in the trail left by Jimmy's overwhelming evil. He followed Jimmy down a dead end alley. In the trash and filth Jimmy looked nervously at his watch.

"Where the fuck is that nigger?" he cursed.

Robby walked out of the shadows and smiled at Jimmy as if he were the ice-cream man, and Robby had two quarters.

Jimmy jumped, startled by the suddenness with which Robby had appeared. "You! What the hell are you doing here?"

"I want you to give back our money," Robby said.

"Yeah…Well, you know what they say, boy, wish in one hand and shit in the other…"

"Ya fucking bastard, give me our money!" Robby screamed. Inside he could feel the power building, rolling like storm clouds in his belly.

Jimmy rolled up his sleeves.

"Now I'm gonna have to kick your worthless half-breed butt." As he spoke, he moved quickly to grab Robby.

Robby smiled even bigger and struck out with the power.

Jimmy flew backwards striking the side of the building and sliding down it. Dazed, he looked up at Robby who had moved to stand just in front of him.

"What the fuck!"

Robby laughed, exhilarated by the power that surged through him. Power that not only could destroy Jimmy but that wanted to, needed to.

"Give me back the money," Robby ordered.

Jimmy got shakily to his feet and dug in his pocket. He pulled the money out and threw it at Robby.

Robby caught it easily and put it into his own pocket. Then he just stood there staring at Jimmy.

Jimmy cringed. He seemed to know what he was up against.

"Now go on, get out of here," Jimmy said. He was too obviously nervous for the order to carry any weight.

Robby smiled again and shook his head no. "I've seen what you've done and what you have a mind to do. I'm not going to let you do that to my sisters. I'm not going to let your darkness touch even one more soul."

Jimmy laughed nervously. "So what ya gonna do, kid?"

"This." Robby unleashed the power. It hit Jimmy like a red hot Mack truck, slammed him into the brick wall at his back, and all but blew him to pieces.

Robby searched, but could find no remorse for his act. Jimmy was going to hurt his sisters. He couldn't—wouldn't—allow that.

The police found just enough of Jimmy to figure out who he had been. They asked his mama about Jimmy. What was he doing in the alley? Who were his friends? Had he acted like he was afraid of anyone? But they never asked why Robby was home in the middle of a school day, or why she was stoned out of her head with three babies in the house. No one gave a damn about a coked-out nigger tramp or her bastard children.

His mother cried because Jimmy was dead. She screamed at Robby and the other kids because she said it was their fault that he'd left. That was when Robby knew he had to get those kids and himself out of there. She didn't care about them, and it would only be a matter of time until she brought in another man. Maybe he'd even be worse than Jimmy.

Robby called his maternal grandmother. She was old and frail and poor as a church mouse, but she put together the bus fare and sent it to them.

Robby waited till his mother went off again, then he loaded up the kids and their few belongs, and at fourteen he left LA and traveled half way across the country to Shea City.

His grandmother had hugs for every one of them, but the house was small—only two bedrooms and one bath—and in bad need of repair. The kitchen sink drain didn't work, there was no hot water, and several windows were broken.

Grandma said the damage came from raising four kids in a little shack. The house was also filthy, and Robby soon realized why—his grandmother wasn't in much better shape than the house. It was winter, and the cold blew through the walls like they weren't there. It was no wonder; half the underpinning had crumbled away, and there were cracks in the walls you could throw a cat through.

Robby started boiling water on the cook stove and found what was left of the cleaning supplies. Then he went to work. He got Evan and Janice to help while Granny told them it wasn't necessary and played with the babies.

All in all, Robby had decided it was the greatest place he had ever lived. For one thing there was a yard for the kids to play in. But best of all, for the first time there was an adult around who actually loved them and cared what happened to them.

The next day Robby sent the kids off to school, left the babies with his grandmother, and went out to find work. He got a job at a local grocery store sweeping floors and cleaning out the warehouse. It didn't pay much, but it was a great job. It was only a block from their house, and Robby brought home produce, milk, and bread when it was too old to be sold. He told them it was for his uncle's pigs, and they pretended to believe him. They even let him take home boxes, pallets, and metal shelf sets they weren't using any more, which Robby used to repair the damage to the house.

Some old plastic displays he measured, cut, and used to repair the broken windowpanes. He used the cardboard boxes to cover holes on the inside walls and tore the wooden pallets apart and used the wood to repair the holes on the outside. He cleared the sink drain and fixed the holes in it with duct tape. He got the hot water heater running with a simple good cleaning.

After he finally got the house squared away, Robby found his grandfather's truck and all his tools out in the shed. The truck hadn't run in years his grandma said, but Robby had a knack for fixing things, and he got the truck running and kept it that way.

Robby helped his grandmother with the utility bills. When he was sixteen he got a real driver's license. That was when he noticed how much good stuff people threw away. He started to collect the things he found in alleys and used them to fix their home up right. He even found enough paint to paint it inside and out—even though the outside was painted an odd green color because the only way he had enough paint from all that he'd found thrown away was to mix them together.

Just when things were starting to get good their mother called, wanting to send them two more babies. Robby took them on the condition that his mother send with them a document proving that she'd had her tubes tied.

Robby had worked long and hard. His grandmother couldn't take care of the new babies during the day, so he started his trash hauling business at night so that he could be home during the day. Evan and Janice would be there to help watch them at night.

Robby had more than his fair share of responsibilities. He had a lot of people depending on him and a power that wouldn't be denied.

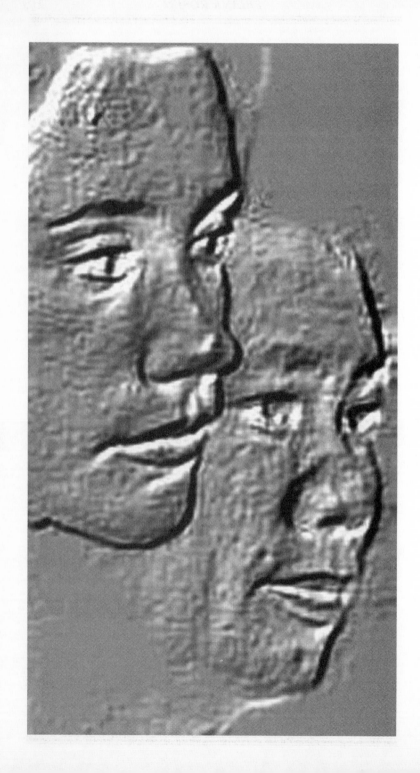

CHAPTER THREE

"There is one alone, without a companion; yea he has neither son nor brother: yet is there no end of all his labor; neither is his eye satisfied with riches: he may say, For whom then do I labor, and bereave my soul of good? This is also vanity; indeed it is a sorry business." Ecclesiastics 4:8

"IT'S MOMENTS LIKE this that make this job bearable," Tommy said as he rounded the corner.

"It's like a bandage on a bullet wound, but it's better than nothing. God, I really need this to go down right," Spider said, crossing her fingers as Tommy parked the car.

"Okay, but remember…why are we here?"

"Because they're hiding a fucking suspect in a double homicide in there."

"But we couldn't prove that, so they wouldn't give us a search warrant. So…Why are we here?"

"Because the sleaze-ball is here."

"Why are we going to break in without a search warrant?"

"Because the stupid fucking judge wouldn't grant one."

"Come on, Spider, work with me," he said with exaggerated patience.

"We heard a woman screaming for help," she said without any enthusiasm.

"Exactly." He looked at his watch. "And that should happen any time now, so…Comlinks on; it's show time."

They hung their comlinks around their necks and turned them on.

"We are staking out a warehouse where we believe Justin Kent may be hiding. He is a suspect in the shooting deaths of his ex-girlfriend, Katie Cando, and a business associate, Bill Smith. The time now is eight o'clock," Tommy said for the comlink's sake.

"Was that a scream I heard?" Spider asked woodenly.

Tommy shot her a heated look, and she shrugged. A minute later the woman screamed.

"Yes, I did hear a scream."

The woman yelled for help.

"It seems to be coming from the building. Let's go," Spider said in the same wooden tone. She smiled broadly at Tommy and jumped out of the car.

Tommy was a few feet behind her when she burst through the front door, and he knew even before he saw the fifteen big hairy guys inside that this was a mistake. Spider was on the jazz, and when she was "rock'n" you couldn't expect anything but pure insanity from her.

"Where's the girl?" Spider screamed.

The fifteen men inside just froze in place. There were boxes everywhere. One man held a big bag of what could only be coke.

"You're under arrest for possession with intent to sell, and..." Tommy looked around till he found Justin Kent. "You're under arrest for the murders of Katie Cando and Bill Smith."

"Where's your search warrant fuzz?" a big man asked.

"We heard a young woman yelling for help, and..." he saw one of them move.

So did Spider. She didn't fire her gun. Instead, she landed a flying kick into the guy's head. As his gun spun out across the floor, she smashed her own gun and her abnormally large fist into the face of another man.

Tommy took a deep breath and started kicking some ass. He wasn't a big guy, but he was a martial artist of superb ability, and the way he figured it, the odds were in their favor even if the big shots back at the station wouldn't be. By the time the back-up units got there, all fifteen men were nursing serious wounds, and all the uniformed officers had to do was cuff them and put them into cars—some of which happened to be ambulances.

Tommy heard his comlink buzz and cringed. Spider walked up to him and smiled broadly with her badly bleeding mouth. He shook his head. The real problem with the woman was that she had a serious death wish and a great deal of tolerance for pain. Tommy answered his comlink while Spider ignored hers and walked over to talk to the other officers.

"Chan!" the lieutenant nearly yelled. "You and your partner get your asses down to the station right now!"

"Just our asses, Sir?" Spider asked over Tommy's shoulder.

"What's that, Chan?" the Lieutenant asked.

"Be there as soon as we can, sir," Tommy said with mock enthusiasm.

"Spider!" Tommy turned to glare at her and she just smiled back. He turned off his comlink and made sure hers was off, too—which it was. "You're either going to get me killed or shit-canned. Come on, let's get back to the station."

Spider nodded. She knew the lieutenant wanted to scream at them. No big deal. It wasn't the first time, and it wouldn't be the last.

"They were all over me," the Latino girl cried to a uniformed officer taking her statement on his comlink. "Thank God the officers got here when they did."

Spider looked at her and winked.

She nodded back carefully. She knew they were good for the money.

"YOU BETTER BE damned glad that this all looks legit," the lieutenant said. He looked at Spider, and more pointedly at her swollen, bloody lip. "Do you think you could wash your face, detective?"

"Not just yet. I'm savoring the moment," she said, smiling broadly.

"Look at you two. Don't think I don't know what you did out there, because I do."

"We brought in a murder suspect who was right where we said he was. Just for gravy, we brought down one of the biggest cocaine rings in the city. Not bad for a day's work," Tommy said.

The lieutenant sighed. "I understand all that, but I think what we're talking about with you two is serious burn out."

Spider looked at her nails and picked at a broken one. "There isn't a cop that's been on the force for over ten years that isn't a burn out. And everyone knows why. You bust some poor *schmuck* for something you don't really think is a crime—but that the book tells you is—so you gottah bust them. When you take them in it'll stick like flies to shit, and those poor bastards—who haven't really done a damn thing—will rot in jail, and the brass will all tell us what a good job we did. Meanwhile when we do something like we did tonight to bring some scum-sucking leeches a little justice, instead of saying those fuckers are as guilty as sin and however you got them is all right by me, you immediately start worrying about *their* fucking rights, looking for any reason to put them right back on the street."

Tommy buried his face in his hands and wished his partner could ever just think something without saying it.

"Everyone starts looking for little pockets of the law that they can hide in and save their fucking filthy little asses. You want less burn out? It's simple. Leave decent people the hell alone, and put the fucking bastards away for life, or gas them, or just blow their brains out. But don't waste my tax money and my time letting them dance out of the charges on 'technicalities.' If they had given us the friggin' search warrant that we asked for, there would be no questions asked right now. But to get a search warrant anymore you have to walk on fucking water, or be a cable guy and say someone's a terrorist. Screw that! Instead of berating us you ought to be praising us, because this time the good guys found a way around the system. This time we used the freaking loophole!"

Tommy could see the look on the lieutenant's face change from one of irritation to rage, and he knew what was coming next.

IT WAS COLD, and they were sitting in the middle of the park on a concrete bench that was apparently created for the sole purpose of giving hemorrhoids the size of grapefruits to anyone who sat on it for any length of time.

And they were sitting here for the third night in a row.

Tommy turned and glared at Spider. "I hate you," he said through chattering teeth.

"Me? Why me?" Spider asked innocently. "It's the friggin' lieuten…"

"All you had to do was sit there and let him bitch. Why can't you ever sit there and just listen, without saying anything?"

"Because he pisses me off."

"He pisses *everyone* off. That's his fucking job," Tommy all but shouted. "Hell, even his wife hates him. But you don't have to open your mouth. Just once couldn't you keep your mouth shut?"

"Laura still mad at me?" Spider asked.

"It's our anniversary, and I'm sitting on a friggin' bench on the coldest night of the year on some bullshit stake-out. What do you think?"

Spider shrugged.

"She thinks you are the friggin' anti-Christ."

"Is that bad?" Spider asked.

"It is to her," Tommy said. "I can't feel my hands. My toes are like frozen rocks in my shoes, and do you know why?"

"Well, apparently, if I understand your bitching correctly, it's because I don't know when to keep my mouth shut."

"Both of you shut up. The frigging suspect is in our sights," a voice inside their ears said.

"Ah! A voice from above," Spider said.

"See? That's what I mean. Talk, talk, fucking talking all the time," Tommy scolded her.

"Tommy, would you shut up? The suspect is looking at you," the voice in their ears said.

"Ah, ha!" Spider said triumphantly.

Tommy saw the suspect then; he was eyeing them. In fact, he had stopped walking. Shit! If they blew this on top of all the other crap, they'd be on shit detail for the next year. He grabbed Spider in an embrace and kissed her. They exchanged a long, passionate kiss, and the suspect started walking again. They parted and looked at each other lovingly.

"Where the hell did that come from?" Spider cooed.

"I was thinking about my wife," Tommy cooed back.

Spider smiled wickedly. "That's funny, so was I."

Tommy shook his head in disbelief. "You are a twisted bitch."

The suspect passed them. They waited a few seconds and then got up, clasped hands and followed him.

"Think he'll bite?" Tommy asked.

Spider nodded silently, watching every move the unsuspecting man made. She was like a predator stalking prey, ready to spring. As usual, she seemed to know when things would happen, when the guy was going to move and how. She knew which way the suspects were running before they did. It wasn't just luck; she *knew*. Tommy knew she did. He just wished he knew how.

"At least now the circulation is going back into my feet," he whispered lovingly.

Ten minutes later he felt Spider's grip on his hand tighten, and he followed as she pulled him into the shadows. Tommy watched the suspect. Another man was approaching, and he was looking around to make sure no one had spotted him. If he saw them he was doing a damn good job of hiding it.

"He's taking the bait."

"I've been waiting for you for three days! You got it?" the bait asked. They'd caught the weasel dead to rights, and he was giving up his partner in crime to cop to the lesser plea of accessory instead of murder one.

The suspect took an envelope out of his pocket and handed it to the stoolie. "Take the money and get the fuck out of town. I'd better never see or hear from you again."

The stoolie took hold of the envelope, but the other guy wasn't letting go.

"I mean it, jerk face. You try to blackmail my ass again, and you'll be damned sorry." He finally let go of the envelope.

"You mean the way you made Eddy sorry?"

"That stupid fuck!" Spider hissed.

She started to move out fast, and Tommy followed instinctively. Tommy heard the suspect's voice in his earphone.

"You're fucking wired! You fucking set me up!"

Then Tommy saw the gun peel out of the suspect's jacket pocket. He pulled his own weapon and screamed without really being aware he was doing so. "Police! Drop your weapon!"

He heard Spider yell into the link. "Move in! Move in! The suspect's got a gun!"

The suspect, startled by all the commotion, fired wildly at the stoolie as he turned to face them. Before he could even finish turning, Spider had shot him once, twice, three times in the chest. She holstered her gun before the body fell and before the other officers could reach them.

Spider turned to look at Tommy, and he saw the fanatical gleam in her eyes. She grinned and then turned quickly away.

LAURA RUBBED AT his tired shoulders. "You're so tense," and added in soothing tones, "Relax, Baby. Relax."

Easier said than done. Tommy closed his eyes, took a deep breath, found his center and let his breath out slowly. He did it again, and was finally able to relax a little.

"I don't know what's with her lately. She's like a friggin' hair trigger—a twitch and she goes off. It scares me. She shot that guy three times in the chest."

"It sounds like she did what she had to," Laura said, trying to work the kinks out of his shoulders.

It felt good. It felt better because he knew that she cared about him and that she cared about how he felt. It didn't hurt that he thought his wife was the most beautiful woman in the world. He loved her long blond hair and fine regal features. Her figure was perfect. Spider had once suggested that Laura's breasts were too large for her five foot four inch frame. Tommy had explained that a woman's breasts could never be too big. His first wife's breasts had been really small; she'd hated Spider, and she had been a cold, uncaring bitch. Laura was her exact opposite and in a lot of ways his, too.

"You don't understand, Laura. Spider Webb is a decorated war veteran. Decorated for sharpshooting among other things. I've seen her knock a penny off a fence post at a hundred feet without nicking the post. She could have shot him in his arm with enough accuracy to snap his arm in two. She could have placed a shot to the ball socket of the shoulder. She could have shot him once and incapacitated him. But she wanted to make sure the man was dead. Three times in the chest in a triangular pattern—that wasn't an accident; it's her training.

"True, he was scum, and he deserved to die. If we had taken him in, they probably would have found some way to cut him loose. At best, they would have given him a life sentence. He would have served a few years in jail and walked for good behavior. The justice system sucks. I don't like what it's doing to us. I especially don't like what it's doing to Spider. I looked at her tonight, and I could see her teeth shining. She was smiling. When I realized that she was standing there grinning over blowing a softball sized hole in a man where his heart should have been, I was actually glad that something could make her happy."

Laura rubbed at his shoulders harder, obviously trying to think of something helpful to say. Laura would not be giving him a long emotion-filled speech all geared at getting him to quit. She herself had been a cop until her routine physical showed that she was diabetic. They had put her on a desk job, and she had stayed there just long enough to work her way through college. Now she worked as a legal secretary in the prosecuting attorney's office. She didn't like it any better than he did when a crook walked. Laura understood Tommy in a way that no one else ever had.

"It's enough to wear anyone down, Baby. We work our asses off to get scum off the street, and some greedy lawyer sets them free again." She sighed. "Spider's breaking faster than the rest of us, because, face it, what the hell else does she have?"

"What do you mean?"

"What does Spider do? Does she have somebody in her life? Something besides work? Does she have family or friends, besides you?"

It was a good question. He'd known Spider Webb from academy days. He'd spent more time with her than any other person he'd ever known. Not just from work, but hours spent fishing and bar hopping and sitting around in her apartment or his house staring at the tube. But while he often spilled his guts to her, she rarely did the same with him. Tommy thought for a moment. They joked about it all the time, but there had to be something in Spider's life.

"Her mother died when she was like—three. Her father was an alcoholic, so she was raised mostly by an older brother. She went into the service right out of high school. While she was in the service her brother died. She's never said how, but she must have blamed her old man because she hasn't seen him since her brother's funeral. As far as I know, there's no other family that she's close to. As for friends," Tommy shrugged and could feel that his shoulders were loosening up, "the only people she ever talks about are the guys we work with. So I don't know. If she's got friends outside of work she doesn't talk about them. She writes to a couple of her old army buddies, but that's about it."

"Does she have a girlfriend?"

"I don't know. Like I've told you before, I'm not even a hundred percent sure she's gay. I *think* she is, but she's never really said one way or the other..."

"And of course you'd never think to ask. You're such a guy. Take my word for it; she's gay." Laura quit rubbing his back then and sat down across from him. "As you know, our new assistant DA, my new boss, is a lesbian. Carrie's worked in the DA's office for the last two years, and I always thought she was really cool, but now that I'm working with her...she's just a really nice person. She's in her late twenties, sharp looking, very intelligent, great sense of humor, and...well, she would really like to meet Spider away from work..."

"No! Absolutely not!" Tommy screamed, laughing. He swung his hands in front of his face, stood up, and headed for the bathroom. "We are not fixing my partner up with one of your friends from work. It's just too creepy."

Laura followed him into the bathroom. "Why not? Spider needs…well, I don't know, something. And Carrie…well, she's like totally obsessed with Spider. She keeps wanting me to introduce them."

"No," Tommy said emphatically.

"Ah, come on, Tommy. What could it hurt? Carrie's my friend. Spider's your partner. It might be fun."

"Yeah, like fucking heartburn," Tommy said. "We don't even know for certain that Spider is gay. How stupid are we going to look if it turns out that she's straight, and we fix her up with a woman?" He looked from her to the toilet and back. "Now, do you mind?"

"Not at all." Laura crossed her arms across her chest, smiled and just stared at him.

Tommy laughed, shook his head, pushed her out of the room and shut the door.

SPIDER LOOKED DOWN at him. "I know it's late, Henry, but I had to talk to somebody. I couldn't just go home."

She fixed his pillows, sat beside him and took his hand. "I got wired tonight. I do that a lot lately. It's like my brain is on fire." She paused a moment, then continued in a whisper. "I killed the perp on purpose. I'll get off because it was a righteous shoot, but I didn't have to kill him. I did it because I wanted to, and I enjoyed it. It gave me a rush…yeah, I know it's sick. But whoever said you could do the right thing and keep your hands clean? I am tired…and lonely."

She brushed the tears from her eyes and took a deep breath. "Look at me, would you? It must be PMS…In those trenches in Baghdad…the guys I was killing…they were just like me. They thought they were right…on the right side, you know? That was their only crime, and I killed them for it. But here on the streets…the scum out there. Their crimes aren't just that they're on the wrong side; their crimes are against mankind. But them I'm expected to let go…to just let them slip between the cracks. Sometimes I just can't.

"It's crazy, Henry. I'm damn near forty, and I haven't done a damn thing with my life. No partner, no kids. Hell, I don't even have dishes, and I can't remember the last time I used my fucking cook stove. I live on cold cereal, Ramen soup, and salad. What the hell for? I can't remember the last time I felt any joy, the last time I even really felt alive…Henry, you're lying here unable to move, to talk, and I'm the one who doesn't know how to live. Something's got to change, but I'm damned if I know what—or how to find out."

SHE'D DRIVEN AROUND for an hour and finally wound up at a bar looking to pick someone up. But it was early in the morning, the pickings were slim, and when it came time to put up or shut up, she went home alone. She should have been exhausted, but she wasn't. She lay in her recliner and stared at the ceiling. The TV was on, but she wasn't watching it.

Her apartment was small. A tiny bathroom, a kitchenette, and the combined living/bedroom—that was it. She had it fixed up nice and kept it clean. Which was more than you could say for the hallways and the other apartments. The landlord wouldn't fix any-thing. But for the rent she was paying she didn't mind fixing things when they broke, or replacing the steam heater with electric base-board heaters when the steam became erratic, or buying new appli-ances when the old ones died.

Usually just being at home, a place that was hers alone, made her more relaxed. Not tonight—or morning, rather. It just felt empty, as empty as her life. She looked at the clock hanging on the wall. It was five o'clock in the morning. She wished she was tired. She looked at the wall of shelves full of books, but couldn't make herself get up to go get one. She stared back at the TV. Mindless drivel. Eventually it succeeded in numbing her brain, and she went to sleep in the recliner.

She dreamt about *her* again, the woman without a face. About noon she woke up with a crick in her neck, feeling more frustrated and empty than she had the night before. She wished she had to go to work, but she didn't. *Two whole days off, two days with nothing to do.* If she had a life, that would have been great. Since she didn't, it was a living hell. At three o'clock she got a call from IAD asking her to come in so that they could run over the incident report one more time, and she was more than happy to go. Even though the whole thing was in the computer, and she knew damn good and well that all they wanted to do was get her to say that she killed the guy on purpose. Which she wasn't crazy enough to do—yet.

CHAPTER FOUR

*"Two are better than one; because they have a good
reward for their labor. For if they fall, the one will lift
up his fellow. But woe to him that is alone; for he has not
another to help him up."* Ecclesiastes 4:9&10

ROBBY WENT IN the bar to see if the manager had a pick-up for
him, to return the barstool he had repaired, and to pick up the money
owed him.

The manager looked the stool over, nodded in appreciation
and paid Robby. Then he told him where the trash was, and Robby
turned to leave.

Just then the man walked into the bar, a big black hole sucking
in the energy from all those around him. A great big evil. Robby's
flesh crawled, and then he was filled with righteous anger. He saw
the man beating women, making them do things they didn't want to
do with him and with other men. He saw him hooking them on
smack so that he could keep them in line. Robby all but ran out of
the bar. He picked up the load and then he waited in the shadows.
The guy had to come out sooner or later, and when he did Robby
would be waiting.

THE 'CRIME' SCENE was like all the others. This time it was Houston
Jenkins, a big time pimp with a history of assault charges. None of
his 'girls' seemed to be too terribly upset. Their only concern seemed
to be that they weren't sure who was going to get them their horse
now. The man was sitting in the big middle of his own bed with his
eyes cooked and bulging out and slime running out his ears.

Spider covered the corpse back up then looked at Tommy and
smiled. "It's shake and bake, and I he'ped."

Tommy sighed and shook his head. Having a weekend off had
done nothing for Spider's attitude. Neither had a one-hour meeting
with IAD, which while it hadn't caused her any real trouble, was a
drag under the best of circumstances.

Tommy pulled her to one side. "Could you maybe try to at least
act repulsed?" Tommy hissed.

Spider shrugged. "There's a reason I ain't an actress. This bastard was a hell of a lot more repulsive alive than he is with his cooked eyeballs bulging."

"What's up with you?" Tommy asked, momentarily losing his cool.

Spider shrugged. How could she explain to him what she really didn't understand herself? "I'm not getting much sleep. For some reason I keep looking at my life. Since it mostly sucks, always has sucked, and is always going to suck, I'm kindah in a blue funk."

She was talking in her best idiot voice and making faces, and that could mean only one thing—that she wasn't comfortable with the subject matter and was making a joke about something that really wasn't a joke at all.

Tommy's brow creased in thought. "You really think your life sucks?"

"Yep. Shit just keeps raining on my head," Spider said with a smile. She walked away and started checking out the crime scene. Houston had been a big man, and unlike all the other victims he had apparently had a chance to thrash around a bit. Before he died he fell back onto the bed, and the impact had broken two legs off of it. She pointed it out to the photographer who took pictures of the broken things in the room and the bed.

Tommy joined her.

"The weapon must take longer when there is more mass," Tommy said. Spider shrugged noncommittally.

"OK, Spider...what do you think it is?"

She smiled at him. "If I told you my theory, you'd be calling the men in the white coats to come and take me away to the Ha Ha Hilton."

THEY HAD SPENT the better part of the day pretending to follow up leads in the case. It wasn't very hard to make sure that everything they found lead to yet another dead end. This guy didn't leave many tracks, and no fingerprints or DNA. Whoever he was, he knew what he was doing.

Now they were heading towards the courthouse to testify against Justin Kent, and Spider was acting weird. Weird even for Spider. Tommy was glad he was driving. Spider's color looked bad, almost pasty-white, and she was jerking at the collar of her shirt and mumbling something under her breath that was inaudible.

"You OK, Spider?" Tommy asked.

"Trying to remember all the details, except the ones I want to leave out, of course. Trying to sort those from the others. Trying to think of every screwy question those fuck lawyers are going to throw at us so I don't trip up." She looked at him and sighed. "The usual shit. I'm a little more spent than usual because, like I said, I haven't really slept in days. I don't want to trip up."

Tommy nodded, and said nothing. Now *he* was nervous. If she fucked up, heads would roll—theirs. "You can do this. We did the right thing even if we did it the wrong way…"

"I'm not having an episode of guilty conscience here, Tommy. I have no problem with anything I've done. I just know that the fucking attorney would rather burn me at the stake than see his client convicted."

He knew that wasn't all of it. There was something else. Something she wasn't going to tell him. But if not him, then who? Who did Spider talk to? Because Laura was right, Spider didn't talk to him. At least not about anything that mattered. There was just too much he didn't know about her, and to say that about someone you'd known for fifteen years was to admit defeat as a friend.

What he did know, was certain of, was that if you didn't talk to someone, eventually you exploded. Maybe that was what was happening to Spider right now. Problem was he'd never been very good at getting people to open up. Truth was that he wasn't sure he wanted to hear Spider's problems, even if he could get her to talk.

THEY COULDN'T GO in the courtroom of course, so they had to sit in the hallway waiting to be called. It reminded Tommy of school. He'd spent a lot of time in the hall. Being smaller than the other kids, and the only Asian in a small Southern town, he'd caught a lot of hell. Since he came from a long line of martial artists who'd been eager to pass on the tradition to the next generation, he'd given their hell right back to them.

Being his father's only son, and in fact the only son born to the first American generation of Chans, he'd been showered with attention from all sides. He was the pride and joy of his family, and they never scolded him for getting in fights at school. At the time he had wondered why, but now he realized that they wanted him to be tough. He started competition at six, and by twenty he had won Grand Nationals. He successfully defended his title two years running. Then one day he'd been shopping with his first wife when two gunmen tried to rob the store they were in. The gunmen made them all lie on the floor. When the old man behind the counter reached for something, one guy spooked and shot him. About that time the cops showed up with sirens blaring. The guys were squirreling out, and Tommy didn't hesitate. He jumped off the floor in a single fluid movement, ran and landed a kick to the nearest gunman's head. As his gun rattled to the floor Tommy swung, kicked, and the second one went down.

Tommy was in all the papers; he was a hero. It was on that day that he decided to become a cop, thereby disappointing his family for the first time.

Now, years later, he was still spending time in the hall for breaking the rules.

Spider looked cool now. Almost aloof. Seeing this, Tommy relaxed. He handed her his coke, she took a drink and handed it back.

A stiff in a coat walked out of the courtroom. "Detective Spider Webb!" he called.

Spider stood up, looked down at Tommy and smiled. "Won't be long now, Tommy boy."

He watched her walk in, thinking how he hated this part of the job worse than anything. Worse than going to the victim's house and telling his family. Worse than having to look at—and smell—half-decayed bodies, or dealing with the IAD. It was the worst of everything all rolled together. You had the perp, and the victim's family, and all the suits, and pictures of the crime scene. Then to make it even better you had to get up on stage and answer a bunch of stupid questions that had purposely been rigged to trip you up. All the time you knew that chances were when it was all said and done the fucker would walk right out, scott-free, to kill or maim or abuse another day. It made him understand why Spider had just killed that guy in the park. No chance *that* guy was going to walk. The real bonus was—no day in court, 'cause court days sucked.

When Tommy walked in the courtroom he saw Laura hovering around the DA's desk, and he smiled. Spider sat behind the DA's desk looking shaken but not stirred, and he relaxed.

Most of the questions were routine, but then out of the clear blue the defendant's attorney said, "Detective Chan, did you hear the scream your partner Detective Webb claims to have heard?"

He played back the video and audio taken at the time of the bust. Comlink videos were always grainy, half pictures, random, and—more times than not—of your shirt. But computer technology he didn't understand allowed them to clean them up and have a more or less complete picture of a bust or crime scene. It was amazing technology, and Tommy for one hated it.

Tommy didn't flinch. "I heard the second scream, but not the first. My partner has very good hearing." The attorney played the tape again.

"It may be just me, but this looks like a part Detective Webb is playing out—and not very well I might add."

Tommy couldn't agree more, and he made a mental note to scream at Spider the next chance he got.

"Spider has very good instincts—uncanny really. When she gets the feeling that something's going on, she becomes very nearly inanimate. She's watching, listening, and her speech patterns often become almost mechanical."

The attorney laughed. "So, what you're saying is that Detective Webb has not set our client up at all, but is just incredibly intuitive."

"Yes, Sir," Tommy answered unblinkingly.

"So you claim that you and your partner were not trying to get around the fact that you were not issued a search warrant for the properties in which you arrested my client and ten other men."

"Correct, sir."

"You weren't trying to bend the law, even a little bit?"

"No, and I resent your implication." *I said that rather eloquently,* he thought.

"What if I told you that Ms. Tourlliony told us that you and your partner paid her to be there and to scream?"

"Objection! He's leading the witness." The new assistant DA had a nice voice, and she was as Laura had described her—stunning.

"I'd call her a liar," Tommy said, just as the judge yelled sustained.

"No further questions."

The assistant DA stood up. "I'd like to ask this witness a couple of questions in re-direct."

The judge nodded, and the assistant DA approached him. Tommy smiled in spite of himself. He'd seen her around before, but he'd never really looked at her, which he figured proved his incredible fidelity. She had a sexy walk, and nice legs, too. She was just slightly shorter then he was, with auburn shoulder length hair and dark green eyes, incredibly sensual lips, and the delicate features and build of a model. Tommy was thinking that she just didn't look like a dyke, so he missed her question.

"Excuse me?"

She smiled indulgently, no doubt used to men stammering like idiots around her. "Did you see Detective Webb in contact with the witness, Ms. Tourlliony?"

"Not until after the bust."

"How many years have you served with Detective Webb?"

"Fifteen," he said, wondering where this questioning was going. He didn't have to wait long.

The assistant DA turned to the jurors. "In fact, Detective Webb's service record is un-marred. Twice decorated for bravery, once as a police officer, and once in service to this country as a paratrooper in Desert Storm III. I agree with Detective Chan. For Mr. Levits to accuse either her or her partner of misconduct is an insult. No further questions. The evidence in this case, however obtained, speaks for itself."

The judge dismissed him, and he went to sit beside Spider.

"Wow! He was really after your ass!" he whispered in her ear.

She nodded and whispered in his, "He asked me the same questions about you. He was trying to get one of us to implicate the other."

"What a dick!" Tommy said too loud. Everyone at the DA's table turned and gave him a dirty look. He shrugged and muttered an apology.

Spider chuckled and he elbowed her.

A few minutes later the judge recessed the case till the next day. They were half way out of the building when Laura ran to catch up with them. She slung an arm around each of their shoulders.

"Where you booger heads off to?" she asked.

"You're sure that's a term of endearment?" Spider asked, giving Tommy a skeptical look.

Tommy laughed, shrugged, and then answered his wife's question. "Gonna go clock out for the day, and then we were going to go by Kelly's and have a couple of beers. Why?"

"I've got a couple of things to finish up, and then I'll meet you there."

"Great! Then maybe we can go to dinner." Tommy looked from his wife to his partner.

"Spider?" Laura asked.

"Can't go to dinner. I've...I've got plans."

Laura let go of them and moved into Spider's path she looked up at her. "What sort of plans?"

Spider looked at the floor. "Ah...I've got laundry and... stuff...you know...Stuff."

"Yeah, I know," Laura laughed. "I know that 'laundry and stuff' can wait. Come on."

Spider looked at Tommy, who just smiled and said, "Don't look at me. I know you don't have a fucking life. Come on, we'll eat at..." He looked at his wife.

"Bartelo's," she answered, knowing it was Spider's favorite Italian restaurant.

Laura looked at Spider expectantly, and Spider nodded, feeling as if she were trapped. She really didn't feel like going out, but if she didn't she was just going to go by the hospital and talk to Henry. Then she'd go home, stare at the ceiling, and think about the suckiness of her life till she finally fell into a fitful sleep and had the fucking dream again.

Still, she hated being the fifth wheel, and no matter how good your friends were, when you went out with a man and his wife, you were really on your own.

"Good! Then it's settled. I'll meet you at Kelly's." Laura ran off before Spider could talk herself—and them—out of going.

SPIDER AND TOMMY slid into the corner booth.

"It was close there for a minute, but they're gonna cage him."

"No thanks to your stellar performance," Tommy whispered. The waiter walked over and set the beers in front of them. They were regulars, and he rarely bothered to ask them what they wanted anymore. He just brought them a couple of cheap drafts.

"Anything else?"

"When Laura gets here bring her a raspberry wine cooler, and bring us each another beer."

"Put it on my tab," Spider said.

Tommy looked at her with raised eyebrows; they usually went Dutch.

"My way of saying I'm sorry, and no I'm not picking up the tab for dinner."

"You're getting off awful cheap." Tommy laughed and took a drink of his beer. "All right, but don't do it again. You put our asses on the line for a laugh."

Spider nodded, and then she did something Spider rarely did, she was silent. He kept waiting for her to talk, but she didn't. This put Tommy on the spot, because usually Spider started the conversation and then they were…well…talking.

"Ah, you catch the game last night?" he asked.

"Ah…what game? You know I don't watch sports. What planet are you from?"

That was it. She still wasn't talking. Just staring at her beer, looking like someone crushed her puppy. God! She was pathetic!

"Your life doesn't suck, Spider," he tried.

Spider laughed loudly and ran a hand down her face. She looked at him and shook her head. "My life sucks, Tommy. Take my word for it. You can count the number of times I've been laid since I got out of the army on the fingers of…" She thought about it for a minute. "Well, you'd have fingers left over. Last time was about two years ago. I'm living from hand to mouth; I barely have enough money left over to exist."

"Spider, you make decent money! Where the hell does it go? Left over from what?"

She just glared at him. He'd asked this question many times, and she never answered it. No reason she should now.

"You know, Spider, you could tell me anything."

Spider laughed, even as tears came to her eyes. "No, I couldn't, Tommy. I love you, but face it. The minute I start talking about personal stuff you're uncomfortable."

Was he? He didn't think so, but maybe he was. She wasn't the first one to accuse him of that. "I'm trying now…"

"Let's just talk about something else. I can wallow in my self-pity on my own time. What about that Fry Guy?"

"Gonna tell me your theory?" He hated to admit it, but she was right about him. The minute they changed the subject he felt relieved. He guessed he really wasn't a very good friend. Growing up all he'd had was his family, no real friends, and his family hadn't been big on discussing personal matters. Now he didn't have his family, so he needed his friends, loved them, but didn't really know how to listen to them. At least not to their problems. Spider's problems.

"No," Spider said with a smile. "You do realize of course that our man is not a serial killer."

"You're the one who reads all the books. Probably why you're so depressed. Who wouldn't be with the crap you read? Serial killer profiles, books on the occult and cults and mass murderers. No small wonder you have nightmares, either."

She ignored him. "This guy kills his victims quickly. He doesn't even get close to them. Maybe—no probably—they don't even see him. Then he doesn't mutilate the bodies; he just kills them and then he goes on his way. That is not a serial killer's MO. The serial killer likes to torture his victims, to mutilate them, sometimes before death—sometimes after. To exact, if you will, ultimate control for as long as possible. This guy's not into that. He's into getting these guys off the street…"

Tommy thought he knew where she was going with this. "So, according to your theory, the killer is sane."

"Well, at least as sane as I am. After all, I killed a guy just to save myself a day in court."

"Shsh! Jesus, Spider!" Tommy said in disbelief.

"Well I did," she said matter-of-factly. "You have to ask yourself what sort of person wants to get this kind of scum off the street? Most of the victims are child molesters, drug dealers, murderers, pimps who prostitute minors, rapists, and wife beaters. Who wants to see these people dead?"

"Everyone," Tommy said with a shrug.

"A *family* man," Spider said, shaking her head adamantly. "Someone with kids, or who feels responsible for kids. A parent, a teacher, or a social worker. Someone like that."

"How would any of those people get their hands on this kind of weapon or that kind of information?" Tommy asked. "It's got to be someone who has at least had access to police files."

"Why?"

"Because how else would they know that these people are criminals?" Tommy asked.

"What is your *chi?*"

"Something inside me, a place I go…"

"Explain it to me."

"I...I can't. It has to be experienced."

"Yet you have no doubt that it exists?"

"I know it does." That was it. She wasn't going to tell him anything else. She was just going to sit there and drink her beer. "You are a maddening piece of shit, Spider Webb. Just tell me your damned theory. Doesn't matter how screwy it is. I already think you're nuts, so what do you have to lose?

She shrugged. "I think this guy exists in the *chi* or its equivalent. I think he sees people in a way that most people don't, and I think that because of this he has power. Power he pulls from his *chi* just like you do, except I think his power comes straight out of that place. I think this guy is pyrokinetic."

Tommy didn't laugh. His father had taught him not to laugh at crazy people. "You left out the part about the little green men."

"I thought it was best that way...okay. All right. I'll admit it's a little farfetched. But it's no worse than the 'stolen from the army' theory the Feds keep popping on us. By the way, I don't see them making any breaks in this case, either, and supposedly they're at least trying."

"So, what we're looking for is a teacher with a wife, two kids and a really big *chi*." Tommy did laugh then, but mostly at his own pun.

Spider frowned. "Gee! I can't imagine why I wouldn't feel comfortable coming to you with my problems."

This only made him laugh louder.

She sipped at her beer and wished she hadn't told him anything, ever. Just when she thought that things couldn't get worse, she looked up and saw Laura walk in with the way-too-sexy assistant DA in tow. She looked at Tommy and scowled.

"So, I guess the fact that your wife has brought me a date means that you have finally admitted that you know that I'm gay."

Tommy looked up. "If it was supposed to be a secret, it wasn't a very good one, but I never knew for sure until right now." Tommy wanted to crawl under the table.

Spider drew a deep breath. She always figured Tommy knew. After all, she never really tried to hide it. She just didn't broadcast the fact, something the military had taught her.

"If you'd asked me, I would have told you. You didn't have to do this. What if I wasn't? That would be even more awkward than this is."

"That's what I told Laura. It wasn't my idea; I told her not to do it. And between you and me, I don't see how it could *be* any more awkward," Tommy said.

"That woman is…well she's way out of my league. I only ever date really homely women; there's less heartache and rejection that way," Spider mumbled.

"Rejection's good for the soul."

"Then I must have a huge fucking soul."

"Let's just try to make the best of it, all right? Laura said she wanted to meet you."

"Why?" Spider asked in disbelief.

"I don't know. Maybe she only dates ugly chicks because there is less fear of rejection."

Tommy waved. Laura and Carrie saw them, and they started over. He looked at his partner, who had turned a cool shade of green. He felt for her. He'd been set up before, and—at least in his experience—it was never a good thing.

"How do I look?" Spider asked.

"Green," Tommy said truthfully.

"It's a good color for me," Spider said nervously.

"SHE'S JUST TURNED green," Laura said in answer to Carrie's question.

"Maybe this wasn't such a good idea, Laura," Carrie said nervously.

"If you really want to go out with her, this is about the only way it's going to happen," Laura said. "She's just nervous. I don't think she gets out much; mostly she just works."

"Maybe if *I* got out a little more I wouldn't be trying to pick up girls I meet at work. She's going to think I'm desperate or just plain weird. I think this was a big mistake."

"We'll pretend like it was all my idea. What have you got to lose?"

"My dignity," Carrie mumbled.

A few seconds later they reached the table. "I hope you don't mind," Laura said. "I brought Carrie along. You kind of know each other from work, but Carrie Long this is my husband, Tommy Chan."

They shook hands.

"And this is his partner, Spider Webb."

Spider took the outstretched hand. Long, delicate, well-manicured fingers clasped Spider's huge, scared, chapped, sweaty palm in a firm, friendly grip. Spider looked up at the woman. Carrie smiled at her, and Spider's head spun. The assistant DA was breathtaking. It wasn't the first time she'd noticed that. It was, however, the first time she had allowed herself to take a really good look. She looked again at the woman's hand, her arms, her...

"Spider, let go," Tommy whispered in her ear.

"Ah, yeah. Sorry!" Spider felt like an idiot. She let go of the woman's hand. Carrie sat beside her.

Spider stiffened. *I'm a fucking idiot. Pull your head out of your ass, your foot out of your mouth, and say something coherent that doesn't have anything to do with her tits or her ass.*

The bartender came over, bringing Laura's drink, their beers, and apparently to save Spider's life.

"Would you like something to drink?" Spider asked.

Carrie looked at Spider and smiled, seeming to immediately relax. "So, you buying me a drink, sailor?"

Spider started breathing and smiled easily back. "Actually, I was never a sailor, ma'am."

Carrie looked at the waiter. "Bourbon and branch."

The waiter nodded and left to get the drink.

CARRIE CHECKED SPIDER out as inconspicuously as possible. She sure did like the package. She'd dated a cop before. She'd been a decent lay, but fucking brain-dead otherwise, and about as interesting as a turnip. She knew that wasn't the case with Spider Webb. This woman was vital and alive. She was also wired and impulsive, and those were never bad things in a lover.

"So, did you pay the girl to scream?" she asked Spider matter-of-factly. Across the table Tommy spit beer, and Laura quickly cleaned it up, avoiding their eyes.

Spider looked right into her eyes and without flinching asked, "What if I did?"

"I'd tell you to get some acting lessons before you do it again," Carrie said, taking her drink from the waiter.

"I'll take that under consideration." Spider took a sip of her beer.

Carrie smiled her very best *I already have you* smile and moved closer to Spider.

Tommy wanted to curl up and die. He didn't want to be here when they were doing whatever it was that they were doing, and he wasn't really sure what that was. Either they were flirting or Carrie was fixing to indict Spider. Either way he hated it, and he hated Laura for making him be there while they were doing it.

"This sucks," he whispered in Laura's ear.

"No, no! They're hitting it off," Laura whispered back.

"And you can tell, how?" Tommy asked.

Laura worked it masterfully so that Spider and Carrie were in a car alone. Well, not actually a car, Spider's Isuzu pickup truck.

At least it's clean, Spider thought.

"So, you lived here long?" Spider asked. *Oh, God! What a lame ass question. What's next, asking her sign? Someone, please save me from myself! At this rate it will be another five years before I get laid again.*

"I've lived here most of my life, but I just started working in the DA's office about two years ago, and I only took over as assistant DA six months ago. I was working and living in LA for a while before that. You know how it is, I was born here, grew up here, went to school here, so I just wanted to be *anywhere* that wasn't *here*. After five years in LA I was ready to come back home."

"I...I was born here in Shea City. I've lived here all my life except when I was in the service." *Do I sound like a total fucking idiot or what?*

"Nervous?" Carrie asked.

"A little...no, that's a lie. A lot."

"If you'd rather not do this..."

"No, no that's not it. I admit that at first I was a little weirded out, but...there's a reason I don't date. You see, any time I'm really attracted to a woman, my IQ drops about a hundred points. I'm afraid I'm going to say or do the wrong thing, and so of course I do. I'm so afraid that she's going to think I'm a dork that I act like, well...a total fucking dork."

Carrie laughed. "And so you just don't date?"

"Not on purpose," Spider said with a smile.

Carrie laughed again. "Will it help if I tell you that I don't think you're a dork?"

"Ah! But you haven't really given me a chance yet."

DINNER WENT SURPRISINGLY well. To Tommy it seemed that Carrie and Spider were talking easily. The veins in Spider's temples even stopped throbbing. Seeing that Spider had calmed down allowed him to relax a little, but he didn't feel any less embarrassed. He felt he'd dealt better with his partner's sexuality when they just didn't talk about it. Tommy glared at Laura every time their eyes met, and she just smiled back at him, completely undaunted. Which made him want to scream.

They had finished their dinner and were now all just sitting around, talking over coffee.

"So, how did you get a name like Spider Webb?" Carrie asked.

"My mother was apparently a wild child. My father picked my brother Scott's name, and so he had this really normal Scott Webb thing going on. My mother named me Spider. I didn't really know her because she died in a car wreck when I was real young, two or three. I always thought that my name was the way my mother made sure she'd always be with me. Everything I know about my mother I know because of my name. My father never talked about her, and wouldn't allow us to, either. To this day I don't know why." Her voice changed took on a bitter edge. "Maybe just because he was a mean, bitter old son of a bitch." She looked around then, seeming to realize that she had been speaking aloud.

Tommy was shocked. Fifteen years he'd known this woman, and he hadn't known any of that. He'd never even thought to ask about her name; it was just her name.

"Carrie," Spider said, looking at Carrie and obviously wanting to change the subject. "That's Celtic isn't it?"

"Yes, it is. It means…"

"Dark one," Spider said.

"Yes," Carrie said with surprise and slightly raised eyebrows. "How did you…"

"She reads too much," Tommy answered.

CARRIE LOOKED ACROSS the truck at Spider. She was taking her back to the courthouse and Carrie's car.

"Dinner was good," Carrie said conversationally. "I like Italian food."

"Bartelo's is my favorite restaurant."

"So Laura said," Carrie said with a smile. With Spider's attention on the road she gave her a good looking over without fear of being caught. Externally she couldn't find one thing she didn't like. The woman's hands were freakishly large, but she didn't necessarily think that was a bad thing, not if she knew how to use them—and Carrie had a feeling she did. But there was no doubt that Spider Webb was trouble, a person carrying baggage filled with secrets. Carrie had a suspicion that there were things you'd never know about Spider Webb, no matter how intimate you became. Of course all these things that should have been ringing all her warning bells only made Carrie want Spider that much more.

Carrie had long ago accepted that she was a decidedly unhealthy girl.

She could tell Spider was attracted to her, too. It had been a long time since anyone had looked at her the way Spider Webb had tonight, with something more than just lust. Carrie was having those 'this might actually be something' feelings which were usually nonexistent on a first date.

Involuntarily she started thinking about all the things she could do to Spider. All of the things she wanted her to do to her. *I wish she wasn't hell-bent on taking me back to my car. I know it's too soon, but I really want to be with her. The last thing I want to do tonight is go back to my empty house and an empty bed. I wish she'd pull this car over, and...*

Suddenly Spider flipped a big U-turn in the middle of the road and headed back the other way. Carrie expected her to pop a light on the roof and activate a siren, but she obviously wasn't in pursuit of anyone.

"What the hell?"

Spider swallowed. "Want to go to my place?" she asked nervously.

"Ah...what?" *My god! I sound like a fucking idiot.* "I'd love to."

CARRIE LOOKED AT the clock. It was one in the morning. She had an early court date and no change of clothes, and she just didn't give a damn. She lay more on Spider than beside her, enjoying the feel of Spider's hands where they caressed her back.

"Can I stay?" she asked, surprised to find that she suddenly felt shy.

"Yes." They kissed again. This time gently, lovingly.

Spider turned out the light, and Carrie moved to wrap herself around her. She couldn't bear to let her go. *How can I feel like this? I hardly know this woman, yet she knows me, what I want, what I need. Please God don't let me be reading her wrong, don't let this be a one way thing.*

"You can stay as long as you like," Spider whispered.

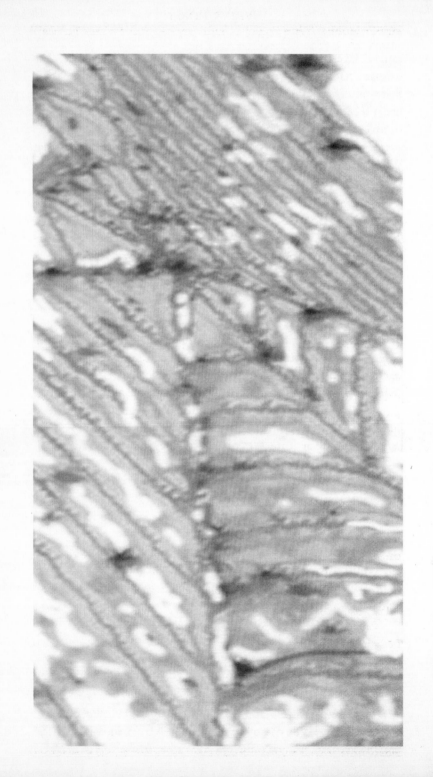

CHAPTER FIVE

"Better is a poor and wise child than an old and foolish king, who no longer knows how to take care of himself."
Ecclesiastes 4:13

CARRIE SKIDDED IN to work twenty minutes late. Her hair was a mess, she was wearing the same clothes she had worn the night before, she was hurried and hustled, and grinning from ear to ear.

Laura laughed at the sight of her. "Someone got lucky."

Carrie waved her in and motioned for her to shut the door.

"My God, Laura!" Carrie sat down at her desk, and started digging through her purse looking for her comb and primping necessities. "It was amazing! Like nothing I've ever had before." If it was possible, an even more stupid grin came across her face. "And now I will say something that's going to make me sound like an utter lunatic, so you have to forget I ever said it. I know it's crazy, because I don't really even know her, but...I think I'm in love with that woman. It's such a lesbian cliché, to go out on one date and start saying you've met your soul mate, but I've never done it till now, I swear."

Carrie worked on making herself look presentable, and succeeded to a degree that made Laura want to hate her.

"I think that's great," Laura said. She couldn't wait to tell Tommy. He'd kept her up half the night, bitching at her for dragging him into that shit. Complaining that his poor partner had looked like a deer caught in headlights. Tommy had refused to back down even when she had reminded him that they had left together and no one was holding a gun to anyone's head. She couldn't wait to tell him that she was right and he had been wrong.

Carrie stood up, took off her suit jacket, and straightened out her shirt. Then she rolled her skirt so that it was at least two inches shorter. "So, does it look like a different outfit?"

Laura nodded in appreciation. "You do this a lot?"

Carrie smiled. "Never for such a good reason."

"Tommy's a little bent over the whole thing. He knew Spider was gay, but he didn't know, if you know what I mean. Now he's afraid they'll have to have a conversation which gets beyond 'Uh huh' and 'want another beer'."

Carrie laughed. "I don't think he needs to worry about it. If she hasn't talked to him about it before, it's not likely that she's going to start now. Well...I'd love to talk for hours and hours, but I'm late already. So bring me the McGillicutty files and lots and lots of coffee."

TOMMY DIDN'T KNOW why he let her drive. It was almost better when she was depressed and sleep deprived. She zipped in and out of traffic, humming tunelessly until finally he couldn't stand it any more.

"OK! All right already," Tommy said, throwing up his hands. "So did you do the DA?"

"Assistant DA," Spider grinned wildly, and Tommy growled back, so she answered his question. "Many, many times. Then I slept, really slept, for the first time in weeks. Then I woke up and we did it again."

"So the 'my life sucks, it's always sucked, and it's always going to suck' of yesterday is now behind us?"

"Right now they could drop a bomb on the hood of this car, and I'd say look at all the pretty colors."

Tommy laughed, shook his head, and changed the subject. "So, have you given up your teacher, fire starter, family man theory?"

"Nope, that was not merely a delusional thing caused by my depression."

Their comlinks buzzed and a message came through from central. This time the body was in an alley again.

Barney Jones had not been a nice man. He'd been busted three times for selling narcotics to minors. Just six months ago they'd had to watch him squirrel his way out of a murder rap. The victim had been a sixteen-year-old girl that he'd gotten drunk. He'd been screwing her when she'd died of alcohol poisoning, and from the coroner's reports he hadn't stopped screwing her even then. Her genitals were all but mutilated by his constant pounding. They should have taken him out and hung him from his dick. Somehow he weaseled his way out of the murder rap and they convicted him of statutory rape, for which he had served a whole six months. Then the courts put him right back on the streets again. But he hadn't been out long when the Angel of Death had swooped down and microwaved his brain.

The coroner pulled back the sheet for Spider and Tommy.

"Ding dong the wicked witch is gone," Spider muttered, laughing a little. Even Tommy couldn't wipe the smile from his face.

"You know him?" the coroner asked.

"Barney Jones. A real low life, and a candidate for the hit parade," Tommy said and explained about the young woman whose life had been ended by him.

Spider was talking to the bartender. "...Strange Robby was here. He's the guy that picks up our weird trash. You know, the stuff the garbage guys won't take. He may have been out here when this happened."

"Why do they call him Strange Robby?" she asked curiously.

The bartender shrugged. "I don't know, they just do."

"Do you know where he lives?" Spider asked.

"Better than that; I got his card."

Spider followed the guy into the bar. It was a real dive. The people inside looked more like caricatures of scum than real people. The guy handed her the card, and she took it wishing she'd left her latex gloves on. One look at the card told her why they called him Strange Robby; the guy's real name was Robert Strange.

Spider was already in the driver's seat, so that meant Tommy had to ride shotgun again. Tommy slid into the car and closed the door. "Poor Barney Jones, couldn't happen to a nicer guy." He laughed. "I love this Fry Guy, Spider."

Spider nodded. "We got a potential witness. I figure if we talk to him we can maybe keep the Feds from doing it and finding something out."

Tommy nodded. "It may be wrong, but it sure feels right."

ROBBY WAS WORKING IN the shop, trying to fix an old refrigerator. Elvita and Duane played on the floor in front of him with some blocks he had made for them out of scraps from a construction site. He'd cut the wood into workable lengths, shaped some into cars and trucks and animals, and painted them with bright colors. No kids had ever enjoyed a set of Leggos any more than these two enjoyed their blocks. The skyscraper they were making looked wobbly at best.

When a deep but definitely female voice from the door asked, "Are you Robert Strange?" Robby jumped, and the blocks went crashing to the floor. The toddlers laughed, clapped their hands, and started construction all over again hardly taking notice of the newcomers. After all, people were in and out of Robby's shop all the time.

Robby knew looking at them that they were police, and he swallowed hard. "I'm Robert, but most folks just call me Robby," he said wiping his hands on a shop rag as he scrambled to his feet. "How can I help you?"

"I'm detective Chan, this is detective Webb." They both showed their comlinks. "We're investigating a murder that took place behind Frank's Tavern. We were told you might have been out there at the time," Tommy said.

Robby was silent, watching the woman. She was watching the kids play. Then she looked at him. Looked him right in the eyes because they were exactly the same height. He saw *the blood and the trenches, heard her anguished cries as she watched in horror as those around her died. Exhausted, wounded, running through streets filled with fire and explosions and death fighting a war she didn't really understand for a freedom that didn't really ever trickle down to her. Saw her righteous anger so strong. Like his, and yet not.* She understood him. Hell, she *was* him, and as he was looking into her soul, she was looking into his. Even as his brown eyes were staring to her blue gray ones.

"Mr. Strange?" she asked in a quiet voice.

He looked away from her. "I didn't see anything," he told Tommy and shrugged. "I wasn't in the alley long. I got the trash and I left."

"Your kids?" the woman asked.

"No, my brother and sister. I take care of them. All of them, actually. There's seven all together," Robby said.

"That must be quite a job," the woman said.

"It keeps me out of trouble," Robby said with a smile. "I'm sorry I can't help."

The woman looked at him and smiled a big, friendly smile. "No problem. Thanks for your time."

Robby watched them go. That was it. They weren't going to ask him any more questions. He had thought someone was helping him, and now he was sure he knew who.

"WHAT THE HELL was that all about?" Tommy asked.

"What?" Spider asked innocently.

"You bloody well know what! Back there, with the garbage man. I think he knew something, and you looked like you were fucking on another planet."

"Would if I could," Spider said with a smile. Then answered the puzzled look on her partner's face. "Fuck on another planet."

"Come on, Spider, you saw something. What the hell was it?"

"I didn't see shit," Spider said. "Just…well, didn't you ever meet someone that you felt you were destined to meet?"

Tommy thought about that and had to answer truthfully. "My old Jujitsu instructor, you, and Laura. But the black garbage man, Spider?"

She shrugged. "That's the way I felt; I think he felt it, too."

"What else, Spider? There was something else—something to do with the Fry Guy. What was it?"

"I think you're right. I think he does know more than he's letting on, and I think he's not talking for the same reason we're not."

She didn't tell him what she really thought. After all, they all wanted the same thing.

SHE GOT HOME late. She'd felt bad about not seeing Henry the day before, and so she had spent extra time with him. It had been a long day after a long night, and her butt was dragging out her tracks.

She walked in and froze; there was someone in her bed. Then she saw the briefcase and overnight bag and smiled. She was a little surprised by the wave of relief that swept over her. All day she had wondered if what had happened last night was even real. If it was, did Carrie really want to see her again or was it all in her head? How should she approach her? Did they have to start all over again at square one, or were they past that? Now she could start to relax.

Spider closed and locked the door behind her and walked over to the bed. She stood and just watched Carrie for a minute. In sleep, with all the stress of life washed from her face, she was—if possible—even more beautiful. Spider took off her shoes and crawled in beside Carrie, pleasantly surprised to find that she wasn't wearing any clothes. She took Carrie gently into her arms and as she stirred, kissed her on the back of her neck. Carrie stretched and rolled in her arms to face her in one fluid motion, and they kissed.

"So, who's this sleeping in my bed?" Spider asked, as their lips parted.

"Is it all right, or is it just too crazy for you?" Carrie asked. The confidence Spider had come to associate with Carrie's voice seemed to have temporarily departed. She was putting herself on the line, letting her emotions dictate her actions maybe for the first time in her life. Spider knew the feeling, it was like jumping out of a plane not having packed your own shoot, you just didn't know whether it was going to open or not.

"It's more than all right." Spider pulled her closer. "I like crazy, and you can surprise me like this any time."

"Can I...I mean...what are we doing? We hardly know each other..."

Spider held a finger against Carrie's lips. "We know each other." She moved her hand and held it palm open against Carrie's chest, over her heart. "In here we know each other. Finding you is like finding a piece of myself that I didn't know was missing."

Carrie melted into her arms as all fear of rejection left her.

SPIDER RUMMAGED AROUND the kitchen until she finally gave up and yelled, "Ramen soup, grilled cheese, or I could send out for pizza or Chinese."

"Chinese would be nice. Chicken Chow Mein?"

"Sounds good to me." Spider called the Chinese restaurant on the speed dial. She walked back into the living/bedroom where Carrie, wearing a skimpy black robe tied at the waist, was looking at Spider's books. Carrie pulled out one entitled *History of the Paranormal* and held it up.

"A little light reading?"

Spider took the book and put it back. "I like to read."

"Apparently so. Nothing fictional?"

"I don't have time to read the things I want and still read strictly for pleasure; if that makes any sense...I put on some tea." Spider walked over and sat down in her chair.

Carrie came over, sat in Spider's lap and wrapped her arms around her neck.

Spider laughed and held her close. "I'm not complaining, but when the food gets here I'm eating and going to sleep."

"Can I stay? Wake you up in the morning?" Carrie asked with a seductive smile.

Spider laughed. "You know I've never been a sex object before. I think I like it."

"I really don't hop into bed immediately with every woman I meet," Carrie defended.

"I know that," Spider said.

"You do, don't you?" Carrie said. It was obvious that she had something more in mind.

"What do you mean?"

"I mean you *do* know. You're psychic…or something."

Spider laughed nervously. "Ah, come on, Carrie. You're an intelligent, professional woman…"

"Exactly, and part of my job is solving puzzles. Everyone has seen things in their lives that shouldn't have happened and did. I don't think you have to be an idiot to believe in the paranormal. I'm serious. You're psychic, aren't you? At very least you feel what I feel. That's why you're so good in bed."

"You think I'm good in bed?" Spider was very pleased.

"Please. You know you are. Don't try to change the subject. Are you psychic?"

Spider took in a deep breath. "Carrie there is no such…"

Carrie caught Spider's glance and held it. "Don't give me any shit, girl."

"Maybe…I don't know," Spider said with a shrug.

"Oh, how very, very noncommittal, Detective Webb. Yes or no?"

"I seem to know what people are…not thinking…but, what they're feeling. I seem to be more empathic than just about anyone else. It's not always a plus in a relationship, or in life for that matter."

"It's a plus as far as I'm concerned."

Carrie kissed Spider on the neck, then moved to her lips. When they parted Carrie looked deep into Spider's eyes.

"Do you know what I'm feeling now?" she asked in a low tone.

"Lust," Spider said with a smile.

"No," Carrie got up and moved to sit on the coffee table in front of Spider. "You don't really know me. If you did, you'd know that this is not like me. Begging to be set up with someone. Sleeping with a woman on the first date or coming back the next night and flashing my DA badge to get into her apartment. Waiting naked in her bed. I just don't do that. Or I didn't till I saw you. The first time I saw you I wanted…no, needed you. I needed to be with you. So I asked Laura to fix me up with you. I don't have any trouble getting dates."

"I didn't figure you did. I'm very flattered."

Carrie felt like there was a fist in her throat. She wasn't going to say it, but then it felt like it was choking her, and she said it before she really knew she was. "I…I know this sounds crazy…I love you."

Spider didn't hesitate. "I love you, too, and you're right, it is crazy."

THEY SPENT MOST of the night making love and talking.

Carrie rolled over and looked at the clock. It was eleven o'clock in the morning. She almost panicked before she remembered it was Saturday. She yawned, stretched, and rolled back over. When she saw that Spider wasn't there she was mildly annoyed. Spider walked out of the bathroom carrying her comlink, and it was then that she realized that it must have been Spiders comlink that had woken her up. Spider sat on the edge of the bed and let Carrie drape herself around her waist, which made them both happy.

"…Uh huh, uh huh…you're fucking shitting me!"

Carrie jumped a little, startled by Spider's sudden outburst.

"Our serial killer…you're sure?" She sighed, obviously resigned. "Okay I'll get dressed and meet you there." She closed transmission. "Fuck!"

"Have to go to work?" Carrie asked, unable to mask the disappointment in her voice.

Spider lay down on the bed and kissed her. "I'm sorry. Dammit, I could happily lay here all day." She got up and walked back into the bathroom.

"You have a serial killer?" Carrie asked carefully.

Spider poked her head back out the door. "You know the Fry Guy is one of our cases?" Stupid question, really. As the assistant DA, she no doubt knew as much about the case and who was on it as anyone. "He fries bad guys' brains in their heads, so I personally think we ought to be giving the guy a round of applause instead of trying to find, stop, and prosecute him. Anyway, that's one of our cases. Well, ours and the fucking Feds. He just broke his pattern. He killed a cop."

"Maybe the officer was on to him…"

"I doubt that. I think this guy has a very good sense of justice. I don't think he'd kill someone just because he was afraid of being caught. Maybe the cop was dirty. Maybe there's something we don't know about this cop, and that's why our boy killed him." Spider was waiting for Carrie to be appalled by the way she was talking about this killer, as if he were one of the good guys. But if she was upset, she sure as hell wasn't showing it.

"How would he know?" Carrie asked.

"Same way he knew the other guys were bad." Spider shrugged and went back into the bathroom.

"You think maybe he's an ex-cop?" Carrie asked, walking after Spider.

Spider shrugged, slipped out of her robe and turned the shower on. "Might be, but I doubt it." Spider screamed over the water.

Carrie had a thought.

Spider was scrubbing the last of the sex off her body when Carrie crawled in the shower with her. Spider laughed. "I have to go to work, Baby."

"This won't take long."

"Where the fuck were you?" Tommy asked.. Spider grinned stupidly, and Tommy shook his head. "No, don't tell me. I don't want to know."

Spider shrugged and walked into the crime scene. Officer Lambosto was lying in the middle of his shop floor. Fried-eyed just like the others. Spider looked around at the workbenches and tools and smiled. Five hundred dollar chain saw. New radial arm saw. Brand new motorbike.

"Why are you smiling?" Tommy asked. Then added in a whisper. "This guy was one of us. Maybe if we had done our jobs this killer would be off the streets right now. This is our fault."

"The guy's wife work?"

"How the hell would I know?" Tommy asked.

"Why would our boy change his pattern now?"

"Because this guy was on to him," Tommy answered.

"Oh, please! Like this blue jerk could figure out what neither we or the Feds could."

"We aren't really trying, remember?" Tommy said in a whisper. "It wouldn't be the first time a uniformed officer tried to get a promotion by cracking a really big case." He punched up Officer Lambosto's files. "See, he's tried to get a promotion to detective class three times."

"And he couldn't, so he went on the take. It wouldn't be the first time that has happened, either. Look around you. Look at this shit. He was a uniformed officer, so where's he getting the money to buy this crap?"

"God! I can't believe you. This guy is dead, and you're trying to fucking ruin his reputation to justify the actions of your precious serial killer."

"Our guy hasn't whacked anybody yet who didn't deserve it, why would he start now? Besides, he's *our* serial killer. I don't remember you bitching about him yesterday when he whacked Barney Jones."

"Barney Jones was the scum of the earth. This guy was a cop. Maybe Lambosto figured out who he was, and…"

"Lame, Tommy. Five will get you ten that if we start checking on this guy he's a low life just like all the others…"

"Spider, for God's sake! He's a cop."

"There is no reason for the Fry Guy to break his pattern, so either this stiff was a creep, or we've got another wako with the same weapon."

"Detective Webb," one of the uniformed officers called. Spider walked to where he was. "Look at this, Sir." He pointed at something behind the workbench. "Looks like you were right."

"Five will get you ten that's the missing coke from last weeks bust," Spider said.

"How the hell…" Tommy started.

"Elementary, my dear Chan. He was one of five people who went into the evidence locker on the day that the coke came up missing." She pulled up the information on her comlink. "This same locker came up short six months ago, but there was so little missing that they couldn't be sure it wasn't just a counting error. He's probably been doing it for awhile, just taking a little here and a little there."

"But he only signed into the evidence locker once, the computer…" Tommy noted.

"Is easier to get around than an attendant in a lot of ways. He could have gotten in without being logged in. It's not all that hard to do." Spider turned her attention back to the officer. "Good work. Take it down to the station and have it tested. See if it really is the stuff out of the evidence locker."

She turned to Tommy. "Let's go talk to his old lady."

"God please don't let her ask the widow if he dealt smack to first graders," Tommy mumbled as he followed her to the house.

The woman who opened the door had obviously been crying, and she'd also obviously just taken one hell of a beating. Spider looked at Tommy and smiled.

"You're a sick bitch," Tommy whispered in Spider's ear as they walked in.

The woman motioned for them to sit down on the couch and they did.

"We're very sorry to hear about your husband," Tommy said.

"Yeah," she cried.

Spider, never one to beat around the bush, looked right at the woman, smiled warmly, and asked, "So, did your old man beat the dog shit out of you, or was it the perp?"

"Christ on a crutch!" Tommy swore.

The woman looked at Spider and snarled. For a second she was silent, and then she started to cry. "That bastard!" She was shaking now. "When I saw him lying there…like that. You know, all burned up, I figured God had finally heard my prayers and struck the fucker dead."

Tommy sat there for ten minutes with his jaw in his lap while the woman poured her guts out to Spider. Spider had that effect on people. For some reason complete strangers would tell her things they wouldn't normally tell another soul. It was like she could break through their politeness zone, get them to say exactly what they thought instead of a stream of niceties. The widow explained that a few months ago, Elvis—yep that was the guy's first name—had started coming up with extra cash. She didn't know where he got it, but when she asked he got mad, and when he was mad he liked to slap her around, so she didn't pursue it.

Along with the coke they found a key to a safety deposit box. In the deposit box they found a sixty-kilo bag of smack and twenty thousand dollars in cash.

But this time there was no way anyone could have known. Hell, the police department had dismissed him as a suspect when the coke came up missing, stating that he couldn't be suspect because of his flawless record. Even the guy's partner passed a polygraph test when asked if he knew his partner was stealing drugs from the evidence locker and selling them.

One of the Feds pulled Tommy and Spider aside. "If you guys have got something on this Fry Guy, tell us now. How could he have known this guy was dirty? It's got to be someone in your department. Maybe someone in the IAD?"

"We don't know any more than you do," Tommy said. Then added suspiciously, "Probably a hell of a lot less. Why don't you just tell us what the fuck the weapon is, and how someone could get a hold of it?"

"For the thousandth time, Chan. We don't know!"

He stomped off, and Tommy turned to Spider. "You believe him, don't you?"

"You know what I believe."

WHEN SPIDER GOT home at about five o'clock, Carrie was gone. She'd left a note.

> *Spider,*
> *Got buzzed as soon as you left. Had to go into the office for a couple of hours, same reason you had to go in. Be back around six o'clock. We could go out, or stay in. Or I could go home to my lonely bed and lament the fact that I'm not in your arms. Whatever you'd like.*
> *Love, Carrie*

Spider cleaned up and went to the hospital to see Henry for a while.

"I met someone. Can you believe it? I'm in love, Henry. I never thought it could happen to me, but it has. Her name is Carrie and she's beautiful, inside and out...yeah, it's kind of sudden, but then maybe again it's not. You know me, I've spent most of my life looking for someone, so when I finally found her, I knew.... want to hear something weird? The first night I slept with her I didn't dream at all. At least not that I remember. Last night I dreamt about Carrie, not the faceless bitch from my nightmares. I think things are going to come together for me now. Well, I gottah go. I've got a date, but I want you to know I'm not going to forget about you, Henry. I promised I wouldn't leave you alone, and I won't."

WHEN CARRIE GOT back to Spider's apartment Spider still wasn't home, but she'd left a note.

> *Carrie,*
> *Gone out for a minute. Be right back. Please don't start without me.*
> *Love, Spider*

Carrie flopped down in the chair more than a little disappointed. She wanted to see Spider, and she wanted to see her now.

She should be home, her home. Her nice, comfortable home. Instead she was here in this hole-in-the-wall in one of the worst sections of town, waiting like a lovesick fool for Spider to get there and 'complete' her. She felt like a total idiot. She had laughed at friends who had acted the way she was acting now.

So this is love—desperate, needy, scatter-brained. Damn good thing this didn't happen to me before now or I'd never have made it through law school. Where is she, what could be more important than being here with me?

She felt insecurity creeping in on her. It was too quick. She was being too clingy; she was driving Spider away. Carrie wasn't used to feeling insecure and vulnerable. Her parents had raised her to be independent, self-assured, and self-reliant. She'd always been completely in control of her destiny; everything she'd ever wanted had been hers for the taking.

Now she was in love and she found the situation to be as unnerving as it was exhilarating. Spider could decide to end it at any minute, and Carrie was afraid she couldn't just walk away. Maybe she'd become one of those women who kept going to their ex's houses calling and crying, "Why, why can't you love me, I love you."

The door opened and Spider walked in with two bags of groceries. She smiled when Carrie jumped, and then she carried the bags into the kitchen and set them down. When she turned around to walk back in the other room Carrie all but tackled her. They kissed long and hard, as if they hadn't seen each other in weeks, and Carrie was reassured.

"So," Carrie released Spider and started going through one of the sacks. "I guess this means we're dining in."

"Yes…well, you might as well know right now that I don't have a hell of a lot of money. I've got a lot of expenses, debts my brother left me."

"You know, Spider…I make good money. It doesn't always have to be your treat or Dutch treat. Some times I could pay, all of the time I could pay, if you want to go out."

Spider did her best to look offended. "Like a kept woman?"

"Would that bother you?" Carrie asked. "Does it bother you that I make more money than you?"

Spider thought about it for a moment. "I don't know. Truthfully, it makes me a little uncomfortable to have anyone pay for anything for me. Logically, if we're going to wind up together, and I sort of hope we are, it's a relief. Because, as I said, I'm not very flush for cash. Now don't get me wrong, all my bills get paid and all that, but there isn't a whole lot left over for extras."

"Then let me pay for the extras. As far as I'm concerned we're already together. If we're going to have the kind of partnership I want, we don't need to worry about where the money comes from, just how we're going to spend it. It's not like I make more money because I work any harder or I'm any smarter. I make more money because my parents were rich lawyers and they put me through law school so that I could follow in their footsteps."

"So, are your parents okay with…"

"Me being gay? They think so. They want to be, and they do their best. They're more upset that I went into criminal law instead of joining them in private practice as a divorce attorney. After all, that's where all the real money is, don't you know?"

Spider started putting the groceries away in an almost tangible silence.

"What's wrong?" Carrie asked.

Spider shrugged and didn't look up from what she was doing. "When my brother died, I'd been away at war for three years, in heavy combat areas, and God knows I'd seen a lot of death. In Baghdad, I'd killed men in the trenches on the end of my bayonet, close up and personal. I'd watched the people beside me, people that were my friends, die. We fought all day and all night, and when it was all over the blood was ankle deep, but we still held our ground. At least some of us did; only five people from my unit made it out of those trenches alive. At the time I thought that was the worst day of my life, but it wasn't even close.

"My father showed up at my brother's funeral drunk. When I saw Scott's coffin being lowered into the earth I felt like my soul was being ripped out of my body. The only person who had ever cared about me was dead, and I knew I was alone. At the time it felt like such a permanent thing—the being alone. I reached out blindly, taking my father's hand to give and take comfort. He jerked away and screamed for the entire crowd to hear, 'Get your filthy hands off me! My son, my Scotty is dead. But you, a fucking worthless dyke, are still alive. There is no justice.'"

"My God, Spider! I'm so sorry."

Spider looked out the kitchen door seeming to focus on nothing. "I called him a sorry son of a bitch, and I left. The worst part of it was that I didn't think he knew. I didn't think any of them knew. Don't ask, don't tell and all. In those days I thought I was completely hidden, totally closeted. But apparently everybody knew, even Scott. I never talked to him about it, and he never talked to me. I realized what that meant; that he knew and said nothing meant that he didn't really want to know. We never got a chance to talk about it—to work it out. For him to grow to accept who I am. It's made it very hard for me to be open about my sexuality. I look at you, at the ease with which you express yourself as a woman and a lesbian, and I envy you. I wonder if I'll ever be that comfortable in my own skin."

Spider wiped the tears from her eyes and tried to swallow the lump in her throat. Carrie just stared at her, obviously at a loss for words, and close to tears herself.

Spider forced a laugh. "I must be premenstrual. Excuse me." She worked her way past Carrie and into the bathroom.

Carrie rushed over to the kitchen sink and washed her face to calm herself down. *What do I say? I should say something. There should be something I can say to help her. How long has she been carrying that around? Is it a story she tells everyone who gets close to her—or just me, now? Is she even close to anyone else? What about Tommy...no she did the same thing to Tommy that she did to her brother; she didn't tell him. She doesn't tell anyone. That was what she was saying.* Carrie dried her face on a paper towel and noticed that she took off half her makeup.

"Damn!" She washed her face and dried it again. She had just finished when Spider walked back in the room.

"I'm sorry. I don't know what the hell got into me. No one wants to hear that kind of shit." Spider started putting the groceries away again.

"You're wrong. I want to hear. I want to know everything about you, Spider, good and bad—all of it. You...we, have nothing to be ashamed of. There's nothing wrong with us. Hell! We're wonderful.

Don't let the way a fistful of uptight bigots look at you make you afraid to be yourself. You have lived an exemplary life, and you have nothing to be ashamed of."

No one had ever said that to her before. No one had ever given Spider permission to be herself. You wouldn't think it would be necessary, but for Spider it was.

That night she had the dream again, but this time the woman had a face and it was Carrie's. Then she saw Robby, and he was calling to her, begging her to join him in his fight.

Spider woke with a start; she knew what the dream meant. For her everything was coming together—and coming apart.

CHAPTER SIX

*"Keep thy foot when thou goest to the house of God; to
draw near to hearken is better than the sacrifice of
fools: For they consider not that they do evil."*
Ecclesiastes 4:17

ROBBY HAD BEEN working on the damned stove all day, and he
was no closer to fixing it. It needed parts, parts that he didn't have
and couldn't make. At five o'clock he gave up and went to start
dinner. It was Evan's turn to help, but he wasn't home yet, even
though the bus had arrived an hour ago.

"Where's Evan?" Robby demanded.

"I'll help," Donna offered.

"Where's Evan?" Robby asked again with even less patience.

All the kids were real quiet. They could tell when Robby
was mad.

"Where is he?"

"He's been hanging out with some bad boys," Janice said.

Robby looked at Donna. "What's she mean?"

"A gang, Robby." Donna started to cry. "Evan joined a gang."

"We'll see about that."

They made dinner, ate, watched TV, and did their homework.
All the kids were in their beds before Evan got home. Robby could
smell the pot on him, and see the darkness licking at his heels. He
looked at the clock. It was midnight.

Evan turned on the light and saw Robby sitting there. He wanted
to look tough, but as he saw the anger in his brother's eyes, all he
could do was start crying.

"Where the hell were you?" Robby asked in a low, throaty growl.
"Donna said you haven't been in school for two days. That you
think you've joined a gang."

"I...I don't have to answer to you," Evan spat through his
tears. "You...you're just my brother. You ain't my daddy, and you
ain't God."

"You worthless piece of shit." Robby didn't raise his voice as he
hoisted himself from his chair. Without using his hands he popped

his brother against the wall and held him there with the strength of his will. "Can't you feel it? The darkness is oozing up around your soul trying to claim you. Can you look me in the eye and tell me that's a good feeling?"

Evan felt the force shove him hard against the wall again and was terrified into silence.

"Answer me!" Robby screamed. He took his hand and ripped the do rag from his brother's head.

"No!" Evan cried as he wet himself.

"You think you want to be a part of this gang. They aren't nothing but crap. I have given up any life of my own to make sure that you guys get the breaks I never had. Do you really think that I would let anyone do this…" he shook the rag in Evan's face, "to my family? Do you really think that I would let you ruin everything that I have worked for? How *dare* you bring the drugs and the darkness into my home with these babies! I'll kill you myself before I let you destroy my family. Take me to them, Evan. *Show them to me.*"

"Robby!" Evan cried louder. "I'll quit the gang. I won't smoke pot no more. I'll go back to school. I'll…"

"You don't understand what you've done. You can't just walk away. They won't let you walk away. Do you think people stay in gangs because they like it? No. They stay because once they're in, they're afraid. Afraid that their so-called friends will kill them if they try to leave, and if they don't some other gang will. And it's not just you Evan, you've put us all in danger, that's how it works. You try to walk out of the gang, they kill one of the kids. You've created a situation that can only be cured one way. Take me to them…*NOW!*"

Evan didn't want to, but he led his brother to his friends. The party he had left earlier still raged. It was in an old abandoned shack at the end of a slum street. There was so much pot and crack being smoked in there that it was coming out the windows. The bitter cold had driven everyone inside.

Robby got out of the truck and donned his "costume". He turned to Evan and snarled at him. "You stay here, don't you dare move. And always remember that everything that happens tonight is your fault."

Evan nodded silently. As Robby walked away Evan sank down into the floorboards, where he covered his ears and tried to block out the screams. Several minutes passed and then Robby opened the door and got in. He started the car and headed home. He looked at Evan quaking in the floor. "You can only belong to one gang, Evan, and that's us. Do you understand?"

"Yes, Robby."

CHAPTER SEVEN

"A good name is better than precious ointment;
and the day of death than the day of one's birth.
It is better to go to the house of mourning, than
to go to the house of feasting: for that is the end
of all men; and the living will lay it to his heart.
Sorrow is better than laughter: for by the sadness
of the countenance the heart is made glad."
Ecclesiastes 7:1-3

THIS TIME IT was bad. These bodies weren't neatly brain-fried; they were blown up. At least fifteen prominent members of the Skulls, a local street gang, had died in the carnage last night. Five people had lived through it, and the stories they told were... well, ludicrous.

"I'm telling you...a purple ski mask and a red cape," the punk said for the fourteenth time.

Tommy shook his head. "Humor me, and tell me again."

"This dude came through the door wearing a purple ski mask and a red cape. Big Jerry yelled 'Who the fuck do you think you are, weenie boy?' He yelled back 'The Angel of Death!' and *BOOM!* Jerry blew up, and then the dude just went around the room blowing people up."

"What did the weapon look like?"

"Man, for the thousandth time. There weren't no fucking weapon, at least nothing you could see. When he had finished he looked at us'ns and said, *This is the only chance I'm giving you. Turn back from the course you are following or fry like the others."*

The kid was scared—terrified and shaking. No doubt coming down off some drug, but he told the same story that the other four had. To the letter.

Tommy watched as Spider drove up. She got out looking more than a little perturbed. "What took you so long?" Tommy asked with a smile.

Spider looked back at him and snarled. At two o'clock in the morning she didn't feel like joking. Mostly she felt like sleeping. Carrie was trying to kill her; not that it wasn't how she'd always dreamt of going.

"What we got?" Spider asked.

Tommy pointed at the door. "You tell me."

Spider walked over and looked in. She took one look around and almost chucked. The smell, the look, the dark.

"INCOMING! OH GOD! It's gonna hit us!" she yelled as she ran. The others ran, too, but most of them weren't fast enough. The blast knocked her to the ground and sent her flying into the wall of the trench. Something soft and wet and sticky hit her in the side of the head. There was a glimmer of realization as the smoke and flames filled the air. That something that hit her was part of Becky. The rest of Becky was lying at her feet. She didn't have time for it to sink in; didn't have time to deal with it because then the bastards were in the trench with them...and it was shooting and stabbing and blood, so much blood—her blood, Becky's blood, the rag heads' blood. James came up beside her, trying to hold the bastards off. A bullet hit him, two, three. She hit the ground and rolled, finding a safe place behind a piece of a car.

"Spider, help!" He held a hand out to her. She reached for him, and something hard and hot hit her shoulder, throwing her back. She tore a piece of her shirt off and packed her own wound as she watched a bullet splinter James' skull. She grabbed her gun, got up and ran towards the enemy. It wasn't courage, it was rage that empowered her. Rage, and fear. Sarge screamed, "No Webb!" But she ran in, firing, and now he was dead and she was still alive. Another bomb hit. This time it hit behind the Iraqis line. The cavalry had come. Seven of her unit joined her, only four lived to see morning. Only the five of them waded through the blood and carnage and survived. It was idiotic. They gave them a medal for living, but then they gave everyone else a medal for dying, and how much more stupid was that?

"SPIDER!" TOMMY SCREAMED again. "Spider!"

She turned away from the scene towards Tommy. She must have looked as shaken as she felt.

"You okay, Spider? You're looking a little green."

"I'm...okay."

"You hear my question?"

She shook her head no.

"I asked if you thought it was the Fry Guy."

She didn't have to think about that one. It was a no-brainer. "Yes."

"Why so sloppy? Why such a mess?"

Spider thought about the mess he was talking about. Thought about what had happened to her in Baghdad.

"Killing Rage. This time he was mad. He didn't really think; he just struck out. Apparently—at least in his mind—they did something personal to him."

"He left five witnesses," Tommy told her.

She looked at him in disbelief.

"And this is what they all said." He punched up the data and showed it to her. She watched all five interviews, and then Tommy repeated the description. "A man of unknown ethnic origin wearing a purple ski hat, a red cape and leather work gloves."

"He knew there was a chance that not everyone here would be truly bad, evil if you will. The five he left alive he must consider redeemable. See if they had any previous records."

Spider seemed disconnected. Maybe she was just tired, but somehow Tommy didn't think so; there was something wrong. It was cold and she was sweating. He looked for the files anyway.

"You're right. None of those five have a record that includes anything harsher than shoplifting. Three of them have no record at all."

"And what do you want to bet that all those corpses do. Or if they don't, that they were deeply into the gang—totally corrupted. We should interview some of the families of both the victims and the survivors see if there are any similarities…"

BODIES, SO MANY *bodies, and somebody had to move them. No one ever thought about that.*

The flies. That's what she remembered—the flies. Like black air they were so thick, and the smell—sweetly putrid. They sent them in on what was supposed to be a routine relief. They were to go in and take over the post; that was what they were told. Their sergeant never told them that everyone there had been killed by some biological or chemical weapon that they weren't at all sure had dissipated. Life was cheap to the boys at the top; that was a fact that never changed. Some dick way up the food chain was always willing to put someone else's life on the line to prove some stupid point.

She didn't sleep the first three days they were there, and any food she ate came right up. By the fourth day they had most of the corpses cleaned up and she had become desensitized, or at least that was what the military fucks like to call it. It was a nice clean way to explain that they had killed part of your brain. That they had stolen away part of your humanity.

Becky never did "desensitize," and it made things that much harder for her. Spider tried to make things easier for her and in doing so wound up making things harder for herself.

Who cleaned up Becky's body? Who cleaned up James's? What good was life when, in the end, you were reduced to nothing more than a mess someone had to clean up?

Body after body, day after day, the heat and the sand and the damned flies...

"GODDAMN IT, SPIDER!" Tommy all but screamed.

She looked at him, took a deep breath, and rubbed a sweaty hand down her ashen face.

"What the hell is wrong with you?"

She checked first to make sure her comlink was off, and then took a quick look at Tommy's. He had apparently severed the link before he screamed at her.

She laughed nervously and started to lie, but she was shaking and felt sick to her stomach. She looked at Tommy, her teeth chattering, suddenly cold.

"Sometimes when you see things, Tommy...things people shouldn't have to see...it changes you, and you're never quite the same again. You have to bury those things real deep or you can't even think to lead anything close to a normal life. But they're never gone, and when you least expect it, they'll jump right back up in your face."

She looked into Tommy's eyes. "You can see too much, Tommy." She wiped the tears from her eyes with the back of her hand. "Things that will keep you up at night, things that won't let you sleep. I'm having a PTS episode. I'm going home, Tommy."

"You okay to drive?"

"Yeah, I'll be all right as soon as I put some distance between me and...*that*. You got things here?"

"Yeah. Sure, pard." Tommy watched her go. He saw her bend over to pick something up; he couldn't see what. Then she got in her car and drove off. He knew he shouldn't have let her leave alone, but he turned around and went back to work.

"YOU DID WHAT!" Laura screamed at him.

Tommy didn't want to do this. If he went back to bed right now he could get an hour's sleep before he had to get up and go back to work again. "She wanted to go home. I let her."

"Damn it, Tommy, she's your partner. It's not like this is the first time she's had one of these PTS episodes. You know she's not safe to drive."

"She's a grown woman. She's never had trouble driving before, she said she just needed to get away," Tommy defended.

Laura picked up the phone and dialed Spider's apartment. Carrie's sleepy voice answered.

"Hello?"

"Hello, Carrie, it's Laura. I'm sorry to call so late. Is Spider home?"

Carrie looked around. Spider wasn't in bed, and as far as she could see, not in the apartment. "No, why?"

Laura took a deep breath. "Ah…Tommy wanted to ask her something about the case, that's all."

"Is everything all right?" Carrie asked. "Is Spider all right?"

"Yeah, she should be home soon. Sorry I woke you. Good night." She hung up the phone and glared at Tommy.

Tommy dialed up Spider's private comlink number. He sighed a sigh of relief when she answered, then frowned when he realized she was in her car. "Spider, what the hell are you doing?"

"It's okay, I'm going home now. I just had to calm down, that's all."

"All right. Go straight home and call me when you get there."

"Will do."

CARRIE GAVE THE phone a weird look and hung it up. She looked at the clock, frowned when she saw the time, and rolled over to try and go back to sleep. It wasn't happening. About fifteen minutes later Spider came in. She looked up at Spider and patted the bed beside her. Spider shucked her clothes and crawled under the covers. Carrie snuggled around her.

"My God, Honey! You're so cold and sweaty. Do you have a cold?"

Spider turned around to face Carrie. "I had a girl friend in the service, you know."

Carrie laughed. "That's okay, Honey. This may come as a shock, but you're not exactly my first, either."

"No, Carrie, let me finish." Spider swallowed hard. "Becky and I were close. It wasn't like you and me, but at least we thought we were in love. We cared about each other. We were entrenched just outside the heart of Baghdad when a bomb landed in our trench. It literally blew pieces of her all over me. For just a second I thought about just standing there till something hit me, too. It was too horrible to imagine living through. But something inside me, somewhere deep down, some instinct took over and I just kept going. She was my lover and my friend, and I wiped her blood off my face and kept fighting. I never looked back."

"If you had, you'd be dead, too," Carrie said quietly.

Spider looked at Carrie. "Don't you see, Carrie? I never told anyone about her. About what she meant to me. She died, and God only knows who buried her—if anyone. I went on with my life, and I left her there—body and soul—in that trench."

"You want to talk about her?" Carrie asked carefully.

"That would be too weird," Spider said.

"Why? Because she was your girl friend? I'm not going to feel threatened. I am one cocky bitch, and I have an almost too healthy self-image. If you loved her even a little, she must have been pretty special, and I want to hear about her."

Spider hesitated for a second. "Becky had delusions of grandeur; going in, she wanted to be the first woman three star general. Two weeks into basic training she was trying to find a way out..."

"For the fifth time, what did you take from the crime scene, Webb?" the lieutenant boomed as he showed the damn comlink video from detective Levits' unit for the fifth time.

"And for the fifth time that is not—technically—part of the crime scene," Spider answered through clenched teeth. "Who says I'm picking up anything? The view is obstructed by a fucking car. I bent over to look at something. I didn't pick anything up..."

"Detective York said he saw you put something into your pocket."

"That's called my hand," Spider hissed.

"He makes a strong accusation, Webb. He says he thinks you took evidence. He says he believes you have been doing so all along. Did you take something from that crime scene?"

"No I did not," Spider gritted out. She looked at Tommy then. "Go ahead. Tell him."

"I didn't see her pick anything up," Tommy lied.

"Not that. Tell him about last night. What kind of shape I was in."

He looked at her for confirmation. Did she really want him to tell the lieutenant about the PTS episode? It would mean a trip to the department shrink at the very least—medical suspension at the most. She nodded at him. He looked at the lieutenant, but just couldn't.

"Ah...crap, Spider."

"Just tell him!" she nearly screamed.

Tommy took a deep breath and let it out, but still stammered when he started talking. He'd never had another partner, and he didn't want one now. "She, ah...she occasionally suffers from a minor form of post-traumatic shock syndrome. She had an episode last night after viewing the crime scene. She wasn't really out, but she didn't really seem to have a handle on present events, either. She wanted to go home, and I told her to do so. She certainly wasn't up for tampering with evidence."

The lieutenant gave Spider an angry look. "Why didn't you report this incident immediately?"

"It's not like it's not a matter of record that I have them. I need to work," Spider said pointedly. "I have debts, and I can't afford any time off. It's more unnerving than anything else. I've never put myself, my partner, or anyone else in danger. I don't think I should be punished for something I have very little control over. Truth is, I might have picked something up—a rock, a piece of broken glass. I don't really remember. But if I had picked any thing of any significance up, I'm sure I would have found it by now, and I would have turned it in."

The lieutenant seemed to think about it. He took a deep breath and exhaled. "I'm not going to take your word for it that these episodes aren't dangerous. You'll be expected to go to the department shrink for evaluation and then treatments. If you fail to make appointments you will be suspended without pay. Do I make myself clear?"

"Yes, Sir."

Tommy was surprised to see the relief cross Spider's face. It wasn't like her to give the bastard what he wanted. Then to his dismay the lieutenant turned his attention on him.

"The FBI seems to think that we are mucking up the crime scene. They are blaming this department for the fact that they have no leads..."

"They're blaming us because they don't want to admit that they are as stumped as we are," Spider hissed.

Tommy smiled. Now that was the Spider he knew and loved.

"This guy has some kind of weapon he probably stole from Uncle Sam. They know a hell of a lot more than we do, and they aren't any closer to catching him than we are. They're looking for a scapegoat."

"That may be so, but you two have made no bones about the fact that you think this guy is doing a public service…" They started to protest and he held up his hand. "You're on too much vid-tape to deny it. God only knows what you say when you've got your comlinks off. My point is this. This guy is breaking the law. He's killing people. He's a murderer. As cops we shouldn't care who he's murdering. If I find out that any of my officers, even one who has been decorated for distinguished service," he glared at Spider, "is tampering with evidence, I'll be the first one to testify against them. Do I make myself clear?"

They nodded silently.

"OK, bugger off then."

Tommy glared across the car at Spider. He couldn't tell what she was thinking, but then he rarely could. He had to look back at the road, because he was driving, after all.

"What did you pick up, Spider?" Tommy more hissed than said. He didn't like being left out to dry when he didn't even know he was wet. Spider started humming and stared out the window as if she hadn't heard him.

"What did you pick up, Spider!" he screamed.

Spider must have known he was about to scream, because she didn't jump even a little. She turned her head slowly to face him. "Nothing."

"Lying bitch," Tommy swore. "This isn't a game any more. This guy is killing more and more people. Some of those gang members were just kids…"

"They were all hoods, every last one of them…"

"They didn't deserve to die like that. I'm not sure anyone does. This has got to stop; it's gone too far. At first I was right with you. Hell, it may have even been my idea. But we can't keep covering for this guy. We're going to have to start looking for him. Now, what did you pick up?"

She started humming again and continued staring out the window.

"Goddamn it, Spider…"

She spun on him, fast and hot. Tommy jumped at the fury in her voice when she started to talk. "I saw what he did last night. I saw it, too. It dredged up shit I thought I'd put to sleep. But that doesn't change the fact that everyone who got slammed had it coming. If they hadn't already raped, mutilated, or killed, they would have. He knows that. Somehow he sees men's souls. I understand that you don't want to cover for him anymore, and I won't ask you to, but don't ask me not to."

Tommy pulled the car over and parked so he could safely glare at her across the car. "Are you going to tell me what you picked up?"

Her silence answered his question.

"Damn it, Spider! You could burn us both with this shit. This guy is a loaded cannon. A man with a very powerful weapon he probably stole from the government. He is not some avenging angel sent to do God's work. Get that through your head."

Spider didn't look at him as she answered. "When I was in the military it was easy. We had one kind of uniform; they had another. We were the good guys, we knew who the bad guys were, and we killed them, even though we didn't really know why they were shooting at us or we were shooting at them, it was easy. All black and white—no grays. Now I'm here in the streets and I don't know who the good guys are any more. Everything is in shades of gray."

Spider turned to look at Tommy then, and the look in her eyes scared him more than a little.

"But not to this guy, Tommy. This guy *sees* evil. He sees it like you and I see color. I'm not going to do anything to stop him. I'm not going to do anything to help them stop him. I'll go through the motions, but that's it. It wasn't that long ago that you agreed with me. Sometimes the ends *do* justify the means. The end isn't a room full of mutilated corpses. The end is good kids that will be alive tomorrow because those bastards didn't live to turn them on to drugs or kill them outright."

Tommy nodded, not because he was sure he agreed, but because he knew there was no changing her mind, and no sense in trying.

"OK, but I'm not playing any more."

Spider nodded back. "I wouldn't ask you to."

For some reason her answer bothered him. He got the idea that what she was really saying was that this was out of his league.

IT HAD BEEN a week since Robby had managed a good night's sleep. The scene in the crack house still haunted him, and the news and every paper was filled up with it. Everywhere you looked you saw something about it. Everywhere he went people were talking about it, and there were cops and G-men all over their part of town asking questions of every gang-banger they came across.

Evan had never done his chores so quickly or completely. Never been so eager to please. Robby blamed himself for Evan's short trip into trouble. He should have been watching him closer; he shouldn't have dropped his guard even for a minute. You couldn't afford to do that with teenaged kids. Worse than the guilt and the fear was the knowledge that his brother now listened to him, not out of any sense of love or loyalty, but out of fear. Because he knew now that Robby harbored some terrible power.

Robby loaded the old air conditioner into the bed of his truck and collected his money from the man. The man smiled and thanked him, and Robby smiled back and thanked him for his business. He got in the truck and headed for his next pickup. Normally the pickup of an air-conditioner would have put him in a really good mood. Old conditioners could almost always be fixed and resold for good money. But today he couldn't stop thinking about how close he had brought the cops to his own door. He had let his anger get the best of him, but then what else could he have done? Written Evan off? Worse, let him bring that scum into his house to infect the other children? He had to stop it; he just wished he could have found another way. He frowned then. The evil never gave you any other way. They backed you into a corner where you could either kill them, or let them live to do what you knew they were going to do. Let them repeat the crimes of their past. And it seemed that lately there had been more of them than ever before.

He was sure that some people might call what he had a gift, but it was a double-edged sword. On the one hand, he had the power to make the world a better place. On the other hand, it meant he constantly had to make decisions he'd rather not make, and he lived in constant fear of being caught.

His family relied on him. He had a responsibility to them, a duty to feed, clothe, house, and love them. He couldn't do that if he was in jail. Every time he killed someone he ran the risk of being caught.

Mankind needed him. He had a responsibility to free them from fear, to protect them from the pestilence that would prey on them. To remove from their midst a danger only he could truly see.

He didn't take either responsibility lightly.

THE FRY GUY hadn't killed anyone in three weeks, and things at work were getting more relaxed. Tommy and Spider were even able to work on some of their other cases.

Tommy drove at break-neck speed through traffic, the light on top flashing, the siren whaling.

Spider was eating a hamburger, not without some effort, and they were talking about the Fry Guy.

"So, why did he stop?" Tommy asked.

"He had to. He knew he'd pushed the envelope on that mass killing, and he knew it was time to back off. Maybe he made himself sick, or scared himself," Spider answered, breaking the rule about talking with your mouth full.

"So, will he kill again? Or have we seen the last of him?"

"Oh, he will undoubtedly kill again," Spider said. "He won't be able to stop himself. Imagine that you had the ability to look at a man and know that he had killed and would kill again if given the chance. Could you let him walk away?"

"I don't know," Tommy said truthfully. "I wouldn't want to, but I might to save my neck."

"What if you realized that the person he might rape or kill was you or Laura?"

"I'd have to kill him," Tommy said without hesitation.

"Our killer sees every potential victim as if it were one of his loved ones. He feels responsible for everyone."

"Or he's just someone who found a really cool weapon and knows that as long as he's butchering gang members and baby-rapers no one's going to really come after him..."

"Except that the FBI is..."

"Which may be exactly why he's backed off now," Tommy said. "In fact, it makes perfect sense. He realized they were getting too close, and he did the gang-bangers the way he did because he wanted to go out in style. For all we know he may have thrown his weapon into the bay and is half way across the country right now."

"Hate to ruin your little theory, but we were nowhere near finding him, and neither were the Feds," Spider said.

"He didn't know that. Maybe he was smart enough to get out before we got close."

Spider shrugged, obviously bored with the conversation. She wadded up her hamburger wrapper and threw it into the bag her lunch had come in.

"Carrie asked me to move in with her."

"Are you going to?" Tommy asked.

"Do you think I should?" Spider asked.

Tommy stared at her for a minute. He hated this; she was asking his opinion on something that could change her whole life. What if he gave her the wrong answer? He could screw up her whole life! If he didn't answer then he was being a dick; it would seem like he didn't care. He stumbled in. "Ah...do you love her?"

Spider seemed as shocked as he was that he was answering her, even if it was with a question. "Yes, I do. Very much."

"She's at your apartment all the time. She never gets a chance to relax; that's got to be a pain." He was proud of himself; this was easier than he thought.

"Yeah, it is that. Seems like I never get anything done, and I'm sure it's the same for Carrie. And with both of our schedules...I don't see her nearly as much as I would like to."

"Do you want to move in with her?" Tommy asked.

"Yes, I do," she said after a moment's thought.

"Then why the fuck did you ask me?" Tommy asked with a laugh.

"I guess I wanted to hear you say that I wasn't crazy. I mean, I've only known this woman a little more than a month."

"What's the worst that will happen? You'll have to look for a new apartment if it doesn't work out," Tommy said. He was good at this. In fact he was enjoying giving sagely advice.

"You're exactly right," Spider said. She slid across the seat and into him as they braked to a stop. They jumped out, slapped on the comlink intercepts, and drew their weapons. Five other cars were already on the scene. The captain was there, and so was the riot truck.

Five perps had held up the bank. Some fucking militia group—which meant they had kevlar and AK-47's. An idiot security guard had tried to stop them. Now he was dead, the robbers had nothing to lose, and fourteen hostages to use for shields.

"Fucking black and whites," Spider cursed as she crouched behind her open door.

Tommy knew why. Just once he wished the black and whites wouldn't rush in so quick. Let the bastards get into their cars and drive away. Chances were you'd catch them. Even if you didn't, it was just fucking money, not lives. The last thing you wanted to do was give the perps nowhere to run when they had a bank full of people.

More police cars roared in, followed by the DA's car. Spider saw DA Richards get out of the car, and Carrie got out right behind him. Spider's stomach churned, and her heart was in her throat. She'd never thought about this, and she didn't like it.

By the time Tommy saw the gunman in the bank move, Spider was already around her door and over the hood. Tommy opened fire on the gunman, and so did everyone else.

Spider ran across the hoods of the other cars as the bullets sprayed. Then she jumped. One arm hit the DA, the other caught Carrie, and she dragged them both to the ground with her.

"Stay the fuck down!" she ordered.

She jumped back up behind the door.

"Spider! No!" Carrie screamed.

Spider aimed and fired. The gunman went down with a hole through his forehead. As the captain screamed for a cease-fire, Spider dropped behind the door. It was deathly quiet. No one was firing now.

Spider looked at Carrie. She looked OK.

"Do you have to be here?" Spider asked.

Carrie nodded and moved to hide behind the door with Spider, as did DA Richards. He looked peaked and was breathing heavily. Spider noticed then that they were both wearing flack jackets; her heroics had probably been unnecessary. Still, better safe than sorry.

"Thanks," Richards said.

Spider just nodded.

"Tommy, you OK?" Spider asked over her comlink.

"Yeah, you?" Tommy came back.

Spider checked herself. Her leg was bleeding, but it wasn't broken. It wasn't bad. "I'm fine."

Carrie noticed the blood and temporarily lost it. "My God! You've been hit! You're bleeding! You're going to die!"

Spider laughed and shook her head. "Thanks for the vote of confidence, Honey."

The Captain was talking to the perps over his loud speaker, but Spider was a little too concerned with her own drama to worry about what he was saying. The ambulance was there, and she was aware that they were taking a couple of the uniformed cops away. She reached out suddenly, took hold of Carrie's chin and turned her to face her. She had a scratch on her forehead, but other than that she seemed all right. Spider kissed her gently on the lips.

"I've got to go. Please keep your lovely ass down."

"Spider, you're hurt…"

"Not bad. Bye!" She kissed her again, released her and ran behind the cars in the direction of the captain.

Richards loosened his tie; his color didn't look good.

"You OK, Sir?" Carrie asked.

Richards nodded. "A little shaken, that's all." He smiled at Carrie. "So, was that the little woman?"

Carrie nodded with a smile. "That's the problem with avoiding the dinner party thing. Everyone winds up meeting your lover under the worst possible circumstances."

THEY HAD REACHED a very guarded truce. Richards was good at negotiating, but these guys weren't really into negotiating, so the best he could do was keep them talking.

The ringleader was screaming now, "We got one of yours, and you got one of ours. That makes us even!"

"Sorry, it just doesn't work that way, Peterson," Richards screamed back. "Why don't you just walk out of there? Give yourselves up, and no one else gets hurt."

"Because he's a fucking lunatic," Spider mumbled shaking her head. She was in the back of the riot truck, being fitted into a titanium kevlar jump suit—as was Tommy. Her leg had been field dressed. Spider put on her helmet to block out the sound of Carrie's protests.

Carrie addressed the captain. "She's wounded; she should be going to a hospital, not into that building."

"I'm sorry, Sir. But Detective Webb volunteered for this assignment, and she is part of our SWAT team. Her wounds have been adequately dressed, and it has been determined that the damage is minimal. She and detective Chan are the only members of my team who have ever done anything like this before. These guys have promised to start killing people in an hour, and since they've got nothing to lose, I can't imagine that they won't keep that promise. Unless, of course, we give them everything they're asking for, and I just don't see Richards doing that any time soon, do you?"

Carrie nodded, then turned her attention back to Spider.

Spider addressed the worry on Carrie's face with the biggest smile she could muster. "It'll be all right," Spider assured her.

Tommy looked on in disbelief as Carrie's expression changed from one of fear and anger to relief and acceptance. Tommy tested his direct comlink to Spider by saying, "Some day you've got to show me how you do that."

Spider smiled at him and shrugged.

"Are you up for this? Because if you're not, a lot of people could get killed," the captain warned.

They both nodded.

"All right. Everyone else is in position. The food should arrive any minute. They'll send one of their men out into the street to pick it up. That should cause a little chaos, and give you a window of opportunity. We'll try to keep you posted on where they are."

"Let's rock and roll," Tommy said. He was wired; this was why he had joined the force. Today he'd make a difference or die trying.

They started out of the truck.

"Spider, I swear to God…" Carrie started.

Spider turned, looked at her and smiled. "Yes, I'll move in with you."

THEY DROPPED THEM on the rooftop by copter. Not too conspicuous considering that there had been news and police copters flying around the scene for the last hour. After that, it was simply a matter of getting down the building without alerting the perps to their presence. Which also wasn't too hard, since they had a recent diagram of the building and all the keys. It was a credit to the people concerned, and the police department as well, that they had been able to empty the building so quickly and so nearly completely.

Using the elevator was out of the question, so they took the staircase.

They walked carefully down the hall towards the bank's back door that the diagram showed opened into a small storage room. From there it was a short trip down a short hall to the bank itself.

Spider focused all her attention on the space behind the door— not an easy thing to do with the captain barking the locations of the terrorists in her ear. There was someone on the other side of the door. Someone scared, wired, and crazy. She pulled Tommy back down the hall again.

"There is one just on the other side of the door. The bank has been taken off system, so the only real problem with the door is getting it open. But with the guy on the other side…"

"I didn't hear that," Tommy said.

"They can't see through walls. He's there, Tommy, take my word for it. If we start fiddling with the lock on the door, he's going to know we're here."

Tommy walked quietly forward and took a closer look at the lock and the door. Then he walked back to Spider.

"I can kick the door…"

"Are you sure? Because…"

"I'm sure," Tommy promised.

In their ears the captain said. "Don't take any chances, goddamn it!"

"I can do it," Tommy promised Spider.

She nodded and they moved back up to the door.

Again Spider focused all her attention on the air behind the door, but the captain was screaming. "Goddamn it, Webb…Chan, no fucking cowboy shit! We're talking civilian lives." When they didn't respond, he continued, "All units at ready! All units at ready! Get ready to move in on my word."

Spider reached up under her helmet and tapped the earpiece implanted just beneath her skin, turning it off. Without the captain screaming in her ear she could focus.

Tommy didn't question her. He'd been here with her too many times to do that. He didn't know how, but she would pull this off without the earpiece or apparent knowledge of the location of the terrorists.

"Can you take out the guy on the other side of the door?" Spider asked him.

Tommy nodded.

Tommy watched Spider for several breathless moments.

"Now!" she whispered.

Tommy kicked the door at the lock. It opened swiftly as Spider's body hurled into it. She kept running as Tommy landed a swift killing blow to the startled man's head. Tommy headed down the hall the way Spider had gone, his rifle at the ready.

Spider was in the room before the terrorists really had time to respond to all the noise. The leader was standing there, still holding a Burger King bag. She shot him first, one neat little hole right in the middle of his forehead. As fast as she could squeeze off four rounds, the other four terrorists fell—all killed with the same precision. One of them had a chance to pull his trigger, but the hail of bullets landed harmlessly in the wall and ceiling.

Tommy strode up beside her as the SWAT team rushed in and pulled up short, realizing that there was nothing for them to do.

The hostages who had been lying face down on the floor were all screaming, sure that they were about to be killed.

As Spider breathed in the moment, Tommy told them, "It's all clear; you're safe now. Please get up and leave the building in an orderly manner."

The comlink had already told everyone outside the building that the mission was successful.

Spider looked at him then and frowned. "Tommy?"

"Yeah."

"I'm gonna pass out." And she did.

SHE STARED AT the TV.

"I could go home," she told Tommy.

He nodded as he munched on an egg roll.

She grunted, and he handed her one.

"Stop being such a baby. They're just holding you for observation…"

"Cost a fucking fortune," Spider mumbled.

"Who cares? You're not paying."

"Oh, yeah! That's right," Spider said, relieved. She ate the egg roll and stared at the TV again. "But I'm so fucking bored, Tommy."

"What a little pussy baby you are, whining all the time." Tommy laughed and shook his head. "I'll be glad when Carrie gets here. Then she can listen to your crying."

"No one has to baby-sit me," Spider said hotly. "I'm perfectly capable of being bored all by myself."

"And listen to Laura bitch all night? No, thank you."

Spider laughed. "You have to go home sometime."

"But I'm delaying it as long as I can," Tommy said.

Carrie walked in. "How are you feeling, Baby?" She sat down in a chair beside Spider and took her hand.

"It hurts," Spider whined.

"Oh, my poor baby," Carrie cooed.

"I'm gonna hurl!" Tommy said in disbelief. He stood up then and grabbed his sack of egg rolls. "I'm going, and I'm taking my egg rolls, too. I'll see you tomorrow."

Spider laughed, then said on a serious note, "Thanks, Tommy." Tommy smiled back. "Any time, pard."

Carrie waited till she was sure Tommy was gone. "What the fuck were you thinking? Are you fucking out of your tiny little mind? You never told me you were on the fucking SWAT team! Of all the stupid shit. And how dare you use that what-ever-the-fuck on me…"

"OK, I was right up with you till then. What are you talking about?"

Carrie glared at her. "You know damn good and well what I'm talking about—playing with my brain. I don't know what you did or how you did it, but I was a virtual zombie till it wore off at about three o'clock. If I'm mad, I prefer to be mad, and if I'm scared, I prefer to be scared."

Spider frowned. "All I did was give you a little *push* so you'd be less stressed. Everyone does it…"

"Everyone does it!" Carrie screamed. "You're kidding, right? Do you really think everyone does that? Because I'm here to tell you that they don't. They can't."

"They can't?" Spider could do it; it didn't even seem very hard. Not like feeling people out or knowing what they were thinking. It was just a little *push*; she didn't even have to focus to do it.

"Did anyone ever do it to you?" Carrie asked, calming down as she settled into the chair.

It was a good question. Spider thought about it for a moment, then shrugged. "I don't know; I think so. People have gotten me to do things I didn't really want to do."

"Take my word for it, Spider, there is a difference between talking someone into something and that thing that you do. It literally altered my thinking. Made me feel perfectly all right with you walking into a building full of terrorists. Made me think the captain had made the right decision instead of hating his guts. I was perfectly calm through the whole damn thing."

Spider didn't understand Carrie's anger. "And that's a bad thing?"

"Yes...yes it is. I'd rather be scared shitless and have my own feelings, thank you very much." She paused, seeming to calm herself down. "Don't you ever do that to me again." It was a warning.

Spider nodded and looked down at her hands. They had taken so much blood she had holes all over her hands and forearms, and then there was the damned IV. She swore it hurt more than the bullet wound, but right then there was something on her mind more important than pain. She couldn't even look at Carrie.

"Did I make you love me?"

Carrie laughed, shook her head no, and kissed Spider gently on the cheek. "Most assuredly not—this is not wearing off. I can't explain it, but this felt different. I wasn't myself. It was like part of me was shut down. It was creepy, and I hated it."

"I'm sorry that I played in your brain. I won't do it again."

"Good, now go to sleep. I need you fully functional as quick as possible. I have to admit that as stupid as it was, your climbing over three cars and hurling yourself through the air to save me was really a turn on."

HE DIDN'T LIKE it. He didn't like it at all. Who the hell did these jokers think they were, shoving their fifth-level government security code in his face and dragging him down here at two in the morning to access his files?

"Download it," the bigger one ordered. Something in the hours of old vid-audio files they had just viewed had obviously pleased him.

"Excuse me?" The captain couldn't believe his ears. "This is her entire record, some of which even I don't have access to. Her psych profile, for instance, is supposed to be completely confidential..."

"We have the clearance, Wainwright," the bigger one said. The smaller one just seemed to sit and watch the door, his eyes jerking around in a squirrelly fashion.

"We're talking about a woman's personal life. An officer who just today put her ass on the line to save a bank full of people. Why the hell are you so interested in her, and what right do you think you have to peer into the most personal aspects of her life?"

"Mr. Wainwright, this is strictly on a need-to-know basis. You don't need to know, and believe me, you don't want to. As for Detective Webb's personal life…She lives in apartment 6R, Blue Rock apartments on the corner of 5th and Elliot. She's a lesbian who is currently doing the assistant DA. In fact, it looks like they may be setting up house. Her mother died when she was three. Her father was an abusive, overbearing alcoholic. She signed up for military service when she was seventeen, and was stationed to the Middle Eastern theater when she was eighteen. You probably know most of her service record by heart, but did you know that she had a lover in the war, and that the woman was blown to pieces right in front of her? Did you know that she was a prisoner of war for five weeks, and that she escaped from a camp that everyone else died in? She suffers from post traumatic shock syndrome. Her brother was murdered when she was still in the service. A Henry Chambers tried to save him from his attackers and wound up in a coma for his troubles. Spider Webb pays to keep this man in the finest rest home in the city. She visits him almost daily and has long talks with him, although he has never showed one sign of consciousness in sixteen years. She is obsessed with serial killers, mass murderers, and the paranormal, and has probably one of the largest personal collections of books on these subjects in the state…"

"Is there a point to all of this?" the Captain asked. "If you already know all that, why do you need the files?"

"The point is that we already know all about Webb's personal life. We're looking for something else in her files, and as I said, you don't want to know what."

"Is that a threat?"

The big one looked at the smaller one, and the smaller one smiled for the first time. The big one looked back at the Captain and smiled; an expression that chilled Wainwright to the bone. "Well, yes. Yes, it was. Now, download the fucking file, and I wouldn't tell anyone anything about any of this if I were you. People who fuck around with this particular—shall we say—*problem* the government is having, have a peculiar propensity for ending up dead."

"You can't threaten me!" The captain was more than a little flustered. "I'm fucking Captain of the Shea City police force."

The man and his colleague laughed, then the big one said, "Tell you what. File an incident report on us, and see if you still have a wife and kids by two o'clock tomorrow afternoon. This is bigger than you can imagine. The government doesn't care who they have to off. You, me, Webb, we're all way down on the food chain. People have been killed for knowing a hell of a lot less than you know right now. The best thing you can do for yourself and your family is download the fucking file and forget this entire conversation."

The captain downloaded the file.

He didn't tell anyone.

"THE DOCTOR HAS to sign your release, dear," the nurse said for the third time.

Spider looked at Carrie and swung her legs out of the bed. "Screw that; I'm going home."

"You'll play hell, too." Carrie pushed gently but firmly on Spider's shoulder. "Don't be in such a big-assed hurry. Another hour or two isn't going to hurt you."

"Don't you have to go to work?" Spider lay back down. She didn't want to admit it, but sitting up that fast had made her a little dizzy. Not to mention nauseous.

"Under the circumstances, Richards gave me the day off," Carrie said.

"I want to go home. Goddamn it! Where is the fucking doctor already?"

The nurse snuck quietly out of the room.

Carrie laughed and sat on the bed next to Spider.

"What's so damned funny?" Spider asked.

"You're the biggest baby." She leaned over and kissed Spider on the cheek. "Why can't you just calm down and relax?"

"I hate being in the hospital."

"Nobody likes being in the hospital." Spider looked at her with a raised eyebrow, and Carrie laughed. "Well, nobody sane, anyway."

"It goes a little deeper than just normal dislike. Weird shit happens every time I'm in the hospital. Every time I have a fucking check up, any time I see a fucking doctor, the weirdness factor just shoots straight up there," Spider said.

"Superstition?" Carrie laughed in disbelief. "You're superstitious!"

"If you had my track record with medical personnel, you would be, too. Let's just say that I'm surprised that anyone will even look at me with the bad luck I seem to heap upon medical professionals."

The doctor walked in, then, his leg up to his hip in a cast. "Sorry I'm late." He laughed nervously. "I had a bit of an accident yesterday."

The doctor looked over her chart, checked her pulse, took her temperature and released her.

"How'd you break your leg?" Spider asked.

"Fell down the stairs at home. Damn clumsy of me." The Doctor turned and started to leave, but he turned back around at the door and looked at her for a little while. "You know, you...better stay off that leg for a couple of days anyway. Take it easy on it for a couple of weeks. A nurse will be up shortly to check you out." He left.

Spider smiled at Carrie. "What did I tell you?"

Carrie had to admit that was pretty weird. "You're cursed."

SPIDER WASN'T SURE that she liked this. She knew she'd told Carrie she would move in with her, but the idea that someone else had packed her things kind of creeped her out. Some of those things were personal, private. The thought that some strange moving company had packed her 'stuff'...Well, except for the fact that she still had all her shit it was kind of like being robbed.

Then there was the other thing. She had never been to Carrie's 'place' before. She had thought Carrie lived in an apartment, however nice.

She didn't. Carrie owned a house, and not exactly a very modest one. It was located in one of the best neighborhoods in Shea City. A house with a pool and 'grounds,' yet. As soon as she saw it, she felt instantly uncomfortable. She sat in an armchair that no doubt cost more than every piece of furniture that she owned, watching the forty-eight inch screen TV, and trying to take it all in.

"I can't fucking believe this," Spider mumbled. "I really *am* a kept woman."

She could hear Carrie in the hallway ordering the movers to take Spider's things into this room or that room. She barely won the battle, but she didn't scream, *Put my shit back in my apartment, I'm going home!*

This was all too fast, and it was scaring the hell out of her. Why had she agreed to this? Why hadn't Carrie given her a little time to think about it? Really think about it, not rush in blind. Hell, she'd never felt less comfortable in her life. Which was really saying something, since she had been a prisoner of war.

You don't move in with someone you've only known for five weeks. It's insane.

She liked to be in control, and now, suddenly she wasn't in control at all. Someone else was making all the decisions that affected her life. Where were her books, and why didn't she get to decide where they went? *Because, birdbrain, this isn't your house! You don't have a house any more! You don't have anything except a pushy, domineering woman who is going to take over your life, and make it a living tormentuous hell!*

"Damn it, Carrie!" Spider screamed. When she didn't get any response, she tried to get up and couldn't. She fell back in the chair with a thump. Some sadistic bitch of a nurse had put a brace on her leg so that it couldn't bend at the knee.

"Goddamn it, Carrie!" There was still no response. She screamed still louder. "Goddamn it Carrie!" When there was still no response, she started to undo the brace.

Carrie ran into the room, out of breath. "What the hell do you think you're doing?"

"What does it look like? I'm taking this fucking shit off so that I can get up and move around. Where the fuck were you? Didn't you hear me?"

It didn't take a genius to figure out that Spider was mad. Carrie sat down across from her and tried to look at her.

Spider looked away.

"I was upstairs, I came as fast as I could. What's wrong, Baby?" She took Spider's hands to stop her from unwrapping the leg further, and to get her complete attention. "Honey, the doctor said not to bend your leg."

"Don't tell me what to do!" Spider screamed back.

Carrie looked at her and smiled. "I'm not telling you what to do, Baby. We decided to move in together, remember? We talked about it."

"But…"

"I admit it. I had your stuff moved while you were in the hospital, before you had a chance to change your mind, because I need you with me all the time."

"But…"

"You can put your stuff wherever you want it when you get better. Right now I'm just having them put it out of the way. And, no, I'm not going to make you part with anything. It's your stuff, and it belongs in our house."

"That's just it, Carrie...this isn't our house. It's your house. I couldn't afford a faucet in this house."

"My grandfather left me a small fortune when he passed away. It was either invest it, or lose the money to taxes. So I bought this house. And this *is* our house. I finished the paperwork this afternoon..."

"Don't do that, Carrie. I don't want you to do that."

"Why not?" Carrie smiled. "You going to leave and sue me for the house?"

Spider looked horrified. "Of course not."

"Then what's the problem? We're together, we're going to be together forever, so...can't you just enjoy the fact that we are together? That we can afford a nice house and a pool? Do you have to worry about where it came from, whose money bought it? If it doesn't matter to me, why should it matter to you? Laura told me you put your death benefits in my name, and you don't see me bitching about it. I know that means commitment to you. Well, guess what, Baby. I'm just as committed to you."

"Tommy!" Spider hissed then muttered. "I guess he tells her fucking everything."

"That's what couples do."

Spider calmed down. She was glad that she was with Carrie, and she supposed she could learn to live in luxury. She forced a smile and nodded. "It'll take some getting used to, that's all. I'm not used to having someone else make decisions for me. You have to admit that it's pretty sad that the only way I can give you anything is if I die"

"You give me things I've never had before, Spider."

One of the movers walked in then. He made Spider immediately uncomfortable. He was on edge, worried or something. She looked right at him and he looked away.

"That's got it, ma'am," he said to Carrie.

Spider, still hung over from the drugs they'd given her in the hospital, couldn't quite fix on the guy. She hadn't taken any drugs since she got home and didn't plan to. She'd rather have pain than be

groggy. As it was, it was hard to say what might actually be bothering the guy.

Carrie paid him, and he and his partner left.

"I didn't like him," Spider said. "He was worried or something."

Carrie looked in the direction the two men had gone. "He seemed
like a nice enough fellow. A good worker."

"I'm still so groggy. I can't be sure, but…I think he was hiding
something."

Carrie laughed. "Welcome to the world of the mere mortals,
my sweet. Imagine never knowing exactly how people feel. Having to trust what they tell you is true." She looked with meaning
at Spider.

It took Spider a minute to get what she was hinting at. "You
know I love you."

Carrie smiled. "Yes, I think I do. But the point is that you know
how I feel about you, and yet you still question my motives."

"I guess I still have trouble believing that anyone as amazing as
you could actually love someone like me."

"Did it ever occur to you that maybe I ask myself that same
question? Why do you keep selling yourself short? You, my love, are
amazing, and I am very fortunate to be loved by you."

"As long as you keep believing that I guess I've got it made."

CARRIE WOULD HAVE a fit, but she was at work, and what Carrie
didn't know wasn't going to hurt her. So Spider had taken off the
offending leg brace and driven to the nursing home.

Spider fixed the pillows behind Henry's head. He didn't sound
good today; his breathing was raspy.

"Hey, Henry! You don't sound so good, bud. I'm sorry I didn't
get by for a couple of days, but I got a little shot. Nothing bad, just
grazed, but Carrie's treating me like a fucking invalid."

She told him all about the hostage situation and moving in with
Carrie. She told Henry things she couldn't tell Carrie; things she
couldn't tell Tommy. As she always did, she looked for any sign that
he might open his eyes and come back to the land of the living.
There was nothing, just the raspy breathing. Yet she felt him, felt his
presence, could feel his emotions as they changed during the course
of their one way conversation and knew that on some level he heard
and understood her.

When she was leaving she stopped by the nurses' station. "Henry sounds bad to me."

"He's had a bit of a cold," the nurse answered. "We all have. As long as it doesn't turn into pneumonia, he'll be all right."

All right. He was never going to be all right. *Maybe it would be better for everyone if he just died. And maybe his soul lives a very full life in a world we never see or touch or feel, and maybe he needs this body to be alive to live in that world.* Who could tell, who knew? Henry was not brain dead. Who knew what went on in his mind? Maybe his life was like one long dream, sometimes bad and sometimes good. Just like her life. She would rather be dead than be like Henry, because you just didn't know. You just couldn't be sure what his life was like. If it was like anything at all.

She had seen horrible things, lived through nightmares. But the unknown was the most terrifying thing of all.

CHAPTER EIGHT

"The wise man's eyes are in his head; but the fool
walks in darkness: and I myself perceived also that
one event happens to them all. Then I said in my
heart, As it happens to the fool, so it happens even
to me; and why was I then more wise? Then I said in
my heart, that this also is vanity." Ecclesiastes 2:14&15

A LOT OF people came to Ninth Street, but not many of them stayed. James Filbert the First was an exception to the rule. Ninth Street was his domain, his turf. He did whatever he liked here, and no one seemed to give a damn.

He slammed the man's head into the wall again. "I told you, you old fuck," he liked the wet sloppy sound the old gook's head made when he struck him against the wall, so he did it again, "I need my money, and I need it now."

"I not have money," the old Korean man said. "You said you protect, but you not protect. Last week robbed two times, so have no money."

James laughed. "You were protected from me, you stupid old fuck." He let go of the old man for a minute and he slid down the wall to fall to a heap on the ground. James pulled on gloves and looked down at the heap without pity. "Guess I'm gonna have to make an example out of you now."

He was about to grab the old man when a shadow fell across him. He looked up and saw a guy standing there in a red cape and a purple ski mask. He had read the papers, and he'd heard the stories, so he was not amused by the man's ridiculous appearance.

Suddenly he was seeing every evil deed he had ever done play out before him as if it were being pulled from his mind. Then there was a sudden tormentuous burning sensation in his brain. He crumbled to his knees. The burning intensified till his brain felt like it was going to explode, and then he pitched forward onto his face, dying. James cried out as his soul was ripped from his body. He looked down and saw his body, the man in the cape, and his former victim. For a hopeful minute he thought he was ascending into heaven, but the next there was pressure all around him—a dark place full of pain. He was swimming in blood, fighting to breathe. He was dying all over again. He couldn't breathe, and then suddenly there was a bright light in his face. Now he was cold, freezing cold, and something foreign was placed into his mouth. For a moment he thought they were going to suck his lungs right out of his chest. Everything was distorted like a bad acid trip. A huge man was holding him by his feet.

"It's a girl," the man said.

A woman with a big, ugly red face glared up at him and screamed. "A girl! I don't want a fucking girl! They said it was going to be a boy this time. My husband is never going to talk to me again."

"Don't you want to hold your baby?" the man asked.

The woman cried loudly and screamed, "Get it away from me!"

James tried to scream out at them, to say that this was all wrong, but all that came out was one loud, long cry.

ROBBY ADJUSTED THE ski mask to make sure that he was covered before he offered a hand to the old man.

The old man took his offered hand, never taking his eyes off Robby.

"You save miserable life. Kim Chung Lee not forget you save life."

"I wish you would," Robby said. He released the old man when he saw that he was on his feet. "You'd better get some medical attention."

Robby started to move away fast.

"Kim not forget you, masked avenger. You ever need help, you ask Kim."

Robby walked quickly to the truck, counting on the cover of darkness to hide him. He quickly took off his costume and stuffed it behind the seat. He breathed in and smiled. It felt good after all this time to have unleashed the power. Besides, how could he have justified watching as that scum beat the hell out of a defenseless old man? Still, he'd taken a risk. It was always a risk. He knew that now. He started the truck and took off. He couldn't afford to get caught.

He remembered the tortured look on the scum's face as he died and smiled. He'd had to let too many of them slip away. It seemed unnatural for him to do so. Right now he felt high as a kite. This guy had been a really bad son of a bitch; now he was just one more stiff. Still, Robby couldn't afford to fall back into the pattern he had gotten himself into before. It was just too dangerous.

He'd have to go back to the way he had been in the beginning. He had been careful and discreet, killing only as he had done tonight when the need to protect overpowered him. Once or twice a year. Since he had killed people that deserved it, no one had even looked for a killer, not really.

But not getting caught had made him feel invincible and cocky, and he had gotten more and more reckless, till he was killing anyone he saw who was evil. He'd gotten careless and brought the investigation too close to his neighborhood. Too close to himself and his family.

Still…he was a man who had very little control over his own life. His whole life seemed to be governed by other people's faults and their failure to hold up to their responsibilities. Responsibilities that he had to rush to fulfill before he was even old enough to know what he wanted for himself.

His life was filled with obligations and duties. The whole world wanted a piece of him, and he felt like there was nothing in the world that was just for him. Except this, the rush he got when he changed the whole world by removing a pimple from the ass of humanity.

Still…he had to be careful; he couldn't afford to get caught. That guy he passed in the bar last week, the slimy dick-wad who had mutilated an old lady and cut up cats just for the hell of it. He shouldn't have let him walk away. Maybe he could just kill him, too, tonight. Maybe no one would really notice. Or if they did, they wouldn't know it was him. He'd be more careful.

OH, GOD! SHE was hot, and so close. "Please, Baby! Please!" she screamed. The fucking comlink went off. "Ignore it, please."

Spider ignored it, the problem was that Carrie couldn't, and the moment was gone. She sighed, frustrated. "Oh hell, get the fucking link!" she screamed. Then she laughed and flopped back onto the pillow. "I hate those things."

Spider got up, wiping her mouth on the back of her hand. "Sorry."

She picked up her comlink and pressed the reply button.

"This had by God better be good."

"Sorry, Detective, but the Fry Guy is back full guns. We've got six corpses, each in a different section of town," he said.

Spider looked at Carrie and winked. "You owe me a hundred bucks."

"The Fry Guy?" Carrie asked, getting up and throwing on her robe.

Spider nodded as she started to record the locations.

Carrie's comlink went off then. She knew why; Richards had been having her do a whole lot more of the legwork lately. She glared at her reply button.

"This guy picked a hell of a time to start offing people again," she mumbled.

Spider walked in, pulling on her shirt. "What's that, Babe?"

"I was this close," she said, holding up two fingers.

Spider laughed. "Duty calls."

"At times like this I wish we were meter readers."

Carrie punched the reply button. "Hello...you called me..." She looked at Spider and smiled. "Yes, I had just heard...no, I don't mind at all going out to the crime scenes...just so happens I was up anyway."

CARRIE SLID ACROSS the seat towards her. "Something's not right with Richards. Lately he...well, he used to be very hands on, and now it's like he's having me do everything important."

"Tell him it's too much," Spider said.

"I'm not complaining, in fact I like it," Carrie shrugged. "It's just weird, that's all."

"He's sick. His heart, I think," Spider said matter-of-factly.

"Come on! He just had his county physical. He's fine."

"If you say so." Spider let it go. She drove at a quick but even pace, no sense squealing the tires off when you were going to look at corpses. Especially when you were hoping you wouldn't find any evidence.

"What is it?" Carrie asked.

"What?" Spider didn't understand her question.

"Something's bothering you. Now what is it?" Carrie asked as she pushed Spider's hair back away from her face.

"Do you really think it's such a good idea for you to show up with me at six o'clock in the morning at a crime scene?"

"You mean because," she put a hand to her mouth, widened her eyes with a mock look of horror, and took in a deep breath, "someone might figure out that we're lovers!"

Carrie laughed at the disgruntled look on Spider's face. Spider didn't really like to be teased, at least not about this.

"It's not funny, Carrie. I mean, you're the assistant DA, for God's sake. A lot has changed since the days when you could be fired for being gay, but the way most people feel still hasn't changed that much. Some day you could have a shot at DA if you don't blow it by..."

"...looking too gay," Carrie finished for her. Carrie just smiled and shrugged, undaunted by her mate's worries. "Someday I will be DA. Which is why I can't afford to have a secret life. People will only trust me if I don't lie to them. If I'm not ashamed—and I'm not—then I show people that it's okay to be gay. In fact, that may be my campaign slogan—Vote for Carrie for DA! After all, it's okay to be gay."

Spider laughed in spite of herself. "Catchy...But seriously, Carrie..."

"I'm dead serious, Spider. I have never been in the closet, and I'm not crawling in there now. I am a public figure, and I am just going to get more public, so you're going to have to come out, too. Are you ashamed of me?"

"Ah, come on, Carrie, you know that's bull shit." It was hard for Spider to get used to the idea that you could be open about your sexuality. "All right. If you don't care, I don't care."

"No, I do care. I want people to know."

"OK. Then I want people to know, too."

TOMMY GOT TO the first crime scene before Spider. He thought about the twenty-five dollars he now owed Spider, and gritted his teeth. He looked at the body, and then had the officer cover the face again.

He had really hoped that it was over, but it wasn't. The Fry Guy was back. It was his MO; scum ball with his brains fried in his head, no witnesses, and five would get you ten no evidence.

Spider had said he'd be back. Just once, he wished the bitch would be wrong. He didn't want to catch this guy, but he didn't feel safe hiding him anymore, either, and he knew Spider knew a lot more than she was telling him.

Spider drove up then. As usual, she was in no hurry. Carrie got out before Spider, and Tommy watched as all the ballistic boys and the detectives looked up and took notice. They were all staring and whispering, and he could guess about what. Carrie went to talk to the coroner as Spider walked up to Tommy.

Tommy smiled. "Tongues are wagging."

Spider shrugged. "Let 'em wag. If she doesn't care, why the hell should I?"

She walked over to the body and raised the shroud, then quickly lowered it. "Yep, that's our boy all right. FBI here?"

"Not yet," Tommy said. "I expect them in full force in the next couple of hours. We're spread a little thin right now, with crews at all six sites."

Spider started walking and Tommy followed. He didn't know what she was looking for. Hard to leave foot imprints in pavement, and this guy never left any fingerprints. Even if he did, it'd be hard to pick out in an alley full of prints and partials. DNA? Well he'd have to actually get involved in some sort of struggle with his victims to get enough of that to be detected, and this guy didn't get close enough for there to be a struggle. Without knowing what kind of weapon he was using...there were no casings, bullets, or poison to be traced. Even if they were really trying to find this guy, Tommy was sure they couldn't do it. Except of course he wasn't at all sure that Spider didn't know exactly who the killer was.

"So why six? It's been two months with nothing, and now all of a sudden we've got six corpses. Does that number mean anything? The amount of time in between?" Tommy asked.

"No. He saw someone he couldn't let slip through, and once he had killed one, thereby alerting the cops that he was back anyway, he might as well finish his list."

"His list?"

"He hasn't killed anyone in two months, but he must have run into lots of people who needed to be killed. Remember that our government decided the prisons were overcrowded. He wouldn't have forgotten about them. He would have made a mental list, maybe even worked at figuring out what their patterns were. You know— like when they went out, where they lived. After all, four of these scum were killed in their own apartments."

"We're on candid camera, Spider. Just because we're not tapped in yet doesn't mean that other people aren't. You've got to stop referring to the victims as scum," Tommy said, shaking his head. He looked away from any comlinks he could see and whispered, "We've got to start trying to solve this case."

"No, we don't. We just have to look like we are," Spider said with a smile. When she took a quick look around, everyone stopped talking and tried to look anywhere but at her or Carrie.

"Yes!" she screamed in a loud, clear tone. "Yes! I am sleeping with the assistant DA. In fact, I am living in the assistant DA's very lavish home. Yes, we do have sex, and, yes, she does look every bit as good naked as you all think she does. Now, do you think we could maybe get back to work? We've got six of these scenes to check out, and I'd like to get it done before the bodies start to rot."

Spider noticed that Carrie laughed, shook her head, and then went right on talking to the coroner as if nothing had happened. Spider started walking around again and Tommy followed.

"Oh! That was very tactful." Tommy laughed.

Spider shrugged. Then she smiled and walked up to the wall. She looked at the bloodstain.

"He started here tonight. I'll just bet that blood doesn't belong to our scu...victim."

"Our killer?"

"No. How's this scenario. This scu...uh the victim is roughing someone up. He was an extortionist, so that isn't too terribly hard to believe. Our killer sees the attack and he decides to stop the scumba...victim. He kills him, and once he had killed him he decided to clean up his list. Kind of like you make a list of things you have to do around the house, and you put them off, and put them off, but then once you've done one of them you feel compelled to do everything on the list."

Tommy looked at her with raised eyebrows.

"Well, I do, anyway." She turned her comlink on then. "Forensics, I want a man over here."

A man came over and Carrie followed him.

"What you got?" Carrie asked.

"Some blood on the wall there. I think the scum..."

Both Carrie and Tommy scowled at her.

"The victim may have been trying to extort money from someone. Then the Fry Guy saw that and killed the scu...victim. Whoever this guy was, he might have seen the Fry Guy. I'd like to take samples of the blood and run the DNA."

"That's a long shot," Carrie said. "There still isn't that much DNA on file yet, just criminals, municipal employees, and the military. You know what the odds are that you'd find a match?"

"True," Spider said. "But in the meantime we can look around the neighborhood for people who've taken a beating. Ask around. See who the sc...victim had been extorting money from. When we find him you can check to see if his DNA matches."

"Very good," Carrie said.

The forensics guy looked up from scraping the bricks. "Why don't you just run a spot on TV asking this guy to come forward? Offer a reward for information about the Fry Guy?"

"Because..." Carrie and Spider started at once.

Spider nodded and Carrie finished, "...the Fry Guy saved this guy from a beating. Maybe even saved his life. There is already a reward for information leading to the capture of the Fry Guy, and everyone knows that. If this guy was going to give the Fry Guy up, he would have left the crime scene immediately and called the station. As it is, a delivery man found the body."

"Isn't there a chance that this might actually be the Fry Guy's blood?" the pathologist asked.

"Well, duh, Flaggerty," Carrie said without much charity. "I have a weapon which fries people's brains in their heads at long distance, but I'm going to get close enough that you can knock me up against a wall. Get real."

She looked at Spider and Tommy's comlinks, obviously in the on position.

"Damn!" she muttered and walked away.

"I was just wondering," Flaggerty mumbled.

"It's OK, man," Spider said. "She's in a pissy mood. Comlink rang just before she reached climax."

"Jesus Christ!" Tommy cursed and stomped away.

"I hate it when that happens," Flaggerty said laughing.

THE CORONER'S REPORTS would prove that, indeed, the alley guy was the first one dead. The other crime scenes turned up no evidence and no witnesses. They were investigating the third crime scene when the FBI showed up.

Then there were the other guys. Two of them, from some agency they'd never heard of, but that the FBI seemed to know all about. The SWTF—short for Strange Weapons Task Force—turned out to be legit, and to have a higher clearance than anyone else on the scene. They hung around not really looking at anything. They didn't even ask any questions. They just stood around, watching and listening.

"Those So-what-if guys are giving me the creeps," Spider said.

Tommy nodded. "What the hell are they even here for? I expected to see them checking for weapon residue or something—anything. All they're doing is watching and listening to the rest of us. They don't even take their friggin' hands out of their pockets. There's something about them…It's all I can do to keep from walking over there and kicking their asses."

Spider nodded in excited agreement. "That's so funny! That's the way they've been making me feel all day. Listen, this is the last corpse. What do you say we go and see if we can find the witness?"

Tommy nodded and they left.

Carrie saw Tommy and Spider leave. The So-what-if guys watched them go, too, and then they started whispering. Carrie discretely called one of the policemen over.

Jacobs ran over only too willing to serve. "Sir?"

"I don't like the way those So-what-if guys…"

"So-what-if guys, Sir?"

Carrie quietly cursed Spider for giving them a nickname that was going to stick in her head better than their real one. "The SWTF guys. I don't like the way they're acting. They're spending more time watching our investigation than anything else. I want you to keep your comlink focused on them whenever possible. You understand? I want you to keep an eye on them while they're here."

"You mean spy on them, Sir?"

"It looks to me like they're spying on us. I think a little cautious scrutiny is in order. We didn't need them before this, so why are they suddenly here? I have a feeling that they know something we don't, so keep an eye on them. That's all."

He nodded and started to walk away.

"Jacobs!"

"Yes, Sir?"

She pointed to her own comlink. "A link-eye, Jacobs. I want this on the record."

"Understood." Jacobs walked happily away. A personal assignment from the assistant DA! Acting on behalf of the DA! It wasn't every day that something like that fell in the lap of a rookie detective.

The So-what-if guys started to leave then. Jacobs looked at Carrie, and she nodded for him to follow them. He grabbed his partner and did so as discretely as possible.

HE SHOOK HIS head no, smiling, and seeming distressed at having to disagree. "Kim not know what you mean. Kim fall down stairs, have accident. That is all Kim know. Kim very clumsy old man."

Spider knew the old man was lying. She could make him tell the truth, but there was no profit in that for her. "Come on, old man, who do you think you're kidding?"

"Kim not good at English. Not understand what mean," Kim said.

Spider laughed. Tommy was not as amused. He took the old man's playing dumb as a lack of respect for his intelligence. The old man was staring at Spider's hands again. It wasn't unusual for some one to notice; it was pretty hard not to. But most people were polite enough that they didn't stare. He was a rude old fuck, and Tommy didn't like him. He reminded him too much of his father.

"Do you think we're stupid?" Tommy hissed in Korean.

The old man looked more than a little perplexed.

"Here's the shit," he continued, still in Korean. "They got your blood off the wall in the alley. We get a little blood from you, match it, and we know it was you in the alley when the victim was killed. We know that James Filbert was extorting money from you. If you're not careful, you could become our one and only suspect in the Fry Guy killings. Are you the Fry Guy?"

The old man seemed to think about that for a moment. Then he stuck his frail wrists out to Tommy and answered. "Yes, yes I am. I am the Fry Guy."

He had confessed to the Fry Guy murders, so they had to take the old man in whether it made any sense or not. The old man was weaving a tale about ancient ways passed down from the generations of his father. Telling how he looked around him and saw the corruption in the city and decided to lash out against it. It was a good story, but of the twenty-odd detectives, cops, and G-men that were hearing it, there wasn't one of them that believed it. They did, however, believe that he knew something. Finally, after four hours of intense questioning, the old man's story began to fray.

"Your store was open at midnight the night the murder of Jason Reeves took place, and witnesses saw you in the store. So how did you kill a man half way across town?" Carrie asked. She'd started getting tired of this two and a half hours ago.

"The ways of the ancients are mysterious and..."

"Cut the crap, old man," Spider screamed at him.

Carrie and everyone else in the room glared at her.

"Give me a big, fucking break. We all know he ain't the Fry Guy." She was hungry, and tired, and she wanted to go home some time this week.

"Are you the Fry Guy?"

"No," Kim answered, and wondered why he had.

"Do you know who is?"

"No."

"Did you see him?"

The old man started to sweat. He didn't want to answer the question. He didn't want to hurt his benefactor.

"Ye...yes."

Spider carefully worded her next question.

"Was he wearing a mask and cape, so that you couldn't see what he looked like?"

Kim was relieved. He wouldn't have to tell them anything they didn't already know, and that thing had left his brain so he could lie. "Yes, yes he was. He was very tall, very fair. I could see that around the mask."

"Why didn't you just say so from the beginning?" Carrie asked with a sigh. "Why did you pretend that you were the Fry Guy?" she demanded. She was tired and hungry, too. Besides, it had been a long day that had started with the ultimate frustration. When and if she ever got the bitch home, she was going to...

"He saved my life. I didn't want him to be punished. He is a good guy. Why you go after him and let bastards like Jimmy Filbert go free? Is this justice?"

It was a good question.

Carrie lectured the old man, slapped him on the wrist, and let him go; much to the astonishment of the detectives and G-men there assembled.

One of the G-men pulled Carrie aside. "You can't just let this guy go. He may have vital information…"

"This is my jurisdiction, and I can do whatever I damn well please."

"He could be our only witness…"

"We have five other witnesses that have seen the same thing. After extensive interrogation they told us no more. Less, in fact, than this man. He at least seems to have some idea of height and skin color, although I wouldn't trust anything he says."

"Why do you say that?"

"He was willing to go to jail for this guy. Do you really think he's going to give us anything that might really help us catch him?" Carrie asked.

The G-man nodded; she made good sense.

Carrie walked out of the room and doubled her speed to catch up to Spider and Tommy. She put her arm around Spider's waist.

"I'm done for the day. What about you, soldier?" Carrie asked with a wink.

Spider smiled down at her. "Do I have to warn you again about sexual harassment?"

"I think maybe I'll have to be debriefed," Carrie said.

Tommy threw up his hands and started walking away quickly. "That's it! I'm outtah here. See you tomorrow."

Spider laughed. "See you, Tommy."

TOMMY DROVE HOME the long way. Kim had stirred something in him he thought was long dead.

He was thinking about his father. Something he tried very hard not to do. *Too many bitter memories. Too much guilt.* He knew he shouldn't feel guilty. It was his life, and he had a right to live it any way he liked. Intellectually, he knew that, but emotionally the loss of family and heritage seemed a high price to pay to go your own way. Still, it hadn't been his decision to be disowned.

When he had given up martial arts to take up a career as a cop, his father—and therefore the rest of his family—had separated themselves from him. If he went back to the constant training and the competitions, if he restored the family's honor, all would be forgiven.

Tommy didn't come back. Then when he divorced the wife his father had picked for him to marry a 'round-eyes,' there was no going back. He had been completely disowned and disinherited. Attempts to contact family members by mail were unanswered. Attempts to call were met with silence and slammed receivers.

To them he was little more than a nagging memory. In his father's mind, he had given Tommy everything, and Tommy had slung it back into his face. Tommy remembered a childhood of ritual and routine. Schoolwork and friends were placed in a position of little importance. Training and discipline were all that really mattered.

Tommy still trained, but not with any regularity. He took time to live, to feel, to love—his father never really had.

For all that they were lacking, he still missed his father and family and wanted to be a part of their lives. But they had cut him off and thrown him away, like a tumor that had been removed.

Did they even think of him? If they did, did they ever remember anything pleasant, any of the happy times they had shared? Or did they remember only that he had gone against their wishes and their customs; that he had broken discipline.

With a little help from Spider Webb, he'd become quite good at breaking the rules.

Laura had taught him how to relax and enjoy life. More important, she had made him believe that it was all right for him to be his own man. Laura believed that he had worth, no matter what he wanted to do, and so it wasn't hard for him to believe, either.

If you lived long enough you eventually learned the inevitable; sometimes to win is also to lose.

"IT IS NOT!" Carrie laughed as she walked across the kitchen to the refrigerator.

"It most certainly is!" Spider flopped down on a chair at the table.

"You want a beer or a coke?" Carrie asked, still laughing.

"Coke…. and voyeurism *is* a victimless crime."

"How can you say that? Many victims say they feel as if they have been raped," Carrie insisted.

"That's because they haven't ever really been raped. Besides, my point was that if you don't know you have a peeper, then it is a victimless crime."

"It won't hold water in a court of law, detective," Carrie said.

"We're not talking a court of law, madam DA, Sir. We've already established that the person involved doesn't know they have a peeper. So we're talking about the real world. If a woman or man doesn't know they're being watched, why should I bring it to their attention? As long as they don't know, they're not victims. I tell the perp to quit and I check to make sure he does. It's that simple."

Carrie sat down across from Spider. "OK...all right. I'm too tired to argue with you tonight. You hungry?"

Spider shrugged. "I could eat a sandwich. Want me to make you one, too?"

Carrie smiled. "I'd love you forever."

"You're easily bought." Spider got up and headed for the fridge. She pulled out the ingredients, and started making sandwiches.

Carrie looked down at her hands nervously. "You make judgment calls a lot, don't you, Spider?"

"What do you mean, Hon?"

"You...make up your own law, and you abide by that even if it's against the written law."

"Where is this coming from?" Spider asked with a laugh. "I thought you knew what kind of cop I am. You've seen my record; it more or less speaks for itself. No, I don't always play by the books, but I think I'm just. I'm not dirty, if that's what you mean."

"I know that, but...you know who he is, don't you?"

When Spider dropped the knife she was using, that was answer enough.

"You can't do this, Spider. You can't protect him. You've got to give him up," Carrie said. "I understand your frustration—believe me I do. But, Honey, they're bringing in the big guns. These SWTF guys look like they play for keeps. Did you know that they followed you today? I know because I had them followed. I don't like them, Spider. I think they're the kind of people who make people disappear, and I don't want you to be involved in this."

Spider quit what she was doing and looked at Carrie without really seeing her. How much should she tell her? How much did she dare...

"Carrie, I'm...I think I'm already in too deep."

"What about Tommy?"

"Tommy's not involved."

"Oh, please, Spider. Don't try to lie to me; you're horrible at it. You can't do this, it's too dangerous..."

"I'm not going to tell you what I know, Carrie. Not because I don't trust you, but because it's better for you if you can truthfully say you don't know. Plausible deniability and all that. There is nothing I can do now that will make this any less dangerous for me. I've reached a 'damned if I do damned if I don't' point. This is a lot bigger than I thought it was. Bigger than the government wants anyone to know. I don't know how, but the Feds are in it up to their beady little eyeballs, and so am I, whether I want to be or not."

IN THE NEXT two weeks there were no Fry Guy killings, and no new leads in the case. There were fewer and fewer G-men, but the two SWTF guys were stuck on Tommy and Spider like glue.

Spider didn't like them. She tried to feel them out, but she could never get a real good handle on them. Worse than that, they seemed to be more interested in Spider than the case, and she was pretty sure she knew why.

Like Carrie and Tommy they must suspect that she knew who the Fry Guy was, and that she was protecting him, and unlike Carrie and Tommy, Spider was pretty sure that the SWTF guys knew exactly why. Well, if they were waiting for her to take them to him, they had a long wait, because she didn't plan to go anywhere near him, ever.

She had told Carrie the truth. She was damned either way. In fact she was pretty sure that the best way to make sure she wound up dead would be to actually bring the Fry Guy in.

She was driving in spite of Tommy's protests, as she had been all week. This way she could keep an eye on the So-what-if guys. She looked in her rear view mirror, and there they were. She could lose them in traffic any time she wanted, but she didn't want to just now. Right behind them she could see Jacob's car. She was pretty sure that the So-what-if guys knew they were being followed, and that they knew that she knew that they were following her. They just didn't give a damn. That worried her.

It was, without a doubt, the most futile waste of the taxpayers' money that she'd seen in years, and she told Tommy so.

"I don't think it's so fucking funny," Tommy said. He looked nervous. "Those spooks give me the creeps. Why don't you just shake them?"

"Because they give me the creeps, too, and I don't want to give them any reason to shoot my ass," Spider said.

Tommy nodded; he supposed that made sense. He decided to change the subject. "So, Laura tells me your in-laws are coming in for the weekend."

Spider mumbled something incoherent and Tommy laughed.

"It won't be that bad."

"I really don't think I'm ready for this." Spider took a deep breath. "I can't believe she sprung this on me. Maybe I'll get shot."

"What are you so worried about? They know that Carrie's queer, so when she invited them to come and meet you I'm pretty sure they weren't expecting you to have a dick…"

"And did you know that you can't rent one for the occasion?" Spider asked, facetiously.

Tommy laughed and punched her in her upper arm. "You know what I mean. It won't be a shock. You're a good catch…I guess."

"Are you kidding? These are rich people, Tommy. I'm living in their daughter's house. It's going to look like I'm living off her. Which, guess what, I am! It's going to be the most uncomfortable weekend of my life."

Tommy laughed. "Worse than a pit in a prisoner of war camp."

"Hey! At least there I didn't have to worry about impressing anyone," Spider answered.

"You don't have to worry about impressing anyone now, Spider. You're a good person. Anyone should be proud to know you. Few people have done the kind of things that you have done. Personally, I have never known anyone I was more impressed with. You are courageous, loyal, and you always have minty-fresh breath."

Spider was more than a little taken aback, and embarrassed. "Well, thanks, Tommy. I feel the same way about you, except for the breath part."

"If you can make it through the weekend without farting and yelling *Thar she blows!* the way you always do, you ought to be OK."

HENRY HAD BEEN breathing funny again, and while trying to get him sorted out she had forgotten what tonight was. It wasn't until she pulled into the driveway and saw the strange car that she realized what she had just done.

"Holy fuck!" She looked at her watch. It was six thirty, and Carrie said dinner would be ready at seven o'clock. But she had expected Spider to be home at five thirty to help. She got out of the car and looked down at her clothes—on top of everything else she was filthy.

She rushed in the house and tried to get upstairs unnoticed so that she could get a shower and change.

"Honey, is that you?" Carrie's voice rang out from the living room.

"No, it's a fucking burglar. I just happened to have keys to your door," she mumbled to herself, then replied, "Yes. I had to work late." It was just a little lie. She still hadn't gotten up the courage to tell Carrie about Henry. Wasn't at all sure that she would understand, and didn't think now was the time to talk about it. "I'll just run upstairs and get cleaned up…"

"Well, come and meet Mom and Dad first," Carrie yelled.

"And when you're done meeting Mother and Father, I'll just run my fingernails across the black board about four thousand times," Spider mumbled as she dragged her way towards the living room.

She'd seen pictures of them before, so there were no shocks. Tall, slender, slightly gray people who'd obviously had everything lifted and tucked at least once. They were attractive in a generic way, impersonal in a plastic-wrapped furniture sort of way, and looking at her as if they expected a genie to pop out of her butt.

"Hello," she said nervously.

"Mom, Dad, this is Spider. Spider this is my father, Robert, and my mother, Jill," Carrie said. Then she walked up and hugged Spider. If it were possible, Spider felt even more uncomfortable. She sort of hugged Carrie back without ever really touching her.

Robert walked up to Spider and shook her hand. "Pleasure to meet you. We've heard so much about you. Saw all your service medals—most impressive."

Spider met his wet-noodle handshake with a firm, confident grip that she didn't really feel. "Thank you, sir."

Carrie's mother, Jill, hugged Spider. Spider tried and failed to figure out what to do with her own hands until she was released.

"I'd better go up and change," Spider said. "Excuse me."

SPIDER LEFT AT what she no doubt thought was a nice, even pace, but was in reality almost running.

"She seems very nice," Jill said.

Carrie sighed. She was beginning to wonder if this was a mistake. Spider was obviously miserable.

"Mother, all she said was hi."

"A police detective…" Her father said thoughtfully. "What kind of money does that bring in?"

"Don't start with that, Dad," Carrie warned. "It bothers her that there is such a difference in our incomes, so let's please just not talk about salaries."

"I was just interested," Robert said. "So, what can we talk about?"

Jill looked at Carrie and said, "She's not all sulky and sullen like that last friend you had, is she? I hate to see you going after the same type over and over…"

"Do we have to talk about every old girl friend I've ever had every time there's someone new in my life?" Carrie said, shaking her head in disbelief.

"There's something else we can't talk about," Robert said. "Better start making a list, Jill."

"Honey, you do tend to rush into things. You've known this woman for what, four, five months now? And, look, you've moved her into your home," Jill scolded.

"Could you just maybe give her a break?" Carrie screamed. She lowered her voice. "I love Spider. I want to spend the rest of my life with her."

"Well, gee! There's a new one," Jill scoffed.

"Do we have to do this? Christ, I've never done this before. I've never even lived with someone before. I've certainly never gotten this close to anyone after knowing them for such a short period of time…" Carrie realized she wasn't exactly helping her case. "If I said anything like that before it was…well it was bullshit so that you wouldn't bitch at me for sleeping with someone…" This also wasn't particularly helpful. "I love you, I want to see you. Why do you have to make me crazy?"

Her parents laughed.

"I'm sorry, Carrie," Jill started. "But did it ever occur to you that it isn't any easier or more comfortable for us to meet your new friend than it is for you, or for her? We love you, and we want what's best for you. We're not here all the time, so we have to find out as much as possible while we're here."

"I notice she's got really big hands," Robert said with a laugh. "I suppose that's got to be a plus."

"Robert!" Jill shrieked in disbelief.

Carrie blushed, but laughed anyway and shrugged. "It certainly doesn't hurt."

SPIDER PICKED AT her dinner, not so much because she was nervous, but mainly because Carrie was a horrible cook.

"It's very good, Carrie," Jill said.

Spider was surprised when she realized Jill wasn't lying. She looked at the old man, and one look at his face told her that he felt the same way about the food as she did. This could mean only one thing; that Jill was as bad a cook as Carrie.

"What a world, what a world," Spider mumbled.

"What's that, dear?" Jill asked.

"Out of this world," Spider said.

"You are such a shitty liar," Carrie said with a smile. "Spider's a good cook," she told her parents. Then said to Spider, "I should have let you cook."

"I will next time," Spider said.

"So, working on any interesting cases?" Robert asked.

Spider opened her mouth.

"None that she should talk about at the dinner table," Carrie said with a warning look. The only case that Spider had that was interesting besides the Fry Guy cases was a mutilation down by the docks. Neither made for very pleasant dinner conversation.

"So..." Robert said with a smile. "How many girl friends have you had?"

"Daddy, for God's sake!" Carrie said, shaking her head in disbelief.

Spider smiled. "I've really only had one serious relationship besides Carrie."

"So, what happened?" Robert pried. "Why'd you break up with her?"

"Robert!" Jill protested. "You don't ask questions like that."

"Well, excuse the hell out of me, but how am I supposed to keep up? Every time I turn around there's something else I'm not supposed to talk about. You're making my head spin."

"A mortar hit her during the raid on Baghdad; she died instantly," Spider answered, not without emotion.

"I...I'm sorry," Robert said. "I didn't know."

"It's all right..." Spider said with a shrug. "How could you have known? I don't mind talking about her. She was a great gal, but she wasn't Carrie."

Carrie looked at Spider and smiled. She was proud of the way Spider was holding up under her parents' scrutiny.

"Was your father a police officer, or a service man?" Jill asked.

"My dad was a drunken plumber. My mother died in a car accident when I was three. I went into the military to get out of the house. While I was in the Middle East my brother was murdered, and so when I got back state side I became a cop."

Robert looked at his wife and smiled broadly. "So, now who asked a stupid question?"

SPIDER HAD GONE to bed. Carrie and her parents had stayed up talking. After about thirty minutes Robert excused himself and headed for the guest room.

"She's led a very hard life, hasn't she?" Jill asked Carrie.

"Yes she has. But she hasn't let it make her crazy. She's a little nervous tonight. She's normally very animated, very funny."

"She have a death wish?" Jill asked seriously, looking at the wall where all her medals hung.

Carrie thought about that for a moment. "I think she did have. I like to think I've changed that. She...it's hard to explain, Mother. She can't walk away."

"What do you mean, dear?"

"If she sees something wrong, she can't just walk away. I don't think that will ever change. She's very good at what she does. It's amazing to watch her work."

"She must be good if they put her on the Fry Guy case."

Carrie nodded silently. "It's really sad. No one in law enforcement wants to catch him. Except maybe the Feds, and I'm convinced they just want him for his weapon."

"Any leads?"

"Not really." Carrie shrugged.

"I noticed her books…" Jill walked over to the bookshelves and started looking. "Unless of course your taste in reading has changed."

"They're hers."

"I can understand why she'd have an interest in criminals and criminal behavior. I guess that makes sense. But what is the fascination with the paranormal?"

Carrie was not about to answer by telling her mother that her girl friend had psychic powers. "She believes, or would at least like to believe, in the existence of psychic ability. The power of the mind."

"Everyone's had something happen that they couldn't explain. People who say they absolutely don't believe are lying, just as much as the guys who get on TV and tell you they can predict your future. Just because you can't see something doesn't mean it's not there," Jill said.

This started a conversation about the paranormal that lasted for two more hours.

THINGS WERE HAPPENING; *things she couldn't understand. The SWTF guys were all around her. They were like giants. The faceless woman screamed and screamed, but Spider couldn't understand what she was saying.*

The doctor said something to her father, something she couldn't hear. Was she sick? What were they doing to her? Why were they doing it? She felt fine until they kept poking her. Why did they keep poking her?

The faceless woman called to her. She tried to go, tried and couldn't. There was something between them. Something that she couldn't see. All she had to do was reach her.

Where was Scott? She couldn't see Scott. She screamed his name, but he wouldn't come.

The faceless woman said he was OK, told her to come on to follow her, but she couldn't get through the barrier and the SWTF guys were yelling at her and someone kept poking her.

She woke with a start and she was back in the hole. A pit with a lid. It was too hot to breathe. The stench from her own shit wafted up through the air, and the flies were as thick as water. They flew up her nose, and she brushed them away.

She was naked and filthy and filled with black hatred. She looked up and up to the roof of her prison. Twelve feet of sandy dirt. The hole was only six feet across and made out of sand. It didn't take a genius to figure out that if you tried to climb out the walls would cave in and you'd suffocate. Once every three or four days they pulled her out of the pit just long enough to wash her down with a high-pressure hose. They screamed at her to tell them where her base of operations was. Then they fought over whether they should screw her or not. So far the commander's insistence that she was unclean and was not to be touched was saving her from at least that. They'd beat her, kick her through the dirt till she was as dirty as she had been before the spraying, and then they'd sling her back into the hole. She'd tried to mentally push them, and had learned that the language barrier did more than stop her from talking to them.

There was no escape. No way out. Only sand and heat and flies, and yet she still wanted to live. Wanted to live and kill them all.

She yelled for Scott, but Scott was dead, he couldn't help her now. No one could help her now. She yelled for him any way, and the bastards threw rocks on top of the tin covering her hole. The sound was deafening, and she covered her ears and cowered into a corner. Maybe she should try to climb out. Better to die trying to escape than die like a neglected hamster in a cage.

There was light—too much light. She was blinded by the intensity of it, and they snared her by the shackles on her wrists with a curved pole before she had a chance to even put up a fight. At the top of the pit she looked into the eyes of the two turbaned bastards. They were alone. No doubt they weren't afraid of becoming unclean. They had just made a terrible mistake. She grabbed the pole one of them held with both her shackled hands, ripped it out of his hands and slammed it into his head in one movement. Then she spun and hit the other. Both landed at her feet.

Most of them slept during the heat of the day. No doubt these two bastards had decided to use that as an opportunity to wet their winkies. One of them twitched, and she lifted the pole high and slammed it into him, crushing his face with such force that his brains oozed out of his head. She dragged the dead men behind a wall, out of sight. Neither one of them had any keys, but one of them had a knife. After several tries she was able to pick the lock and get the shackle off of one of her hands. She closed the loose end up over the other cuff. She grabbed their side arms first, and then she striped one of them and put on his clothes. She smiled because she knew now that she was very close to freedom. No one had sounded an alarm yet, so no one had any idea she had escaped.

She looked at the hole and then back at the now naked dead man. She quickly dragged him over and dropped him in. Looking from the light into the darkness of the pit they might not even notice that it was a naked man instead of a naked woman. She quickly put the tin over the hole and quietly made her way through camp towards the motor pool. Even the guy in charge of guarding the motor pool was sleeping. The few people she'd seen moving around hadn't seen through her disguise. She got in a truck and turned the key. She was almost out of the motor pool when the alarm sounded. She sped up.

At the gates two guards stepped into her path, firing. She shot one, but before she could kill the other one a bullet struck her in the stomach. It was hard and hot. She crashed through the gates and down the road out into the desert. She didn't know how long she drove or how far. It was hot. She'd packed her wound, but something was wrong, and she was going to need medical attention soon. Problem was, she had no idea where she was. The jeep started to act up, and she realized that she had run out of gas. She looked up at the blazing sun. It was still a long time till nightfall. The jeep sputtered and died.

She dug a pit under it and crawled in to hide from the rag heads and the sun. She had survived the situation, but she was God only knew where, she was badly wounded, and the water stored on all of the vehicles wouldn't last forever. There was a stench coming from the wound that she knew only too well. The bullet had hit a section of bowel. With or without medical attention, infection would set in. Without that attention, she wouldn't survive. It didn't look good. She looked at the gun she held in her hand and decided. She'd take a nap. If she woke up and was in too much pain, she would just shoot herself.

When she woke up she was in the hospital. The SWTF men where there, too. They were arguing with the faceless woman, and people were poking her. Her stomach was better, so why were they poking her?

"She's very important to us," the SWTF men said.

The faceless woman was calling to her, but she couldn't reach her. Somehow she knew that everything would be all right if she could just reach her.

SPIDER WOKE WITH a start and sat straight up in bed. She took several long deep breaths, wondering if she was really awake this time.

"Spider, are you all right?" Carrie asked.

Spider jumped out of bed and ran into the bathroom. She ripped off the T-shirt she was wearing and stood before the mirror looking at her stomach and the scar that ran across it.

"Spider," Carrie said sleepily from the door. "Are you all right?" she asked again.

Spider turned to look at her. She saw the light of false dawn struggling to get through the drapes just behind Carrie. She turned back to the mirror and ran a hand over her stomach.

"Yeah, I'm all right. I just had a nightmare."

Carrie came up behind her and hugged her.

"It was so real. One of those things where you dream that you wake up, but you're not really awake, and then when really horrible things keep happening you think they're real."

"I'm so sorry, Baby."

"The worst part was that part of the dream was something that really happened. So it was like the whole thing must have happened, do you know what I mean?"

"Yes…" Carrie said. "They're the worst kind. Hard to tell for a while where fantasy ends and reality begins. Want to talk about it?"

"Not really." She slapped herself in the head with the palm of her hand hard enough that it hurt, then turned to face Carrie. "I know why I had the fucking dream. I'm going to kill Tommy."

"Why?" Carrie asked.

"I was complaining about your parents staying with us. Tommy said if I'd lived through a prisoner of war camp I could live through a weekend with your parents. That's why I dreamt about the camp. The hole." She was thoughtful then. "But what was all the other shit? With the So-what-if guys and the faceless woman."

"Why were you looking at your stomach?" Carrie asked carefully.

"I don't know." Spider forced a smile. "I was weirded out, and I guess I thought if I saw the scar instead of a bloody wound I'd know I was awake."

Spider looked into the mirror at the scar on her stomach and the one on her shoulder, and hip. Her body was littered with scars, some small and some large, and all of them had a story. Most of the stories weren't pleasant, but they were hers.

"I'm kind of fucking beat up."

"I think you're beautiful," Carrie said. She wrapped her arms around Spider's waist and lay her head on her shoulder. "I like your scars; they're part of you."

Spider laughed. "You're a little sick, Honey, but I was never one to look a gift horse in the mouth, and I'm certainly lucky that love is indeed blind."

"Can you go back to sleep?" Carrie asked.

"Maybe, but I don't want to," Spider said. "Why don't you go back to bed, though? I know you came in late."

"Are you going to be all right?"

"Yeah, I'll be fine," Spider said. "I have a lot of nightmares, Carrie. I always have. Even when I was a kid, way before the war. It's normal for me. Now go on back to sleep. I'll be fine."

Carrie was too tired to argue.

Spider watched Carrie lie back down, and then she found her T-shirt, pulled it on and headed downstairs. In the kitchen she started a pot of coffee, and then she punched up her comlink to see what the night's events had been. Mostly to see if the ballistics information had come in on their case. The whole time she was doing it she was trying to figure out what the fucking dream meant. If she could ever figure out who that faceless bitch was, what her presence meant, then maybe the nightmares would stop forever. At the very least, maybe the faceless woman would move out of her head.

Ballistics still hadn't processed their evidence. No doubt they'd have to wait till Monday now. She turned her comlink off and got a cup of coffee. She looked at the kitchen clock and cringed; it was only six thirty. God only knew when she'd gotten up, or when Carrie finally would. She could spend hours rattling around the house, trying not to make any noise until the rest of them got up. Then she would have to spend a whole day in parent hell. Why couldn't the comlink buzz her in to work now? The fucking thing only buzzed you in on your day off when you were supposed to do something you wanted to do, or were in the middle of sex.

"Life sucks," she muttered.

She'd never really had parents as an adult, so she really didn't know what was expected of Carrie by her parents or what Carrie expected of them. As a child, her father had expected her and Scott to stay the fuck out of his face and she had expected him to be passed out drunk by eight o'clock. Somewhere between her own memories and TV families must lie the norm.

She sure as hell didn't know what any of them expected of her. Was she supposed to make herself scarce for the remainder of the visit? Or was she expected to be constantly there, struggling to act entertained. Or was she expected to entertain them, and if so, how?

"I could show them my scars," she muttered.

She took a sip of coffee; it was too damn hot. So she spit it back into her cup and went to the sink to get a long drink of cold water. After a minute, she decided there was no permanent damage. Sitting back down at the table, she stared at the offensive cup of coffee. It was going to be a long day.

SPIDER HAD NO idea there were this many antique stores in the entire state, much less the city. The first couple had been interesting enough, but how much old junk could you look at?

Carrie moved up beside her and took her hand. "You're bored now, aren't you?"

"No. I was bored three hours ago. I can't even tell you what I am now, because no one has made a word for it yet." Spider forced a smile. "I suppose I'll live. I'm just tired."

"Thinking?" Carrie asked.

Spider nodded. "That damn dream. It keeps playing over and over in my head. I can't understand what my imprisonment has to do with the rest of the dream."

"It's just a dream, Honey. Dream's are like that, weird and…" She shrugged. "Well, distorted. If you try to figure out what they mean, you'll go crazy."

"Oh, Carrie! Look at this," Jill cooed from across the store. "Wouldn't this just be divine in your dining room?"

"No!" Spider said adamantly in Carrie's ear. Spider was damned if she was going to stand by and watch Carrie spend more money on a what-ever-the-hell it was than she made in an entire year.

Carrie smiled and let go of Spider's hand.

"I'm just looking," Carrie said. She started across the store.

After only a moment's hesitation, Spider hurried to catch up to her.

"Carrie, wait!"

Carrie turned to face her.

"It's your house and your money. I shouldn't have said anything, and I'm sorry."

Carrie just smiled at her and shook her head. "It's our house, and you have the right to say what you want or don't want in it. But, for the record, if I wanted the damn thing, I'd buy it." She poked Spider on her chest with her finger. "And nothing you could say would stop me."

Spider smiled back. "So much for my dreams of dominance."

"Carrie, come here," Jill demanded.

"And mine," Carrie smiled helplessly, shrugged, and went to join her mother in ooh-ing over the breakfront.

Spider started looking around the store. She smiled at herself. *I've got to learn to relax. I've got to quit apologizing for everything I do. Carrie wasn't mad at me. She doesn't really get mad. She just lets things slide and...What the fuck!*

Spider took a step back. Then she picked up the picture with trembling fingers. It was an old, antique, sterling silver frame, but that wasn't what was giving her the shakes. It was the picture. It was a picture of a young woman with an infant on her lap. A little boy stood at her knee looking at the infant. The boy was undoubtedly her brother, Scott.

She flipped the frame over, undid the clamps, and took the photo out. On the back of the photo it said *Scott, four & Spider, six months.* She put the frame down and turned the photo over. She looked at the woman in the photo long and hard. She was finally seeing her mother. Tall and slender...*My God I look like my mother!* She quickly dried the tears from her eyes and swallowed the lump in her throat.

"You there! What are you up to?" the shopkeeper asked as he approached her.

She looked at him.

"How much?" she asked.

"Three hundred and fifty dollars," he said, and looked at her as if to say I know you don't have it.

"I don't want the frame," Spider spat. "I just want the photo."

She looked around to make sure that Carrie and her parents weren't paying any attention to her. They weren't. She pointed at the picture.

"This is a picture of my mother, my brother and myself," Spider whispered. She turned the picture over and showed him the back. "I'm Spider, my brother's name was Scott. My mother died when I was a baby, and my father got rid of all her pictures. This is the first time since I was three that I've seen my mother."

The man's expression changed immediately. He looked from the woman in the picture to the woman that held it and had no trouble believing her story.

"Tell you what, kid. The frame is what's for sale. Why would I charge you for the photo when it's obviously yours?"

"Thanks. Thanks a lot," she said.

"I'll put it in a sack for you."

He did so, and she thanked him again.

"So, WHAT DID you buy?" Carrie asked when they were back in the car.

"I'll tell you later," Spider said quietly, but she was smiling, which Carrie didn't really expect.

In fact, Carrie couldn't remember ever seeing her this happy except right after they'd had sex.

Carrie started to look in the sack.

"Please, Carrie?" Spider pleaded.

Carrie put the sack down and nodded.

"Must be for you, dear," Jill said.

"Leave the kids alone, Jill," Robert said. "Can we go home now? My legs are about to fall off my body."

"IT'S TOO WEIRD," Carrie said looking at the picture Spider had handed her a few moments before. "You didn't know what your mother looked like."

"No. Like I said, I was about three when she died. My father got rid of all her pictures, put them away, or sold them. Makes sense that he'd pawn them off for the frames."

"Still, what are the odds?" Carrie said.

"Apparently pretty good." Spider took the picture from Carrie and looked at it. "Is it just wishful thinking, or do I look just like my mother?"

"Except that you'd never be caught dead in a dress, I'd think that was you. Even her hands are…"

"Freakishly large," Spider said with a smile.

"Well, I don't think they're freakish." Carrie was embarrassed, and she was blushing. Something she just didn't do. "I like your hands."

Spider laughed at her back peddling. "Carrie, I'm not self-conscious about the size of my hands. I guess I should be, I mean it's not like I don't know that they're abnormally large, but it just doesn't bother me. Never has. Scott had big hands, but Dad didn't. So I always figured it was a good thing."

Carrie grinned wickedly. "A very good thing."

Spider put the picture carefully on a shelf and lay down on the bed beside Carrie. Spider was quiet, pensive.

"What's wrong?" Carrie asked, brushing a stray strand of hair out of Spider's face.

"I was just thinking how different my life might have been if I'd had a mother, or if Scott were still alive. I spent a big chunk of my life working very hard at not caring too much, because, let's face it, I just don't have a very good track record. Sometimes it worries me that I love you as much as I do."

Carrie thought about it for a second. "I'm glad you love me, and I don't believe that it means I have been marked for impending doom. In fact, I have never felt so safe in my whole life. I don't believe in curses or bad luck."

"Me neither, not really." Spider snuggled close to Carrie. "So, you want to have sex?"

"Oh my God, Spider!" Carrie screamed sitting straight up in bed.

"OK, all right. We don't have to. I understand if you're a little up tight what with having your parents in the house and all," Spider said quickly.

"That's not it," Carrie laughed and turned to look at Spider. "Spider, the faceless woman in your dreams…"

"Yes?"

"It's your mother."

IT WAS SO obvious that Spider could have kicked herself. The dreams almost made sense now. The child inside her equated safety with getting to her mother. Of course she couldn't reach her mother, because her mother was dead. It was kind of disturbing if you thought about it, which Spider tried not to. The woman had no face because Spider didn't remember what her mother had looked like.

The department shrink didn't seem to see any significance in her finding a picture of her mother. Or in Spider's realizing that her mother was the faceless woman in her dreams. In fact, she wasn't even sure that he was awake until he asked a question.

"What do you suppose the SWTF men represented in your dream?"

"I don't fucking know. I thought that was what the department was paying you for."

"And why do you think you dreamt about being a prisoner in a hole?"

"Well, duh. Because I was a prisoner in a hole for five weeks, and my stupid-assed partner reminded me of it," Spider said. "Do I really have to keep coming in here? Because if you're just going to sit there while I answer all the questions, you're wasting my time."

"You don't think that I'm helping you?"

"Well, no," Spider said. *Is this guy a fucking idiot or what? How fucking stupid is he? The fucking department is paying him a small fortune to sit on his ass and look bored. Guess he isn't stupid at all if you think about it. He is, however, a fucking asshole.*

"Why don't you think our sessions are helping you?"

"Because you ask me stupid assed questions and you never seem to be listening to me when I answer them. Also, I'm not any better or worse than I was when I first came in here. So I have flashbacks. Big fucking deal. Everyone remembers stuff. It has never gotten in my way at work, never caused any real problems. It's not like I run around trying to shoot people or anything. I figure that these so-called post traumatic shock episodes come with the territory. If you'd been through what I've been through, and seen the things I've seen, you wouldn't be able to erase it from your brain, either. You try sitting in a fucking pit for five weeks. Smelling your own dung. Getting the crap beat out you on a regular basis. So fucking hot you can't breathe. No idea what tomorrow's going to bring, or even what day or time it is. Then see if you don't change forever. All of the therapy in the world is not going to put me back where I was before I stood in a trench and had pieces of my dead lover's body slap me up-side the head. I'm not sure I would want it to. To be so-called normal after that, to my way of thinking, would make me one sick fuck. The bottom line is that you don't give a damn whether I live or die, and I know it. So how the hell could talking to you help me?"

"What makes you think I don't care about you, or what happens to you?"

I'm fucking psychic, you dork. "I can tell. I'm not a fucking moron, you know."

"I don't think that you are. I am listening to you..."

"You fucking annoy the hell out of me," Spider said throwing up her hands. "I try to tell you something I think is very enlightening, and you're blowing me off. Only to ask some stupid assed question about the So-what-if guys."

"I think you may have trouble with authority figures," the shrink suggested.

"I have trouble with you!" Spider spat back.

"And why do you suppose that is?" he asked.

"Because I don't like you. You're a big, dumb, never-been-any-where, never-done-anything, had-everything-fed-to-you-on-a-fucking-silver-platter *Jerk*"

He looked at his watch, then at her. "Well, that's our time for today. I think we've made a lot of progress."

Spider got up and headed for the door. When she reached it she turned and looked at him. "I suppose if I told you to eat shit and die, I'd be fucking cured."

TOMMY MET HER in the hallway. "Well?" he asked.

"He's a friggin idiot," Spider said.

Tommy laughed. "Why do you say that?"

"He thinks I'm well on the way to recovery because I hate his guts."

"Makes sense to me," Tommy said. Spider just stared at him and he smiled. "If the guy knows he's an asshole, maybe that's how he knows someone else is sane; whether they hate him or not."

"You keep trying, but it's just not working for you, Tommy. Thousands of comedians out of work, and here you are trying to be funny," she said. They were almost out the door when their comlinks buzzed and they were called back into the lieutenant's office.

"COME IN," THE lieutenant ordered.

Tommy wondered why he always did that. Did he really think they were going to stand in the hall like dorks till he told them it was all right to come in?

"Better sit down."

They did.

"DA Richards just suffered a major heart attack. The doctors say it's bad. They're hopeful about his recovery, but in the mean time..." He looked at Spider. "Your...whatever the hell you call her, is the acting DA. Don't think that gives you one damn bit more privilege than anyone else in this department."

Tommy worked hard at not smiling. It was easy to see that this really chapped Toby's ass. It was no secret that he disliked Spider Webb. Toby liked to think that you could do things by the book and get results. Tommy and Spider proved almost daily that you could get a hell of a lot more done if you weren't afraid to bend the rules.

Toby could tolerate Tommy. Tommy wasn't as abrasive or openly insubordinate as Spider. Tommy knew when to keep his mouth shut. He knew how to look as if he had been duly chastised, and to a superficial bastard like Toby that was all that really mattered.

Tommy looked at Spider. She was obviously upset, more than he thought she should have been. He knew she liked and respected Richards, but he doubted that was the reason that she looked like she was going to strangle Toby with his own testicles.

Tommy steeled himself for her attack and the repercussions.

"I call her Baby. I'll be sure to tell her just how much respect you have for her and our relationship." She glared at him. Then she stood up, walked over and put her fists on his desk.

Tommy waited for Toby to order her to get her hands off his desk, as he usually did.

But Toby could see Spider's face, and knew before Tommy did just how mad Spider really was. Toby kept quiet.

"You're way the fuck out of line!" Spider screamed. "If I was the kind of pencil pushing, paper crunching geek that you are, I'd probably be bringing you up on charges right about now. Don't you *ever* accuse me of asking for or receiving special treatment, or I'll have your fucking job. And don't you *dare* bring my private life up when either of us are on duty or in front of my partner. You got trouble with me? Then you meet me after work somewhere, and we'll discuss it then. Not here where your fucking rank protects you."

She stood up straight and left the room.

Tommy looked at the lieutenant, shook his head, and followed his partner. He had to run to catch up with her.

"Pencil pushing, paper crunching geek!" Tommy laughed in spite of himself. "That's pretty bad, even for you."

Spider stopped dead in her tracks and turned to glare at him. "You think this is funny, Tommy?"

Wow! She really is mad! "I'm sorry. I just don't get it. What's the big deal? He's said worse things and you didn't get nearly this pissed off."

Spider started walking again, and he followed.

"No, you don't get it, do you, Tommy? Because in a way you're just like him. You don't really think of my and Carrie's relationship as being the same as you and Laura's. This was a personal attack on Carrie's integrity as well as my own," Spider said. She seemed to calm down a little. "That little crack, calling Carrie my 'whatever the hell I call her.' He wouldn't do that to you, or to any straight person on the force. He obviously has no respect for me—that I can live with. But he doesn't respect Carrie. He thinks he's better than her because he's straight and she's not. As if the true test of a person's worth is who they fuck. I knew he didn't like me, but now in know he hates my guts, and I haven't done anything to deserve that."

Tommy nodded. He understood now. If someone said something he didn't like about Laura he'd have to kick their ass. "Spider, don't lump me with him. I'm on your side, always have been, always will be. Just because I don't wear an 'I love my gay friend' T-shirt and march in a freaking parade doesn't mean I don't understand that you're the same as us."

Spider nodded silently as they walked across the parking lot towards their car. Spider even let him drive without an argument. Tommy slid into the driver's seat as Spider climbed in and shut the door. Tommy started the car.

"If you feel that strongly about it, why *don't* you bring him up on charges? He's a dick; maybe this is our chance to get rid of him."

"Are you nuts!" Spider said.

Tommy shrugged and pulled the car out into traffic.

"If Richards is down for the count—and I hope he's not—but if he is, Carrie's going to be running for DA with less than six weeks left to campaign. She *wants* to be DA. She'd never run against Richards, but if Richards is out…I can't help not having a dick, but I'm sure as hell not going to do anything else to ruin her chances. She'd never forgive me if I did. Hell! I'd never forgive myself." She took a deep breath. "Besides, I have to work here. Most of the guys we work with wouldn't understand why I was making such a big fuss. Hell, most of them aren't any more comfortable with me than he is. If not because I'm gay, then because they know I can kick their fat, fucking, out-of-shape, donut-eating asses."

Tommy nodded. She was right. He would have liked to tell her she was wrong, but he knew it was true, because they felt the same way about him. The ones who weren't uncomfortable around him because he was Asian didn't like him because they knew he could kick their fat, fucking, out-of-shape, donut-eating asses.

"Yeah, if you brought charges whether you won or not you'd lose the respect of every other cop on the force. We have enough trouble getting backup as it is. Unless of course they all hate him as much as we do."

"Even if they hated him…face it, he was out of line, but if I brought charges against him it wouldn't be because I felt that I had permanent emotional scars, but because I don't like him."

Spider grabbed the rear view mirror and repositioned it even as Tommy protested.

"Goddamn it, Spider…"

"Hey!" She repositioned it again. "Well, I'll be damned! The So-what-if guys have stopped following us."

"They were only following us in the first place because they think you know who the Fry Guy is. Which you do," Tommy said, readjusting the mirror so that he could actually see.

"Shush…shush…shush. Don't say shit like that when we're in the car. First off, I *don't* know who he is. Second, how do you know our fucking car isn't bugged?"

Tommy laughed. "Now you're just being paranoid. They wouldn't bug our car."

Spider knocked on Tommy's head. "Hello! Is anyone home?"

"Ow! Stop it!" Tommy pushed her hand away and rubbed his head. "That hurts!"

"Well, wake the fuck up, then. If they're going to follow our every fucking move for weeks, I don't think they are above bugging the car."

Tommy nodded. She had a point—and not just the one on the top of her head. "We'll go back to the garage and have the mechanic run a diagnostic. That should turn up any foreign objects in the car."

"That's not a bad idea," Spider said.

They turned around and went back to the station.

"What did you fuck up now?" Ricky the head mechanic asked.

"Nothing, butt head," Spider said. "We might have a bug in the car."

"So spray a little raid on it…"

"Not that kind of bug, ya fucking moron," Spider spat.

"Could you just run a diagnostic scan over the car?" Tommy asked.

"What good will that do?" Ricky asked, wiping his grease-covered hands on the hood of their car and glaring at Spider as if daring her to say something about it.

Spider didn't give a damn if the car was dirty, but she didn't like the fact that he was trying to push her buttons.

"Ricky, you goddamn weasel faced little creep…"

"Could you just run the diagnostic, Ricky? Then we can go," Tommy said.

Ricky nodded, popped the hood and started hooking the car up to the diagnostic.

"Don't know how this is going to help, but if it will get that bitch out of my hair…"

"Why you little…"

Tommy grabbed her arm and stopped her forward momentum.

"Did you ever hear the old saying, 'You get more flies with honey than you do with shit'?" Tommy asked in a whisper.

"He started it," Spider whispered back. "You'd think they were his fucking cars."

"Spider, the car you hit in the parking lot *was* his car," Tommy reminded her.

"That was five years ago. It was completely his fault, and his fucking insurance paid for the damage. Why can't he let it go?"

"Oh, I don't know, Spider, maybe because you keep calling him a moron?" Tommy suggested.

Spider smiled. "Like it's my fault his fucking parents were brother and sister."

Tommy laughed and shook his head.

"Except for trash and crap in the ashtray, under the seats and on the dash board it looks clean!" Ricky screamed from his place at the computer screen. "Lots of dirt in your carpets."

Spider and Tommy joined him at the computer screen.

"What's that?" Spider asked pointing.

"That's a tiny piece of dust in the overhead light, bright spot," Ricky laughed.

Spider went to the car with a screwdriver and pried the cover off the dome light. It took her several minutes of searching, but she found what she was looking for. She retrieved it and took it over to Tommy. It was no bigger than the head of a pin.

Tommy looked at it. "What the hell is it?"

"I think it's a bug," Spider said.

"Fuck me." Tommy breathed. "Ricky, you have a magnifying glass?"

"Why would I have a magnifying glass in a garage?" Ricky asked, looking over Tommy's shoulder.

"So you could see to pee," Spider answered.

"Oh, you're so funny, Webb," Ricky said without humor. "Why don't you get your own sitcom?"

"Good idea. I wonder if they could get me some fat, balding dickless fuck with thick glasses to play off of—Hey! What are you doing next week?"

"You call me a moron, meanwhile you think a piece of dust is a fucking bug," Ricky said.

"Shut up, both of you!" Tommy looked around, then he grabbed Ricky's glasses off his face.

"Hey!" Ricky protested.

"Just need them a second," Tommy said. He held the glasses over the speck of metal on Spider's finger, and he was looking at a bug. "Damn, we're fucked."

"You're a genius, Tommy," Spider said looking at the bug through the glasses.

Tommy handed Ricky his glasses back.

"What now?" he asked Spider.

"We throw the fucking thing into traffic so that they have to start following us again."

And she did.

"GODDAMN IT!"

Kirk Anderson slung the headphones across the van, as loud street noise filled her ears.

"They found the fucking bug."

Jason Baker rubbed his chin. "It's all right. We still have the others. Sooner or later she's gonna slip and give him up. When she does, we'll have both of them."

"ONE OF THOSE FUCKING things…" Tommy was still whispering as they were driving. They had thrown every spec of trash away and vacuumed the car, but he still didn't feel safe. "It could fucking be anywhere, in our clothes. Hell, there could be hundreds of them everywhere and a normal bug detector would never find them."

"The car scan did," Spider said thoughtfully.

"It's a diagnostic program set up to look for anything—even a piece of dust in a fuel line. It has a complete schematic of the car programmed into it. A normal detection device wouldn't have a chance. That thing wouldn't, couldn't emit enough energy. Who the fuck are these guys, Spider? Where did they get equipment like this, and why the hell are they after us?"

Spider stared out the window, obviously deep in thought.

"Well!" Tommy demanded.

"I don't know," Spider said after a moment's thought. "It's not just the Fry Guy thing. I'm sure of that."

Tommy glared at her. There was something she wasn't telling him.

"I swear, Tommy, I don't know any more than you do."

He glared at her again.

"Not about the So-what-if guys, anyway. They don't know any more than Toby does about what I know about the case—they couldn't. We certainly aren't suspect enough for them to tail us and bug us. So there has to be something else."

Tommy nodded. "But you do know who the Fry Guy is. I know that, and if they've been bugging us, you…then they might know, too."

Spider nodded. "I guess, but I don't think that's all of it."

"So what now?" Tommy asked.

Spider thought for a moment. "Well, I don't know about you, but after much consideration I have decided to take a personal day. Richards is down, and Carrie'll need me."

She punched up her comlink and in put the necessary data into the main computer. "Take me back to the station so I can get my car."

"Spider…." He turned the car around. "What the hell are we going to do about this?"

"Well, I hate to answer a question with a question, but what the hell *can* we do?" Spider said. "If it's any consolation, I don't think they're after you. I think they're my problem. Since I have no idea who they are or what they want, I'm just going to have to wait for them to make their move and hope I can handle it when they do."

SPIDER FOUND CARRIE at the hospital with Richards' wife. Carrie ran to meet her and threw her arms around Spider's neck. Spider held her tight. Carrie'd obviously been crying.

"I was at work, but I thought you might want me here."

"I do," Carrie said. She dried her face on Spider's shirt and then dragged her over to meet Mrs. Richards.

The woman was obviously anxious and upset. Spider felt the woman's pain, and was glad. She had often talked to wives or husbands in hospitals. Too many times there was nothing but relief and a hope that the person would die. Usually, if there was any anxiety, it was because of the bill. For most couples the love didn't last, it got torn apart by promises unkept, dreams unfulfilled, and resentment over lost time. They were trapped in a relationship they couldn't get out of without losing everything they'd worked for, or breaking vows they didn't want to keep. For them death was a welcome answer to their problems

Spider saw a world most people didn't. A world with the niceties and the bullshit striped away. Usually it was a real downer, but Mrs. Richards loved her husband and was hoping that he would come back to her healthy and whole. It made Spider feel good, and she had to work at not smiling.

She'd learned early on that you couldn't let your features show what you were getting from other people. For instance, if a man was telling a supposedly very heart felt, touching story about his late wife, you couldn't snarl at him because the feelings you got from him were joy and a sense of freedom. You had to act as if you believed his bullshit story.

"So, how's he doing?" Spider asked Carrie when they walked down the hall to get coffee, leaving Mrs. Richards behind.

"I don't know. He's still in surgery. It doesn't look good; he's had a pretty massive heart attack. I don't really know what they're doing to him. Someone said something about an artificial valve. They're afraid he's had a stroke, but they really can't tell till he's conscious. I'd like to know what the fuck they do know. At any rate, he won't be coming back to work at any time in the near future. I don't know what's going to happen with the election. If he is able to work it's not likely that he'll be able to convince the voters that he's healthy enough to be DA. His work means so much to him. I don't know what he'll do if he can't work."

There was no triumph in Carrie. Maybe it hadn't even dawned on her yet that she might run for DA. Her only concern was that a man she liked and admired was horribly ill. Her only desire was that he make a complete recovery. Spider was glad. She forgot herself and smiled, which was, of course not what she should have done, and Carrie glared at her.

"What the hell are you so happy about!" Carrie was obviously mad. "It's not worth it to me for Richards to die because I'd like to be DA someday. Hell, I'm not even ready yet."

"I...I know that," Spider stammered. "That's why I was smiling. I was happy that you were so virtuous."

Carrie nodded. "I'm sorry, Honey. I forget sometimes that you're not always on the same page as the rest of us."

They had reached the coffee machine. Spider started getting the coffee as it had been ordered.

"I feel so guilty."

"You...why?" Spider said.

"Because you told me he had heart trouble. I should have said something," Carrie said.

"First off, they would have thought you were crazy," Spider said, handing Carrie one cup of coffee. "That's for Mrs. Richards." She started the next cup. "Second, he knew he had heart trouble, or at least suspected, otherwise I couldn't have got it from him. I can't predict the future. He was worried about his heart...Worried that he was going to have an attack the day of the hostage situation in the bank."

"But his physical gave him a clean bill of health," Carrie reminded Spider.

"Doctors and tests don't catch everything. He knew he was sick." She handed a second cup to Carrie. "That's yours." She started getting her own coffee.

"So, is forewarned really forearmed?" Carrie asked.

Spider grabbed her coffee and they started back.

"Well?" Carrie prompted.

"I'm thinking," Spider answered. She thought only a second longer. "It's saved my life at least twice, and helped me save others. So I can't come right out and say no. But it has made it impossible to lead a so-called 'normal' life, who knows how many wrong turns I've made because I knew how someone felt, so I couldn't say yes, either."

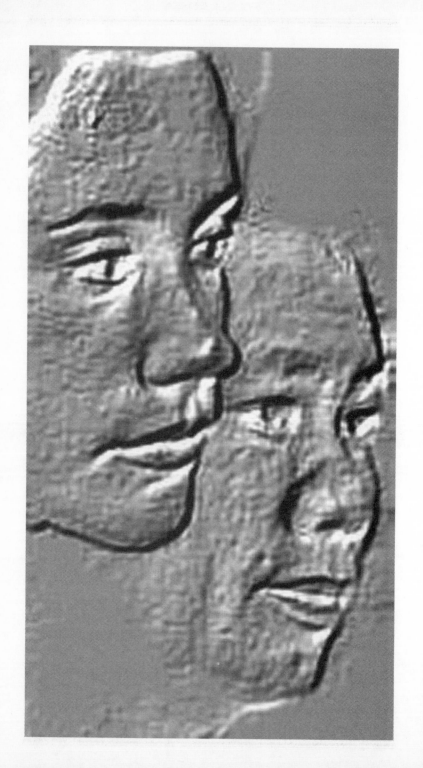

CHAPTER NINE

*"Surely he gives to a man that is good in his sight
wisdom, and knowledge, and joy: but to the sinner
he gives the task of gathering and heaping up, that
he may give it to one who is good before God. This
also is a vanity and a striving after wind."* Ecclesiastes 2:26

ROBBY STARED AT the man at the end of the alley. He watched as the man disappeared around the corner.

Six, six at least. He preys on women, old and young, he doesn't care. He takes from them something that they can never get back; their peace of mind.

He wrestled the washer into the truck. He had work to do, a family to support. They counted on him for everything.

They count on me to keep them safe, and here I stand letting a rapist walk away. I can't do it, and I won't.

He pulled his gloves on tighter and went in the direction he had seen the man go.

TOMMY LOOKED AT the clock. Two o'clock in the morning. "Why can't this guy pick a more reasonable hour to kill people?"

"Scum come out at night," Laura suggested sleepily. "If you prey on scum, you've got to come out in the dark, too."

He looked at his comlink. "I'd better make like a baby and go. Spider's already on her way."

"Poor Carrie, this has been a hell of a day for her," Laura said.

Tommy had to agree. Richards had come through surgery OK, but he had suffered a pretty major stroke, and had struggled to announce that he would not be running for re-election. In a statement dictated at great personal cost, he asked his supporters to vote for Carrie. On her way out of the hospital Carrie had run into a wall of reporters. They asked her if she was going to run. She said yes. They asked her about Richards and about her campaign. Mostly they wanted to know if it was true that she was a lesbian, to which she answered yes. After that they had bombarded her for fifteen minutes until the police were able to pull her through the crowd to her car.

Tommy had finished dressing. He bent down and kissed Laura. "Hopefully I'll be home before I have to get up and go to work."

"Be careful. I love you, Tommy."

"I love you, too."

"How am I supposed to get worked up about the death of scum like this?" Carrie asked Tommy in a whisper.

"You just said a mouthful," Tommy agreed.

Spider had wandered off and was checking out the crime scene. Tommy had worked with her long enough that he knew when she just wanted to be left alone.

"So, things cool off a little?" he asked Carrie, even though he could guess at the answer.

Carrie shrugged. "Before or after Spider tore the phone out of the wall and threw it in the pool?" She sighed. "I don't know, Tommy. Maybe I shouldn't run for office. I think I can take the heat, but I'm not sure about Spider. People were calling all evening. Very few of the calls were supportive. Most of them were…'We don't need no fucking dyke running the country'. Ignorant fucks who don't even know what the DA does. Telling me shit like God's gonna strike me dead. Threatening me, calling me a pervert. I've never seen Spider so mad. I was upset, and she knew it, so she started taking the calls. After the third one I heard this popping sound, and the next thing I knew the phone was flying through the air into the pool. Then she crawled up on the roof with a high-powered rifle and sat there for three hours just waiting for anyone to try anything. So I'm guessing the last one was an actual death threat."

Tommy didn't know what to say. "I'm sorry, Carrie. Listen, I'll talk to Spider."

"Can you talk to every idiot in this city? Because I've got to tell you that I was happy to see the phone gone, and the whole time I was trying to talk her down off the roof I was wondering if maybe she wasn't right where she needed to be," Carrie said. "You know, every time I think we have evolved farther than this I realize that we never should have crawled out of the mud. It's the same old shit. When people have a belief that is hard to defend and impossible to prove, they either persecute or kill the people who disagree with them. That's why mankind becomes more and more stupid. Because all these self-righteous idiots keep destroying anyone with a brain." She walked away mumbling something about breeding a generation of culls.

Tommy started looking over the crime scene just because he wanted to make sure he looked busy.

Spider was talking to one of the Feds, but this time she didn't look agitated. In fact, they seemed to be having a normal conversation, which would of course make it abnormal.

SPIDER HAD APPROACHED Harry Sullivan with caution.

"Harry, can I talk to you for a minute?" she asked. He nodded and walked over to her.

"What is it, Webb?" Obviously he was ready for an argument over something.

"What's up with the idiots in black?" she asked.

"You mean the So-what-if guys?"

"Damn! I thought I coined that."

"Sorry to disappoint you. We've been calling them that for years," Harry said.

"So, what the hell are they?" Spider asked.

Harry shrugged. "I've been doing this for fifteen years, and this is only the third time I've ever seen them. Never for this long, either. They usually come in, a bunch of evidence comes up missing, and they're gone. Every time it was a case like this. Someone was using a weapon no one could identify."

"Anything else?" Spider asked.

Harry looked at her and smiled an all-knowing, smug smile.

She wanted to slap it off his face. She sighed. "All right, all right, but you're going to think I'm nuts. That's the only reason I haven't told anyone what I think."

Harry nodded.

"It's not a weapon. I think this guy, maybe he's some sort of mutant or shit. I think he sees evil. Justice is blind, but this guy isn't. If he was an ex-cop, or even active, he would have shown up on the comlink system by now. It's a simple process of elimination. You know that because you know how the system works. Our boy is not a cop, he knows these people are crooks because he *sees* it."

"Okay Webb. So far what you're saying makes as much sense as anything else I've heard, but what about the weapon?"

"You'd better have some good shit for me, Harry," Spider said. She looked around again to make sure no one was watching them. "All right. First, if there was a weapon like this it would be on file somewhere. There would be some information on it. The FBI would sure as hell know about it, and it's obvious that you are as clueless as we are. The only thing that I could find on my link that would come close to delivering this kind of damage weighs about six hundred pounds. If our boy were carrying something around like that, someone would have seen him—and it."

"I have the same information. We were thinking maybe some other country had developed..."

"And you guys don't know about it? Not very damn likely. I think this guy *is* the weapon. Now, I don't know how he came to be—or why. But I think he's pyrokinetic. I think he sees their evil and has the power to do something about it."

The G-man wasn't laughing. "The SWTF guys were bugging me, too. So I started sifting through some old files. You know, anything I could find that might give me some clue as to why they were here now. I came across a file marked...." He looked around quickly and then, just to be on the safe side, pulled her out of line of sight of anyone. "The project was called Better People through Chemicals. Their idea of a joke or something. It was a locked file, and took a sixth level clearance, which I don't have. I got in, not going to say how. It was a list of names and dates. I thought at first they were dates of birth. But then I came across the word 'fertilization'. I noticed a pattern—five fertilizations at a time. Every three years."

"What the hell was it?" Spider asked.

"I think the government is dabbling in genetic engineering. I think the Strange Weapons in Strange Weapons Task Force are people. I think these guys show up when one of their 'weapons' gets away from them." He looked around again. "They're following you because they think you know who their weapon is. If you do, you'd by God better play dumb, because if you tell them what you just told me, there's a real good chance you're gonna wind up dead."

Spider nodded. "That's what I thought. There is no winning with them. Don't find him and they follow you around, and you don't know what they're going to do. Do find him and they kill you because then you know too much."

"You said it, sister," Harry said, shaking his head.

"Sounds to me like you'd better watch your back, too," Spider said.

"Believe me, I already am."

NEITHER ONE OF them had gotten enough sleep to make them really happy about being at work. Spider was driving. Tommy was almost asleep, and they were heading down to the morgue to talk to the coroner so that he could tell them what they already knew. Microwaved brains.

A bus went by. Someone had hit Richards' campaign photo in the chest with a red paint ball.

"Now, ain't that sweet," Spider hissed.

Tommy looked over to see what she was talking about and grunted his agreement.

"What were you and Sullivan talking about last night?" Tommy asked.

"You really don't want to know that, Tommy," Spider said. "I'll just tell you this. The So-what-if guys that have been following us and bugged our car are nobody to fuck with."

Tommy nodded. Since he wasn't one hundred percent sure that he didn't have one of those tiny little bugs on him, he wasn't going to press the issue. He looked out the window. It was a beautiful spring day. Not too warm and not too cold. He'd like to take Laura and a blanket, go to the park and just hang out. That was the problem with life; 'responsibility' got in the way of enjoying it. You were constantly doing what you had to do instead of what you wanted to do.

Tommy's whole life had been that way.

"When I was a kid, maybe six or seven, Uncle Lop Sing was hiking in the woods. Way off in the middle of nowhere he found this old campground that had been built by the WPA or the CCC, abandoned and forgotten years before. Not even the road had been maintained, so that you had to hike five miles to get there. There were eight small rock cabins and one huge meeting building. It became a family tradition that once a year the whole family would hike up there together and stay for two weeks. It was a beautiful place with a running creek, and it was so quiet. The whole family was together. My mom and my aunts would cook huge meals. My uncles would fish and play ball with my cousins. I always wanted to fish, too. I always wanted to play catch. But my father said it was a waste of time. It was one thing to go on vacation, and another to stop training. So while everyone else was playing, I was training. It was my responsibility. Since all of my cousins were girls, I had to carry on the tradition. It was my duty."

"Duty sucks," Spider said, with no elegance but a whole load of camaraderie.

"I always wanted to go there and just play catch," Tommy finished with a sigh.

"Then why don't you?" Spider asked.

Tommy just stared at her, mouth open for a second, then he laughed. "You know...maybe I will."

Spider readjusted the rear view mirror. The SWTF guys were right behind them. She turned quickly and drove down what she knew was a blind alley and they followed.

"Spider! What the hell!" Tommy screamed as he was thrown up against the side of the car.

Spider braked to a stop, jumped out of their car and ran back to the car that had pulled in behind them. She got there before the SWTF men had a chance to back up.

"WHAT THE HELL is she doing?" Kirk asked.

"Calling our bluff," Jason answered.

Kirk rolled down his window as she approached them. Her partner was not far behind her. "See how well they work together? Now why can't we be more like that, Jason?"

"Because I don't like you, and you don't like me," Jason said bluntly.

Spider knelt on the ground beside their car so that she was looking in the window. Tommy stood at her shoulder.

"OK, I'll bite," Spider started. "Why are you spooks following us?"

"Orders, detective. I'm sure you understand orders," Kirk said heavily.

"No, can't say that I do. Why are they ordering you to follow us? Why did you bug our car?" Spider said.

"Orders. I hate to bust your bubble, detective, but we don't have to tell you anything. We don't have to give you any reasons. We don't even have to smile when we say fuck you."

Spider smiled at him a moment. Then she jumped to her feet, grabbed him by the collar, and jerked him quickly up so that he was half way through the window. She then shoved him into the car roof until his back made a funny little popping noise.

Tommy hurled himself across the hood and slammed the car door into Jason as he got out of the car, successfully pinning him in the doorway. Then Tommy held him there, giving him a look that dared him to so much as breathe funny.

Spider glared down at Kirk. "I know people like you. You've been in my face my whole fucking life. You think you've got some kind of power over me. That you can kill me any time you like. Well listen up you fucking walking carcass. *I* could kill *you* anytime I like."

He tried to look away, and she jerked on him till he was forced to look at her.

"I could snap you in two right here right now, and feel no remorse. So, if you want to play fucking games, then you play fucking games. But let me warn you. I'm like a dog; if you try to corner me, I'll eat your fucking face."

She let him go and started walking away. Tommy did, too, although he kept his eye on Jason, who, for his part, put his hands in the air indicating that he didn't want a fight.

Kirk moved his hand toward his gun.

Spider spun in a single motion, her gun in hand, pointed at his head. She smiled at him. "And *bang! bang!* would make you dead."

Kirk put his hands up, then lowered himself into the car. Jason got back into the car, too, and they backed quickly out of the alley.

Spider put her gun away, and Tommy slapped her, palm down in the shoulder, hard enough to rock her back.

"Are you fucking out of your tiny little mind?" Tommy screamed. "Did you not just tell me that you don't fuck with those guys?"

"I was torn," Spider said.

"Torn!" He popped her in the shoulder again. "What the fuck does that mean? One minute you're telling me that they are bad wuju guys, and the very next minute you're pulling them over and kicking their asses. Which I'm here to tell you is going to piss them off."

"I was afraid to do nothing," Spider said. "I was afraid to do nothing, and afraid to do anything. I was torn. Now whatever happens, at least I'll know what caused it."

"WHAT IS THAT smell?" Jason asked, flagging his hand in front of his face.

Kirk was driving quickly, putting as much distance between them and Spider Webb as he could.

"What is that fucking smell?" Jason demanded again. He saw the color go up Kirk's face, and started to laugh. "You shit your fucking pants!" He laughed harder. "Big bad Kirky shit all over himself. Oh man, that's one for the books."

"Shut the fuck up!" Kirk screamed. He'd never been more terrified in his life.

"Well, one thing's for sure. She has the *push*. No more wondering about that."

Kirk's hands would be shaking if they weren't on the wheel, and he hadn't shit his pants since he was three. So, as much as he would have liked to disagree with Jason, he couldn't.

"I'm gonna go change my pants, and then we'll make a call to Deacon." Kirk glared at Jason. "I swear, if this ever leaks out…"

"What? The fucking seat will be ruined?" Jason laughed uncontrollably.

Kirk didn't think it was funny.

SPIDER DIDN'T STOP by the hospital that day; she went straight home. Carrie wasn't home yet, and probably wouldn't be for another hour, so now was as good a time as ever.

She dug through her drawer until she found what she was looking for. Then she stuffed it in the top of her pants quickly.

She grabbed her old TV, headed for the door, shoved the TV in her truck and headed out. She went the long way, making sure that no one was trailing her. A quick diagnosis of her truck had turned nothing up, and she had made a habit of only wearing clothes after she had run them in the drier on high ten minutes first.

Still, she hoped that she wasn't making a big mistake. Hoped that she wasn't giving the So-what-if guys just the break they needed.

ROBBY WAS WORKING on a microwave. Evan was helping him and telling him about his day. Things between them were seemingly normal, although Robby doubted their relationship would ever be the same again.

"…Roseanna looked at me and asked me if I would help her with her math. 'Cause of me being so much better at it than her."

Robby laughed. "I think you'd better work on your English."

"I'm just excited." He slowed down. "I'm sixteen now, Robby. I got my driver's license. I know you don't want me to work, but the guy at the market said I could have your old job, and I'd help out with the money around here and still have something left over…"

"And then you could buy a car and go out with Roseanna," Robby teased. "Hand me that pair of pliers."

Evan handed Robby the pliers. "Well, yeah," he said more than a little embarrassed.

"What about your grades, Evan? You don't make great grades anyway, except for math. If you start working, you're still going to have your chores here, and then you'll have less time to study," Robby said. He grunted a little as he pried on the screw head. Someone had striped the head out, and a screwdriver wouldn't work on it.

"I swear I'll keep my grades up, Robby. You let Donna and Janice and Devan work, and they're younger than I am," Evan begged.

"Donna and Janice are just babysitting a couple of nights a week here at the house. Devan mows lawns and rakes leaves here in the neighborhood, so that's not really the same. Besides, they make a lot better grades than you do," Robby said. The damn screw finally came out.

"Please, Robby! I'll work double hard."

Robby thought about it. Evan had turned his act around and was acting more responsible. Besides, why shouldn't he bring in some money to help with the family? "All right, but here are the rules. Your grades suffer and that's it—no argument…"

"Deal," Evan said.

"Wait, I ain't finished yet, boy. Second, you still do your chores around here, no questions asked, and no complaints."

"Deal."

"I'm still not finished. Ten percent of what you make goes to the house, and another ten percent goes into your bank account—just like the girls and Devan."

"Great! Can I go tell old man Cooper I'll take the job?"

"Get going," Robby said with a laugh.

Evan took off through the side door for the house.

"Bet that gets to be a handful."

Robby started and turned to face the woman who had just walked in the garage door carrying a TV set. Even if her coloring hadn't been so strange, he still wouldn't have had any trouble re- membering her. She set the TV down.

Robby stood up and wiped his hands. He looked at her and again he saw the visions—remnants of a life filled with war and hell. "Something tells me you didn't come here to get your TV fixed."

Spider Webb pulled something out of the front of her pants and threw it onto the workbench.

He stared at his glove for a moment then looked at her. "I dropped it. I knew where I must have dropped it, but I didn't dare go back after it...If you knew, why didn't you turn me in right then?"

"I never really wanted to turn you in at all. But after I found that I really couldn't, could I?" She held up her hand. "I noticed your hands the minute we walked in. I could feel you in my head, just like I'm sure you could feel me in yours."

Robby walked over and slowly put his hand against hers. It was almost a perfect match, with his fingers being only slightly longer than hers.

"I can never get gloves. Where the hell did you get this?"

Robby moved his hand and picked up the glove. "I make them. See?" He held it out to her. "I take two pairs of work gloves, cut the ends out of the fingers on one pair, cut the whole finger off the other and sew them together. If they had found this..."

"They'd go back up the line with it and sooner or later someone would remember that the garbage man had abnormally large hands, DNA evidence in the gloves. You'd be gone, and I don't think I'd be far behind you," she said.

"Do you...could we be related?" Robby asked. In his whole life he'd never seen anyone with hands like his except in a picture of his father.

Spider shrugged. "I don't know. Maybe distantly. My mother and my brother both had this...I'd call it a deformity, except that besides getting me teased I've never found it to be anything but a plus. Except for you, I've never seen anyone outside my family with these hands before." She paused. "I know that you have psychic ability..."

"And so do you," he said.

She nodded. "It's not lethal like yours, but yes I do." She paused again and then continued. "There are some nasty fuckers hanging around. Call themselves the SWTF, stands for Special Weapons Task Force. They're investigating your case, and they're following me. I'm not going to tell you everything that's going on because I'm not really sure I really understand it. But I will tell you this. I never had any plans to come near you again; it's just too risky. But, Robby, you have got to quit killing people, man."

HARRY SULLIVAN WAS looking over the dock at the water again. A view he was becoming increasingly irritated by. They slammed the plastic pipe into his back again, and this time he threw up.

"I asked you what you sent her," Kirk said.

"And I told you. Nothing!" Harry said through clenched teeth. Kirk hit him again.

He saw stars. They were going to kill him no matter what he said. He knew that, and knowing that, there was no reason for him to tell them a goddamned thing. He just wished they'd kill him and get it over with. He'd tried fighting them, and they'd broken both his legs for his effort. They spun him around, putting pressure on his badly broken limbs, and he almost passed out. Then they slapped him in the face till he was almost conscious.

"I'm going to ask you one more time." Kirk put the barrel of his gun against Harry's forehead. "What did you send the cop? What does she know?"

Harry forced a pained laugh. "It's gonna kill ya man. You'll never see it coming; you'll just be dead. You bastards built this thing, and now it's gonna kill ya—if she don't get ya first." He spit in Kirk's face. "I'll see you in hell."

Kirk pulled the trigger. Harry's body poured over the rail and into the river with a splash. By morning his body would be in the next county, if the catfish didn't eat him outright. But he wouldn't be going to hell.

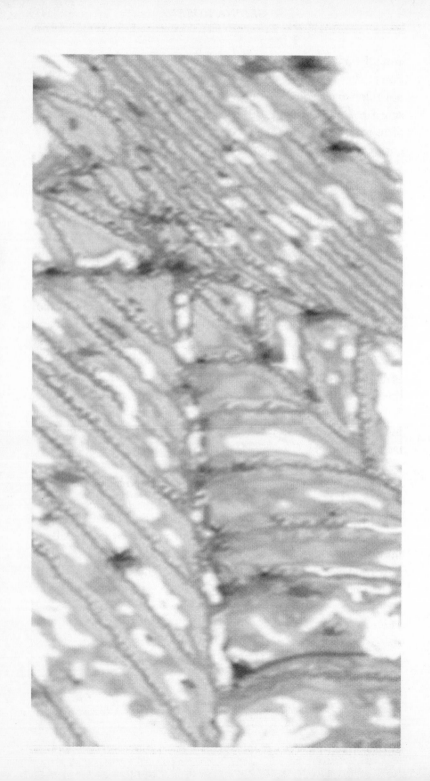

CHAPTER TEN

Better is the end of a thing than the beginning

THE CAMPAIGN HAD been a disaster—for Carrie's opponent.

He had tried to make her sexuality an issue, but these days it just wasn't that big a deal.

Carrie had countered his attacks with information and knowledge, explaining to the voters just exactly what a district attorney did. She pointed out that while she had several years' experience in criminal law, William Barns had never worked in anything but corporate law, and never in any accountable capacity.

Further, she had asked the voters to consider the sick and tawdry things that Barns and his wife might be doing in their bedroom. When his camp protested her tactics, she reminded the voters that he was the one that insisted that a person's sex life was the determining factor in whether they would be a good DA or not.

In the first—and subsequently only—debate held, Carrie had presented a chart showing a definite rise in arrest to conviction rates, and a lowering of the crime rate, explaining that she would continue to run the DA's office as Richards had with his input and support.

Barns had countered, "That's not because of the DA's office, that's because of the Fry Guy. Who, by the way, you haven't gotten any closer to catching."

Carrie had smiled, completely unflapped by his outburst. "The 'Fry Guy' killings would appear to have stopped for the time being. You can hardly accuse the DA's office or the city's police force of shabby work in the case. As you no doubt know, there are at least two federal agencies involved in this investigation as well, and they're no closer to catching this guy than we are. The Fry Guy killings are a high priority, and we're doing everything in our power to apprehend him. I just don't think it's the most important case on the book. Not when there are people out there killing innocents—people without records of violent crime. As DA, my job is to decide which cases get tried and which don't, to make sure that innocent men aren't tried for crimes that they didn't commit, and that convicted criminals are punished to the fullest extent of the law. Richards didn't do a whole lot of plea bargaining, and neither will I."

"Well, isn't that a whole lot of double talk that common people don't understand," Barns said.

"By 'common,' I'm assuming that you mean 'stupid,' and I by no means believe that the voters of Shea City are stupid. Which is why they'll all be voting for me on Election Day."

"So are you saying that anyone who doesn't vote for you is stupid?" Barns screamed. He was losing it—both the debate and his temper.

"What's next, Barns? Are you going to scream 'I'm rubber and you're glue'? Come on. Tell us what you're going to do as DA instead of pointing fingers at me. The people can look up my record. I've got five years of experience working as a prosecuting attorney in the DA's office, three in LA and two here. Richards didn't make me assistant DA because he thought I couldn't handle the job. He didn't ask his supporters to vote for me because he thought I was inept. What can you bring to the DA's office that I can't? That's all the people want to know."

"Family values for one thing. I've been married for fifteen years and have three kids. We go to church every Sunday."

"So do you deal with a lot of murderers there? Because I think what the people want to know is whether you can convict criminals and get them off the street."

"I want to get them off the street. I know how, and I have a family to protect which gives me a little more incentive than you," Barns countered.

"The citizens of this city are my main concern. My partner is a police detective, so it's in my best interest to make sure that I don't put killers back on the street."

"Did you hear that, people? She said *she*. Now do we really want our city represented by a lesbian?"

"I'm not running for mayor, I'm running for DA. It isn't the DA's job to represent the city. If you think that being DA is a really glitzy job, then you're going to be mightily disappointed. You get pulled out in the middle of the night to look at bloody crime scenes, and dragged to the morgue to look at bodies. You spend most of your working hours dealing with the scum of the city. There is nothing at all glamorous about being DA. You have to be dedicated to your work and to the people of this city. You aren't above them, you are their employee, and you have to be able to get the job done. I know I can; I've done it; I'm currently doing it. I don't even think you know what the DA's job actually is, since you seem to think that the only real qualification you need is to be heterosexual."

"You are monopolizing all of the time." He looked at the moderator. "She is monopolizing all of the time."

The moderator shrugged. "Sorry, it's an open topic, one-on-one debate, which is what you asked for, Sir."

"If you can't hold your own in a friendly debate, how do you expect to hold your own in the courtroom day after day?"

Barns had stormed off the stage and out of the building. When a wall of reporters had tried to talk to him he had shoved through them without a word.

The rest of his campaign was one giant homo-hating spread after another.

Carrie had countered by continuing to show the public that she knew what the job was and how to do it.

When a trashy looking hooker went to the news media and claimed that she was the 'family man's' mistress, 'hypocrite' was added to the list of his shortcomings.

Carrie won by a landslide.

At her campaign headquarters the noise was deafening as the final tally came in. There were congratulations from everyone. She gave her acceptance speech, and then Carrie went off to find Spider.

She hadn't seen her much at all the entire evening. Or the last few weeks for that matter. Spider was still very uncomfortable being 'out' in front of anyone, and now she had instantly become one of the most celebrated lesbians in the city. Carrie found Spider in the corner talking to Tommy and Laura. They were all talking and laughing and swilling champagne. She wished she had found Spider talking to some total stranger—as long as it wasn't a beautiful woman stranger. Spider really seemed to have a hard time making friends, and it was mostly because she didn't try.

People moved out of Carrie's way to let her through without being asked. It was then that it really sank in. She had just won the election. From now on people were going to be treating her differently, and she wasn't sure that she liked that idea. Wasn't sure that she liked it at all.

Suddenly there were too many people in the room. The walls seemed to be closing in. From now on, like it or not, she was a public figure. Mikes in her face whenever she turned around, very little personal time, no fucking privacy. What the hell had she been thinking?

Spider pushed her way through the crowd. Carrie felt Spider's hand at her elbow, steadying her.

"It will be OK, Carrie." Spider whispered in her ear. "It's nothing that you haven't been doing all along. Next week the campaign, the election, and everything else will be old news, and you can get back to being DA."

Carrie nodded, took a deep breath and found that she could breath again. Just having Spider there made her feel better. "I'm exhausted. I really just want to go home."

"Then that's what we're doing," Spider said.

They started out of the building, and the press was all over them. Carrie answered as well as her tired brain would let her…Yes, she was thrilled about the election…no, she would not be taking the congratulations call from Barns because she had never been as phony as he was and didn't plan to start now…no, she didn't plan to run for any other public office in the future, she was a prosecuting attorney, and she was very happy being DA.

Spider found a mike in her face.

"Detective Webb! What role will you play now that your partner is DA?"

Spider stared at the mike for a minute, but realized it wouldn't look good for Carrie if she took the mike and shoved it up the reporter's ass. "Well," she stammered, "I guess I'll support her like we support each other in everything. As far as playing any role in the DA's office…decisions or stuff…the answer is none. She's the DA; I'm a cop. There's no reason for our paths to cross anymore at work than they ever have. The people voted for her, not me. And I would appreciate it if everyone would just leave me out of the politics." With that said, she physically pulled Carrie through the crowd and out of the building.

"THAT'S BIG TROUBLE," Jason said through a mouthful of sandwich as he watched the TV screen.

Kirk nodded. "Just what we fucking needed. All the damned publicity doesn't make our job any easier. I really didn't think she'd win the election."

"No one did, or they would have made sure she didn't. Guess people really are becoming more tolerant," Jason said, then washed his sandwich down with some stale beer.

"Or the other guy was just so fucking incompetent that the people would rather vote for a queer," Kirk snarled. "Either way it throws a big fucking monkey wrench into our plans. We're going to have to be a whole lot more cautious. Like Deacon said, we need to reevaluate our methods."

Jason shrugged. "I'd just like to go home. I haven't seen my old lady or the kids in three months now."

"There is a reason why the agency discourages such emotional attachments," Kirk said.

"Because they don't want us to have any heart, any compassion." Jason threw his sandwich wrapper into the trash hard. "Hell, I was bled out a long time ago, Kirk. I thought that I could get my humanity back by having a family. It didn't take me long to realize that by having something that I cared about so much, I had finished selling my soul to the agency. By having a family I'd given the fucking agency absolute leverage over me. That's why I hate your guts, Kirk. Because I know that on the day that I didn't do the agency's bidding you'd be only too happy to hang my little girl up by the hair of her head and torture her until I gave in."

"You never have understood, Jason. This is bigger than any one person. More important than one family. The future of the free world…"

Jason jumped up and glared down at Kirk. "Who the fuck are you trying to sell! Don't give me that 'future of the free world' shit. We're playing with people's lives. A few assholes have decided what is right for everybody. They have created something that has gotten out of control. And the fucking Fed we iced—he was right. We created something that's going to kill us. Between you and me, it can't come fast enough. I was in too deep when I realized just how fucking far around the bend the SWTF is. Now I keep doing shit I know is wrong. I don't have any soul left, but unlike you I still have a conscience, and when we plug some poor fuck like that Fed I don't sleep. I have guilt. But I keep doing it because the agency owns my fucking soul. They got your soul, too, Kirk. You're just too dead to know it."

"If you're quite done psychoanalyzing me, you can run along and set up the equipment. See if we're picking anything up."

"Yessir, Massa. What evah ya say, Massa," Jason said sarcastically as he bowed all the way out of the room.

"SHE DIDN'T LOOK very happy about winning the election," Tommy said as he started slipping out of his monkey suit.

"She wants to do the job, but her doesn't really want the title. She's been worried about the publicity all along. Apparently the campaign has been something of a strain on she and Spider's relationship," Laura said. She stepped out of the shower and grabbed a towel. Whenever she was in big crowds of people she always felt filthy until she showered and washed her hair. "It has to be a really weird time for her. New relationship, new job, new duties."

"Really?" Tommy asked, curious. "Spider didn't say anything about it."

"Well she wouldn't, would she?" Laura said. "From what Carrie says that's most of the problem. Spider would really rather stay in the closet, and now—like it or not—she's out. Everywhere she goes people know who she is and that she's gay. She's having a lot of trouble with it." Laura combed her hair. She started to blow it dry and decided it was too much like work.

Tommy walked into the bathroom to brush his teeth. "A few weeks ago, the lieutenant got smart with Spider—made some crack about Carrie. I've never seen her so mad. I don't blame her. It's nobody's business, and now everybody knows. For a lot of people that's all the reason they need to hate her. It's not fair."

"But it's the way things are." Laura slapped him on the ass and left the bathroom for the welcome comfort of their bed.

Laura smiled and squashed into her pillow. For her, being in their bed was like being in the only really safe place in the world. Safe from the outside world. A place she and Tommy shared alone with no intrusions. The last few weeks with the campaign had been hell for Laura, so she could only imagine how it must have been for Carrie.

Tommy spit the toothpaste out. "Do you mean that Spider and Carrie are having trouble, like they're going to break up?"

Laura waited till he stopped gargling to answer. "No, not at all. Carrie hasn't said anything like that. They're in love, and I think it would take a lot to break them up. It's just been tough, that's all."

Tommy walked in and crawled into bed. He wrapped himself around Laura and she snuggled against him.

"Are you tired?" Tommy whispered in her ear.

"Not at all," Laura breathed, and started crawling all over him.

SPIDER AND TOMMY had pulled a late night stakeout waiting for a little weasel-faced creep named Freddy Brown. They had reason to believe that he might have witnessed the recent murder of a hooker.

"At first the fuckers were everywhere," Spider was saying. "Even found one hiding in that God awful hedge on the west side of the house. A son of a bitchin gnat couldn't squeeze through, so this dick head took battery powered hedge clippers and cut a hole in the fucking thing. He had a fucking camp stool there and had been sitting there God only knows how long filming the house."

"What the hell for?" Tommy asked.

Spider shrugged. "Who fucking knows? Waiting for us to do it in the yard or something I guess."

"How'd you find him?" Tommy asked.

"Well, as you know I've been a little squirrelly lately. I was looking around before we went in the house, and I saw the sunlight reflecting off his lens. I thought he was SWTF, so I freaked out, right? I go back out the gate and sneak around behind him, grab him and start kicking his ass. Carrie is, of course, having a conniption fit, 'You're going to kill him! You're going to kill him!' so I wasn't listening to her. Then I realize she's yelling out that the guy is trying to show his press card."

"What did you do then?" Tommy asked, laughing.

"I punched him in the face one more time and let him go. Carrie called the cops and had him arrested for trespassing. He's threatening to sue me for his injuries, but Carrie says he can't. She was pissed off at me anyway. Said I overreacted."

"Not *you*," Tommy said sarcastically. He took the binoculars and looked at the building as if seeing better would make a person who wasn't there appear.

"So, you think this dickhead is ever going to show?"

"He has to come home some time," Spider said.

"Of course it doesn't have to be till after we give up staking out his fucking building," Tommy mumbled. "Wait a minute!" Tommy removed his binoculars.

Both partners watched as the man got out of the taxi, and both ducked down lower when they saw him looking around.

When he was sure he was in the clear, Freddy Brown paid the cabby and headed for his building.

Tommy and Spider got carefully out of the car and started walking down the sidewalk in the man's direction.

Freddy's head spun quickly around to look at them. He didn't wait even a second; he took off running.

"Shit!" Spider screamed and took off after him.

Tommy was right behind her, remembering to turn on his comlink and to scream, "Stop! Police!" It was procedure, and it was stupid because no crook ever stopped just because you told them to.

"Fuck you, man!" Freddy sped up and turned down an alley; they followed. He hit the fence and was over—no problem. Spider hit the fence first, but Tommy cleared it before she did.

When they reached the other side of the fence Freddy was already gone. They looked around, but there was nothing. A horn blared.

"Let's go!" Spider screamed and took off towards the street. They rounded the corner just in time to see Freddy run through yet another lane of traffic. Tires squealed as the drivers hit their brakes. Freddy rolled over the hood of one still-moving car and was across the street. Spider and Tommy dodged traffic holding their comlinks up and yelling "Police!" as if that had ever stopped any officer from being hit by a car.

They got across the street just in time to see the son of a bitch run into a four story walk up. They started chasing him up the stairs.

Spider stumbled. Tommy stopped momentarily to see if she was OK. Spider nodded.

"I'm too old for this shit," she panted out.

Tommy nodded and they started back up again.

"You little fucker, when I catch you I'm gonna rip you a new asshole!" Spider screamed.

He ran all the way up and onto the roof, and then the little fucker barricaded the door. Spider and Tommy broke through it just in time to see Freddy jump from one roof to the other. They

took off running. At the edge they both stopped, looked at each
other, and then looked down. Then they looked at each other again
and shook their heads no.

Freddy laughed and flipped them the finger.

"You dumb little fucker," Spider panted out. "We just need to
talk to you."

He took off running across the building and was soon out
of sight.

"Lost...suspect...witness," Tommy panted into his comlink.
He reached down and put his hands on his knees, trying to catch
his breath.

Spider grabbed her side and collapsed on the roof.

"I'm...fucking...gonna...die. Wish I couldah...just shot...the
stupid...bastard," she panted out.

"That...would have...sort of...made it hard...to question him."
Tommy flopped on the roof beside his partner.

"WHAT?" TOMMY ASKED. He rubbed his eyes and stared at Spider's
image on the vid-phone through a sleep-covered haze. He turned
to look at his wall clock and started shaking his head. "Never
mind. At six o'clock on Sunday morning I don't care what it is. I
want to sleep."

"Come on, Tommy," Spider begged. "Look at us! We're turning into old, flabby, married people."

Tommy sighed, threw up his hands and walked into the living
room where he flopped down on the couch. She could come in or
not; he didn't give a shit. Crazy damned white woman, six o'clock
on Sunday morning. He'd kick her ass if that wasn't what she was
asking him to do.

Spider walked in but didn't sit down. She was wearing a sweat
suit that was so drenched, she'd obviously already been jogging in it.
"Come on, man! It'll be fun!"

"Nothing's fun at 6:00 on a Sunday morning." He seemed to
realize what she had said before. "And, for the record, we *are* old,
flabby married people."

"I don't think we can afford to be."

"Then go play with yourself!"

"I got a woman for that now."

"You know what I mean."

"Come on, don't you want to be in shape?"

"I'm in perfect shape for an old, flabby, married guy. I work out almost every day, that's more than most guys my age."

"For how long? A half hour a day, an hour on weekends? Wouldn't you like to be back in the kind of shape you were in when you were king of Ju-whatsit?" she asked.

"To tell the truth, no," Tommy said bluntly. "What I would like is to still be asleep. To wake up at 11:00, have a Twinkie for breakfast, then sit and watch the fucking tube until my brain is dead, and…"

"Ah, come on, Tommy. It'll be fun."

"What it will be is insanity," Tommy said. "Why, Spider? In all the years we've worked together you've never had any interest in learning Jujitsu. Why now?"

Spider sat down; she wasn't bouncing around now. "Tommy, when I was in the service I had martial arts training. Nothing close to what you've had, but I had it. I was in perfect physical shape. I felt like I could handle anything they threw at me, and I damn near died more than once. I don't feel like that right now. I need to be able to walk the razor's edge again, and I only know one person who can teach me that."

Tommy nodded. "This has something to do with losing that punk the other night, doesn't it? That guy was half our age, and he makes his living on those streets."

Spider nodded. "That's part of it, but not all by a long shot…The body they found in the river in Forcehaven."

"Yeah?" Tommy said.

"It was Harry Sullivan, the FBI guy I talked to." She whispered in case Laura was up and might hear them. "He had been tortured before he was killed. I think it might have been because he gave me something he shouldn't have."

Tommy took in a deep breath and let it out. "I don't suppose you're going to tell me what he gave you."

She shook her head no.

He stood up and started for his room to change. In the doorway he stopped and turned to look at her. "Will you do what I tell you without questioning everything I say?"

Spider nodded.

"You will have to train every single day."

She nodded again.

"I mean it, Spider, if we start this, you're going to have to go all the way with it, or you might as well not bother."

"Tommy, you're acting like I've never been in training before, and I have," Spider said.

"This will be like nothing you've ever done before."

"Good, I'd hate to be bored."

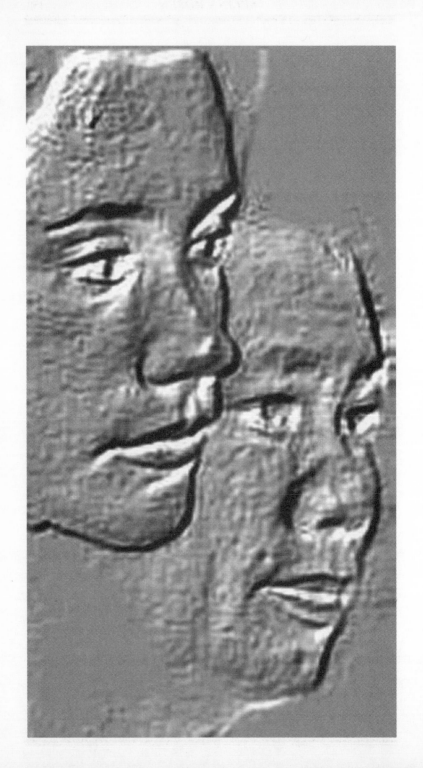

CHAPTER ELEVEN

"That which has been, it is that which shall be:
and that which has been done is that which shall
be done: and there is nothing new under the sun.
Ecclesiastes 1:9

TWO MONTHS PASSED with no sign of the Fry Guy or the SWTF for that matter. Spider had relaxed a little, but she hadn't stopped training.

"I thought the crap would stop after the election," Carrie told Laura. "You know, that things would get back to normal. But for about three weeks afterwards the press were still on me like flies on shit..."

"Don't you love all the wonderful metaphors you learn living with a cop?" Laura laughed.

Carrie nodded. "Thursday in court I almost told the jury to look at the 'fucking' facts in the 'fucking' case and find the 'fucking' scum-bag' guilty. It never ceases to amaze me how many uses Spider can find for the word 'fuck.' Sometimes I think 'fuck' is the only word she knows. Except of course for the ever-popular 'scumbag.' Anyway, I had about decided that I had made a big mistake running at all, and was trying to think of ways—without having a heart attack—that I could just let Chalmers take over for me. But then Congressman Hampton got caught with a transvestite, and suddenly I was old news."

"Thank God for scandal," Laura said with a laugh.

There was a loud thump against the living room wall, and one of the pictures rattled, fell off and landed on the couch. Carrie was glad she had decided not to sit there. Before either one of them had a chance to run into the garage, Tommy poked his head in the door.

"No one hurt." He panted to catch his breath. "No hole... in wall."

"Aren't you playing a little rough?" Carrie asked. Since they had started this martial arts training kick there was barely a week went by that Spider didn't have at least one new bruise. "I don't want to have to take her home in a bag."

"What are you worried about?" Tommy asked, rubbing at his head. "I'm the one who hit the wall." He shut the door and ran back into the garage.

"As if that somehow makes it all right," Laura said, shaking her head. "Tommy says she learns very fast, and she has apparently showed him a couple of moves he didn't know. Just last week he was telling me how wonderfully she was doing, as he held an ice pack over his eye where she had blacked it."

"I'm sorry," Carrie said, shrugging helplessly. "I don't know why she got it in her head to do this, but I know that it's turned your schedule upside down, and I'm sorry."

Laura shook her head. "I'm not. Carrie, Tommy loves Jujitsu. Hell, it's the one thing in this world that he will admit that he's good at, but he had all but stopped practicing. I'm glad he has someone to train and spar with. I have never seen him so self-confidant or motivated. I just wish he'd loosen up a little bit. Have more fun with it instead of being so intense all the time." Laura got up and put the picture back just in time for someone to slam into the wall and knock it off again. She threw up her hands and sat back down as Tommy's head popped in the door.

"No one hurt. Wall not broken," he gasped, and disappeared again.

Laura smiled broadly. "Since he's fighting again he's about three times as horny as he was before."

"And that's almost never a bad thing," Carrie said with a grin.

"Focus, Spider," Tommy ordered.

"OK." Spider took a deep breath. Just how long had she been standing on her fucking hands? Felt like an hour. All the blood in her body was in her hands and brain; her feet were going to sleep. Sweat was running down her cheeks and into her eyes.

"Focus!" Tommy ordered.

"I am!" Spider spat back.

"No you're not. Your mind is all over the place. You're thinking about how much your arms hurt, and how much your back hurts, and how the sweat is stinging your eyes. You're thinking about how long you've been on your hands, and how much longer I'm going to make you do it. Don't think about anything but standing on your hands."

Spider thought he was ridiculous. *Standing on my hands, that is what I'm thinking about. Hell! That's all I am thinking about. Standing on my hands. My hands are on the floor, my feet are in the air, my head is hanging free. My back is straight. I breathe in and I breathe out—nothing else matters except that I am standing on my hands.*

"Spider you can come down now," Tommy said. "As you come down, tuck into a ball, roll across the floor, and then jump onto your feet."

She did it with little or no trouble. She looked at him and smiled.

He smiled back. "You have learned much, Grasshopper. Just don't get too goddamned cocky."

They walked into the house together, Tommy on his hands.

"Show-off," Spider said as she plopped on the couch next to Carrie. "I'm dead, I don't know how you can do that."

"I don't know how either of you can do any of it," Carrie said. "Show Laura your muscle, Baby," Carrie said grabbing Spider's arm.

"No," Spider laughed as her face turned red.

"Come on, Baby," Carrie taunted. "You showed me."

"Come on, Carrie." Spider tried half-heartedly to pull away.

Tommy laughed as he grabbed two beers out of the fridge. He grabbed one by the neck, threw it up and spun it till he was holding onto the body of the bottle, and then he hurled it bottom first at Spider without announcing that he was doing so. Carrie and Laura both screamed, but Spider caught it with her free hand without so much as a fumble. "I can't believe you're embarrassed about anything," Tommy said.

"I can't believe you're throwing full beer bottles through our living room at her head. Don't do it again," Laura warned.

"I am so impressed by the amount of testosterone in this room," Carrie said jokingly. "Come on, Baby, show Laura your muscle."

Spider laughed. "Only if it will make you leave me alone."

Spider made a muscle, and Laura clapped her hands in appreciation. "Fucking impressive, huh?"

Tommy promptly started putting on a whole show, flexing everything that he could flex in front of company and singing "I'm too sexy." Then he started swinging his shirt around his head.

They were all laughing at him, he was the center of attention, and for the first time that he could remember, he felt comfortable with it.

Tommy felt good, he felt ready, although he wasn't sure just what he was ready for.

IT WAS A nice night for a drive, so Carrie was glad when Spider decided to go home the long way around the lake. The moon was full and glinted off the water. It looked deceptively warm. It wasn't. At the end of January, the temperature was thirty-five degrees, and with the brisk wind it felt like twenty below outside.

"What's wrong?" Spider asked.

Carrie laughed. "You know, every once in awhile I'd like to have a thought all to myself."

"I'm sorry," Spider apologized.

Carrie patted Spider's leg. "It's all right. I was just thinking how much I like spending time with Tommy and Laura, but..."

"But what?" Spider asked when Carrie didn't finish.

"Why don't you have any other friends? Why can't we ever visit any of my friends?" Carrie asked. "Most of my friends have only seen you when they come to the house, and then only for a few minutes, till you find some lame excuse to leave."

"It's not lame. I'm training..."

"You started this shit before you were 'training.' Besides which, just what the hell are you training for? It wouldn't hurt you to miss a day or two. I hardly ever see you anymore..."

"That's not all my fault. You've been working a lot more."

"There's not a whole lot I can do about that, Baby. Then when I bring people to the house to help me so that I don't have to stay in the office, you leave rather than have to get to know some of the people I work with."

"I'm not very good with people, Carrie. People don't like me."

"You don't know that."

Spider gave her a side ways glance.

"You don't give them a chance, Spider. You're cold and abrupt with new people, and when you sense they don't like you, you never give them another chance. Do you have even one friend besides Tommy?"

"I still keep in touch with Helen, Victor, and Terry from my old unit in the service. We E-mail back and forth. There's a couple of guys at work. I talk to them, and they don't hate me. I'm sort of friends with them. Jamie, the girl who runs the dispatch desk, I like her, she likes me. But I don't hang with any of those people."

"Why not?" Carrie demanded.

Spider shrugged. "I'm not like you, Carrie. I can't be like you." She was starting to get mad. "It's not easy to be friends with people when you know how they feel about you. Not easy to have friends and to feel their pain. It's easier not to get close."

"Easier, maybe, but not better," Carrie said. "What do you expect? Of course if you blow people off, they're not going to 'feel' very charitable about you."

Spider thought about that for a minute. Carrie might have a point, which of course did nothing but piss her off more. "I'd rather be around people I can trust. Tommy likes me, no matter what I do. So does Laura."

"And that equals safety to you?" Carrie didn't really understand. "Don't you ever want to let anyone else in?"

"I let you in," Spider countered.

"Come on, Spider, you know what I mean. I would like for us to have more friends. To have more of a social life than you and Tommy beating each other up while Laura and I talk about work and watch movies. There are a lot of people in the world. We're getting invited to a lot of parties. I'd like to go to some of them."

"Then go," Spider said. "I never said you couldn't go."

Carrie sighed. "The point is that I'd like to go with you. You'd have a good time if you'd let yourself."

"Ah, come on, Baby. These parties you're talking about aren't really my kind of thing—or my kind of people," Spider said.

"You don't know that. Do you have any gay friends?"

"Helen's gay, so is Terry."

"And they live?"

"Helen lives in Atlanta and Terry lives in San Diego."

"Run into them all the time do you?" Carrie asked. "It's only ten o'clock. Let's go to a club. Go dancing. I'm going to call a couple of friends to meet us there right now."

"I'd rather not," Spider said.

"You know what?" Carrie smiled at her. "I don't care. We've been together for almost a year. Do you realize that we have never been out dancing? You can dance can't you?"

"Of course I can."

"Then let's go."

"OK, all right." Spider gave in. She shouldn't keep Carrie from going out if that's what Carrie wanted to do, and she really didn't want Carrie going without her. Besides, Carrie was letting her fight all the time. So it seemed only fair. "Could we go home so I can change first?"

Carrie looked at Spider's soaked sweat suit. "Oh, all right."

She pushed the buttons on her cellular phone. "Hello, Jenny? Why don't you and Francis meet us at the Rainbow Lounge…yes, it is me, and yes I did…maybe if you're really nice she'll show you her muscles…Great! We'll see you in about an hour then. Bye-bye."

She looked over at Spider who looked like she was about to take a really big pill with no water. "Come on, Baby, it will be fun. You'll see."

"That's what my army recruiter told me," Spider scoffed.

THE CLUB REMINDED her of her single days when she would occasionally drop in to see if she could pick up a late night snack. She usually chickened out, went home alone, and let her fingers do the walking. So it wasn't necessarily a good memory.

Spider had to admit this was a lot nicer than any of the dives she'd ever gone to. It would be just her luck that now that she was in a permanent relationship she would finally find out where all the good- looking, successful women hung out. Carrie caught her staring at someone and slapped her in the shoulder.

"I was only looking." Spider laughed. "You said you wanted me to have a good time."

"With me," Carrie said. "I wanted you to have a good time with me."

Someone waved at them across the room.

"There's Jenny and Francis."

"Good. I was beginning to think I had something stuck between my teeth," Spider said.

Carrie took her hand and pulled her through the crowd.

Spider and Carrie sat down. Carrie introduced Spider to her two friends as she greeted them. As Spider slid into the booth next to Carrie she stifled a yawn. She'd worked out for three hours that day, and she didn't really feel up to meeting new people in a strange place.

"Well?" Carrie screamed in her ear.

Spider looked at her. She could feel that Carrie was anxious about something, but didn't know what she was really asking her.

"What?" Spider screamed back.

"What do you think of the club?"

"Great. Really…great." Spider said, happy that while she could read people they couldn't read her. Looking around at the clientele made her feel like she was about a hundred and eighty, and the damn music was so loud it was literally hurting her ears. She wondered how Carrie thought she was supposed to get to know her friends if they couldn't actually hear each other. Besides, it was hard to make friends with someone when you knew they were lusting after your old lady and thinking you weren't nearly good enough for her, which was exactly what Carrie's friend Francis was feeling.

The band stopped playing, and Spider's ears quit ringing. The waitress came over to take their drink order. They all ordered some fruity shit Spider didn't recognize, so she just ordered a beer. When she did, the waitress screamed, "Spider! Spider Webb! Well, I'll be damned," she said. "Well, you just stand yourself up here and give Maggy a big ole hug."

Spider stood up and hugged the woman who seemed reluctant to let her go. Maggy Jerrick, of all the luck, she'd slept with maybe three women in the entire state, and Maggy was one of them. Fifteen years older than Spider and fifty pounds overweight, she'd taught Spider a thing or two right after she'd come home from the war. Spider still thought of her fondly.

"Maggy! Good to see ya. You haven't changed a bit."

"Unfortunately." She laughed. She released Spider and Spider sat back down. "Saw ya in all the papers with your lady," she winked at Carrie. "Ya got yerself a live one here," she said and walked towards the bar, to fill their drink order.

Carrie looked at Spider, who was blushing purple. Spider looked back at her and shrugged. "I was young, I'd just gotten out of the army…"

Carrie gave Spider an accusing, if amused, look. "I thought you didn't know anybody in town."

"You said that, not me," Spider reminded her.

Maggy brought them their drinks, and it was she who noticed that Spider wasn't really with them.

"Spider, you all right, girl?" Maggie asked.

Spider looked up at the mention of her name. "I...ah...excuse me." She stood up and started to make her way across the bar. Slowly at first, and then at a dead run.

"Spider, what the hell!" Carrie screamed.

She saw Spider turning on her comlink and immediately looked around. Then she saw it, the gun in the man's hand as he swung away from the bar. As Carrie hit the floor she saw Spider grab an unopened beer bottle from a table.

"Get down!" Carrie screamed.

Carrie wondered why police even bothered trying to save the bystanders. The majority of the people in the room just freaked out. Carrie couldn't see, but she could hear the gun going off. She was on her comlink at once.

"This is DA Long. We have a gunman and people down." She didn't know if there were or not, but she knew they came faster if there were injuries. She didn't have to give a location. Her and Spider's comlinks would give them that.

SPIDER HAD MOVED quickly but quietly, and the uzi-wielding lunatic hadn't seen her. As she ran the last few feet to close the gap between herself and the gunman she grabbed a beer bottle off a table by its neck. No time to go for her gun, not where it was hidden on a leg strap in her boot.

"Hey fuck head! Over here!"

The lunatic turned and started firing.

Spider threw the bottle up, grabbed it by its body and hurled it butt end at the gunman. The bottle smacked into the side of his head and broke, sending beer and glass flying. The gun slipped from his limp hands, and a second later the gunman crashed to the floor as the weapon rattled across it.

Spider looked around and found Carrie hiding under a table, seemingly unharmed. Spider grabbed the gun first, and then she checked the gunman for signs of life. There weren't any. Weren't any at all. She scanned the room quickly in search of another assailant and saw and felt nothing. The side of the perp's head had a very smooshy-looking spot on it. *Shit, I didn't mean to kill the bastard. I don't care, but I didn't do it on purpose. The press is going to love this.* "*Gay DA and lover caught in gunfire at gay night club. This can't be just a coincidence. It has to be the SWTF, has to be some sort of test, but for what I wonder."*

"We just got the bastards off our backs," Spider mumbled. Then she continued loudly, "Is anybody hurt?"

Before anyone had a chance to answer, the cops broke in followed by a crew of EMTs with stretchers. Three people had minor wounds. Another had a belly wound.

Since everything seemed to be under control, Spider went to help Carrie out from under the table.

"Well, this has been a lot of fun. We'll have to do it again real soon," Spider said sarcastically as the reporters ran in.

CARRIE TRIED TO go to sleep, she really did. But every time she almost got to sleep she'd see people falling and hear the gunfire. Knowing some of what Spider had been through, Carrie wondered how she slept at all.

"It would have been my fault," Carrie said. "You didn't want to go; I made you go."

Spider sighed. Carrie couldn't blame her, every time Spider almost went to sleep, Carrie started talking again.

"It wasn't anyone's fault, Honey. Think of it this way. If you hadn't wanted to go to the club, that cuckoo might have killed a lot of people tonight."

"If you couldn't feel him, or whatever you do, we might have been some of the people dead, and it would have been my fault," Carrie said. "I dove under the table like a coward, and let you go off to get shot and…"

"I didn't get shot. If I couldn't count on you to use your head and go for cover, then I might have gotten shot trying to cover your ass. Please, Baby, I'm tired. Couldn't we just go to sleep?"

Carrie moved to curl herself around Spider. She kissed Spider's neck, then whispered in her ear. "Make love with me."

"Ah, come on, Baby." Spider groaned. "I'm tired, it's the middle of the fucking night…"

Carrie moved her hand down Spider's body, and Spider shivered.

"Come on, Baby," Carrie breathed.

Spider wasn't terribly hard to convince.

SOMEONE WAS BANGING on her head, a ringing in her ears, a…

Fucking doorbell.

Spider forced herself out of bed. She looked at the clock. Damn! It was eight a.m. She was late, and on Sunday morning, too. She pulled on her pajama bottoms and headed for the door. She knew who it was before she heard him yell.

"Damn it, Spider!" Tommy screamed so loud he might have been on the same side of the door that she was.

Spider opened the door quickly. "Tommy, I'm so sorry. Give me a minute to get dressed. You would not believe the night I've had."

"Forget it!" Tommy screamed. "I waited in the park for you for two hours! You promised me when we started this that you would do what I told you. That you would follow my rules. If you want to do this, it can't be haphazard or sloppy. There are certain routines, rhythms." He realized then that Spider was just staring at him as if he'd gone mad. That, and that she wasn't wearing any shirt. There were scratch marks on her stomach and her shoulders, and he was temporarily distracted. "What the hell happened to you?"

Spider smiled stupidly. "Carrie."

"You were fucking! I was waiting for you for hours and you were getting a piece of ass. That's it! I'm not doing this. This isn't a game. This is…"

"Insane," Carrie finished for him as she came down the stairs tying her robe closed. She handed Spider a T-shirt. "What the hell are you screaming about?" she asked Tommy.

"I was supposed to meet him at six. I forgot to set the alarm," Spider said as she pulled on her T-shirt. "I'm sorry, Tommy…"

"You're apologizing to him," Carrie said in disbelief.

She looked at Tommy. "Tommy, we almost got killed last night. Didn't you check your link this morning?"

Tommy shook his head no.

Carrie briefly filled him in on the events of the night before. "…We were filling out statements and dealing with the press until three this morning. I," she pointed at herself, "turned the fucking alarm off so that she could get some sleep, because she needed it. The world will not come to a screeching halt if you miss a day of practice. Or even two or three. I would like to wake up just one morning and not be alone, and I imagine Laura feels the same way."

Tommy heard about half of what she said. "There is no excuse! When you break the rhythm you lose everything. She wasn't doing anything at six in the morning, so she should have been there."

He glared at Spider. "You should have been there. You should have at least called to tell me that you weren't going to be there so that I could start without you."

"I'm sorry, Tommy," Spider said though at this point there was a certain, 'bite my ass' quality to her voice.

"If it happens again that's it. I'm not doing this. You're too undisciplined as it is."

"This is fucking insane!" Carrie said throwing up her hands. "You need a reality check, dude. Didn't you hear a word I said?"

He didn't have to listen to her. She wasn't part of this. She should mind her own business. She had no idea what was going on. He ignored her. He looked at Spider. "I expect to see you at six. If you're not there I'll start without you, and that's it." He turned and stomped out of the house.

Spider and Carrie just stared at each other.

"What's with him?" Carrie asked.

Spider shrugged. "He really doesn't like to wait? Hell, I don't know. He's never been that mad at me before."

"What are you doing answering the door without a shirt on?" Carrie asked slapping at Spider's shoulder.

Spider shrugged. "I was tired…I…I really don't know." She rubbed at her eyes. "I think maybe I'm a little punchy after last night."

"Want to go back to bed?" Carrie asked.

"To sleep," Spider said starting up the stairs.

"If you say so," Carrie said wickedly.

"You're not going to let me sleep until I give you sex, are you?" Spider said with a sigh.

"No," Carrie said wickedly.

"Well, come on then, let's get this over with."

TOMMY WAS STILL fuming when he got home. He walked in and slammed the door. Laura was sitting watching TV.

"What's wrong, Baby?" she asked.

"Spider never showed up! Started whining about having some kind of trouble in a bar last night!" Tommy screamed.

Laura looked at the clock. It was only 8:30 now. She knew that was way too early for Carrie on a Sunday morning. "You went over to their house?" Laura asked carefully.

"Of course I did!" Tommy screamed. "I had to make her understand what she had done! You can't break the rhythm. You can't…"

Spider was on the TV. He sat down and grabbed the clicker from Laura to turn the sound up.

"…that is what I said," Spider said, obviously agitated.

"You took down the attacker with a beer bottle?" the reporter asked.

"Yes, a beer bottle. What about that is so—*beep*—ing hard to understand!"

"Why didn't you use your weapon?"

"Because the bottle was there, and my gun was hidden in my—beep—ing boot. I wasn't on duty."

The picture turned back to the reporter in the studio. "That's what the detective said. A beer bottle. And, once again for those of you who missed it. Here is the footage shot on the bar's surveillance camera."

They played the tape, and Tommy watched, mouth open.

"Between you and me, I think Detective Webb pulls that off with a lot of style, not to mention bravery under fire," the reporter concluded.

Tommy turned the TV off and slumped back onto the couch. That was what Carrie had been trying to tell him, and he had been so consumed that it really hadn't registered. He had tuned her out because she was the "insignificant" woman.

Laura stood up and looked down at him. "You OK, Tommy?"

Tommy shook his head no. "You know…I almost hated my father because he put training and discipline above everything else. I always swore I'd never be like him. I told myself I didn't continue doing Jujitsu because it reminded me of him, but the truth is I was afraid of becoming him. Now look at me. I am my father. Screaming at my best friend over something as insignificant as missing an hour of running. She could have been killed last night! She'd probably had little or no sleep, and all I could think about was that she had kept me waiting. That she had broken training, messed up my rhythm." He looked up at Laura. "I love to fight. I didn't realize how much I missed it. I love the challenge, and Spider is a challenge. I think she could win competitions right now. She already knew hand-to-hand; she's just adapting what she already knows. She's coming up with an all-new system. It's Jujitsu, but it's not. But I don't love it enough to let it turn me into a single-minded monster like my father. Should I quit?"

Laura sat down beside him, and then she put her arm around his shoulders. "I think training with Spider has been very good for both of you. I also think you both need to put it into some perspective. It is just a game, a sport, and since neither one of you are interested in competing, I think you might calm down just a little bit."

"You think I should apologize to Spider?" he asked.

"Yes, I do. Then I think you should cancel the Sunday night fights and spend some time with me. But I don't think you should quit fighting." She kissed him on the cheek. "By the way, while you're in such a good mood, Mom and Dad are coming to dinner." She laughed at the look on his face, then got up and started for the kitchen. "I'll get you a cup of coffee. Why don't you call Spider?"

"Because they're probably having sex. They are always having sex." Tommy got up and followed Laura into the kitchen where he stood in the doorway and watched her as she poured him some coffee. "When I got there this morning, Spider came downstairs to answer the door. She was topless, and she was all scratched up. Looked like she'd been mauled by an animal."

Laura handed him the coffee. "Topless? How do you mean."

"Topless, as in her boobs were hanging out."

Laura smiled. "And how were they?"

"Surprisingly good actually, which was kind of disturbing. Imagine walking in on your sister in the shower and she turns around and she has this dick."

Laura made a face. "I can imagine. Breakfast?" she asked.

He nodded, sat down at the table and watched as she started making it. He helped with the housework, but he didn't cook. He sure hadn't learned how as a child, and as an adult he'd never had to. He'd always made enough money to eat out or had a woman to do it for him. He supposed this was sexist; he just didn't care as long as he didn't have to cook for himself...or do his own laundry.

"I asked Spider what happened. She said Carrie did it, and she was grinning like an idiot." He took a sip of his coffee. "I'll just wait a couple of hours and then I'll call. Maybe they will have gotten it out of their system by then."

"I hope not. Then they'll be as boring as the rest of our friends," Laura said.

"I don't think Bud and Judy even smell at it any more," Tommy said matter-of-factly. "Not that you can blame him. She's gotten so goddamned fat."

"Tommy! What a horrible thing to say," Laura said angrily. "You mean you wouldn't love me anymore if I got fat?"

"Were not talking fat here, Laura. The woman broke our fucking couch, remember? They had to cancel their trip to San Francisco at the last minute because she couldn't get her fat ass into an airplane seat. That's not just fat. Hell, he'd have to roll her in flour and look for the wet spot, or just put his peter in a wrinkle and coast."

"That is such a guy thing, Tommy. Did it ever dawn on you that maybe it's his fault she got that fat? They don't have the best marriage you know…"

"Because she is a big, fat bitch. All that woman does is whine, bitch, and eat. I love that shit she does where he always has to get up and go take care of the kids. Says she's resting. Resting from what? Last time I looked, eating a Twinkie was not all that tiring. Bud used to actually be a happy guy. We used to have some good times. Now that bitch won't let us be alone for more than five minutes without her or a screaming, fucking kid."

"She told me she doesn't think Bud loves her anymore," Laura said. "She's miserable, and that's why she's fat and angry."

"He doesn't love her because, once again, she is a fat bitch. Give me a break! You know as well as I do that she has never had what you would call a sparkling personality. If she was thin, she'd still be a bitch…"

"Ah! But if she was thin she'd still be fuckable," Laura said. "Because she's fat, she's not even good for that."

"It's the double threat that makes Lenny go limp. You can handle bitchy, or you can handle fat, but fat and bitchy? No way."

Laura laughed in spite of herself. "Well, she was bitchy when he married her."

"Ah…but she wasn't fat."

"You're horrible," Laura said as she set a plate of eggs on the table in front of him.

"Oh. I'm sick to shit of all this politically correct bullshit. People are fat because they have no willpower and are lazy."

"It's been proven that there is a fat gene..."

"It's not like it's incurable, Laura. All they have to do is stop eating like fucking pigs. Judy claims she doesn't know how she put the weight on, because after all she doesn't eat as much as anyone else. Next thing you know she's stuffing her face full of fucking doughnuts."

"That's what I love about you, Tommy, you're so compassionate and understanding," Laura said, shaking her head in disapproval.

"That's me! I'm a sensitive guy."

"You know, Tommy, some people don't mind being fat. It's not like it's illegal or anything. Some men actually like fat women."

Tommy shrugged. "I don't have anything against fat people as long as they aren't bitches."

She wanted to be mad at him, but she'd have to work at it, and it just wasn't worth the effort. Especially when, try as she might, she couldn't quite clear the politically correct fat hurtle herself. As much as she might want to, she just couldn't sympathize with people who said they couldn't stay on a diet. After all, her entire life from the moment she'd learned that she had diabetes had been one long diet. Every day was filled with things she wanted to eat that she couldn't, and things she didn't want to, but should. Reading the ingredients on everything she bought, asking in every restaurant, measuring her food at home. When she went to the bar and her sugar was all right she could have one wine cooler or a beer; that was it. It was a pain in the ass, but she did it to stay off of insulin and away from needles. Of course she knew diabetics who couldn't stay on their diet, so maybe it really was all a question of willpower after all.

"Will power challenged," Laura mumbled.

"What's that?" Tommy asked.

"Just thinking about how you never know what to call people any more," she said. "You know, all the new labels that are supposed to be better than all the old labels. Like Native American, for instance. That has always bugged the piss out of me."

"Why?" Tommy asked.

"Well, tell me how stupid is this. We don't call them Indians any more because that's wrong since they aren't from India. But we're going to call them Native Americans even though I'm fairly sure that the 'Native Americans' didn't call this country by the name of an Italian explorer."

Tommy thought about that for a minute. "That is pretty stupid now that you mention it. Why couldn't we just continue to call them Indians when we're talking about all of them, since we all know what we mean, and call them by their tribal names when we're talking about an individual?"

IT HAD TAKEN Spider awhile, but she'd finally gone back to sleep. Later she would wish she hadn't.

The faceless woman screamed and screamed. She was in pain. She wanted Spider's help, but Spider couldn't reach her.

They were poking Spider again. Poking her and talking, but she couldn't really understand what they were saying. The SWTF men just stood around and watched.

The faceless woman screamed again. Spider was wrong, the woman wasn't in pain, she was mad and afraid.

"Let her go, stop it!" the woman screamed.

Spider became aware of her own tears now. She was scared, and it hurt. The poking hurt and she didn't like it; it was scary.

"It will hurt less if you hold still," one of the men said.

The car rolled over and over and over. She went out the window.

There was fire, so much fire, and the woman screamed. She was trapped in the car. She needed help, but none came. Scott was running in circles around the car crying, "Mama! Mama!"

Then everything was black and it was dark. Scott was crying and crying. She couldn't see him, but she knew it was him. She was scared, terrified, but she couldn't scream, couldn't even cry out, and she was trapped. A single light pierced the darkness, and then there were others. She knew what they wanted, what they wanted to do. They were going to poke her again, and she didn't want that. Finally she screamed.

"Honey?" Spider heard Carrie's voice, felt her hand on her shoulder and felt reassured. "You OK?"

"The club...it was no coincidence, it *was* some sort of test." Spider was sitting straight up in bed, drenched in a cold sweat. Her throat was a little raw and she realized she must have screamed out loud.

"What?" Carrie asked.

"Nothing, I'm sorry I woke you up," Spider said. She lay back down slowly, and Carrie curled herself around her. "Just paranoia, me trying to make sense of what happened—and the dreams."

"Don't worry about me. It's about time we got up anyway. Who would be testing you, us, for what?"

"I wish I knew. Dammit! It means something...I think the dreams are some kind of memory. Something to do with my mother." She shook her head. "Some kind of memory that I've buried or...I don't know."

"I know a hypnotist. Good one. Works with us sometimes on potential witnesses. He could do a regression on you, and maybe see what you're repressing."

"I don't think that's such a good idea. I'm fairly certain that knowing whatever I have forgotten could get you killed."

The phone rang, and Spider was only too glad for the distraction. She answered the phone.

"Hello."

"Hello Spider, this is Tommy...listen. I'm sorry about this morning. Sorry that I've been such a prick. Let's take today off. Give me a chance to put things back into perspective."

"But what about the rhythms?" Spider teased.

"I said I was sorry," Tommy said.

"Apology accepted, and I'm sorry I didn't at least call."

"Under the circumstances, I really couldn't blame you. Tomorrow morning at six o'clock?"

"I'll be there," Spider said.

"Great! I'll see you then...Oh, and Spider?"

"Yes?"

"Great tits."

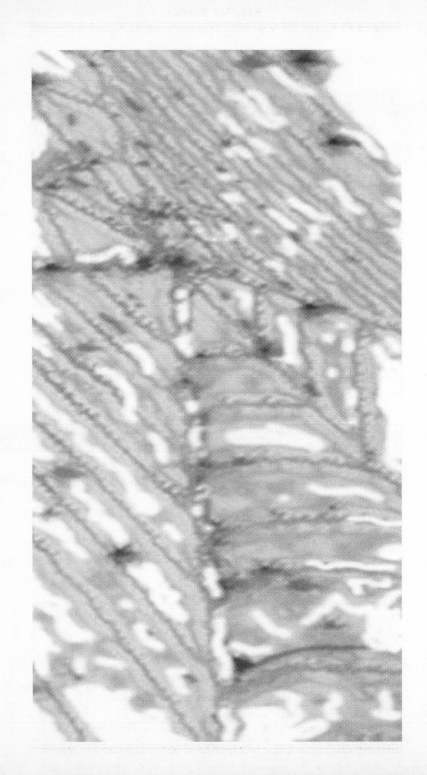

CHAPTER TWELVE

"As he came forth from his mother's womb naked
shall he return to go as he came, and he shall take
nothing for his labor, which he may carry away
in his hand." Ecclesiastes 4:14

MARK TRIED TO leave a little early so that maybe they wouldn't find him. He tried to take a back way, a short cut he knew about that they probably didn't. Maybe then he could get home without getting beaten up.

He hadn't meant to make them mad, but he wasn't going to give in to them again. His father had told him to stand up to them, but he was afraid. Afraid of what he might do if they started hitting him.

He was fairly certain that he'd managed to shake them when someone hit him in the back of the head with God only knew what.

"Hey, dickhead! Where the hell do ya think yer goin'?"

Two sets of hands grabbed him and dragged him into the alley. They slammed him against a wall and his pack broke, spilling its contents all over the ground.

"Do...don't mess with me," Mark stammered out.

They laughed at him and the bigger one, Johnny 'Round House,' the only thirteen-year-old in the fifth grade, shoved him in the shoulder so that he hit the wall again. More of the contents of Mark's pack rained onto the ground.

"Stutter why don't ya, ya whinin' little flinch." He laughed. "Oh, I'm gonna love kickin' your pussy ass."

The other kid was a lot bigger than Mark, but he was only a year older. Everyone knew that Teddy Miller wasn't the real menace. He just didn't like getting teased for being fat and stupid, and being Johnny's best friend meant he didn't have to worry about that.

"L...leave me alone. I...I'm warning you!" Mark stammered out.

Johnny punched him in the mouth hard, and his head spun.

"Hey, Johnny! That's enough, man," Teddy said. "You said we was jus' gonna scare him a little."

"Get on outtah here if you can't hack it, Teddy," Johnny said.

"Don't hurt him, Johnny. He ain't a bad dude," Teddy said.

"Get the fuck outtah here, Teddy!" Johnny screamed.

"Fuck you, Johnny," Teddy turned and left.

Mark watched him go. No hope that he'd run to get help, didn't have the balls for that. He didn't want to be part of beating Mark up, which made him better than most. But he was too worried about his own skin, too afraid of breaking the playground code to help Mark.

Mark was scared. This guy was a dark void sucking in any light that touched him and diminishing it. Johnny had it in his mind to hurt him. Hurt him bad.

Mark had the power to stop him. He could stop him the same way he'd stopped Mr. Ryan's damned old pit bull from biting him.

Johnny pulled back to hit him again. Mark didn't stammer this time. He stood up as straight and as tall as he could.

"If you hit me one more time I'm gonna kill you, Johnny Round House," Mark hissed.

Johnny laughed and hit him.

Mark stared at Johnny and smiled. "That's three," he said mimicking Principle Whitters. Johnny went flying across the alley, hit the wall and exploded.

Mark picked up his stuff and ran.

"You know, like you'd say that the American Indians inhabited most areas of the United States, but then you'd say that your friend Joe is a Choctaw. Or the Cherokee of western Oklahoma had their own written language," Tommy said.

"You make fun of me for having 'Too much sex,' as if that could ever really happen, and then you and your wife spend your spare time figuring out shit like this?" Spider said with a laugh.

"Don't you think that would be better?" Tommy asked seriously.

Spider shrugged. "I guess. I never really thought about it one way or the other. No blood in my brain, don't you know?"

The call came in on the car's comlink.

"Hey guys! Fry Guy's back. Alley directly behind Harvest School."

"That's fucking impossible!" Spider swore.

Tommy could tell by the look on her face that this was completely unexpected.

"Shit!" She looked out the window so that he couldn't see her face.

"We're on our way," Tommy said into the link. He turned the link off and stared at Spider. "I thought you said he'd always kill. That he couldn't help it."

"Yeah, but I…" Spider let the sentence die.

"You what, Spider?" Tommy asked. "What did you do?"

"It's not important."

But it was. She thought she'd taken care of the problem, gotten the SWTF of their backs. Now the nightmare was back.

SPIDER SAW WHAT no one else did. A smashed down place in the garbage where someone had been standing, and a couple of broken pencils on the ground. She purposely didn't walk over and check it out.

"He was…well, I hate to speak ill of the dead, but he was a bad kid," Principle Whitters said. "A bully really."

Spider glared at the man. He was one to talk; he was nothing more than a bully himself. A scrawny, ugly, short guy, he no doubt couldn't hold his own with his peers. So he got a job where there were people he could push around. Some graffiti scrawled across the alley wall told how the kids felt about him. In big red block letters it read 'Child Molester Whitters, humps all sorts of critters.'

"Who the hell are those guys?" the principle asked.

Spider looked up and saw the SWTF guys. She frowned, then said to the principle, "It's OK, they're supposed to be here. You were saying about Johnny?"

"He…well, he'd already been in juvey twice for…well beating people up. Johnny put a twelve-year-old boy in the hospital when he was only eleven."

"And he's still in school?" Tommy asked in disbelief.

"Not my fault." Whitters shrugged. "According to the state law, as long as the kids are of school age they have to be in school."

"Were there any kids in particular that he was messing around with?" Spider asked.

The principle shrugged. "Who wasn't he bullying would be a better question." He snapped his fingers then. "He has a friend, Teddy Miller. He's always with Johnny; he might know something."

"Thanks." Spider walked away and Tommy followed. She punched in the kid's name and in seconds her comlink spit out an address.

"Or maybe he's in the alley being scraped off the wall with Johnny." Spider knew what Tommy was thinking; he didn't have to say anything. "How did they identify the body anyway?"

"Kid had a fake ID," Spider said nonchalantly. She walked past the SWTF guys and they smiled. "Let's go talk to the Miller kid."

MARK DIALED THE phone with trembling fingers. Most days he hated it when he came home to an empty house, but today he was glad.

The phone rang once, twice. "Come on, you stupid mother fucker! Pick up the phone," Mark hissed.

"Hello?" a woman answered.

"Hello, ma'am. Is Teddy home?"

"Teddy!" The woman screamed. "Phone!"

Mark waited. It was only a few seconds before Teddy answered.

"Yeah," he said, obviously around a mouthful of food.

"I killed Johnny. You'll know that's the truth in a little while," Mark said. "If you tell anyone about me, I'll kill you, too." Mark hung up quickly.

TEDDY LOOKED AT the phone and shrugged. Some kind of stupid joke. He hoped Mark *did* kick Johnny's ass. It would serve Johnny right for being such a prick.

The doorbell rang.

"I got it, Mom!" Teddy screamed and took another bite of sandwich. He walked over and opened the door still chewing. He looked up at the two people standing there. "What?" he asked around a mouthful of sandwich.

The man and woman showed him their comlinks. "Is one of your parents home, son?"

"Mom!" Teddy screamed. His mom came, and she and the cops went into the dining room to talk. Teddy sat in the living room and pretended to watch TV, but he was sweating. They must have found out that it was he and Johnny that tagged the school. His mom was going to kill him.

"Teddy, come here please," his mother called.

He could tell she was crying, but she didn't sound mad.

Teddy walked slowly into the room. His mother jumped out of her chair and ran over and hugged him tight.

"Wha...what's going on?" he asked.

She sat him down in a chair and dried her face with the backs of her hands. "Teddy..." her voice broke and she calmed herself down. "Teddy, something terrible has happened. Johnny has been killed."

Teddy dropped his sandwich. He remembered the phone call. He was sad and terrified all at the same time. "Somebody killed Johnny?" Teddy cried.

"Yes, son," the chink cop said. "I'm sorry, but we're going to have to ask you some questions."

"I don' know nothin'!" Teddy cried. He held his stomach. He felt like he was going to barf. "I didn't see nothin'. He was fine when I left him."

"When is the last time you saw him?" the man asked.

"At school," Teddy lied. He couldn't believe this. That little sissy Mark had killed Johnny? If he could kill Johnny, he could kill Teddy easy. But if the cops took Mark in he'd be safe. "Who killed him?" he cried. Maybe they already had Mark, then it would be safe to tell the truth.

"A criminal the papers and TV have been calling the Fry Guy." It was the woman who answered his question, and he really looked at her for the first time. He saw her hands and couldn't look away. He jumped and moved quickly away from her, still staring at her hands.

"I...I didn' see nothin'. I wish I did, but I didn' and now my best friend is dead." He looked the woman in the eyes. "Please, I don' know nothin'. Jus' leave me alone." He ran out of the room.

He hid in the hallway where he could hear, but couldn't be seen.

"I'm sorry," his mom said. "But they were very close. You must realize what a shock this has been for him."

"It's all right. I understand," the man said. "Doesn't look like Teddy can help us anyway. I'm very sorry about your son's friend. Thank you very much for your cooperation."

Teddy poked his head out as he heard the front door open. The woman turned quickly and stared right into his eyes. He couldn't look away. It was like when Child Molester Whitters looked at him when he was in trouble—only this was worse. His flesh crawled. He was glad when she turned around, and gladder still when the door closed behind her.

Teddy collapsed in a puddle on the floor, crying, and his mother came and held him. He had a good mother, the best mother; she would be ashamed if she knew the kind of things he had been doing. No more, he wasn't going to do anything bad anymore, because he didn't want to hurt his mother. Because if he did something bad, *they* would come and get him, and now they knew where he was.

"YOU'RE AWFULLY QUIET," Tommy said.

Spider heard it in his voice. He was mad. She could feel his anger and frustration. He blamed her.

"It's not my fault, Tommy."

"A kid is dead!" Tommy said. "A thirteen year old kid. Your precious avenger killed a kid."

"Hitler was a kid, Jim Jones, Jeffrey Dahlmer," Spider said. "Who knows what Johnny Pots might have become?"

"We'll never know because he's dead now!" Tommy shook his head. "He was a school yard bully. So what! Are you suggesting that we just go around and kill every school yard bully?"

"I'm suggesting that psychotic behaviors start in childhood. The Fry Guy knows who is truly evil. This child was evil, and he killed him," she said.

"How can you rationalize this?" Tommy said. "He blew that kid up all over the alley."

"Maybe it wasn't him," Spider said.

"You're saying there's more than one of them?" Tommy said. Spider was silent.

"That's what you're saying, isn't it? We have a second killer."

Spider shrugged. "I don't know, maybe. I do know one thing. That kid was lying. He saw something, and he's too scared to say what."

"We should pump him, then. Break him down till he tells us what he knows," Tommy said.

Spider shook her head no. "Do that and I'm afraid we'll have more than one dead kid."

MARK SNUGGLED INTO his bed, pulling his covers up over his head, hoping to keep everything out. It wasn't working, because he was the scariest thing he knew. He shouldn't have killed Johnny, shouldn't have blown him up.

He'd warned him, and Johnny just wouldn't listen. Wouldn't stop. He never did. He was mean to everyone, and he didn't think there was anything wrong with it. He had been dark and bad, and he deserved to die. Mark had to make himself believe that, or he was going to go crazy.

His mother came in flipping on the lights and he jerked violently. She sat down on the corner of his bed.

"Honey, are you all right?" she asked.

He uncovered his head slowly. "I'm scared," he said. "Real scared."

"It's OK, Honey, nothing like that's going to happen to you. You're a good kid, and this Fry Guy only kills bad people."

Mark nodded silently. He looked at his mother. He looked nothing like his mother or father, and nothing like his baby sister. They were all blonde, and he had black hair. They had brown eyes; his eyes were a weird, almost-blue color. They tanned, and he didn't. He knew he was adopted, but he didn't tell them that he knew.

When you were adopted that meant your real parents didn't want you, but that your adopted parents wanted you more than anything. He loved his mom and dad. He was glad that they pretended to be his real parents.

His mom hugged him then. "We wouldn't let anything happen to you," she said, rocking him back and forth. She kissed him on the top of his head and started to leave.

"Mom?"

She turned in the door. "Yes, Baby?"

"I am good, aren't I?"

She smiled at him. "Very good, now try to get some sleep." She turned out his light and left his door open.

"Is he all right?" he heard his dad ask his mom.

"He's scared. Can't say I blame him," she answered.

"I hate to say this, because I know he was just a kid, but the way he's been bullying Mark, hitting him. I figure he got what was coming to him," his father said.

"Jared! What a horrible thing to say!" Mom scolded him.

"Kid shouldn't have been in school with the other kids to begin with. He should have been in prison. I mean, just look at Mark's face."

"With this lunatic running around. Well, maybe I ought to have mother pick Mark up from school for awhile."

"That's not a bad Idea, although I don't think the Fry Guy would be interested in Mark. He's a good kid."

Mark smiled and snuggled into his bed. Mom and Dad thought he was good. Dad said Johnny Round House got what was coming to him, and everyone thought the Fry Guy killed him, so everything could get back to normal now. If he could just quit thinking about it.

THE DOORBELL RANG.

"I got it!" Carrie called out.

"Good. Freaking Tommy! I think he broke every bone in my body." Spider groaned from her chair. The workout had been rougher than usual. Probably because Tommy was holding her personally responsible for that kid getting blown all over the alleyway.

Carrie looked through the peephole. "Spider, some strange black man is standing on our porch holding a TV."

"Oh shit!" Spider jumped up and ran to the front door, temporarily forgetting how stiff and sore she was. She shoved Carrie aside, none to delicately, and looked through the peephole. "Ah shit! Ah shit!" She ran her hands down her face. The doorbell rang again. She opened the door and jerked Robby inside, TV and all. "What the hell are you doing?" She spat at him.

"Br…bringing your TV back. I fixed it."

"Mind telling me what the hell is going on?" Carrie asked.

"Ah…Robby had my TV," Spider said quickly. "He was fixing it." She quickly thought over what she had said and assessed the situation. "He's had the damned thing for months, and now he delivers it in the middle of the night."

"I'm…I'm really sorry."

"Sorry, I'll give you sorry!" Spider took the TV and set it down on a table in the hallway. "Come on outside and let's talk."

"What the hell is going on?" Carrie demanded.

"I can take care of this, Carrie."

Spider grabbed Robby by the arm and dragged him outside. She closed the door behind her leaving Carrie in the house.

Spider jerked on Robby's arm and whispered. "What the hell were you thinking coming here, around Carrie? That's really stupid, Robby. Really, really stupid."

"I'm sorry, but I wanted to let you know that I didn't ice that kid. I didn't break our agreement. I wouldn't."

Spider sighed deeply. They had reached his truck, so she turned him loose and he turned to face her.

"I don't want Carrie put in the middle of this. I don't want her to become a target."

"I'm sorry. I thought if I brought the TV back that would be good cover."

Spider nodded. "It was. I'm just a little paranoid. Don't know why, but a simple thing like having a serial killer drop by the house in the middle of the night when I'm living with the DA and have the SWTF breathing down my neck makes me tense."

"I'm sorry," Robby said. "I didn't know what else to do. What do I do now?"

"We'll never get rid of the bastards if they find out there are two of you. Unless of course they know about this one." Spider was thoughtful. "Robby, you got a shopping list?"

Robby smiled then, his teeth shining in the moonlight. "Just say the word."

CARRIE WATCHED OUT the peephole. She couldn't see too well, but she could tell that they weren't fighting. She moved to a window and peered cautiously out. If Spider caught her spying on her, she'd have her hide.

They were having some sort of very serious conversation, and it lasted for almost thirty minutes. At one point they were even laughing. As the young man started to leave he reached out to grasp the car door handle, and it was than that Carrie noticed his hands. They were like Spider's.

Carrie moved quickly away from the window, sat down and picked up the paper pretending to read. What the hell did it mean? Who the hell was that man?

Spider came in and walked into the living room carrying the TV. "Young people these days have no work ethic."

Carrie planned to say nothing, to just pretend like she bought the whole little drama, but she had never been able to play stupid even when it was in her best interest to do so. Carrie put down the paper.

"Can the shit, Spider. I was watching you. All right, pitch a little bitch, I don't care. I saw you talking to him. You weren't mad, and neither was he. I also saw his hands. So you want to tell me what's going on?"

All right. Her first instincts had been correct; she should have kept her mouth shut. It was obvious even before Spider started screaming that she was pissed.

"Goddamn it, Carrie!" Spider screamed. "I'm trying to protect you and you just won't allow it. Don't get into this shit! I don't want you in it. It has nothing to do with you and I. It only has to do with me."

"If it involves you; it does involve me. Can't you see that? Now just tell me what the hell is going on."

"Just!" Spider threw her hands in the air. "I don't know what the hell is going on anymore. All I do know is that it's dangerous to know anything, and the last thing I want to do is put you in any danger. *Please* don't ask me to tell you. *Please* don't try to figure out what's going on. I'm only asking you to do one thing for me—stay the hell out of it. It's none of your business."

"I'm the DA. My office offers me some protection. I'm not afraid. Crime in this city is my business!" Carrie screamed back.

"Being DA will not protect you from these people, Carrie. The only thing that can protect you is total ignorance. So quit prying around." Spider stomped up stairs.

Carrie started to follow her, and Spider spun on her. "Can't you see? I love you, and I don't want you to get hurt."

Carrie started crying then. "And can't you see that I love you, and I don't want *you* to get hurt? Don't you think I have a right to know what's going on? If the tables were turned, would you want to be left out in the dark? Maybe I could help."

Spider walked back down the stairs and took Carrie into her arms. Carrie held her tightly.

Spider didn't let go of her. "When I was young, I had all these big dreams, goals. I was going to find true love, get everything I wanted, stop crime and cure cancer. Then one day realization slapped me in the face, and I knew that I already was where I was going. I gave up any dreams and desires I had and fell into a rhythm of complacency. I was never going to have more than I had right then, and I was all right with that. I wasn't happy, in fact I was miserable, but it was comfortable misery. Then right when I had given up my last shred of hope, I met you, and…everything changed. Suddenly I had everything I'd ever dreamt of. I just want to be here with you forever, but if you keep snooping around I'm going to have to leave. Because if you figure them out, they'll kill you."

Carrie moved her head to look up at Spider checking her face for any sign of insincerity. There was none. "You're serious?"

"Yes."

THEY FOUND THE first body at four in the morning, and by ten they'd found four more.

Carrie surveyed the last murder site. "At this rate, being DA will be a nothing job because there will be no criminals left to prosecute," she told Laura and then screamed. "Except of course for the Fry Guy! About whom we have no clue!"

She glared across the vacant lot at Spider who just smiled and shrugged.

Carrie couldn't get what Spider had said out of her head. Spider meets with some mysterious stranger last night, and now they had five more fried repeat offenders. She wanted to think it was a coincidence, but she knew it wasn't. Spider was mixed up in this up to her neck, and by turning a blind eye to it, so was Carrie. But if what Spider alluded to was true, there really was no satisfactory alternative.

One of the So-what-if guys approached her. She was a little surprised, because they had never taken any interest in talking to her before. In a flash Spider had moved herself between Carrie and the man. He tried to go around her and she put a hand on his shoulder. Damn it! What the hell was she doing now?

SPIDER PUT HER hand palm down on Kirk's shoulder.

"Stay the fuck away from her," Spider hissed.

Kirk smiled at her. "You're very protective, aren't you? She's the DA here. I just wanted to ask her a couple of questions. Unless, of course, you're willing to answer them."

"You know everything I know," Spider said.

"Somehow I doubt that, Detective Webb. I'll only keep her a couple of minutes...I'm not going to hurt her...yet."

Spider grabbed him by the collar and glared at him. "You stay the fuck away from her."

He jerked free of her grasp. "That's only going to work once, Webb. I'm going to talk to her, and unless you want to try to explain to her and everyone else here why you're accosting me, I suggest you get the hell out of my way."

Spider moved reluctantly.

Tommy walked over to Spider. He'd seen the whole thing. "What's going on?"

"That's what I'd like to know," Spider said. She didn't take her eyes off the So-what-if guy.

CARRIE WAITED WITH bated breath as the man approached her. She'd seen the whole altercation, and was not looking forward to this meeting.

"DA Long, my name is Kirk Anderson, SWTF." He held out his hand. She didn't shake it, and he withdrew it.

"I know who you are. What do you want?" Carrie asked bluntly.

He nodded his head to the side indicating that he wanted to talk to her alone, and behind him Carrie could see Spider flinch. Carrie left Laura behind, and she and Kirk walked a few steps away from the crowd. The guy gave her the creeps, and she was glad to see that both Tommy and Spider were keeping an eye on him.

"If I may be blunt," Kirk cleared his throat and looked over his shoulder at Spider. "Ms. Long, Carrie…"

"Call me Sir," Carrie corrected.

"Sir, your partner, Detective Webb, has information which is vital to our investigation. It would be in her best interest to speak with us. In fact, it would be in your best interest for her to talk with us. You might tell her that," Kirk said.

His expression never changed. Over his shoulder she could see Tommy holding Spider back with an effort. Carrie hoped she was doing a better job of hiding her feelings. It *wasn't* all in Spider's head. There was a real and present danger, and here he was. You didn't have to be an empath to know that.

Carrie was surprised at how confident she sounded when she spoke. "I'm sure that if Spider had any information she would have given it to you."

He laughed then. "Why would she give it to me when she hasn't given it to you?" He walked away then without further explanation. The meaning of his words sank in as she watched his departing back, and she looked at him with black hatred.

Spider walked quickly over to her. "You all right?"

"They're who you're afraid of, aren't they?" Carrie whispered. Spider nodded.

"They've bugged our house, Spider," Carrie said, lowering her voice still more.

"Are you sure? How do you know?"

Carrie told Spider exactly what he had said, then held onto Spiders arm when she swore and started to run over and kick his ass. He waved at her and smiled, then he and his buddy walked over, got in their car, and drove away.

"The bastards!" Spider cursed.

"Maybe you should tell them," Carrie whispered. "Tell them whatever it is they want to know and get them off our back."

"That won't happen, Carrie. They don't work like that. Please stay out of this."

"I can't, Spider. Don't you understand? I can't! *They won't let me.*"

WHEN CARRIE GOT home the house was in ruins. Everything was ripped apart and stuff was slung everywhere. There was a lump in her throat as she pulled the mace from her purse. Spider's truck was in the driveway. She turned her comlink on.

"Spider!" she hollered. Spider walked out of the den carrying a pillow. Carrie sighed with relief and punched a cancel code into her comlink. She ran over and hugged Spider. "What the hell happened?"

"They bugged the whole house. The movers must have done it. Remember? I told you I didn't trust them. So far they were all in my stuff." She pulled a pimento jar filled with water and eight tiny little bugs out of her pocket. "I'm gonna sling them down the disposal."

Carrie walked past her into the living room and flopped down in a chair. She looked around her at the carnage in the room. "You did this?"

Spider looked around her. "I'm sorry, Baby, but I had to. I'll put it all back when I'm sure I have them all."

"You can never be sure, Baby, they're not much bigger than a pin head. They could be anywhere." Carrie buried her face in her hands and started to cry.

Spider knelt beside her and patted her back.

"I'll get all of them, Baby. I know it's a mess, but I'll clean it all up. It's not as bad as it looks. I'm pretty sure I got all the ones out of our bedroom."

"Not as bad as it looks!" Carrie pushed away from her and stood up. She glared down at her. "You're pretty sure you got all the ones out of the bedroom! All this time those bastards have been listening to every word we said, everything we did. What the hell have done to us, Spider? What the hell have you done?"

"Shush!" Spider said.

"I won't shush. They're going to kill us all anyway, and I don't even know why. Now I want to know why my privacy has been invaded! Why our house is in a shambles! Why those fucking So-what-if guys think they can walk up to me, and threaten us—threaten you without fear of repercussion? What the hell do they think you know that they are willing to take these kinds of chances? What the hell are you playing at?"

"I'm not playing at anything!" Spider yelled, standing to her feet. "These guys," she shook the jar in the air, "they're the ones who decided they wanted to play, and the only way I can save any of us is to try to keep the secrets I have. Don't you understand? If you know, then that makes you a target. If Tommy knows, he's a target, and if I tell them what I know, then they've got no reason to keep me alive. The only reason I'm still alive now is because they think I'm the only one who can tell them what they need to know."

"Who the Fry Guy is." Carrie flopped back into her chair and wiped her face. "He's got a weapon they want."

"Please, just leave it the fuck alone."

CHAPTER THIRTEEN

"There is no man who has power over the wind to retain the wind; nor has he power over the day of death: and there is no discharge in that war; nor shall wickedness deliver those who are given up to it." Ecclesiastes 8:8

"YOU DID WHAT!" Deacon screamed from behind his desk.

"It seemed like it might be more expedient..." Kirk started.

"This woman is the brand new lesbian DA. Every fucking camera in this country is turned on Carrie Long right now. You don't do shit to her. You don't talk to her. You don't even look at her. I thought I made that crystal clear."

Kirk glared at Jason who just grinned. Kirk didn't have to ask who had told Deacon what he had done. The goddamned weasely-eyed little dwarf.

"Sir, with all due respect, we are getting nowhere this way..."

"If there is one thing that the agency has never been, Anderson, it's in a hurry. You get in a hurry and you make mistakes. Webb wasn't kidding. If you back her into a corner she'll rip your face off. That's a fact. You push her too hard and she'll blow this whole thing wide open. I told you what the science boys said about her."

"That's why I'm recommending termination," Kirk said.

"Then we'll never find out who the Fry Guy is, and he's our real problem—not Webb. Hell, we know all about Webb, she's part of the program. This guy's *Not!* He's the one we really have to worry about. Besides, the boys at the top have made it real clear they don't want Webb killed."

"How can we get her to tell us anything if we can't put the pressure on?" Kirk asked. "I guarantee she's not going to just give us the information."

"We can put pressure on her, Kirk. But we can't afford to be stupid about it. Look what your stupidity cost us. She's found every bug in the house. We had ears in there, and now we got nothing because you got ants in the pants. You're going to have to be subtler.

We move on nice and slow, and if that doesn't work, *then* we get vulgar. But even then we don't get sloppy."

"Yes, Sir," Kirk said through gritted teeth.

Deacon stood up then, put his fists on his desk, and looked down at Kirk. "I know you'd love to think otherwise, but you are not in control of this operation. Hell, I'm not even the boss, which would make you a fucking peon. Don't go off half-cocked again. When you do, you make me look bad, and I don't like to look bad. Do I Jason?"

"No, Sir," Jason said.

"From now on if you need to take a shit, Kirk, you check in with me first. You got that?"

"Yes Sir."

"Do you think it's fucking funny?" Kirk asked as he drove.

Jason grinned broadly. "Yes," he said simply.

"I ought to kick your fat, fucking…"

Jason shook a finger at him. "Better call Deacon first."

"Someday I'll be where Deacon is, Jason, and then you'll be sorry you weren't more respectful," Kirk said.

Jason laughed. "And that's it for you, isn't it? That's the whole tamale. To become a high ranker in the agency. To be a bigger peon than you are now. That's fucking pathetic."

Kirk laughed back. "That's kind of the pot calling the kettle black, isn't it?"

"Ah, but at least I *know* I'm pathetic," Jason said.

"You make me sick," Kirk spat. "You are completely without ambition…"

"I had ambition once and look where it got me. I'm a fucking hired goon for a secret government agency, which never should have existed in the first place. Stalking someone who's no doubt going to kill me, in the company of a man I cannot stand, and who can't stand me. When you have a job like ours, Kirk, ambition isn't a good thing; it's a bad thing. Just look at what you're willing to do to get a crappy office like Deacon's."

Spider looked down at Henry. He looked so peaceful. He always looked so peaceful.

"Hey, dude!" She sat down beside him. "Boy, have I gotten myself into a big heap of crap…" She talked to him for about half an hour. When she started to leave a nurse at the front desk called her over.

"There a problem, Karen?" Spider asked.

"No. A man came in and left this. He told me to give it to you." She handed Spider an envelope.

"Thanks." Spider forced a smile and then went out to the truck with the unopened envelope in her hand. She looked in her rear view mirror, spotted the SWTF men, and wasn't too surprised. She started to just wad the envelope up and throw it away, but curiosity won the day and she opened it.

It read: *How touching! Wouldn't you like to know once and for all what really happened to your brother and Henry Chambers? If you show me yours, I'll show you mine.*

Spider had a pretty good picture of what had happened to her brother and Henry. She'd like to follow these bastards to whatever rock they crawled under at night and see if they could take it as well as they could dish it out. But she couldn't afford the luxury of anger, no matter how righteous it might be.

She wadded the note up, used her car's cigarette lighter to light it, and then threw it out her window.

THE DOORBELL RANG and George stupidly opened the door without even asking who it was.

"Hello, can I help you?" George asked the middle-aged man who stood in the doorway.

"Yeah, ah," he cleared his throat. He looked past George into the hallway. "You the butler?"

George was more than a little offended. "No, I'm the assistant DA. Can I help you?" he asked again.

"Spider Webb live here?"

George began to think he had screwed up badly.

Carrie walked into the hallway then, a stack of papers in her hand. "I haven't got all night, George…" She saw the stranger in the door then and right away started wondering how many steps it would take her to get to her gun. She still had the mace, but now it had a friend.

"Who are you?" she demanded.

"I'm looking for Spider Webb," he said.

"Who are you?" Carrie demanded again.

"Cecil Webb...I'm Spider's father. Man at the station house told me she left for home an hour ago. Said she lived here."

CARRIE DIDN'T KNOW what to do with him. She got him a cup of coffee and showed him to the den where she and George were working.

Was Spider going to be glad he was here? Was she going to be mad that Carrie had let him in the house? What the hell was he doing here? Why now of all times?

He was walking around the room looking at Spider's service photos and the medals that lined one wall of their den.

"How long does it usually take her to get home? Hell, it only took me about twenty minutes, tops."

It was a good question. It wasn't the first time Carrie had noticed a discrepancy in the time between Spider's leaving work and getting home. It took her anywhere from thirty minutes to an hour longer than it should have, and she wasn't always at the bar with Tommy.

"She should be home soon," Carrie said.

"So...I take it...you must be her girlfriend." He didn't even try to hide the sarcasm in his voice.

"That would be me," Carrie said.

"She's done very well for herself, hasn't she?" He indicated the medals, but Carrie knew what he meant.

"She's worked very hard," Carrie said through gritted teeth.

She heard the front door open, wondered if she should warn Spider, and if so—how. Too late, Spider was walking in the room.

"What a fucking day I had...Hello, George."

"Spider," George said.

Spider walked over and kissed Carrie on the cheek. "So, how was your day?"

"Average," Carrie said. "Spider, your..."

Spider turned before Carrie could finish and stared at the man standing in the corner. She glared at him. "What the fuck do you want?"

"Spider, for God's sake!" Carrie muttered.

Carrie looked at George who indicated that he had to leave the room. She nodded at him, and he all but ran out.

"Is that any way to great your old man, girl?" Cecil asked with a laugh that was anything but pleasant.

"Oh, I've graduated from 'worthless dyke' to girl, have I? We got nothing to say to each other, so why don't you bugger off, old man?"

He was shaking with anger. "I thought maybe we could put all that behind us, but you're not going to let me do that, are you?"

"What's in it for me?" Spider hissed.

"OK, girl. I can be blunt, too. There's really only one reason I'm here. Two government bullyboys showed up at the house. Hadn't seen anything like them since right after your mother died. They asked a bunch of questions about you, your brother, and your mother. I didn't tell them too much. I sent them on their way, or I tried to. They weren't in any hurry to go, and made it real obvious that they'd rough me up if I pushed the issue."

Spider's attitude changed. "What exactly did they want to know?"

"Stupid shit, really. Were you a happy child? Did you have friends? Nightmares? Were you afraid of the dark? Asked the same things about Scott. They wanted to know why your mother left me…"

"Mother left you? You never told us that," Spider said.

"It wasn't anything you needed to know. I don't know why she left, and I told them so. I just came home from work one day, and she had taken you and your brother and gone. Didn't leave so much as a note. Two weeks later she died in the car crash…"

"Where the fuck were Scott and I?" Spider asked.

"You were both thrown clear. When they found you, you were still in your car seat. Didn't have a scratch. Or so they said. When I looked at you, you had little bruises all over. Nothing too bad, but I wondered how you got them."

"We were in the car!" Spider screamed. "We were in the car, and you never told us that." Spider rubbed her head and tried to process the information. "Were these men SWTF?"

He shrugged. "They said they were some kind of weapons experts or somethin'. Government goons in black trench coats show up at your door, you don't ask too many questions."

"Did it ever dawn on you that maybe Mother didn't leave of her own free will?" Spider asked.

Cecil looked at Carrie. "There she goes again, the wonderful mother thing. I took care of her most of her life, fed her, clothed her. Me, she hated, but the wonderful mother…Always fantasizing about her. About how great she was. Spider and her brother both.

Till the day Scott died he blamed me for everything. You ever try raising two thankless kids on your own? It ain't easy...."

"Shut up! Shut the fuck up!" Spider screamed. Her fists were wrapped so tightly that her fingernails were biting into the skin of her palm. "I'm thirty-nine years old. Most of my life we haven't even been on speaking terms. Didn't you realize that these fuckers were after me? They want to play with my brain. What did you tell them about me?"

"Don't you scream at me, girl!" Cecil's rage seemed more potent than his daughter's. "What the hell have you done that these guys are asking about you? What the hell are you into, girl?"

"What did you tell them?" Spider hissed and pushed. She'd never pushed him before. But now she realized just how completely the parent/child bond between them had been severed, and didn't consider even for a moment that she might owe him the courtesy of not playing with his brain

"I told them the truth. That you were a moody, miserable child. That you had nightmares constantly. There wasn't much to tell..."

"Because you never really knew me. You were always fucking drunk off your ass. You're a belligerent, drunken piece of shit. Always were and always will be. Get out of here! Just get the hell out of my house," Spider ordered.

"I want you to get those goons off my back," Cecil said, standing his ground. "It's your fault they're bothering me. I want you to stop doing whatever the hell you're doing so that they'll leave me alone. Better still give me some money so I can get the hell out of town. Yer girl's got enough cash to spare."

"It will be a cold day in hell when I'd give you anything." Spider laughed at him. "Don't you get it? They've never left you alone, and they never will. This time it *is* my fault, and I don't give a damn. Get out of my house, or I'll throw you out. If you're wondering if I can, or if I really will, then just try me."

CARRIE PUSHED A drink into Spider's trembling fingers. "You OK, Spider?"

Spider nodded and downed the drink before she avoided answering Carrie's question.

"The dirty bastard has a hell of a nerve coming here. All my life I've been plagued by nightmares. The filthy creep knew exactly what

I was dreaming about, and he never told me that we were in the wreck that killed our mother. Never sent us to counseling. Never even tried to help us get through it."

George walked slowly into the room. "Carrie…can I help here?"

"If you'd take those papers and work on them tonight I'd appreciate it," Carrie said.

George walked over and collected the papers, sticking them into his briefcase. He started to leave, then turned at the door. "I'll see how much of it I can do on my own. If you guys need anything…"

"Thanks, George," Carrie said. "Would you lock the door on your way out?"

"Got it, boss." He left.

Carrie waited till she heard the door close. "Why do you think they went to him? They must have known the two of you hadn't spoken in years. What was the point?"

"They're squeezing me from all sides."

Spider put her hands behind her neck and tried to rub away some of the tension.

Carrie moved her hands and took over.

"Thanks," Spider said. She could feel the calm slowly returning to her body as Carrie rubbed her neck and shoulders.

"It's a military tactic. Not unlike some of the crap you do to people in the courtroom. They want to make sure that I have no place to turn; nothing that they haven't touched. My woman, my car, my house, everywhere I go, my estranged father. They are systematically touching everything I have ever touched." She was thoughtful. "Apparently they mean to interrogate me. That's why they're compiling all this data. The more you know about a person the easier they are to break."

"It's hard to get answers out of someone when you know nothing about them," Carrie agreed. "It's easy when you know everything about their past and their psyche. If you know the way their mind works, then they can't hide anything from you."

"Problem is I have a feeling they know more about me than I know about myself," Spider said thoughtfully.

Spider gently pushed Carrie's hands away, stood up and started pacing the room.

Carrie sat down where Spider had been.

"What do you mean by that?" Carrie asked. Spider looked down at her and Carrie threw up her hands. "Don't say it; I already know. You can't tell me without putting my life in jeopardy. Honey...don't I already know too much? Aren't I already a target?"

"They would have to be pretty desperate to do anything to you right now."

"You mean because I'm in the public eye?"

Spider nodded. "If a secret agency wants to remain secret, and believe me these pecker-heads do, it doesn't run around nabbing government officials."

Carrie nodded. That made sense. "What about you?"

"I want you to make me a promise..."

"Absolutely not," Carrie said, shaking her head frantically.

"Hear me out, Carrie..."

"No. I know what you're going to say, and I don't want to hear it."

"If I go missing..."

Carrie got up and stomped out of the room.

Spider followed her, grabbed her arm and spun her around.

"Damn it, Carrie, listen to me!"

"No! You listen to me! If anything happens to you, I'm going to do everything in my power to take these bastards down, and nothing you can say—no vow, or promise, or oath you make me take—is going to stop me. Maybe you should go away. Hide out with one of your army pals for a while or something. Wait for things to cool down."

"I can't run from this, Carrie. If I do it'll only follow me—or worse. This, whatever the hell it is, and please believe me when I tell you that I'm not exactly sure of all the details myself...it isn't going to go away. Sooner or later it's got to be dealt with." She took Carrie's face between her hands. "You have to be strong. Sometimes you have to play the game by their rules, but at least then when you win the game is over." Spider let Carrie go.

"You're saying things that make no sense and scaring the hell out of me, Spider," Carrie said close to tears.

"You're going to have to use your head. If you screw up trying to play the hero, you'll just get me killed. You'll get us all killed. You're an intelligent woman, Carrie, a hell of a lot smarter than I am. I'm trusting you to use your head and do the right thing. Don't let me down."

"I'll try not to, but it would help if I knew what the hell I was supposed to not be doing and why."

CHAPTER FOURTEEN

"There is a vanity that is done upon the earth; that
there are just men, to whom it happens according
to the deeds of the wicked; again, there are wicked
men, to whom it happens according to the deeds of
the righteous; I said that this also is a vanity."
Ecclesiastes 8:14

CARRIE LOOKED AT the memo in her hand. No doubt the bastards had decided to bring out their big guns. She threw the memo down on the desk and started pacing back and forth.

What the hell did she do now?

There was really only one thing she could do. She sat down again and pressed the button on her intercom.

"Yes?" Laura's voice answered.

"Laura, send George into my office. Then get hold of Spider and have her sent down here."

"Anything wrong?" Laura asked.

"Everything's wrong."

"WHAT DO YOU mean?" Spider asked, pacing the floor.

"His lawyers have asked that his case be reviewed, and their petition has been granted by the state supreme court. There's nothing I can do about it." Carrie sighed. "It gets better. I can't work this case because my relationship with you creates a conflict of interest."

"You're not going to stand as prosecutor at his parole hearing because of some stupid ethical shit? The bastard helped kill my brother."

"It's *because* he killed your brother. It's a conflict of interest, and it's not just an ethical thing, it's the law. I can help George set things up, get ready for trial…"

"I can't believe these bastards can do this. They're going to free the asshole who killed my brother, and I can't stop them."

"George is a good attorney, Spider. He'll do his best. With your testimony he shouldn't be paroled."

"But he probably will be." Spider stood up and shook her head. "They'll make sure that he is. They think I'll go nuts and make a mistake, and then they can pick me up legally. Well, I don't know when they think I was born, but two can play at this game." Spider started for the door.

"Spider."

Spider turned to look at Carrie.

"Don't sink to their level. Maybe they don't have as much clout as they'd like to believe. Maybe we can keep him in jail."

"And maybe my ass is a tambourine and if you smack it, it will play music."

Spider went out slamming the door.

Carrie leaned back in her chair. "Gee! That went better than I expected."

AS THE VERDICT came in Spider jumped out of her seat, walked to the back of the courtroom and slammed the doors open with her hands.

She was fined a hundred dollars for her trouble—contempt of court—and warned by the judge that being the partner of the DA did not give her special rights and privileges.

"Obviously not, since you stupid worthless bloodsucking bastards just let my brother's killer walk out of here."

She was fined another hundred dollars and warned that her next outburst would land her in jail.

Carrie grabbed her by the arm and pulled her from the courtroom before she told the judge where she could stick her gavel. In the hallway Spider glared down at Carrie.

"The whole fucking thing sucks. They couldn't do this if the whole fucking system wasn't corrupt."

"Spider, please calm down," Carrie whispered as she continued to pull her down the hall away from the courtroom. "This is what they want. They're trying to make you hang yourself. That's why you have to promise me you're not going to go after this guy."

Spider stopped and stared down at Carrie. "He's not going to just walk away, Carrie. I won't let that happen. But if you don't want me to go after this guy, I won't." She started walking again, and Carrie let go of her arm. "I'll beat them at their own game. I'll get them yet."

WHEN SHE GOT back to the station there was a message waiting for her. Lieutenant Toby wanted to see her in his office.

"Sorry to hear about the verdict. I know it must be very hard for you," he said.

Spider was silent.

"I'm warning you, for your own good. Stay away from this guy. He's legally out, and if you do anything…"

"I'm not a fucking idiot," Spider said, levering herself to the front of her chair.

"You been giving me nothing but attitude lately, Webb! You got a problem?" Toby all but screamed.

Spider stood up and stared down at him. "Problem? There's no problem! Just you and me trying to get through life without bumping into each other." She pushed just enough to make sure Toby was too scared to scream at her or call her back into his office, and then she walked out.

She located Tommy and waved at him that she was ready to go. Tommy ran to catch up with her and met her at the front door.

"It fucking reeks!" Tommy said. His answer to being supportive.

Spider nodded silently and slammed the front door open.

"Spider! What the hell!" Detective Jacobs started as Spider damn near hit him. She ignored him and walked towards their car. Obviously she intended to drive, and Tommy cringed at the thought.

"What are you going to do, Spider?" Tommy asked.

Spider turned to him and smiled. Not the most pleasant expression he'd ever seen. "What do you think I ought to do, Tommy?"

"Wait for a while. Wait for everyone to forget that you have any interest in this guy. Then we find him out one night, he happens to be mugging a little old lady, and we accidentally beat him to death."

Spider laughed and gave Tommy a real smile this time. "You know that would be poetic and very cleansing. But I don't want to wait."

THE TYPE WRITTEN letter had been addressed to him. Inside was two hundred dollars in cash and a note that said *Take the kids to the zoo.* And a date on which to do it.

The postmark was from Piedmont, but Robby knew who'd sent the letter and the money, and he wasn't about to pass up a chance at meeting with her or going to the zoo.

He slapped the camper shell on the truck and loaded up the kids. They were all really excited. None of them, including Robby, had ever been to a zoo before. When he told them they were all eating at Waffle House for breakfast as well they went ape-shit crazy.

Robby took one of his siblings to work with him each month. At the end of the day's work he took them out to eat at the Waffle House. Then he took them over to Wal-Mart and gave them ten dollars to spend any way they liked. It wasn't much, but it was a hell of a lot more than he'd ever had.

The kids marched into Waffle House single file and sat down where Robby told them to.

The waitress hurried over to wait on them. "My goodness, Robby! You got all the children with you today."

Robby smiled back.

"We're going to the zoo," Colistia told her.

"We're going to see the monkeys," Elvita said, clapping her hands together.

"They'll put you in a cage if you aren't careful," Devan taunted.

"You!" Elvita screamed.

"That's enough now. You children promised to be good," Robby reminded them.

"Yes, Robby," Devan and Elvita said together.

"Well, it sounds like great fun," the waitress said. "Same as always?"

Robby thought about that for a moment. He usually brought them in and ordered them a short stack because it was the cheapest thing on the menu. He'd called and found out that the zoo cost five dollars each for him, Evan, Janice, and Donna, and it was only three dollars each for the other kids. That was only going to cost him thirty dollars. With drinks...and if he let them each get something at the gift shop...

"Let them order whatever they want."

The kids let out little excited noises.

He looked at them. "Get what you want, but eat what you get." They all started ordering at once.

"Shush!" Robby ordered. "Mary can't hear herself think. Now, do this one at a time, starting with Evan and going around."

ROBBY HAD THOUGHT that he would enjoy the zoo, but he had thought he would be too old to experience the magic of it. He wasn't. The kids were done looking at one exhibit and ready to go to the next way before Robby was.

There was a playground beside the ape habitat, and while the kids ran around playing on the equipment, Robby watched the apes. He studied a display showing ape handprints and humans. He looked around to make sure no one was looking, and then he held his own hand over the ape print. He successfully covered the entire print.

"Funny, I used to do that same thing when I was a kid," she said. "Don't turn around. I don't think I've been followed, but it doesn't hurt to be careful."

"Thanks. I never could have afforded to do something like this for them without your help."

"Well, I kind of need your help, kid." She slipped a piece of paper into his hip pocket. "I made out a shopping list. Take care of it when you can. These are some really bad guys who slipped through the cracks. The guy on the top of the list I want you to pay particular attention to. Make a record of the things in his brain—all his crimes. He killed my brother, and I want you to see if he just did it for fun, or if someone paid him and his buddies to do it. I put a picture of my brother in your pocket with the paper, and the paper is self-explanatory."

"Who do you think wanted your brother killed?" Robby asked.

Spider pointed past him into the ape habitat at a huge silver backed male. "You see that guy sitting there?"

"Yes."

"He was born and raised here in this zoo. Do you think he knows he's in a cage?" she asked.

Robby thought about that for a minute. "I guess not, but…"

"There's a group of people who…well, I think that's what they did to me and my brother. I think my brother figured out that he was in a cage, and so they killed him. I think you are like an ape running wild who hasn't been put into a cage yet, and that's why they are looking for you. Because they don't know how you got out of your cage."

"I don't get it," Robby said.

"If you're lucky you never will. Good luck, Robby."

"I don't need luck, Spider," Robby said smugly.

"Don't get cocky, kid." That said, Spider left.

Elvita walked up to him and started jerking on his arm. "Let's go see the elephants, Robby. Let's go…"

Robby laughed. "Okay, okay already. Let's go see the elephants then."

As they were leaving the ape house, his eyes focused on the book that cataloged all the different apes by name and told their genealogy. Robby stumbled a little as he realized what Spider had been saying.

SPIDER HAD MADE his job easier than ever. She told him exactly where these guys would be and at what time they would be there. But he didn't kill them in the order they appeared on the list. He put Sammy Two Toes—so-called because he had two toes cut off—Franklin in the middle of the list. He waited outside the back door of a club called Hoochies. At eleven forty-five, just like clock work, the sleaze walked out and made his score. His dealer went back in the club and Sammy started down the alley towards Robby. Robby backed up into the shadows and waited. When the guy was close enough, he stepped into his trail.

"Hey, nigger," the black man snarled, "don' get in Sammy Two Toes's way."

Robby concentrated and started pulling a catalogue of the man's crimes from him. He saw him in prison, beating a man to death then framing another prisoner. Saw him raping a series of young men who had the misfortune of being put into his cell. Back, back through his crimes, he got what Spider wanted. Then he fragged the guy and moved on. He still had two more to do before morning.

CARRIE WOULD HAVE liked to have been surprised to find that Sammy Two Toes was among the dead found last night. But she wasn't, and now she knew for certain—beyond a shadow of a doubt—that Spider knew who the Fry Guy was.

Spider looked at the body on the ground and kicked at it with her toe. Then said in her least convincing bit of acting to date. "Oh! Look! If it isn't Sammy Two Toes."

Carrie wondered when everything had gone so horribly wrong. This thing was spinning out of control, and there was nothing she could do about it.

The So-what-if guys pulled up, and Carrie's flesh crawled. They got out of their car and headed straight for Spider. No beating around the bush this time.

Carrie'd had everything she had ever wanted, ever even dreamt of, and now she was going to lose the only thing that really mattered. Their exchange was—if quiet, very heated. She was the DA, and she had never felt so powerless in her whole life.

"You want to talk now, Webb?" Kirk asked in a hiss.

Spider could feel his frustration, his anger. He had hoped for one response and had gotten another. It didn't help that she was smiling smugly at him. "Talk about what?"

"Where is he? Who is he?" he spat back.

"Who can see through a super hero's clever disguise? A super hero only keeps his superhuman powers as long as no one knows his true identity. I can't believe that you idiots haven't moved on to greener pastures. Surely if I knew who the fuck he was I would have brought him in myself. Me being a thrice-decorated law officer of this city and all. I don't appreciate the implication…"

"Cut the shit, Webb. This guy just iced one of the guys who helped kill your brother. Now either you had something to do with that, or it's the goddamnedest most convenient piece of murder to take place in this city in a long, damn time."

"It would have to be the latter, dirt bag. Because obviously I, a trice-decorated law officer of this city, would not be in cahoots with a cold-blooded killer," Spider said. She made her face a mask of calm. "What I'd really like to know is why you stupid trench coat wearing fucks are so goddamned sure that I know something. So sure, in fact, that you would bug my car, my home, interrogate my father, follow me, and threaten my old lady. There is certainly no evidence that points to me knowing one goddamned thing more about this case than you or anyone else. So there has got to be some reason, something the rest of us don't know, that makes you so damned sure that I know something. And you know what? I'd give almost any amount of money in the world to know what that is."

"Quit fucking with me, Webb," Kirk hissed. "You had better quit fucking with us, or…"

Spider stood toe to toe with him. "Or what…I'll tell you what. You had better not fuck with me. You had, *by God*, better not fuck with me, because you bastards may kill me and everyone else, but before I go, I'm going to make damn sure that I take you with me."

She walked away to join Tommy in looking at some piece of dirt he'd found.

Kirk walked over quickly and got into the car. Jason got into the car beside him. He made a face and opened the window.

"Goddamn it, Kirk!"

"Shut up! You shut up right now! I've had just about all I'm going to take out of you!" Kirk screamed.

"Nothing came out of me, Kirk." He waved his hand in front of his nose. "Christ on a crutch, Kirk! What did you eat?"

"That fucking bitch is going to pay. I swear, I'm going to wipe that smug look off her face, if it's the last thing I do," Kirk hissed.

"While you're at it, you can wipe your ass, too."

APPARENTLY NO ONE thought Sammy Two Toes death was a simple case of serendipity. The FBI talked to her, the captain called her on the carpet.. Fortunately she had an airtight alibi; she had been in bed with the DA. Their home security system recorded people exiting and entering their house by time and code, and no one had entered or left the house after nine o'clock. Neither Carrie nor Spider's codes had left the house for sure.

Spider guessed it was his turn to ask.

"I'm sorry I have to ask you these questions," the lieutenant said. "I know everyone and his brother has already asked them, but…"

"No, I don't know who the Fry Guy is. No, I did not have anything to do with Sammy Two Toes's murder. Yes, I am glad he's dead. Last night I was in bed with Carrie all night. I most certainly do not possess a weapon that will do anything like this. As I have said, you can search my house any time you want."

"Well, that basically covers everything I wanted to ask. Except…I know we never really liked each other, but why are you giving me such shit lately?"

She started to scream at him that it was because he was a narrow minded little bigot, but then she felt the genuine confusion coming from him. "Because you never liked me, but as soon as you found out for sure that I was gay, that was all the reason you needed to hate me. You treated me with no respect, and I demand respect. I deserve it. But then you dared to question Carrie's integrity, and that's what really burnt it. I thought I made that pretty damn clear when it happened."

He nodded. "I didn't hate you. I hated that you were gay. I've always been very uncomfortable with the whole thing. When you partnered up with DA Long...Well, I'd never really liked you from the get go because I figured you were queer, and because you're a fucking cowboy. I figured you were going to rub the gay thing in my face and I...well, I jumped to some pretty despicable conclusions, and I acted like a complete jerk. I've been going to the department shrink and he's helped me to see that my homophobia is just a manifestation of my insecurities as a man. I'm sorry that I reacted in the way that I did, and I would like for us to call a truce." He held out his hand.

Well, he was full of shit, but at least he was sincerely full of shit. She shook his hand.

TOMMY BOUNCED OFF the side wall. He held up his hands and gasped for breath. "Enough," he said. "We have practiced enough for tonight."

Spider looked at the clock on the wall. He was right. It was almost ten o'clock. She nodded, took a few deep breaths and realized that her ribs were tender where Tommy had kicked her.

"Remember, your kicks are fine, but your hands are your best weapon. No one expects that kind of impact from a hand."

Spider nodded, grabbed up her Gatorade and took a long drink. Then she looked at Tommy.

Tommy caught her stare and held it. Something was obviously on her mind. "What?"

She walked over to her bag and pulled out a CD case. She handed it to him. It was sealed with scotch tape. "Here."

"I don't really like Metallica"

"It ain't a freaking music CD, numb nuts." She took a deep breath and let it out. "The dead FBI guy?"

"Harry Sullivan."

"Yea...he sent me some stuff. I didn't understand half of it. Funny if you think about it, they killed him for sending it to me and most of it meant nothing to me. What he sent me plus everything that I know or even suspect about what is going on is on that CD."

Tommy started to open it, and she slapped his hand.

"Don't open it. Leave the case taped closed. I couldn't give it to Carrie, because I know she would look at it. I'm trusting that you won't. To take away some of the temptation to look at it, the name of the Fry Guy is *not* on that CD. This is about what our government has been doing behind our backs." She looked at him again. "Take it and give it to someone that you trust. Preferably someone who lives out of state. Tell them not to take the tape off. Have them rent a safety deposit box and put it in there. Do not use the phone or the mail to make this transaction. If anything happens to me, I want you to get in touch with that person and tell them to take the disk to a computer—any computer with internet access—and slam this information onto the world wide web. If this goes down, the only way to save your asses will be to expose the bastards. A secret is only worth protecting if no one knows it."

"Why don't we expose them now?" Tommy asked.

"Because if we expose them, we expose me and a whole lot of other people to a brand of persecution the likes of which the world has never seen before," Spider said. "Having that disk puts your life in danger. If they find out that you have it, they'll kill you. But if you don't have it…It's kind of a catch twenty-two."

"I understand." Tommy paused. "Spider, how did you get into all this? It can't be because of the Fry Guy. Hell, I was covering for him as much as you were. Hell, in the beginning I was covering for him more. If you look guilty then so must I. I just don't get it, was it something that happened in the service?"

Spider shook her head no. "I didn't chose to get into anything. I didn't have any choice. I thought I did, but I didn't." She paused and looked into her drink bottle. "I knew…I always knew that there were an awful lot of unanswered questions about my life, about me. Simple things like…look how fair I am. I don't tan, but I don't burn. How many times have we been fishing, Tommy? How many times did you go home with a sunburn? Didn't you think it was funny that I—who am a damn sight lighter than you—never got so much as pink?" She didn't give him time to answer. "I obviously didn't want answers, because I never pursued any. Now all those questions are being answered, and I realize I was right not to ask the questions in the first place. But now it's too damn late. Comes a time in every venture where you've met the point of no return. Remember we talked about that once?"

Tommy nodded.

"Well, I was way past that point before I even had a clue what was going on."

SPIDER COULDN'T SLEEP, so she stared at the ceiling. Carrie lay curled around her sound asleep. Even Spider gently caressing Carrie's shoulder didn't cause her to stir.

Spider wished things could stay like this. But she had to look at reality. These So-what-if-guys were not going to go away until they got what they wanted. Then, if they let her live, which was doubtful, they were still not going to really leave her alone.

She hoped she was right about Carrie being safe. Hoped she was right about Tommy being able to protect himself and Laura. She hoped there would be a time when they would be sitting around drinking some beers and talking about the whole thing as if it were no big deal.

She'd pray, but she'd tried that before. If God was there, He wasn't listening to her.

She was worried about Robby, about all his brothers and his sisters and his ageing grandmother. They needed him around, but he wouldn't be around if the So-what-if guys found him.

She worried about Henry. Who was going to take care of him if she was gone? Who'd go visit him…

She was aware of being asleep, which was in itself a weird beginning to a dream. She was asleep, and she was watching herself and Carrie sleep. Then she was flying out of the house over the rooftops of the city. She made out the park and the hospital where Henry was. Henry was sitting on the hospital roof; he waved at her. She flew over and sat down beside him.

"Henry, man…I didn't know you could get out of there!" she said excitedly.

"Well, I'm not staying in *there* all day. It's fucking duller than shit. This is pretty cool, though. I kind of float around the city at night and look in on people. Saw a couple having sado-masochistic sex the other night, that was entertaining."

"You're a voyeur!" Spider laughed.

"Hey! When you can't do, you watch. Do you think it's wrong?"

"Nah! I think it's a victimless crime as long as the person doesn't know they're being watched," Spider answered. "Carrie disagrees, but what the hell does she know? Henry…Why did you try to save Scott?"

"You've asked me that a thousand times. It took you long enough to get up here so I could answer. I don't really know why; I didn't know him. I can tell you this, though, I don't know if I would have been as heroic if I had known one of those assholes had a gun. I saw three guys beating up one guy and I figured I was closing the odds. I always did have the shittiest luck. I was engaged once. Caught my fiancée having sex with my retarded cousin, Brian. I got dysentery the night of my senior prom. It kind of makes sense that I'd run in to help a guy in a simple fisticuff and get myself shot. Then here I sit—or lay, rather for…how many years?"

"Sixteen," Spider said.

"Wow that's a bitch. If I'd had to lay in that fucking bed all that time I'd be nuts, and if you didn't come to visit me every day I'd be nuts anyway. Of course, talk about dull! Until this last year you had less of a life than I did."

"Henry…you know, lots of times I felt like you were the only one I could really talk to…"

"Which is really pathetic considering that I couldn't talk back."

"I've tried to do what's best for you, but I'm admitting it now, I don't really know what the hell that is. Are you happy like this, or would you rather be dead?"

He seemed to think about that for a minute. "Well, floating around watching other people was kind of like the ultimate TV. I can even go to other countries and other worlds. It was a real trip for about the first ten years, but after awhile…Well, watching isn't doing. I can't feel anything, touch anyone, and vicarious pleasure can only get you so far. I run into someone else floating around up here every once in awhile, and I've had some really great conversations, but we're mostly in agreement. We're ready to go on."

"Go on where?" Spider asked.

Henry shrugged. "Who knows? I just know there's something, and I'm ready to go now if you can let me go."

Spider looked at him. "I know it's stupid, but by keeping you alive it was like I was keeping Scott alive. He was the only one who ever really cared about me."

"It is stupid, and now there are people who care as much about you as Scott did. So it's time for you to go on, too."

When Spider woke up she felt rested. She remembered the dream and smiled.

"What?" Carrie asked. She was pulling on her robe.

"Just thinking how lucky I am. To be with you, to love you and to have you love me. Whatever happens now they can't take this time that we're having right now away from us. Do you know what I'm saying?"

Carrie smiled back at her and nodded. "Let's worry about what's going to happen when it happens." She took off her robe and lay back down beside Spider.

Spider held her close, enjoying the way she felt in her arms, imprinting it in her memory for a time when she might not be able to hold her. "I want you to meet a friend of mine."

"Right now?" Carrie asked in a disappointed tone of voice.

Spider laughed. "No, not right now."

CARRIE LOOKED DOWN at the sleeping man in the bed. "Maybe we should come back later when he's awake," she whispered to Spider.

"He doesn't wake up. He's in a coma. He's been in a coma for sixteen years. For that sixteen years, ever since I got out of the service, barely a day has gone by that I didn't come and visit him. He's where all my money goes. Henry is why I never have any extra spending money."

"Henry. This isn't Scott, then. Excuse me, Honey, but I don't get it."

"Scott *is* dead. Henry wound up here because he tried to save Scott. He had no parents or siblings, only distant relatives none of whom were interested in him. I didn't know where he was, but I did know that he thinks, that he feels, because I can *feel* him. He has normal brain function. Henry got like this trying to protect Scott, and if I had been here maybe I could have saved Scott. Maybe Henry would be married with three kids right now. I didn't want him put into some filthy state home. It just didn't seem right."

Carrie looked at Spider for a minute and then started to cry.

"Why are you crying? I'm really not insane…"

"That's the most wonderful thing I've ever heard," Carrie cried. "You're one of a kind."

"Maybe yes, and maybe no." Spider smiled. "At any rate, I figured there are enough things that I can't tell you, so I wanted you to meet Henry. So…you don't think I'm crazy?"

"Oh, this is definitely crazy." Carrie laughed, drying her eyes. "But it's exactly the kind of thing I would expect you to do."

"He wants to go now. I always wondered whether he did or not, and now I know that he does. He wants to go, and his body won't let him."

Carrie nodded, trying to pretend like she didn't think that was the most insane thing Spider had said yet.

They sat and talked to Henry for some fifteen minutes and then they left.

Spider drove home.

"Well, at least now I know you're not spending all your money on some trollop," Carrie said. "I was beginning to wonder just where the hell you went after work. I figured it must be one of those *Don't ask or they'll kill you* things, so I didn't ask."

"Carrie, I…" She took a deep breath. Damn, this was hard.

"What is it, Baby?"

"I need money."

"How much?"

"I…About five thousand dollars in cash," Spider said. "Do you have it?"

"I…don't have it readily available, but I can get my hands on it in an afternoon's time. All I have to do is cash a CD. Can I ask what you need it for?"

Spider shot her a look.

"OK, stupid question." Carrie shook her head, and once again wondered when she had lost control of her life.

ROBBY OPENED THE manila envelope carefully and away from prying eyes. He counted the money and then counted it again. The instructions were simple but clear.

Obviously, Spider thought things were going to get worse before they got better. He burned the note and pushed the money down deep in his pocket. He'd never seen that much money in his life. All the things he could do for the kids with that money! But the money was earmarked for something else, her instructions were clear.

He owed her. After all, it was his fault she'd been caught up in this whole mess. He ran his hands over his head. She was where she was partly because she had laid her ass on the line covering his. Now he had to play by her game plan; put his life into her hands. He wasn't used to doing that. Wasn't used to not being the one to have to make the big decisions. It was a relief, and it scared the hell out of him at the same time.

The only real decision being left up to him at the present time was how he was going to make sure that his family was taken care of. He didn't know how much time he'd have, but he was pretty certain that it wouldn't be a lot. Not enough to put back any huge amount of money.

After a few more minutes thought he did the only thing he could do. He walked into the house. "Kids, Grandma, we have to have a meeting!"

HE LOOKED AROUND at them. By the looks on their faces they knew something was going on. He took a deep breath, held it for a few seconds, and then he looked straight at Evan and started.

"I might have to go away. I don't know for how long. Doesn't matter why. Just know that it's not because I want to, and it's not because I'm going to jail or anything like that. Here's the thing— there's a little in savings but not a lot. It won't last you long at all if you start digging into it."

"We can manage on my check if we have to, Baby." His grand-mother was close to tears.

"Evan can run my trash route, and since he'll have the truck he won't have to save the money for a car."

"I can keep my job at the store, too…"

Robby cut Evan short shaking his head no violently.

"No, you take time off. The trash business makes good money, and if everyone pitches in there is no reason that you can't go to school, date, have a life. You do have to grow up, Evan, but not all the way, and not all at once."

"Janice, maybe you can get Evan's job at the store."

She nodded, looking sad. "What are we going to do without you, Robby?" She cried, got up, ran over and hugged him. "We haven't ever had to do it without you before."

Robby patted her back, swallowed the lump in his throat, and pushed her to arm's length. "Janice, I've always counted on you to do what's right. To be the little mother. You just keep doing what you're doing. See if you can't get Evan's job in the grocery store and things will be great. Now go sit down. If you want permission to do any-thing you'll have to go through Grandma. Does everyone understand?"

"Yes, Robby," they said in unison.

"We've only existed this long because you've listened to what I told you. Don't forget what I've tried to teach you and you'll be fine. If you treat my being gone like a holiday, you won't make it, and that's a fact."

He spent the rest of the night lining things out for them. When he was done he went out to the truck ready to start his night run.

Janice and Evan followed him.

"Well?" he asked.

"Robby..." Evan started but couldn't finish.

Janice did it for him. "Are we going to be like you?"

Robby laughed. "No, you aren't going to be like me, and no one will come after you. If anyone asks about me, tell them I'm going into the service like I told you. Now go on back in the house."

They left. Robby smiled, shook his head and popped the hood. He checked the oil, added some, and slammed the hood closed again. He saw Donna standing there looking worried. Like the weight of the world was on her shoulders. Donna had always worried too much.

"Everything will be all right, Donna."

"For us. But what about for you?" Donna walked over, jumped up and sat on his workbench. "I'm worried about what will happen to you, Robby."

"Don't you worry about me, Donna. I can take care of myself."

"Sometimes it makes me cry," Donna said.

"What, Donna? What makes you cry?"

"That you take care of everybody and no one takes care of you. You spend all your time fixing things and cleaning up other people's messes. What's going to happen to you now, Robby? What's going to happen to you?" She sniffled and wiped her face on the back of her fist. "It's not fair, Robby. It's not..."

"Donna, if there's one thing that I have learned, it's that life isn't very often fair. But sometimes the things that you think are the worst turn out to be the best. Look at us, look at me. I didn't ask to raise seven kids, but I wouldn't change things. I love you all because you're my family. I hope that I have at least helped get you on the right path, and if I have, if you grow up into healthy happy people, then what else do I need to accomplish with my life? I'm counting on you, Donna, more than anyone else."

Donna sniffled again. "Me! Why me?"

"Because you're the smartest, Donna. Have been since the day you were born. Grandma's smart, but she's old and she forgets things, and it's getting harder for her to get around. Evan's a good kid, he's got a good heart, and he means well. But, as we all know, he's got piss poor judgment. Don't be afraid to tell him if he's screwing up. Janice is good with the babies, and she's got a lot of love to give, but she's a pushover. Tell her to stand up for herself. Colistia, now Colistia has talent. With the right encouragement she'll be a great singer someday, I'm sure of it. Colistia loves us because were her family, but her head is too much in the clouds most of the time to help much with worldly things."

Donna laughed, and Robby smiled.

"We need to encourage her, but don't forget to make her come down to earth every once in awhile. Devan…now that boy is a worker, a mover and a shaker. He'll always make a living, but don't let him forget to have fun sometimes. Elvita likes to laugh—a happier child was never born. But we both know that Mama's drug habit left its mark on her brain. She's never going to be very bright, and people will try to push her around and use her. She's going to have to learn early in the game that she can't take anything at face value, not to trust people till they have proved they can be trusted."

Robbie paused for a moment to clear the frog out of his throat. "Duane is mechanical, so he's going to be able to fix things like me and like Granddad did. He already knows how to take things apart and put them together, but he's got a temper on him. You'll all have to work real hard at teaching him that kind of behavior won't take him very far."

"You, Donna, are the shiniest apple in this barrel. You're smart, and you're good-looking. You've got a good head on your shoulders. You've got good instincts and people like you. You can be anything that you want to be, Donna. Don't let the family down, they need you, and I need to know that you'll be there for them. But don't let them stop you, either. You can soar with the eagles, girl, there isn't any doubt about that. Don't worry so damn much. Let me tell you something else that I've learned. If something can be fixed, then you can fix it. If it can't be fixed, then no one can fix it. So there's no need to worry about it. You work with what you've got and you go on."

She nodded, jumped off the workbench, ran over and hugged Robby tight. "I love you, Robby, better than anything."

"I love you, too, kiddo. Don't forget what I said. When people put you down or don't believe in you, then you pick yourself up and believe in yourself. Because I don't count myself a fool, and I sure have faith in you."

CHAPTER FIFTEEN

*"I returned, and saw under the sun, that the race
is not to the swift, nor the battle to the strong, nor
yet bread to the wise, nor yet riches to the understanding, nor yet favor to men of skill; but time and
chance happens to them all."* Ecclesiastes 9:11

NO NEW FRY GUY killings in two months. Jason had assumed
they were being called back to the main office to be debriefed and
sent home. He knew that wasn't the case as soon as he saw the look
on Deacon's face.

"Sit down," Deacon ordered. He picked up the small stack of
papers on his desk and looked at the top one. "Know what this is?"

Jason and Kirk shook their heads silently.

"It's an order from the top. They want the Fry Guy, and they
want him now."

"What?" Kirk said. "But…there hasn't been a Fry Guy killing
in two months! He could be in another country by now for all
we know."

"Well, they don't think so," Deacon said. "For that matter neither do I. Apparently this guy is something of a marvel to them, and
they want him back here for testing."

"We're supposed to bring this motherfucker in!" Jason screamed.
"Are they nuts! I thought they wanted us to shoot him or something.
This guy fries people's brains. How do you catch someone like that?"

Jason never opened up his face in the office, so both Deacon
and Kirk were a little shocked by his outburst.

"They said they'd take care of capturing him when the time
came. All they want us to do is to put pressure on Spider Webb.
They'll have their boys on hand if we need any help."

Kirk smiled. "So they want us to put pressure on Spider Webb?"

"Don't be so fucking smug, Kirk. Between you and me I think
it's a bad idea. I'm just glad I'll be here behind this desk while you do
it. Carrie Long is still off limits, but just about anything else goes.
Here's what I want you to do…"

"THIS IS THE stupidest fucking thing," Tommy swore. "A fucking locker search, fucking haven't gone through this since high school." He waited beside his locker.

"They've had shit come up missing from the evidence room, and there really isn't a hell of a lot left that they can do," Spider said.

"Look at the fucking video on the lock-up area."

"Those can be rigged too easy, remember?" Spider said.

"Then they ought to fix it so they can't." Tommy swore.

"Open your locker, Chan," the Lieutenant said.

Tommy did. Two men and a dog rifled through the contents for some three minutes. "OK, Chan. You're clean."

"Yeah, and everything I own is covered in fucking dog slobber," Tommy mumbled as he tried to put his locker back into some kind of order.

The dog started jumping on Spider's locker, and Spider's heart sank into her gut.

"Webb, open your locker," the lieutenant said.

Spider opened her locker. The dog went ape-shit, and they found what they were looking for in the pocket of Spider's jean jacket. Spider looked at the bag of coke hanging from the lieutenant's fingers.

"Why, Webb?"

"You know I didn't fucking steal that shit," Spider said. "I don't do drugs. Everyone knows that. So why would I steal that? There certainly isn't enough to sell. Besides which, if I wouldn't steal from the evidence room when I needed money, why would I do it now when I don't?"

The lieutenant nodded. She was right. It didn't make any sense. "Will you take a drug test?"

She nodded.

"Let's go to my office."

Tommy went with them. "This is a frame up. You know this is a frame-up," Tommy said hotly.

The lieutenant put his comlink to Spider's arm and pushed a button. He read the results. "She tests clean."

"Don't sound so fucking surprised."

The lieutenant's head swung up; he looked shocked. It was Chan who said it. He ignored the outburst. Everyone was allowed an occasional show of temper, and Chan and Webb were close. It made sense that he would rush to her defense.

"I didn't steal that shit," Spider said. "If I did, do you really think I'd be stupid enough to put it in my own locker? Or anywhere in this building for that matter?"

He looked at her and shook his head. He sat down behind his desk. "I don't think you did. Unfortunately everyone saw it, and it's on the main frame."

Spider ran her hands over her face and sat down.

Tommy just stared at her.

She looked back, and she knew what he was thinking. She shrugged. "It's not the lieutenant's fault. He didn't do it," she said. "I'm worried about how this is going to look for Carrie."

"I'll try to keep the press out of this," the lieutenant said.

Spider laughed bitterly. "Good fucking luck."

"You'll have to be suspended pending an investigation," he said carefully and waited for the explosion.

"I know," Spider said. She stood up and handed him her comlink and service revolver.

"This fucking stinks!" Tommy screamed. He felt that someone should be screaming, and it didn't look like it was going to be Spider.

"OK, Chan, that's enough," the lieutenant warned.

"I'll tell you what's enough…"

"It's not that bad, Tommy. They gottah prove I did it in order to suspend me permanently. I didn't do it, so there is no proof. It's just a pain in the ass for me, and it's embarrassing for Carrie."

"We'll try to keep it under wraps. I really am sorry…procedure, you know." The lieutenant shrugged helplessly.

She smiled at him, feeling his sincerity; maybe he wasn't such a prick after all. She stood up. "Better take me off-line." She leaned forward.

The lieutenant got up and walked around his desk, the wand in his hand.

"This is unfucking believable," Tommy swore.

The lieutenant touched the wand to the lump behind her ear. Spider felt a slight surge of electricity, and the deed was done. She was completely off-line for the first time in years.

"Call me when it's over," Spider said. She turned to walk out, and Tommy followed her.

"That's it!" Tommy said in disbelief. "You're just going to let this happen!"

"There's nothing I can do, Tommy." Spider turned to face him and threw up her hands. "I guess I'll enjoy a little time off and wait for the other shoe to drop."

SPIDER WATCHED THE six o'clock news with bated breath. She didn't know how he did it, but Toby had successfully kept it off the news—at least for now. She turned the TV off and leaned back in the recliner. She heard the front door open and then close.

"Honey, the funniest thing happened to me at work today," she mumbled to herself. She still didn't know how she was going to tell Carrie.

Carrie walked into the room looking exhausted and threw her briefcase onto the chair Spider was sitting in.

Spider grunted as she caught the case.

Carrie spun around.

"Oh, Honey, I'm sorry! I didn't know you were home...where's your truck?"

"Parked out front where it always is," Spider said.

"Ah...no, it's not," Carrie said.

Spider ran past her and out the front door. She stood looking at the blank spot where her truck was supposed to be.

She turned to Carrie. "You're not going to believe the day I've had."

THE POLICE HAD just left from filling out her grand theft auto complaint when the phone rang. They'd found her truck. Wasn't much left—some crunched metal and smashed glass with a license plate that she had to pay to have hauled away.

"Your insurance..." Carrie started.

"Honey, that truck is ten years old and paid for. I don't have anything but liability on it." She sighed. "It doesn't get much better than this."

"You're just having a bad day," Carrie said, forcing a smile.

"I can't believe they're fucking with me like this. I thought this was over. I thought I had overreacted. But it's not over; they're starting right up again."

"Who is doing what, Honey?"

Spider just looked at her.

"Oh, come on, Baby, you're not going to start this again are you? You're just being paranoid."

The phone rang and Spider answered it. "Hello?"

Carrie got up and headed out the door.

"Where you going?" Spider asked, covering the receiver with her hand.

"To the den to use the other phone."

"Hello, Spider?" Tommy could never really tell if it was her or Carrie over the phone.

"Yep."

"You OK?" he asked.

"Yeah, I'm fine. I got no job and I got no truck, but I'm great."

"Truck? What happened to your truck?"

"Stolen out of the driveway and totaled. The cops who came out here to take my complaint were real understanding, though," she said sarcastically.

"Yeah, I bet they were," Tommy said, and added this to his long list of reasons to hate uniformed officers. "Well, they're going to clear you—they have to."

"I know," Spider sighed. "I'm not worried about that. I'm not even really worried about the truck. I'm just worried about what's next."

"Oh, you're not going to start that shit again! I thought we were over that. Hell, there haven't been any Fry Guy killings and no SWTF guys in town for months. You're just being paranoid. Some guy you pissed off at work is trying to get back at you, and it's not the first time some kid has gone to a rich neighborhood, stolen a car and totaled it."

"That's what they want you to think," Spider said.

"Doesn't that shrink do anything for you? I admit it, there for awhile I was getting as squirrelly as you were, but…there is no big government conspiracy, no one's after you, no one's after anyone."

"If you say so. But then that means that my life sucks."

"As long as we're talking about things that suck…I can't run with you in the morning. The lieutenant just informed me that I will be staking out a really stinky section of the dock tomorrow morning," Tommy said.

"Alone?" Spider asked.

"It's just an observation thing. Looking for a witness, not a perp. Guy used to work on the docks. They figure if he's in trouble he might go back there."

"Well, gee! That sounds like great fun, wish I could be there."

"Yeah, right," Tommy scoffed. "Try not to worry."

"Yeah, right," Spider laughed. "Good bye, Tommy."

"Bye."

Spider hung up the phone and flopped into the recliner.

"I got you a car for tomorrow," Carrie said as she walked into the room.

"Suddenly I have become a very high maintenance woman," Spider said with a sigh.

Carrie sat down in Spider's lap and wrapped her arms around her neck. "So, you ready to start working that bill off, chick?"

"My work is never done."

SHE DIDN'T KNOW why, but it seemed earlier when she had to run by herself. It seemed more like work, that was for damn sure. She rounded the corner and ran straight into the So-what-if guys. The big one was standing in the middle of the path, the other one was standing just off it.

Spider didn't give it a second thought; she landed a fist in the middle of Kirk's face and sent him flying. He landed on his ass on the ground, his nose spouting blood like a geyser.

Jason started to move towards her.

Spider took a stance and thumbed her nose at him.

Jason put his hands in the air and moved back.

Kirk screamed and held his nose. He stumbled to his feet, and Spider landed a spinning kick to his ribs that sent him flying onto his butt again. She looked at Jason to see if he was going to move again.

He smiled and held up his hands again.

"Here's the news, goat turd," Spider hissed at the wounded man. "I don't know who the fucking Fry Guy is, and if I did I sure to dick wouldn't tell you. Every time you hurt me, I'm gonna hurt you. Your nose was for my reputation; your ribs were for my truck. You keep fucking with me, and you're going to run out of body parts."

Kirk pulled his gun and pointed it at Spider. To his surprise the gun went flying from his hand. The next time he saw it, it was in the huge hand of Spider Web. Then it was flying into the lake.

"Thiiiiis...is bigger...than you know...Weeebb," Kirk managed to get out.

"And I am meaner than you know, Kirk." She took off running again as if nothing had stopped her in the first place.

Jason walked over and helped Kirk to his feet.

"Why...why di-didn't you he-help...me," Kirk demanded.

"Help you what? Get your ass kicked? If I wanted to be a fucking hero I sure as hell wouldn't be doing this job." Jason started helping him towards the car.

"We'll have to put on a lot more pressure before that one breaks." Kirk groaned as Jason helped him into his seat.

Jason laughed. "I think it's more likely that she'll break you."

"Everyone has a breaking point; we just have to find hers."

THIS WAS THE second morning of this shit. Tommy would much rather be in the park running with Spider. Running and talking was a good way to start a day, lots better than sitting on a dirty dock smelling last week's catch of the day.

To make matters worse, it wasn't cold but they insisted he wear a P jacket and pretend to be fishing. They said it made him look less threatening. He agreed. Only an idiot would be wearing a jacket on a day like this one.

Dawn was just starting to break. The dock was still shrouded in darkness. He heard something move behind him and turned just in time to see five men bearing down on him. He had to be imagining things.

"Nice morning for fish..." He wasn't imagining shit. The bastards jumped him. The first one got a face full of foot for his troubles. A baseball bat was spinning towards his head. He spun quickly, caught the bat with his foot and it exploded into splinters. He ducked under the third one's attack, then rose up throwing him over his back and into the lake behind him. A punch landed in the side of his head and he rolled with it, punching another attacker in the solar plexus hard enough to stop the man's heart, so that he dropped like a rock.

"Come in! Come in! I got trouble!" Tommy screamed. In a few minutes at the most, he would have back up.

With Tommy's attention diverted for just a second one of them landed a punch into his ribs. Tommy spun and kicked the guy sending him staggering back. The other guy swung at him with what was left of the bat. Tommy grabbed it and slammed it back towards his attacker, striking him in the eye. Tommy backed up and got into his

stance, waiting for their next attack. One of them came running at
him, his feet heading for Tommy's face. He grabbed the man's feet
in mid-air, twisted and the man went spinning head first into the
wooden dock. His head making a sick, thudding noise as it struck.

Tommy went for his weapon reluctantly. "You fuckers are under arrest!" Tommy wiped the little bit of blood from his lip.

His comlink buzzed, and then the voice in his ear said. "Cars
are on the way."

"It's about fucking time." He looked at the two men in front of
him. "Here comes the cavalry, when they get here you fuckers…"
They weren't listening. They were focused behind him. Tommy started
moving forward just as something cracked him in the back of the
head. He spun and kicked and the guy went into the lake again. But
the blow had temporarily blurred his vision.

"Finish him," one of them said.

"You finish him. I'm getting the hell out of here."

They grabbed their fallen comrades and took off. Tommy tried
to give chase, but when he started to run the world started spinning.

He sat down and took several deep breaths. He was still seeing
stars and the fuckers were getting away. Damn, how could he have
been so stupid? You never, ever left anyone alive or kicking. He'd
been a cop too long.

When back up finally got there, the perps were long gone.
They loaded Tommy up and hauled him off to the hospital. He
had a slight concussion, and a huge knot on his head, but nothing
that wouldn't pass in a couple of days. Still, he was only too happy
to go home for the day even though it meant Laura had to come
and get him.

Laura looked at his swollen lip. She hugged him and kissed his
forehead. "Come on, Baby, let's get you home."

On the way home Tommy told her all about the fight.

"I don't get it. Why? Why did they attack you?"

"Who knows?" Tommy said with a shrug. "They were thugs,
thugs don't need reasons to do things. Maybe they wanted my money;
maybe they wanted my fish and tackle. Maybe they just wanted the
sheer pleasure of beating the living hell out of someone."

"And maybe it's those So-what-if guys," Laura said.

"Come on, Honey, you're starting to sound like Spider. I should
never have told you anything about it," he said.

"Well, I'll be glad when Spider goes back to work. I feel better when you're working with her. I know she'd never willingly let anything happen to you, and that gives me comfort."

"God! My head hurts," Tommy said.

"When we get you home we'll put some ice on it."

"Oh, good! Then it will hurt and be cold."

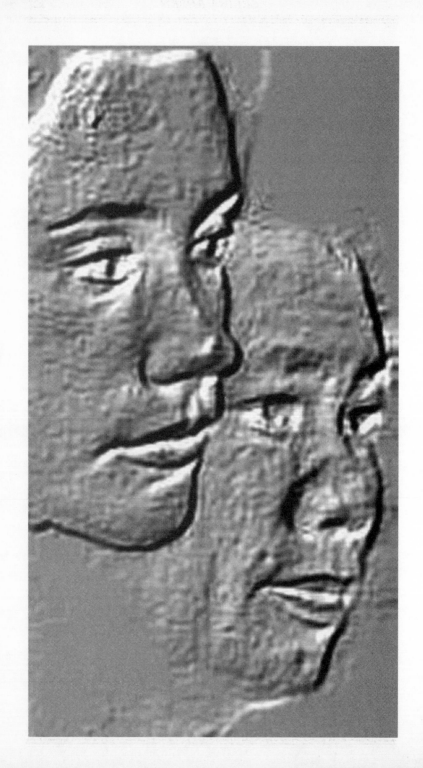

CHAPTER SIXTEEN

"For man also knows not his time: like the fishes that
are taken in an evil net, and like the birds that are
caught in the snare; so are the sons of men snared in
an evil time, when it falls suddenly upon them."
Ecclesiastes 9:12

CARRIE, LAURA AND George had gone to lunch, although it seemed to Carrie that they had done more working than eating.

"Enjoy your meal, DA Long?" the host asked.

"Very much, thank you." Carrie started out the door, Laura followed, and George, as always, was bringing up the rear. Carrie opened the car door and slid in behind the wheel. She had just put the key into the ignition when she heard a strange popping sound. Laura let out a startled scream and fell to the sidewalk. Carrie, thinking that Laura had tripped on the curb, got up and ran around the car to help her up. To her surprise George slammed into her, knocking her to the ground.

"Get down! I think someone's shooting." George sounded like he was talking into a vacuum. For a minute it didn't register. None of it registered.

"Laura! Laura, are you all right?" George screamed

"I...I don't know." She sounded like she was miles away instead of just a few feet across the sidewalk. "I've been hit."

Carrie didn't really remember how she got out from under George, but the next thing she knew she was at Laura's side, and George was crawling along the ground yelling at her for taking chances.

She heard the sirens coming, and the next thing she knew, cops had surrounded them. Carrie saw the wound in Laura's arm and wondered what was taking the goddamned ambulance so long.

"It doesn't look bad," Carrie said.

"Well, it sure doesn't feel good." Laura was panicking, looking shocky.

"George, give me your jacket," Carrie ordered.

George took off his jacket and handed it to Carrie.

Carrie wadded it up and used it to apply direct pressure to the wound. It was bleeding badly.

"How's that?" Carrie asked.

"Better, I think," Laura said.

Carrie was aware of police running around like crazy all around her. No doubt they were looking for the shooter.

"There's a silencer on the weapon!" George shouted to the police. "But I thought I saw something up there." He was pointing at the parking garage across the street.

"Carrie, aren't the paramedics here yet?" Laura asked. She was scared, and who could blame her?

"Where is the fucking ambulance?" Carrie screamed.

"It's on it's way, Sir," one of the officers said. "Should be here any second now. I already called Detective Chan, and he'll meet us at the hospital."

The ambulance showed up then. The paramedics that ran up to help were wearing flack jackets. They started working on Laura. The woman paramedic pushed Carrie gently away. She pulled up the jacket, looked at the wound and smiled at Laura.

"Now that doesn't look bad at all."

The other one was spitting out vital statistics that meant nothing to Carrie, and then they were lifting Laura onto a stretcher and loading her into the ambulance.

Carrie followed. "I'm going with her."

The female paramedic nodded.

Carrie noticed that the police were putting a layer of bodies between her and everyone else, and when she got in the ambulance a cop went with them.

"Carrie?" Laura said.

"Right here, Laura," Carrie said.

"You think...was it the SWTF?" Laura asked.

Carrie realized then what had just happened. Someone had tried to shoot her. Laura just happened to be in the wrong place at the wrong time. Carrie wondered what the hell Laura knew about the SWTF. Carrie laughed nervously, looked at the officer and shrugged.

"Of course not, Laura. Just some lunatic. I get death threats every single day. I'm sorry, Laura, it should have been me."

"Too many coincidences, Carrie. Too many damn coincidences," Laura mumbled and then she was out.

TOMMY PACED THE waiting room. It wasn't supposed to be like this. It was never supposed to be like this. Laura had a "safe" job. She wasn't supposed to be in danger.

"Tommy, she'll be all right," Carrie said from where she sat in the waiting room.

Tommy glared at her. "If you had taken the police escort that they wanted you to have…"

"I don't see what good that would have done, Tommy, but if it will make you feel any better we'll have one from now on."

Spider rushed in then, hugged him tight and released him. "I just heard. What the hell happened?"

Carrie walked over and hugged her. "It was terrible…" By the time she had finished telling Spider everything that had happened she was in tears. Spider held her and patted her back. She looked at Tommy.

"What happened to you?" she asked looking at his swollen lip.

"I had a run in with some thugs down at the dock." He didn't elaborate. The last thing he wanted to hear right now were any of Spider's conspiracy theories. "What is taking so fucking long?"

The doctor walked out then and called, "Mr. Chan?"

Tommy ran over to him.

"You're wife is going to be fine. The bullet didn't hit anything vital, and we were able to remove it without any real trouble. She's up and she's asking to see you."

"Thank God!" Carrie said under her breath.

Tommy followed the doctor closely, obviously wishing he would walk a little faster.

Spider sat down next to Carrie and was silent.

"They didn't find anybody, did they?" Spider asked.

"No, but…"

"And the men who went after Tommy yesterday on the dock?"

"No. What does that have to do…someone just tried to kill me!"

"Shush," Spider ordered. She lowered her voice. "It's them, Carrie. It has to be them."

She looked at the cop who was supposed to be guarding Carrie. Spider didn't recognize him, he felt OK. Wasn't worried, didn't seem hostile, but that didn't mean he wasn't one of them, either. You just couldn't be sure.

"You can't trust anyone, Carrie. Remember that."

SPIDER HAD INSISTED on seeing Laura. Carrie hadn't been sure it was such a good idea. Spider had been acting weird even for Spider, but now she was acting perfectly "Spider" normal, which was almost scarier.

Laura looked tired, but seemed otherwise to be fine. Carrie remembered the last time she had visited someone in the hospital. Then it had been Spider who was shot. She decided she definitely did not like guns.

"I know it probably has something to do with the fact that I'm higher than a kite, but it really doesn't hurt that much at all," Laura said.

"Technology has certainly advanced since the first time I got shot, I can tell you that," Spider said. "Took me about half the time to heal this last time.

"Well, isn't that nice!" Tommy glared at Spider. "My wife is not going to make a habit out of getting shot."

"I didn't say she was," Spider said.

"I have to get back to work." Carrie started for the door.

"You're fucking kidding, right!" Spider screamed. "Some lunatic may be trying to shoot you, and you're going back to work?"

Carrie was a little shocked at Spider's outburst, but managed to keep her cool. "I'm the DA. I have to go back to work. I'll have police escort and full-time security now. I may be hard-headed, but never let it be said that I don't learn from my mistakes."

Spider nodded

Carrie kissed her cheek and then left.

Spider sighed. She looked at Tommy. He looked scared, and Tommy never looked scared. It was more than a little unnerving.

"I wonder if you can get this shit legally?" Laura said looking at her good hand as if she were seeing it in a whole new light.

The phone rang. Tommy answered it. "Hello…" He pulled the receiver away from his ear and looked at it. Then gave Spider a puzzled look.

"It's for you." He handed her the phone.

Spider took it as her stomach finished flipping over.

"Yes?"

"A little to my right, and that could be *your* old lady laying there or in a coffin somewhere. It's all up to you, fly girl. You can give us what we want, or you can watch us pick off your friends one at a time. It's your decision."

Spider walked away from the bed and whispered. "Midnight, same place we met last time. I'll be alone, you be alone, too. I see anybody, and I'm way out of there."

"Sorry can't do that. I'm not about to go in there and let you rip my fucking head off. I'll have people there—lots of people. But they'll stay back as long as you behave yourself."

"No deal," Spider said.

"You don't get to deal, chick. You don't have any bargaining power left. The boys at the top are getting tired of dicking with you. They're ready to play hardball, and I don't think you're up for the pitch."

Spider looked from Tommy to Laura. "All right."

She walked over and hung up the phone.

"What was that?" Tommy asked.

"I need to talk to you," Spider said.

Tommy didn't ask why, he just followed her out of the room. "What's wrong?"

"No one was trying to shoot Carrie. They're afraid to shoot Carrie, or at least that's what I'm counting on. They shot Laura on purpose to make a point."

"For God's sake! Give them this guy," Tommy said, shaking her till her teeth rattled.

"It's not that easy. If I give them what they want, then I become expendable. We *all* become expendable. These aren't the sort of people who ever leave lose ends. You have to get Laura and get the hell out of town tomorrow morning first thing. Pack your car and tomorrow morning when you check her out you just keep going. I don't think they'll try anything in the hospital, but...Just go, and don't tell anyone where you are going. Don't let anyone follow you, either. Make damn sure you don't have any tracers or links on you. You'll also have to get into the lieutenant's office and take yourself off line."

"This is all crazy. I can't do this. I can't give up my life."

"Then you're asking me to give up mine in a very permanent way, because at this point the only way I can protect you if you won't protect yourself is to put a bullet in my own brain. And even that's not a safe bet if they think you know too much."

"This is all crazy. This can't be happening."

"But it is. Please, Tommy..."

"All right, all right, I believe you. It's insane, but I believe you."

"Then you'll do it?"

"I'll do it."

CARRIE COULDN'T REMEMBER when Spider had been any more loving than she had been this evening, and when they had made love it had been a truly religious experience. Now Spider was holding her so tightly that it was almost uncomfortable.

"Laura's shooting today...It really scared you, didn't it?" Carrie asked.

"It changes everything," Spider said quietly. She released Carrie and got slowly out of bed. She walked towards the bathroom and turned as she got to the door. "You know I love you, don't you?"

"Yes, I do," Carrie said.

"That I never want to be anywhere without you?"

"And I never want to be anywhere without you. What does this have to do with anything, Baby?" Carrie asked.

"You never know what's going to happen, and I just wanted you to know." She went in the bathroom and got in the shower.

"What the hell are you doing?" Carrie asked from the doorway.

"In all the confusion I forgot to tell you that they put me back on line today. I've got to go to work." Spider stepped out of the shower and started to dry off.

"Oh, that really sucks! I mean, I'm glad this shit is over, but this sucks. The middle of the night?"

"Tommy was on stakeout on the docks. He's with Laura now, so..." Spider shrugged and started to get dressed.

Carrie looked at her wishing that she could see what Spider was feeling for a change. "Be careful."

"I will be." Spider hugged her tight, kissed her, and then headed out of the house.

Carrie followed her. "It's a little cool," Carrie said. "You sure you're wearing enough clothes?"

"Yeah, I'll be fine." Spider smiled at her. "Take care of yourself, Carrie."

"You take care of yourself, Honey." Carrie closed the door after her. "Hmmm." She'd almost gotten shot today, so she supposed it would be more peculiar if Spider were just taking it all in stride.

SPIDER LOOKED DOWN at him lying there helplessly.

This time of night there weren't many people around. There was an eerie quiet to the room—to the whole hospital.

She hadn't turned the light on, really no need to. She could see him well enough in the glow from the streetlights coming in the window.

"Well, Henry, this is it. This is the last time I'll ever see you. I've got to go, and it's not easy to do." She wiped a tear from her eye. "To go, to leave everybody you care about behind, to step into God only knows what. All I really know is that it's not going to be good. I hope…no, I pray I'm doing the right thing, because I'm not sure I know what that is anymore…goodbye, Henry."

She put her hand over his mouth and held his nose closed with her thumb and forefinger. He convulsed once, twice, and then he lay still. She put her head to his chest; there was no heartbeat. He was gone. Right or wrong, it was over.

"Good luck, Henry, old man."

HE HAD BEEN bound to one place for so long. Now he was finally moving, moving from this warm, welcome place out there into the unknown. Yet he wasn't afraid. He was ready for a change, no matter what that change was.

It was tight and uncomfortable and more than a little scary, and then, just as he was about to panic, he pushed out the other side into the light. Strong firm hands grasped him and pulled him into the world. They wiped him off with towels. It felt good to be touched. Felt good to feel. Then they wrapped him up and handed him to the most beautiful woman he had ever seen. She was crying.

"He's the most perfect baby I've ever seen." She held him close to her bosom, and he felt her warmth. "I love you more than anything in the world, Albert."

A man bent over him then and took his hand. "Do you realize how long we've been waiting for you, little guy?"

Not as long as I have been waiting for you.

IT WAS TWELVE fifteen. Where the fuck was she? Kirk looked around; she was nowhere in sight. He could see his men all around him. They kept contacting him through his link, letting him know constantly that she had not even entered the park yet.

"She's not going to bite." That was Jason for the thirteenth time that night.

"Shut up! Shut the fuck up!" Kirk hissed.

"I see her!" That was Ted at position one. "She's alone, she's coming your way."

SPIDER GOT SLOWLY out of the car. She took a deep breath, let it out and headed for the meeting place at an even pace.

She saw the slimy So-what-if guy and snarled. He was the embodiment of all that she hated. A lazy, deceitful, disloyal, backstabbing monster whose only ambition was to get higher and higher up the food chain so that he could devour all those below him.

Tonight he felt bloated with power. Tonight he looked at her and saw a battle he was about to win. He was smug and without compassion.

Spider smiled smugly as she walked on. She got about ten feet from him before he put his hands up.

"That's close enough, Webb," Kirk announced. When she started to move forward anyway, she could hear the cocking of weapons all around her. Damn! There was a shit pot load of them. Still, she had expected nothing less. She looked at him closely and smiled. His nose was taped, and from the way he was standing she must have really done a job on those ribs.

"You're a frightened, evil, wicked little piece of shit, aren't ya?"

He laughed at her, which wasn't a good idea. She didn't like to be laughed at.

"Just tell us who he is and we can dispose of all this unpleasantness and both go back to our lives."

She laughed at him then. When she stopped it was obvious that she was not pleased. "We all know that when I tell you what you want to know I become expendable. But I can promise you this. Neither one of us will be going back to our lives."

"No more games, Webb. You give us this guy or we take everybody else."

"Did it ever occur to you that I might be willing to die to keep my secret? To protect the people I love." She pulled her gun then and stuck it to her head.

Kirk backed up, seeing any chances for advancement going up in smoke if this crazy woman pulled the trigger.

"All you have to do is give us the Fry Guy. Give him to us and you can have your life back. That's a promise."

Spider lowered her gun. "A promise from a man like you means nothing." She smiled at him. "But I'll tell you what you want to know. It's me. I'm the Fry Guy."

"You! You had alibis every time someone was killed!"

She laughed. "Not every time. Besides, who alibied me? Carrie, Tommy..." She let out a bellow of maniacal laughter. "I just gave them a little push, and they never knew I left."

"This is bull shit! This is bullshit! You're not the Fry Guy."

"Oh, yes. Yes, I am."

Kirk felt a tightness in his brain—a heat. He started running backwards. "Oh God! Oh God noooo!" His brain exploded in his head, and he fell to the earth in a limp pile. A guy she'd seen crouching behind a tree was next, and then the man walking by the dumpster. He was clearing her way, and all she had to do was run. She took off at full tilt boogey. They gave chase. A man barred her way briefly. Then he dropped his weapon, grabbed his head and screamed as his head made a strange popping sound. He staggered and fell, and Spider cleared his body easily. She was almost to the car. If she made it to the car she was practically home free.

Then something hit her in the neck, and suddenly the distance to the car was impossible. As she staggered and then fell she didn't have to wonder what had hit her. Damn! She hadn't counted on tranquilizer darts.

Robby sighed. *She hadn't made it. Damn it! That changed everything. Move to plan two.* He stopped frying people as soon as he saw her go down. He watched helplessly as the men who had been all over the park now ran to her side. Two vans pulled up, and men in lab coats got out of one. They put Spider Webb into a straightjacket, then they put a bucket-looking thing over her head. He knew instantly what the helmet was for, because his mental link to Spider was severed immediately. They hauled her back into one of the vans with them, then the SWTF men loaded their dead into the other van, got in themselves and roared off.

When Robby was sure they were all gone he crawled down out of the tree he'd been in for hours. He took only a second to stretch his tired limbs, then he ran to the car, jumped in the driver's seat and took off. He turned the switch on the box next to him and it started to blip. Now he wouldn't lose Spider.

Of course, he might not find her, either.

TOMMY DIDN'T LEAVE the hospital. Nothing at home was important enough to risk the fact that it might be bugged. All that mattered now was survival.

He wasn't waiting till tomorrow. Wasn't taking any chances.

He watched Laura sleeping. She hadn't protested his staying, and he hadn't had too much trouble talking a nurse into loaning him some scrubs to wear to sleep in. They'd brought him a cot, but he wouldn't be using it.

He looked at the clock. It was one in the morning. Things were quiet on this floor. Not too many people around. He looked out into the hallway—not a soul in sight. He stepped out and headed for the ER. As luck would have it, there had been a four-car pile up and the joint was jumping. In the excitement no one took notice of one more person in scrubs running around doing things.

Back in Laura's room he checked on her. She was still sleeping soundly. He went into the bathroom and locked the door. Then he pulled the pillowcase from the top of his pants and took his stolen stash from inside it, stacking it along the top of the sink.

He pulled his hair up and, using surgical tape, taped it away from his implant. He gave himself a shot of Lydacaine to deaden the area, and then he took the scalpel and cut a single line across the top of the small lump. Using tweezers he pulled the implant from his skin. He ran it under the water, holding it in his hand all the time. He made sure it was in the on position, and then he taped it to his arm. Only then did he see to the wound. He used surgical glue to close it, smeared it with antibiotic ointment, and dressed it. His hair barely covered his haphazard bandaging job. He quickly cleaned up the mess he had made, making use of the biohazards bin he had filled earlier with the clothes he'd been wearing. This done, he headed down the hall towards the extended care ward.

The name on the door said that his name was Brian Green. According to his chart, he had just received a heart transplant and was doing well. He was due to be in the hospital at least two more weeks. That made him the perfect candidate.

He opened Mr. Green's robe, and the guy woke up. He looked straight at Tommy, and Tommy smiled.

"What the hell?" Brian Green asked.

"I'm sorry, Sir, I tried not to wake you. Dr. Parker asked me to put a monitoring device on your back...Just in case."

"In case of what?" the man asked in a panic.

Tommy smiled in a concerned fashion. "You know, just in case. Could you roll onto your side?"

The man did so without another question, and Tommy quickly taped his link securely on the man's back.

"That was it. You can go back to sleep now. I'm sorry." Tommy left, shutting off the light. He sighed with relief and headed back down the hall, grabbing a wheelchair on the way.

Well, so far so good.

Back in Laura's room he shook her gently till she woke up. She smiled at him in a way that let him know that she was still druggy. "We playing doctor, Honey?"

"Yes." He picked her up and put her into the wheelchair he'd brought back with him. "We're going for a ride." He covered her with one of the blankets off her bed.

"What's going on, Tommy?" Laura asked. She wasn't so out of it that she couldn't tell there was something wrong.

"You were right and I was wrong. That should make you very happy, so just shut up and sit still."

He looked both ways before he rolled her out into the hall, so he jumped more than a little when someone called out.

"You there!"

Tommy looked over his shoulder and saw a short, fat nurse with a face that looked like it had been hit with a shovel, heading towards them.

"What's that, ma'am?" he asked.

She caught up with them. "What in God's name are you doing? It's one thirty in the morning. Patients are supposed to be in their rooms."

"Where are we going, Tommy?" Laura asked.

Tommy shot the nurse a half smile. "Escaped from the psych ward. She thinks I'm her husband," he whispered.

"You *are* my husband," Laura said.

"You'd think they could keep these damn whackos locked up. Should have known you were from Psych when I didn't recognize your face. Sorry to bother you."

"No problem."

She went on her way, and Tommy all but ran to the service elevator.

It opened right next to the rear exit, and they were out of the building. He started to breathe again when he saw the car. He rolled Laura over to it. Bud opened the door and helped Tommy put Laura into the car.

"Can you tell me what the hell is going on?" Bud asked.

Tommy didn't answer; he just ran the wheelchair back inside. He ran back a few minutes later and jumped in the back seat with Laura.

"What's going on, Tommy?"

"I can't tell ya, because I really don't know. I just know that someone is trying to kill Laura and me. Now just drive."

Bud didn't have to be told twice.

"You get the clothes like I asked ya?" Tommy asked.

"Yeah. They're in that sack sitting in the floor, but…They ain't gonna fit."

"That doesn't matter." Tommy got in the sack and dug the clothes out. He put them on over what he was wearing.

"Where the hell you want me to go?" Bud asked.

Tommy was watching out the rear window to see if they had picked up a tail. So far it looked clear.

"Tommy?"

"Take me on into Franklin."

"Franklin! Tommy that's a two-hour drive one way! I'll never get home on time. She'll make my life a living hell…She'll…"

"If you don't help us, Bud, we're going to be dead. Tell her you had to work late…"

"If she calls work and finds out I didn't even come in, my life won't be worth living."

"And it is now?" Tommy helped Laura dress, not an easy task with her arm in a sling.

"No…"

"Then what have you got to lose?" Tommy asked.

"And he scores!" Bud laughed. "OK, Tommy. Franklin it is, then. I tell the bitch I had to work late. If she finds out I didn't go to work, I tell her I'm having a fucking affair. What's the worst she can do, leave?"

Tommy allowed himself to get some sleep. When Bud shook him awake, the bone behind his ear was throbbing. The wire from the implant had been stuck into the bone—that's how you could hear with the damn thing. Now Tommy was wondering if he'd gotten all of the wire out.

"What now?" Bud asked.

Tommy sat up and looked around trying to get his bearings. He rubbed his eyes.

"You'll drive us to a car rental place where you will rent us a white sedan. You will get the extra insurance. You will rent it for two days. We'll leave in the white sedan, and you'll go home." Tommy handed him some money. "Tomorrow you will drive your car to a parking lot within walking distance of a Wal-Mart. Don't take a cab, and don't let anyone see you walk in. You will shop at Wal-Mart for about forty-five minutes, and when you walk out into the parking lot, go to any empty spot and start screaming that your car has been stolen. Then you call it in. By then I should be long gone, and since they can't find the white sedan, they will have to believe you."

"Which it has been—by you!" Bud screamed. "I can't do that! You're a fucking cop, for Christ's sake!"

"Which is why I know how to commit a crime without getting caught. Now come on, move it. Remember, not till tomorrow."

"If you say so…Am I going to go to jail?" Bud asked.

"I'm stealing the car, Bud, so don't worry about it," Tommy said. "By the way, Bud, that thing I gave you?"

"The top secret thing?"

"Yeah. Now listen close, this is what I want you to do…"

SPIDER WAS WAKING up. Her feet kicked out from the curled position they had been in and hit the side of something cold and metal. It hurt because someone had taken her shoes.

"Be still or you'll hurt yourself," someone said.

She could hardly hear them; it was like listening through water, and…She couldn't feel anyone. She kicked the cage again to see if he would talk again.

"Please be still, or we'll have to sedate you," he said.

"What the fuck have you done to me!" she screamed. She couldn't see anything. There was something on her head. She tried to take it

off, and that was when she realized that her hands were bound—
and bound good. "Take this fucking thing off my head."

"Must be horrible for her," another one said, obviously talking
to the first one or a whole bunch of them. She didn't know how
many. "Imagine going your whole life being able to feel those around
you, then to be suddenly cut off. It would be as if we were blind."

"Well I can't see shit, either, you stupid dick, but I can still hear
so you can quit talking about me as if I can't. Take this thing off
my head." Her screaming reverberated in her own ears. She could
handle being tied up, even caged, but this thing on her head was
driving her nuts. It was some kind of psychic screen to stop her
from using her 'powers.' Her stomach grumbled and she remembered the transmitter she had swallowed a few hours ago. Hopefully, Robby hadn't done something stupid and gotten himself
caught. Hopefully, he was following and would think of some
way to save her ass. Because right now it was real obvious that she
couldn't help herself.

She tried to scrape the helmet off on the floor, but it was con-
nected to her head by some chinstrap that she couldn't get off because she couldn't get her hands on it.

"Why don't you just kill me!" she screamed, and started banging
her head on the floor. They sedated her again.

THEY WALKED INTO Sears and did something they had never done
before. They charged as if there were no tomorrow. Then they hit
several other stores, doing the same thing before they hit the open
road going back the way they had come.

The car was loaded to the top of the seats.

He would use cash from now on. The plastic trail would lead
the SWTF to Franklin while he was going in the opposite direction.
He had to explain all this to Laura.

Laura nodded. She was tired and her shoulder hurt. She'd felt
like an idiot shopping for clothes while wearing one of Bud's four
hundred pound wife's dresses. Of course she had looked like an
idiot, too. Not that Tommy looked much better wearing six foot
four inch, two hundred fifty pound Bud's clothes. She looked down
at the jeans and sweater that she was wearing now. She looked better, but the little shopping spree had worn her completely out. Not
really astonishing considering she'd been shot the day before.

"I'm sure that I don't want to know, but…just how much money did we spend this morning?" Laura asked, trying to get comfortable.

"I purposely didn't keep track."

"Are we…I know this is stupid because we're running for our lives, but are we going to lose our house, our cars…I mean if we can't make payments…I guess none of that matters as long as we're alive and together."

"It *does* matter," Tommy said bitterly. "Of course it's more important that we are alive and together, but these bastards have no right to take everything that we have worked for, and Spider…God only knows what will happen to her, and for what? No one knows, not even Spider knows. She may be dead already. Well, they haven't seen the end of Tommy Chan. I will run and hide because that is the best thing to do right now, but then I will rise up and strike, and they won't know what hit them."

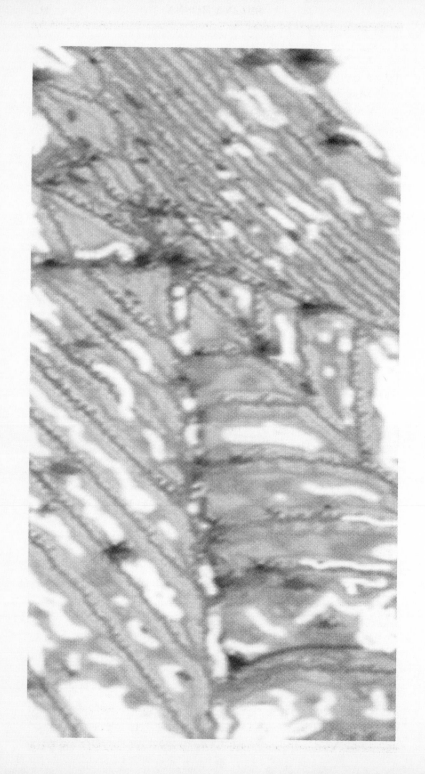

CHAPTER SEVENTEEN

"Remember now thy Creator in the days of thy youth,
before the evil days come, and the years draw near,
when thou shalt say, I have no pleasure in them…"
Ecclesiastes 12:1

THE ALARM WENT off. Carrie reached over and slammed the snooze button. She rolled over to find Spider, and found empty air instead. She was about to panic when she remembered that Spider had gone to work. She started to roll over and go back to sleep, but suddenly she was wide-awake. She sat straight up in bed.

I didn't see her comlink. She thought about Spider's leaving. Replayed it in her head. *I didn't see her comlink; she didn't have it when she left—I'm sure of it. In fact, I hadn't seen it all evening.*

She got out of bed and threw on her robe. She grabbed her own comlink and called Lieutenant Toby.

"Hello, Lieutenant Toby, homicide…"

"Cut the shit, Toby," Carrie said with forced calm. She knew his comlink told him exactly who was calling. "Listen…did you put Spider back on-line yesterday?"

"The hearing is this morning. I'm not expecting any trouble, but…no, she can't be put back on line until after she's been cleared. I'm sorry. I know Spider didn't do this. It's just regulations, you understand…"

"Yes, I do. Thank you, Lieutenant."

As she severed the link, the alarm clock went off for the second time and she jumped. She turned the alarm off.

She sat down on the bed and ran her hands down her face. *That's why she was acting so weird. She's gone off hunting the SWTF. I blew the whole shooting thing yesterday off to a loony, but Spider thought it was them, and now she's gone after them.*

She started to call the hospital and stopped. The phone could be bugged. She'd better get dressed and go down there. If anyone knew what was happening, it would be Tommy.

LAURA'S ROOM WAS empty. She went to the front desk quickly and was told that Laura had not been released yet. A nurse followed her back to Laura's room. She walked in, and seeing no one there checked the bathroom.

"This is most unusual," the nurse said. "Wait here. I'll just run and see if maybe they haven't taken her to X-ray or something. She shouldn't be up yet. Most unusual."

She had two cops with her, so she might as well use them. "Check the room."

"What are we looking for, Sir?" one asked.

"You'll know if you find it," Carrie said.

They started searching the room. A few seconds later one of them called out. "Sir!"

She walked over and looked into the bio-hazard bin. She recognized the clothing Tommy had been wearing the day before as well as his comlink system. In the closet were all Laura's clothes. She got on her comlink and called Lieutenant Toby.

"Yes, DA Long?" he answered.

"Toby. Where does Tommy Chan's link say that he is?"

She could hear him playing with the buttons on his keyboard. "It looks like he's in City General, where you're at, Sir."

"Well, I don't see him. Put me on line. Give me a locator on his frequency. If he's here I'll find him, but I doubt he's here. I just found his comlink in the trash."

"I'll stay linked with you while you check. I'm sending extra units to you now," Toby said.

Carrie opened her comlink to the locator program and started following the signal. She and the two officers wound up in the room of a man named Brain Green, who was in the middle of being catheterized.

"What in God's name?"

The nurse finished quickly and covered him.

"I'm District Attorney Long, officers Grimes and Peterson…"

"I don't care who you are! A man has the right to a little privacy, for God's sake."

"I'm very sorry, but I believe you have something attached to your body that…well, shouldn't be."

"You mean like a bomb! Christ almighty…"

"Not a bomb, sir, the item is harmless," Carrie said. "Has anyone come in and put anything strange on you?"

The man looked through all the wires and tubes running in and out of him and shrugged. "Which time?"

Carrie took a guess. "What about sometime late last night?" Brian thought about it for a moment and then nodded adamantly. "Ya! A guy came in here, in the middle of the night. He stuck something on my back. Said it was some sort of monitor."

"Could you roll onto your side maybe?" Carrie asked. He did. She opened his gown and removed the tape holding Tommy's implant to his back. She handed it to one of the officers, who automatically put it into a plastic evidence bag. "Can you give us a description of the man?"

"He was short, five-six, maybe. He was oriental, stocky, he had long hair." The man shrugged. "I was tired, he was wearing green scrubs."

"Computer! Put Tommy Chan in a lineup program." Pictures of two other Asian men appeared with Tommy's picture and she showed it to Brian. "Was it one of these men?"

He pointed to Tommy. "That one."

"Thank you very much." Carrie started out of the room, the officers following.

"Can I ask what the hell is going on?" Peterson asked.

"No, you can't," Carrie said not even turning to look at him. "You get all that, Toby?"

"Yeah, but...what the hell *is* going on?"

Carrie waited for the officers to step out of earshot before she answered. "I'm not really sure. I don't want this situation to go any further than you and me. Do I make myself clear?"

"Yes, Sir."

"Have every inch of this hospital searched."

"What do I tell the men they are looking for?" Toby asked.

"Not Chan. I don't want anyone looking for Chan."

"What then?"

"SWTF. That's what they're looking for, and if you find one, you arrest him and you call me."

"Arrest him? On what charges?"

"Murder. Kidnapping. Pick one, I don't care! Just bring them in."

"Yes, Sir."

"And Toby..."

"Yes, Sir?"

"I meant what I said. No leaks. I've got direct link to you, and you're mine twenty-four, seven. You so much as blink without telling me, and I'm going to be all over you like white on rice."

"THEY'RE NOT HERE, Deacon. That's the long and the short of it," Jason explained over the Comlink. "And now there are fucking cops everywhere."

"Why?" Deacon asked.

"The DA got here first. I figure she noticed her girlfriend was missing and thought she might have come to visit her partner's wife in the hospital. We got out of there in a hurry when she showed up. No doubt they realize the Chans are gone, and that's why they're scouring the building."

"Damn it!" Deacon swore. "OK, never mind trying to find Chan for the time being. I'll run computer checks and send men in his direction if I get anything. In the mean time the bosses have a contingency plan. It should be easy to carry out, even for you, Jason. They are sending you a science crew now. They should meet up with you at the rendezvous in an hour. Don't screw this up, Jason."

The link was closed. Jason looked out the window of the car and sighed. He'd hated Kirk, but he sure as hell didn't want his fucking job, and now he had it like it or not.

"Sir," Roger said, "shouldn't we be heading for the rendezvous?"

Jason looked at the kid. He might be twenty-five, if that old. Jason started the car and started to roll. "Let me tell you something, kid. The agency isn't what they'd have you believe that it is. If you're smart, you'll get out while you still can. Change your name, take a job in a fucking gas station, but don't stay here."

"I believe that what you are saying is treasonous. I won't turn you in this time, but don't let it happen again," Roger said.

Jason laughed, although he was not amused. "Funny, I thought you died back there in the park."

AN APB HADN'T pulled in Spider's rental car. Carrie paced her office. Spider hadn't called, probably because she couldn't. Carrie fought her tears and her panic. She had to think, and think clearly. Had to keep her head. Being clever under pressure that was what she was best at, so she had to keep her wits about her.

It all made a kind of warped sense now. The So-what-if guys tried to have Tommy beaten up, but when that hadn't worked they went after Laura. Carrie had never been the target, and they had never intended to kill Laura. It was all part of their plan to wear Spider down, and it had worked. Tommy must have been a target, too, and so he had taken Laura and fled. But what the hell had happened to Spider? She had very deliberately left in the middle of the night, but where had she gone, and why had she left her behind? Carrie could have handled life on the lam, could have handled almost anything but being separated from Spider, not knowing whether she was dead or alive. She picked up her mug and smashed it into the wall, which did nothing but bring George and the two cops into the room at a dead run. She held out her hands and forced a smile.

"Nothing's wrong, just…"

"I'll send someone to clean it up," George said, walking out.

The cops followed him. A few seconds later a cleaning lady walked in with a mop and bucket and cleaned up the mess. George was with her. He waited till she had finished cleaning up the mess and closed the door behind her when she was gone.

"You want to tell me what the hell's going on?"

Carrie looked at him. Spider said not to trust anybody, but goddamn it she needed somebody.

"You'd better sit down." She spent the next thirty minutes filling him in on everything she knew or thought she knew about the SWTF, the Fry Guy, and their connection to Spider. "She's gone. Left with nothing, not even a toothbrush. I don't know whether she's running, captured or dead." She started to cry and made herself stop. "I feel so helpless! What does she want me to do?"

"It sounds to me like she wants you to live," George said gently. "I knew those SWTF guys were trouble the minute I saw them, but what the hell is their game?"

"I think…before the SWTF got involved, Spider had some theories about the Fry Guy. Crazy theories that she told Tommy, Tommy told Laura, and Laura told me confidentially. Spider had a theory that the Fry Guy didn't have a weapon…"

"Well, that's what the witnesses say, but…"

"Let me finish…" She told him the little bit that she actually knew. "…even before the SWTF showed up, Spider had stopped making any theories about the Fry Guy. I think it was because she knew who he was. In fact, I'm sure of it, and so was the SWTF."

"Then why didn't she turn him in?"

"Lots of reasons, not the least of which was that he was doing something she thought needed doing. He wasn't killing anyone who didn't deserve it."

"How did she find him?"

"Well, leave your skepticism outside for a minute and I'll tell you. You see, Spider's an empath. If one of their leads got her close to him she would have known it was him. There wouldn't have been any doubt in her mind."

"So the SWTF want this guy because he's a weapon?"

"Well, that's a logical conclusion, but I don't think that's all of it. See, I think the SWTF has been building people. Gene splicing. Genetic engineering. Cloning. Not that long ago these processes were just fiction; now they're all fact. I think the Fry Guy escaped from them and now they've got to get him back before he exposes what they've been doing. Since Spider knows who he is, either she's running from them to keep them from finding out, or they've got her, or..."

"Or?"

"Or she's dead." She sucked in her tears, and swallowed hard to keep her composure.

"What are you going to do, Carrie? You tell me what you want to do, and I'll help."

"I don't *know* what to do. I just have to think. There has to be something."

Just then her intercom screeched.

"Yes?" Carrie said.

"There is a man insisting that he see you, Sir. Says it's urgent. Having to do with Spider Webb."

"Let him in."

SPIDER WOKE UP in stages. Whatever they had given her had wiped her completely out. She had no idea what day—or even year it was. She opened her eyes, and the light stung them at first.

It was at that moment that she became aware of a gentle swaying motion. A look up told her that she was suspended from the ceiling, no doubt by the back of the straightjacket they had put her in. There was a huge mirror in one wall which let her know right away that she was under observation, as she watched her self swaying two and fro like some prize fish on a hook. The rest of the room was stark white.

"Well, this sucks," Spider mumbled. She was grateful at least that her head was uncovered. She reached out to feel around her and got that same blank feeling she had gotten before. The room must be made of the same thing the helmet had been made of.

"I see you've decided to wake up. That's splendid," a voice cooed.

"God? God is that you? Because I'd really like to get the fuck outtah here," Spider said looking at the ceiling.

The voice laughed. "I guess you could call me that, yes. So, you want to tell us who the Fry Guy is?"

"I told that, dumb ass. I'm the Fry Guy," she said.

The voice in the room laughed again. "Come on, now. We both know that's not true. Why don't you just tell us the truth? We don't want to have to hurt you."

Spider kicked her feet until she was spinning in circles. "Cool! Wow! Now I'm getting sick...I am the Fry Guy. You saw what I did in the park."

"We know you didn't do that, that you couldn't."

"And why the fuck couldn't I? Hell! I could do it right now if this room wasn't so fucked. Come in here you cringing yellow dick, and I'll *show* you what I can do."

A door opened in a wall and a short, fat guy in a lab coat walked in. He was without a doubt the biggest geek she had ever seen, and she laughed immediately upon seeing him.

"Do you find something amusing?"

"I was expecting Darth Vadar, and instead all I get is fucking Dilbert. I feel cheated. Go back and get me a real villain."

"We are not villains, Spider. We are not your enemies. In fact, we ask you to give us the Fry Guy to protect yourself as well as the whole program. I'm sure you've figured out that you're different by now."

She caught his eye and glared at him. "Let me down," she hissed.

He frowned a little. "No."

"Let me down," she ordered.

"You can do that till your nose bleeds. It won't do you any good. This room is equipped with a psychic disrupter. I'm afraid your tricks won't work in here. All you'll do is give yourself a nasty headache. Now tell us who he is; we have no wish to damage you."

"I am the fucking Fry Guy!" Spider insisted.

"No, you're not!" His face turned red with anger. "Why do you play me for a fool? The powers are sex-linked. Pyrokinesis, telekinesis, and telepathy in the males. Telekinesis, empathy, and mental push in the females. So, while your attempt to give yourself up in your friend's place is noble, it simply won't hold water."

"What a crappy day this is turning out to be," Spider mumbled. She glared at him then. "I'll never help you fucks. You killed my mother, you killed my brother, and now you expect me to help you. You tell me you're not my enemy? Hell, you are my *only* enemy. Don't try to win my trust. Either kill me or let me go right now and forget this whole thing, because I swear to God if you don't...I will get free, and when I do, I'll hunt you down like a dog and kill you."

"The deaths of your mother and brother were regrettable—a great loss to the program. We certainly don't want to lose you, but you must understand that absolute secrecy is imperative."

"You spineless, soulless fuck! I meant what I said. I'll never tell you one damn thing that might help you, and if you don't kill me, I will most assuredly kill you."

He pulled a syringe out of his pocket. "I can see that you're going to make us do this the hard way." He sighed. "Since we're going to find out anyway, couldn't you just tell us and make it easier on everyone involved?"

"I have no desire to make it easier for you, and better men than you have tried to crack me."

ROBBY PARKED AS soon as the blip stopped, got out of the car and walked around with the locator in his pocket. He'd walked for about three miles back and forth before he found the building. When he did he felt like an idiot. It was a huge, white thing. On the front, in five-foot letters it said SWTF. Underneath in smaller letters it said Special Weapons Task Force, and under that in still smaller letters it said Securing the Free World Through Service. Whatever the hell that meant.

Robby had kept his distance. The front doors, back doors, and side doors were all equally well guarded. But that would be a problem only if you found a way to get through the gate or over the wire and past the goddamned dogs.

"Well, they're surely to fuck securing something," Robby mumbled as he headed back. He needed some sleep. He thought better when he'd had some sleep. It wasn't nearly as long a walk back to the car as it had been walking around trying to pinpoint her location. It sure as hell hadn't been easy following and not losing her, especially going through towns. It had been a long drive all through the night, and the sun was starting to come up when he crawled behind the wheel.

The car was small, an old Hyundai, but it was the best he could do. After all, the five thousand dollars she's sent him had to pay for more than a car.

Robby drove to a park he'd seen on the way in, found a spot out of the way, laid his seat back, pulled his shades down, and went to sleep.

When he got up it was already dark, and looking at the clock he saw it was seven thirty. Quickly putting up the shades, he drove back towards the SWTF building, drove past it, then around it, and then he left the area. He sure to shit didn't want to get caught sneaking around. He drove around till he found a little diner where he went inside to get something to eat and ask a few questions.

The waitress brought him a menu and a glass of water. "Hello, I'm Helen. When you're ready to order just holler."

She was smiling at him. He liked that. So few people ever took the time to smile anymore. He smiled back.

"Thank you."

He took the menu, looked at it for a few minutes just to be polite—hell, he'd known what he was getting when he'd walked in the door—then he coughed a little.

Helen walked over, still smiling.

"So, what can we do for you?"

"Burger, fries and a coke," he said.

She nodded and started to go.

"Wa.. wait up."

She turned around.

"I'm sorry to bother you, but I'm new in town. I just passed a big building all guarded up, SWG or SWT…"

"The SWTF building?"

"Yeah, that one. Just what is that anyway? They got it guarded like Fort Knox."

She laughed and shrugged. "I've been asking that same question around here for four years. Ain't no one givin' me the same answer twice. Some sort of government agency. A lot of them come in here for lunch. Real spooky bunch if you ask me. Won't tell you anything that they do, all wear long lab coats and button up shirts with pocket protectors—except the guards. If you ask them what they do they all say the same thing. Research. Whatever the hell that means. There now, you know as much as I do, so you can't be a newcomer any more. Your food will be done in about twenty minutes. I'll bring you your coke." She took off.

She was pretty and nice. Robby smiled. He liked her. He'd never really had the time to date, hadn't even taken the time to look around. He was looking now. She was fine, nice face, pretty smile, great figure...and he was probably going to get his fool self killed trying to save some hard-headed police woman from a bunch of Nazi-like whackos. He wondered if a day was ever going to come when his life wouldn't suck. But at least Helen had given him something nice to think about.

"I SAID I have to pee!" she screamed, then laughed.

"You just went," he said.

Spider winked at the woman technician in the room. "And let me tell you, Honey, you sure know how to wipe a snatch. I have to go again!" she screamed at the man.

"You're not going till you answer the question," he said. He was exhausted. They'd been doing this for hours with several different drugs, and nothing was working.

"Tell that to my bladder," Spider laughed. Then she pissed down her leg.

"Oh, for God's sake!" the man screamed.

"Hey! I warned you!" She laughed hysterically. The drug that should have made her spill her guts was only making her high as a kite.

"Let her come down. We'll try something else."

HER HEAD WAS pounding, and her butt didn't feel that great, either, after passing the beacon. Luckily she had flushed it, and no one was the wiser.

The fucking drugs had left the taste of fermenting onions in her mouth. She felt like six miles of rough, rocky road.

The scientist walked in. This time he had one of the So-what-if guys with him. He had a weapon in his hand that she was only too familiar with.

"So, we've graduated to torture," Spider said dully. She noticed her voice was hoarse. "You fucking creeps. Don't you get it? You can kill me, but you can't break me."

"Why are you making me do this?" the short fat man screamed. "I don't want to hurt you. It gives me no pleasure. Give me this man, and I promise you he will not be hurt, either"

"Unless of course he doesn't do what you tell him." Spider laughed. She licked at her swollen lips. "Then you'll shoot him full of drugs, hang him from the ceiling, and torture him. I can live with my own pain before I could deal with his. That's what makes me different from you. I'm not making you do shit. Whatever you do to me you do of your own free will. I don't see you hanging from a straightjacket being interrogated. On the other hand, whatever I wind up doing will undoubtedly be your fault, because you could have left me alone, and you chose not to."

The man hit her with the cattle prod. After a while she lost track of how many times. Finally she looked down at the little man with glaring hatred. "I'm not going to scream out his name. I'm not going to scream out at all. You can fry me to a crisp with that fucking thing." She looked at the SWTF man who was dishing out the punishment and said directly to him. "I'm going to take that thing and shove it up your ass. Do you hear me?"

The fat guy nodded his head indicating to the other man that he should shock her again. The SWTF guy moved a little closer than he had been before. It was a big mistake. Spider jerked quickly. Her foot landed with a resounding *thud* in the side of the man's head, and he fell to the floor convulsing.

Spider laughed maniacally. "You don't even know who you're fucking with, but then again maybe you do. In which case, you shouldn't be screwing with me!"

The scientist knelt beside the now still man on the floor. He checked him, then screamed, "Medic! Medic!" He glared at Spider. "I think you killed him."

"Let's see…I'm hanging from the ceiling and the bastard was hitting me over and over again with a fucking cattle prod…no, I don't feel one damn bit of remorse."

The medics rushed in, put the man on a stretcher and carried him away.

The scientist looked at Spider and screamed at the top of his lungs. "Just tell me!"

"Just...No!"

JASON DIDN'T LIKE this. The whole thing stank. He slipped on his gas mask and lobbed the canister into the door he had just picked the lock on. He closed the door and waited.

"10,9,8,7,6,5,4,3,2,1."

He and Roger went in.

The gas was still thick, but it would dissipate. By morning there would be no noticeable residue. Jason picked up the canister and pocketed it as he made his way upstairs. He looked in on the parents; they hadn't woken up, and now they wouldn't for at least three hours. He found the boy in his bed and lifted him into his arms.

He couldn't imagine how he would feel if he woke up and found his son missing. How Josh would feel waking up in some strange place, much less where this boy was going.

Jason started to carry the boy on out, but then handed him to Roger. Downstairs and out of the house the lab coats took the boy and shoved him into the van.

Jason and Roger headed for their car. Their work was over here. They'd be following the van back to headquarters as escort. Jason looked over at Roger who looked visibly shaken.

"So, how do you feel about your new job now?"

CHAPTER EIGHTEEN

*"Cast thy bread upon the waters: for thou shalt
find it after many days."* Ecclesiastes 11:1

CARRIE LAY IN her empty bed, praying that the phone would
ring and it would be Spider. She rolled over and looked at the clock.
It was two in the morning. She couldn't sleep and everything sucked.
They still hadn't found Spider's car or any trace of her. To make
matters worse, the SWTF had seen fit to visit her that afternoon.

"WHAT THE HELL do you want?" she'd asked him.

"Oh we've got what we want, DA Long. Now we just want
to make sure that it stays in good health. I think that's in both of
our interests."

"What is that supposed to mean, Mr…"

"Deacon, the name is Deacon, and I thought that was really
pretty plain."

"You're saying you have Spider," Carrie said. "This is insane! I don't
know what you lunatics are up to, but I can, by God, guarantee…"

He was clicking his tongue then. "Oh, come now, all this name
calling doesn't suit you. As for threats…well, we both know how
hollow those are since I hold all the cards."

Carrie sighed. The bastard was right. He had everything. He
knew what the hell was going on, and she didn't have any idea, and
he had Spider.

"That's better. Now, if you ever want to see the object in
question…"

"Is there any chance of that?" Carrie asked with a lump in
her throat. Mad at herself for showing the weakness that she
knew he was counting on. "Because if there isn't, why am I even
talking to you?"

"There's a very real chance if you play your cards right."

"And how do I do that? After all, as you just pointed out I have
no cards."

"You quit looking for Spider Webb. If anyone asks, she's gone
to visit some old army buddies."

Carrie nodded silently then looked up at him. "Why are you ruining our lives?"

The man's manner changed then, and he looked almost sorry. "Because a handful of stupid people think they have the right to make decisions for the whole world, and the rest of us are powerless to stop them. It's easier if you learn not to give a damn, ma'am." With that he got up and left.

No guarantees, but she called off the search. That didn't mean she was going to quit looking, it just meant she wasn't going to be so obvious about it.

SHE ROLLED OVER again. She could still smell Spider on the blankets and pillows. She hit the bed with her fist.

"Spider! Where the hell are you!" She buried her face in Spider's pillow and cried till she fell asleep.

She woke with a start before the alarm had gone off. The light was just creeping into the room, and she didn't have to piss. She knew some noise had woke her up. She rolled over, sat up, opened the drawer on the bedside table, and took her gun out. She heard a car backing out of the driveway, pulled the gun from its holster and cocked it before running to the window. She could just make out the car as it left the driveway, but in the dim light couldn't have made out the make or the model. She did know it wasn't Spider's rental, it had been white, and this car was a dark color maybe even black.

She grabbed her comlink and strapped it on her wrist then slowly and carefully left her room, checking all the upstairs rooms first before going downstairs to do the same thing. She found a Metallica CD sitting on the rug just inside the front door. Someone had no doubt pushed it through the mail slot. She walked over and cautiously picked it up. She removed the tape and slowly lifted the lid, half expecting to find a smashed flat body part. Inside was a CD marked with the words, "Dammit Tommy I told you not to open this," in Spider's handwriting.

Carrie was pretty sure that Spider wouldn't want her to see it, either.

THE ROAD WAS worse than he remembered it. Of course it had had twenty years to deteriorate, too. Still, it was a rental car he never planned to return, and he didn't really care what happened to it. He finally reached a part of the road bad enough that he had to stop. He pulled off the road and into the brush as far as he dared and parked. Laura must have been really wiped out from her injury. They had put her seat back and even the rough ride hadn't woken her up.

He found the sleeping bags and covered himself and Laura, letting her keep both pillows. It would get cold tonight. He looked out the window at the stars. It was clear; it was beautiful.

Whatever else, he and Laura would be safe now.

He wished he could be sure where Spider was.

He hoped he'd done the right thing having Bud take the disk to Carrie instead of having him put the information on the web as Spider had instructed. He was working under the assumption that Spider was still alive, and that she could make it through whatever-the-hell was happening. If she did, and everything she had told him was true, she'd be condemned anyway if what was on that CD got out. He hoped that Carrie would know what to do with the information on that disk.

He wished he had any idea at all what was going on back in Shea city, what, if anything, had happened to Spider.

That was when he realized just how cut off he was. No phone, no comlink. They had radio, but that wouldn't tell him what was happening with Spider. He'd have to get out, go in somewhere and find out. But that would have to wait till he had hidden Laura safely away, until after things had cooled down a little.

He crunched down into the sleeping bag and sighed. It was warm and he was tired. He could worry about the rest of the world tomorrow; tonight he needed to sleep.

HER LITTLE 'ESCAPADE' as they called it had gotten her sedated again. When she woke up this time the thing was back on her head, she was chained by the ankles to something she couldn't see, and her hands were cuffed behind her back. Her shoulders were starting to hurt from being in the same position for so long, so she sat up with no small effort and pretended not to notice the thing on her head.

"I'm hungry! Do you have it in your heads to starve me?" she asked.

Nothing. Not a murmur. She knew what they were doing now. Sensory deprivation.

She had no idea how many hours passed without contact. No one spoke to her. No matter how many times she told them she knew what they were doing they didn't stop doing it.

Finally the creep asked. "Would you like the helmet off?"

"No. Don't care," Spider said and rocked back and forth humming a tune.

"Wouldn't you like to see, too eat, to be a part of the world around you?"

She laughed then. "Ah! But I've never really been part of the world around me, have I? If you're asking me If I want to come out and play, the answer is no."

"Goddamn it!" he screamed. "Why are you making this so hard?"

"Why are you being such a weenie? The fucking Iraqis tortured me for five weeks and you're getting tired after a couple of days. At this rate it looks like you'll crack before I do."

She heard him walking away. The silent treatment again. She lay down and went to sleep.

When she woke up again someone was taking the helmet off her head. She tried to head butt the person taking the helmet off and got tazed for her troubles.

"Ouch! That smarted."

With the helmet off her head she looked around. Everyone was way out of reach. It took a second for her eyes to adjust, although it was hard to say if it was because of the sleep, the deprivation helmet, the tazing, or all the fucking drugs. Everyone was leaving the room. It made her wonder if she was free. She jumped up, started to run after them, came to the end of her tether, and fell with a clatter of chains to the floor. She rolled onto her back and looked at the ceiling.

"Now that was fucking stupid."

She heard someone crying. She turned and saw the back of what she assumed from the size and the haircut was a small boy.

"Ah, come on…What are you twisted fucks up to now!" Spider swore, getting to her feet.

"Turn around, Mark, she won't hurt you," the man said from the control booth.

"Don't turn around; it's a trick," Spider said. "They aren't your friends."

"I know that!" the boy screamed back. "Don't you think I know that?"

"Do what we tell you, boy," the man ordered.

"This shit isn't going to work," Spider started. "You twisted bastards aren't…" The boy turned around to face her, and she jumped back and screamed at the men behind the mirror. "That isn't Scott! Do you think I'm an idiot? My brother was a grown man when he died. You should know that—you killed him."

The man laughed. "You're right, this boy isn't your brother, Spider. The boy is your son."

SPIDER WALKED AS close to the boy as the eight-foot chains on her ankles would let her. She looked at him, and as she did the dreams and the memories flooded back in on her.

The doctors and the lab coats, all that poking and prodding. It all made sense now. She fell to her knees and stared at the boy. She had no doubt that what they said was true; she could almost feel her blood coursing through him.

"All these years, the nightmares…You bastards were harvesting the eggs from my body," she hissed.

The head scientist walked in then. "So, you believe me, then."

"Whether what you are saying is true or not, I have no bond to this boy. I don't know him, and he doesn't know me. If you mean to torture him to death to get me to talk, then kill the boy and have it over with."

The boy cried loudly and made a run for the open door, where one of the SWTF guys grabbed him.

"The boy means nothing to me." Spider stared past the fat fuck into the hallway behind the door. She could feel the other guy standing in the doorway. He was scared, scared to be so close to the experiment, and he hated the fat guy. A gentle push— just add to the hatred that was already there. She'd never tried it without speaking except up close, but when the guy turned an expressionless face to her she knew she'd broken through. She wasn't going to try anything big just now, but maybe she could play this card later.

"That's why we're going to allow you some time alone together. To get to know each other," he said.

"It won't work," Spider said. "I'm not too overly sentimental when it comes to kids—mine or anyone else's. Besides, if you've made this one, you've made a dozen just like him."

"The children of the program are so funny." The scientist picked the boy's chin up and looked into his face as the security guard tried to hold the squirming boy still. The boy jerked his head away. "They are transplanted into a suitable candidate in the embryo state. No one—not the children—not the surrogate mother and father—nor anyone else should be able to figure out that they are not with their proper parents. Yet all of the children of the program know that they are not with their true parents. Isn't that right, Mark?"

"You go to hell!" the boy cursed.

"When you look at this woman, you can tell that she's your real mother, can't you?"

"Leave me alone!" Mark screamed.

"Why don't you leave the boy alone?" Spider said.

"Do you want to tell us who the Fry Guy is?"

"I've told you a million times. I don't know who the Fry Guy is."

"Why do you insult my intelligence!" he yelled.

Spider screamed back. "Because it would be wrong to insult your face!"

Mark started to laugh. So did Spider. The scientist's face got redder, and he stomped out of the room. The SWTF man threw the boy back in and stomped out after the scientist.

Spider jumped to her feet and managed to catch the boy with her body before he could make contact with the floor. Now Spider would have sworn she didn't have a maternal bone in her body, but as the boy's flesh met hers, there was a knowing and a oneness that she had never felt with anyone before. She knew beyond a shadow of a doubt that the boy was, in fact, her son.

She waited for him to steady himself, and then moved quickly away from him.

Mark turned around and looked at her.

She looked away. The last thing she wanted them to know was that she had any feelings at all for him.

"Are you...are they telling the truth?" he asked.

"About me being your biological mother?" Spider asked sitting down. Her head was spinning, and she felt like she was going to vomit.

"Are you?" he asked.

"I think so. Yes," Spider said. "We're an experiment." She looked up at the window. "You, me, and a whole lot of other poor fucks out there. They believe they own us; that we belong to them, and that therefore they can do whatever they like to us."

Spider looked up at the window and then down at the floor. She concentrated, and then slowly and carefully she started to move her cuffed hands up her back.

Mark sat down, close to her. "Why?"

"Quiet, boy, you'll break my concentration," Spider said quietly.

"WHAT THE HELL is she doing?" Don asked Fritz.

Fritz couldn't be bothered to answer; he was too busy watching.

Spider Webb walked her hands up her back and then over her head till her hands were in front of her. Then she slowly manipulated one hand out of the cuffs and started on the other.

"We have to stop her!" Don said. "She'll be loose!"

"I don't think she can get her feet loose," Fritz said. "She is amazing. Is she not amazing?"

Spider pulled the other hand free, then slung the cuffs into the window, and answered the boy's question by screaming at the two-way glass.

"Because they got nothing better to do with the taxpayers' money! Trying to make some kind of absolute soldier. Who knows how they did it or why? I only know that the stupid fucks seem to think it's perfectly okay to screw with people's bodies and their lives." She jumped to her feet and glared hard at the glass. "You kill people, and I'll kill you! Do you hear me? *I'LL KILL YOU!*"

"My God!" Don said, stunned. "Look at this reading!"

Fritz looked over his shoulder at the dials. The level of psychic activity that had just erupted in that room was… "None of our test subjects to date have been able to break a three. She just broke a six, and her nose isn't bleeding."

"I'm not sure the room can contain her, Fritz," Don said. "The room is only made to contain up to an eight. If she can do a six without trying, who's to say she couldn't do eight or more? The barrier won't hold."

"We can't afford to lose her as a breeder," Francis said. "The children of her first batch test higher than all the others from that same year."

"Mark is from her…?"

"He's from the third batch, Fritz. His Father was William Brackstone. Mark has great potential; I would hate to lose him…"

"We won't lose him, Francis, and we won't lose her. If we get the Fry Guy…Imagine the boon to the project if we crossed him with her!" Fritz said.

"We'd be able to cut our projected outcome time in half. In one generation we could be looking at the future," Don said excitedly.

"I want us to start testing the boy tomorrow," Fritz said. "If he has no potential for the program, then he's expendable."

He watched through the window as the woman moved purposely away from the boy. When the boy tried to follow her she yelled at him to stay away from her. That she wanted nothing to do with him.

"Will she ever give us the Fry Guy?" Don asked Fritz.

"She'll crack. Sooner or later they all do."

A MOTHER AND father woke up in Shea City to every parent's worse nightmare. Their son was missing.

Cops and FBI swarmed their house and asked questions. The neighbors fanned out, putting up flyers. The police put up roadblocks. Rivers were checked and psychics by the dozens poured in to offer their services, He was…'by a river,' 'in a dark box,' 'afraid,' 'not afraid.'

So many questions from so many people. Had they seen anyone hanging around? Had Mark been unhappy? Do they think he ran away from home? Then came the lie detector tests.

"What is your name, Sir?"

"Jared Parker."

"Mr. Parker, did you ever hit your son?"

"I spanked him a couple of times, but hit him?"

"Yes or no, Sir."

"No." He tried to fight his anger. All he cared about was finding his son, and if this was what he needed to do to get the cops up off their asses, this was what he was going to do. But it was hard.

"Did your wife ever hit your son?"

"No."

"Did you take your son anywhere and leave him?"

That question because of all the parents who had run scams over the years. Collecting huge amounts of money to look for children that they had hidden someplace.

"No."

"Did you kill your son, Mr. Parker?"

"Oh my God!" Jared cried out. "Is my son dead? Did you find his body? Is that what this is all about?"

"Yes or no, Sir."

"No! For God's sake, would someone tell me what's going on?"

A red-headed woman walked into the room. "What the hell's wrong with you?" she yelled at the woman who'd been running the test. She looked at the results of his test and then at Jared.

"Sir, no one has found a body. We have no reason to believe that your son isn't just fine. Get him off that thing! I want to talk to him in my office ASAP. And please don't do the same thing to the mother."

CARRIE PACED HER office.

"Well?" Justin Denisten asked. He had been sitting in DA Long's office for almost ten minutes now watching her pace. While he didn't mind the view at all, he had things to do.

"He should be here shortly," Carrie said. "Please, I need you to be patient."

Jared Parker walked into the office.

"Good! You're here. Close the door and sit down please." She cleared her throat before she continued. She seemed to be looking for some sort of inspiration. When she finally spoke again, it was obvious that she hadn't found any. "Except for George, who I have asked to be here as a witness, we have all experienced the fall-out from a giant government conspiracy being fronted by a department called the Special Weapons Task Force, or the SWTF…"

"That's it! I'm out of here," Justin said, standing up.

"Agent Denisten, wouldn't you like to know why your partner Harry Sullivan was killed?"

"Harry got killed because he went snooping around those freaking So-what-if spooks. If we go snooping around we'll be just as dead."

"This room has been run over with every modern bug detection device known to mankind, on top of that I have had a sonic disruptor put in. So even if we happened to miss a bug— we found three and a phone tap—there is no way a clean signal can leave this room. All they'd get is static. So we can talk freely," Carrie assured him.

"You don't know these maggots, Sir. They have ways…they kill people."

"Excuse me," Jared was at the end of his tether. "I have a nine-year-old boy missing. I don't see what any of this could have to do with my problem."

"If Mr. Denisten will sit down, I'll tell you," Carrie said. She sat down and waited for him.

Denisten sat down reluctantly.

Carrie flipped on her monitor. "Now, if you can all just bear with me, I assure you that this concerns every one of us. My partner, Detective First Class Spider Webb came up missing the night before last. That same evening, her partner Tommy Chan and his wife Laura went into hiding. As you know, Denisten, Tommy and Spider had been working on the Fry Guy cases."

He nodded.

"Your late partner, Harry Sullivan, gave Spider Webb some information on the SWTF and a disk with a list on it. He knew more than he should have, and he gave it to the last person that they wanted to know, so they killed him." She punched a button on her keyboard, and the list appeared on the twenty-four inch monitor built into her wall.

"What the hell is it?" Denisten said looking away, as if not seeing might somehow protect him.

"It's a family tree of sorts. You see, the government has been secretly experimenting on people."

"Come on!" Denisten screamed. "Something like that…there would be a leak!"

"There is a leak, right here, right now. And the Fry guy, he's the leak. I had my doubts, too. The notes Spider left on the end of this disk are kind of cryptic. Theories, lots of which contradict each other. Obviously she had been trying to figure this all out for quite some time…"

"What does any of this have to do with my son?" James nearly screamed.

"That's when all of the pieces came together," Carrie said. "When I saw a picture of your son on the TV today. See? This is a picture of my partner, Spider Webb." She punched a few buttons, and the view on the monitor changed. "Notice the size of her hands, Mr. Parker…Now here's a picture of your son…And here is a picture of Spider's dead brother, Scott, as a boy…."

"Christ on a crutch!" Denisten said. "But why? Why make people?"

"These aren't normal people. Spider certainly isn't, you only have to look at her service record to know that. She's empathic, and she has this kind of mental manipulation where she can get people to do things they wouldn't otherwise do. Who knows what else she can do?"

"What does become clear as you read what Spider has written is that the Fry Guy doesn't have a weapon, he *is* a weapon."

"What are you saying about my son?" Jared asked. "My wife was pregnant; I saw him born. He *is* my son. I can't explain the uncanny resemblance, but Mark *is my son.*"

"If you'll look at the list you'll see that all of the women "implanted" had a certain blood chemistry. A chemistry conducive to carrying one of these babies. With the global internet, any government agency with a high enough security clearance can get their hands on any personal information they want. I imagine they find the right women, wait for them to come in for a pap smear—actually, any gynecological exam would do, as long as they aren't on the pill. Hell, you don't ever know what they're doing down there. You don't want to know; you just want it to be over with. It would be almost too easy to implant a fetus in an unsuspecting woman. Since the doctor is obviously already in cahoots, he's not going to say anything when the child has an alien blood chemistry."

"Alien!" George screeched.

"Oh, yes," Carrie punched up a picture of DNA. "This is normal DNA. Human DNA." She punched another set of DNA into the picture and over lapped it with the first one, showing clearly that they were not the same. This is the DNA coded for these children." She got rid of the human DNA. "Spider isn't afraid of very many things, but she's afraid to go to the doctor. Turns out that every doctor who ever treats her meets with some unfortunate accident. Three of them wound up dead, and the last one wound up with his leg broken. I talked to him. He was reluctant, but he gave me this. This is Spider Webb's DNA. As you can see, it is a prefect match. I don't know exactly how, but these people are all hybrids—half human, half some alien species not of this world."

"Where's my son?" Jared asked.

"Wherever Spider Webb is. See, for whatever reason, the Fry Guy is not part of their program. He's slipped away from them, and he's out of control. At least he's beyond their control. Spider is the only person who knows who he is, and she's not going to just give him up. That's the reason Tommy and Laura left. So that they couldn't be used to make her talk. Taking me would be too risky."

"So what are you saying?" Jared asked in a panic.

"I don't think it's a coincidence that your son is missing, Mr. Parker. They needed leverage. Tommy and Laura have disappeared, I'm off limits, and she's just not close to anyone else. I think they are going to use your son to make Spider talk."

"You're saying he's not my son—that he's some kind of alien," Jared said. "He's not an alien. He's a little boy. My little boy."

Carrie ignored his outburst. "The SWTF has got to be stopped."

"Agreed. But how?" Denisten asked. "These assholes have a sixth level clearance. That means there's a good chance that the fucking President of the United States knows exactly what's going on and isn't putting a stop to it. Wherever we go we're going to hit a stone wall. They won't kidnap you and take you away to be tortured because a missing DA causes big problems, but if you think they absolutely positively will not kill you because you hold a public office, then you are dead wrong, sister. If you give them too much grief they are going to decide that you are a bigger headache alive than you would be dead. You've had a lot of death threats, and that opens a big window of opportunity if they decide to dive through it. After all, no one's close to finding out who shot your legal assistant, are they?"

"Because the SWTF leaned on me and I called off the hunt. Just like I didn't go to the authorities about Spider's abduction, just like Mr. and Mrs. Parker are going to miraculously find that their son ran away and is staying with his grandmother in south Florida..."

"You're crazy if you think I'm going to quit looking for my son..."

"I know where your son and my partner are. They are in the SWTF complex in Madrid, Tennessee."

"Then let's go get him!" Jared said.

"It ain't that easy," Denisten told him. "Place is a fortress. Hand imprint coding on all the doors. Dogs, six-foot electric fence, machine-gun armed guards at all the entrances. I don't think you realize, Mr. Parker, what DA Long has been saying. You can't just walk up to the door and say, 'Give me my son.' The way they see it, Detective

Webb and your son are *their* property. They made 'em, so they own 'em. These people tortured my partner and killed him because he had part of the information that we have now all seen. What do you think they would do if you walked to their front door and told them you're on to them and you want your half-breed alien child back?"

"You're suggesting I do nothing? What do I tell my wife?"

"I'm suggesting that you do what I told you to do," Carrie said. "I'm sure the SWTF would be only too glad to make sure that your story holds water. As for your wife, I suggest you tell her that her son is safe as long as she keeps her mouth shut. Your boy is part of their program, and they're not going to hurt him unless you push their hand."

"Don't tell anyone what you just heard," Denisten said. "Knowing this shit could get you killed. Get us all killed."

Jared nodded. It was all so insane that it had to be true. "Can I go now?"

"Yeah," Carrie said. She looked drained. "Please. For all of our sakes. Don't tell anyone anything. They may have your whole house bugged, your phones tapped."

Jared nodded and stood up. "Am I ever going to see my son again? I don't care what he is. I've raised him, he's mine, and my family won't be whole till he's back with us."

"If we are successful, you should get your son back. But I can't make any promises, Mr. Parker. Just remember that my partner is with him...it's in my best interest to do everything in my power to get them back."

He nodded and left, head down.

Denisten looked at her. "OK. So what do you want from me?"

"For someone who didn't want anything to do with this, you certainly seem eager now."

"Yeah, well, I can't get much deader than I all ready am...so?"

"Harry found this information in one of the FBI computers, which means that the FBI knows exactly what the SWTF is doing. It also means that somewhere there is more data. I want you to see if you can't match these dates, this data, with births. Let's see if we can't find their 'people'."

"And do what exactly?"

"I don't know. Maybe activate their army against them."

CHAPTER NINETEEN

"He who digs a pit shall fall into it; and whoever
breaks through a hedge, a snake shall bite him."
Ecclesiastes 10:8

TOMMY THREW SOME wood into the fire and sat down in a fold-ing lawn chair. He looked over at Laura, sleeping soundly on the blow-up mattress. He looked around and smiled. They were well set up here.

The camp had grown up badly, and he had walked past it twice before he finally found it. He'd had to half carry Laura most of the way, and with full pack, even in the kind of shape he was in, it hadn't been a picnic.

When they'd come up here every year when he was a kid, his family had kept the cabins up, fixing doors, windows, and roofs so that they could enjoy them from year to year. His uncles and father had kept the brush cleared out and the paths marked. No one had done that in years, and even the best cabin had obvious roof dam-age. He'd brought a hammer, nails and a tarp with him on that first trip in anticipation of damage.

Of course he'd had to make a ladder from pieces of trees he found lying around. He'd nailed the tarp along the edges, carefully covering the whole roof.

The cabins were small—just twelve by sixteen. He broke up a bunch of wood, brought it in, and started pumping up the bed which was the only thing he had brought with him besides the tools, tarps, bedding and food. Laura had been quiet, sitting and watching him as he worked. The trip and the hike had been rough on her.

Laura lay down on the bed as soon as he got it pumped up, apolo-gizing for not being more help. She went to sleep almost immediately.

The door had a huge gapping hole in it, and the window was missing two panes of glass. Even though he'd kept the fire blazing and they had more than enough bedding, the first night they had still slept cold.

The next morning he dressed Laura's wound, made them some breakfast and went back to get the rest of the stuff from the car. By the second trip, he decided that he had definitely over bought.

That afternoon, using wood and panes salvaged from the other cabins, he fixed the window and the door.

Laura used the camp broom, and despite his protests, swept the cabin out using only her good arm.

Tommy turned the Coleman lantern off. They needed to conserve the fuel, and he could see just fine by the firelight.

He'd bought a shit load of oatmeal, raisins, coffee, dried beans, vitamins and salt, but everything else was in short supply.

The camp was on a creek, so they wouldn't want for water. He had been surprised at all the wonderful fold-up and inflatable camping gear you could get. He'd bought a hang-up plastic bag (a solar shower) an inflatable shower stall, an inflatable sink, an inflatable bed, fold-up cookware, chairs, shovel, broom, etc.

He also bought way too much ammo for his gun, a wrist rocket slingshot, a small crossbow and twenty bolts.

He knew everything in these woods that was edible, and he could live here for the rest of his life if he had to. The bastards could try, but they couldn't out wait Tommy Chan.

The only thing that was really bothering him was that he didn't know what was happening with Spider. He leaned back in his chair and looked into the fire. He couldn't decide whether he wished Spider had told him more, or whether he wished she had told him less. The things he was imagining didn't leave Spider in very good shape.

Laura was still very tired, but then you really couldn't expect her to be doing flips. After all, she was diabetic and recovering from a gunshot wound. Still, it looked better today than it had the day before, so it was healing. Laura didn't complain, but he could tell she was scared and worried. She didn't understand why they were on the run. She was hurt, and she really wanted familiar surroundings and people. She kept talking about how worried her parents must be.

Tommy looked at the bare concrete floor. He remembered doing pushups on that same floor till his arms ached. These woods in which his cousins had played had been a survival course for him. The creek they had kicked, splashed, and had water fights in had meant hours of swimming back and forth till his stomach cramped for him. Still he had loved it here. Perhaps because it was a change of scenery, or because the whole family was together, or maybe it was just the overall feeling of peace you got from being in the woods far away from the mechanized world.

He felt at peace here now and felt guilty about it. Laura was upset, Spider was certainly not enjoying whatever-the-hell was happening to her, and he was happy because he was in the woods with his wife, camping with a bunch of new gear he was never going to pay for.

THERE WAS NO rhyme or reason to the way they turned the lights off and on, and Spider had no idea how many days she'd been there, but they hadn't let her shower. It was dark, and as always the boy was making his way towards her. No matter how many times she shoved him away, he kept creeping closer. This night, or day, or whatever it was, was no different. The next thing she knew the boy was lying against her. She started to shove him away and then had a brainstorm. She couldn't talk to him because they would hear anything that was said. They couldn't contact each other telepathically because of the psychic disrupter, but…

Her back was to the window, the camera would only catch the boy's front. She started to trace out letters on his back slowly.

~Can you read this? Move your arm if the answer is yes.~

For a minute his arm was still, but then it moved. *You bastards! I found a way around your shit again.*

Spider smiled.

~Move your head for no, your arm for yes.~

He moved his arm again.

~Good boy! Did you burn anything for them?~

He moved his head.

~Good! Don't. Don't let them know that you have power. We can get out of here if we use our heads.~

He turned around then and wrote on her stomach. *I thought you didn't like me.*

Spider moved her head and wrote on his stomach. ~I can't let them know.~

I'm scared.

~They should be afraid of us.~

ROBBY DIDN'T MIND sleeping in the car. Of course, he'd spent weeks making sure that the car was as comfortable as most bedrooms. As for bathing in the sink in the men's room, with his bath box, it wasn't that much harder than jumping into the shower at home. He had learned a long time ago, and had pounded it into his siblings' heads that if a person really wanted to be clean, then they could get clean. It didn't take that much time or that much money. All it took was a little effort.

What Robby didn't like was not working; it made his days long and boring. He still had no clue how to get Spider Webb out, but he knew that whatever he was going to do, he was going to have to do it soon.

Every noon he had lunch down at the diner. He told himself it was because he was checking out the SWTF staff, but the truth was he spent more time checking Helen out.

He knew from what he was picking up from some of the lab coats that Spider was in the building in a highly secured section, and that she had a small boy with her. Other than that, most of the bastards were so dark you didn't want to stay in their heads long. Not if you couldn't kill them immediately afterwards.

It was odd; most of the security guys were OK. Some were a little gray, but most of them weren't black. The scientists, though, they were the bad fuckers. Twisted shits, every single one. Then there were the SWTF guys. They didn't come in very often, but when they did, they made Robby's blood run cold, and it was all he could do to keep from frying them. The grimy scientist guys rationalized that what they did was for the greater good—they were insane. But the So-what-if guys just liked the power they wielded and causing pain.

He went to the diner for lunch, and there was a Help Wanted sign on the door. It was his lucky day. Now no one would question his being there to watch either the So-what-if guys or Helen.

He walked straight up to Helen. "Anyone take the job yet?"

"You don't want it," Helen whispered. "It's minimum wage, and it's washing the dishes."

Robby shrugged. "I don't mind doing dishes."

"Then go talk to Rudy; he's in the kitchen. But don't say I didn't warn you."

Rudy hired him on the spot. Then he proceeded to tell him everything that was wrong with the dishwasher—which was basically everything. Robby worked through the lunch rush with it busted, and then brought his tools in and started working on it. By the time the evening crowd hit, the washer was fixed and the job was easy. At least it was easy for Robby, especially when he got to spend so much time looking at and talking to Helen.

He was caught up with his work and helping Helen with orders for the evening crowd when *he* walked in. He was a So-what-if guy—one of the ones that wore black—and when Robby looked at him he saw black, but the black was engulfing, surrounding the light. This was something that he had never seen before. This man was trapped—trapped as surely as Spider Webb was trapped. He wanted out, wanted redemption, and saw no way to achieve it. He wanted another chance, or at least a chance to make things right. He hated doing the things they made him do, and the thing that weighed heaviest on his mind at this time was that he was the one who had stolen the boy from his parents. Robby brought him a menu and their eyes met.

"What the hell are you looking at?" he asked Robby, jerking the menu from his hand.

Robby smiled back at him. "A very troubled man."

The man looked down at Robby's hands then, and Robby let him look.

"Just call the waitress when you're ready to order," Robby said and walked quickly away, sticking his hands into his pockets. That man might be able to help him, but he was going to have to be more careful. His hands would be a dead give away to any SWTF personnel who worked on 'the project' as they all called it.

THE MAN'S NAME was Fritz, and Mark hated him. He was a bad, bad, man, with darkness all around him.

Every day they came and got him. They put the deprivation helmet on him, and then they carried him to this room. They took the helmet off, there was a bale of hay there, and over and over again they told him to burn it up. Over and over again he told them he couldn't. He could see them standing behind the glass, and he knew what he'd really like to burn up. He wasn't sure he could burn the hay even if he wanted to. After all, *it* hadn't hurt anybody, and he wasn't mad at it.

"All you have to do is try. Focus your mind," Fritz said.

"I am!" Mark screamed.

Fritz made a screaming, irritated noise then, a noise that Mark had only ever heard coming out of Fritz's mouth.

"Did she tell you not to do it?" Fritz asked.

"Who?" Mark asked.

"Damn it boy, you know who! The woman."

"Which woman?" Mark asked playing dumb; something he knew annoyed the hell out of Fritz.

He made the noise again. "Spider Webb. Your mother."

"You know everything she says to me," Mark said. "You listen to everything. She doesn't even like me."

"We know you're finding some way to communicate. How are you doing it?"

"I don't know what you're talking about. She hates me." He started to cry then. It wasn't hard to whip up tears when you really were sad and scared shitless. "I want to go home! I want to go home!"

"Worthless boy!" Fritz screamed. "Don't you realize that if you can't make fire you are of no use to us?"

"I want to go home! I want my mom!"

Don looked at the woman carefully but didn't dare get too close. He turned the high-powered hose on again. Fritz said it would dredge up nightmares and past memories that might help break her. Fritz said to knock her down every time she stood up. It didn't seem to be breaking her, though; all it really seemed to be doing was pissing her off real bad.

"You fucking bastard! If I ever get my hands on you!"

He hit her in the face and knocked her down.

Spider hit the floor hard, and they laughed—they all laughed. Then the interpreter asked her again in his broken English.

"American pig! Where is your unit?"

"Up your butt, you filthy bastard!" she yelled. She had just stumbled to her feet and the hose knocked her down again. She hit her head and the world spun.

One of the guards took her by the hair of the head and banged her head into the dirt till there was so much mud up her nose she couldn't breathe. She blew hard, blowing the dirt plugs from her nose, and then she grabbed the filthy bastard by the head and twisted hard and fast. He dropped like a rock. They screamed out, and then there were boots, and water, and darkness.

Spider pulled herself up and ran to the center of the room where the chain that held her was imbedded in the concrete floor. She grabbed it with both hands and started yanking screaming, "I'll kill you! You fucking rag headed bastard! I'll kill you!"

Don watched in terror as the chain started to give. He turned the hose off, there was a snapping sound, and she was free and running at him. Don headed for the doors, but no one was opening them.

"Jesus, God! Let me outtah here! Goddamn! Open the door!" He felt her hands grab the back of his shirt. "Oh dear God!"

The door opened and a crew of armed So-what-if guys ran into the room, but Don was already dead, his head smashed like a melon on the wall of the room.

The door closed quickly behind the crew.

Spider slammed her palm into the nose of one man, driving it up into his brain. As she was grabbing his gun, three darts struck her at once.

Spider looked at them. "Oh fuck!" The gun rattled from her hands, and she fell to the floor.

FRITZ LOOKED AT the tapes over and over again. "Amazing! Her strength is far greater than that of other test subjects. Her sense of balance, focal points—it really is amazing! I'd seen her looking at the chain before, but had no idea that she had been slowly weakening one of the links. Or that she would even be capable of something like this."

"Fritz, I asked you what we were going to do about Don's body," Francis repeated. She'd been hysterical most of the after-noon, and the last thing she wanted to see over and over again was her friend and colleague having his brain smashed out of his head.

"I'm having the bodies incinerated," Fritz said. "Same as we always do. Try not to be so sentimental. Don was a scientist, and he knew the risks."

"You should have had one of the goons doing it, not Don!" Francis cried. "That thing has killed three people since she's been here."

"They're morons, Francis. They have no idea what to look for— the subtle break in a voice, the gentle lift of an eyebrow…it takes a scientist to recognize things like that." Fritz turned away from the monitor and looked down at the scene below. "Ah! The mother and her child. It's a pity that the boy has no real power; all of his siblings have shown such promise. But he doesn't seem to have anything.

The only plus to that being that it allows us to go all the way if we have to."

"She seems to have grown some attachment for the boy. She lets him sleep by her now. He brings her meals without being asked, and she thanks him."

"Still, I wonder if it will be enough for her to give up her friend," Fritz said. "It is a crying shame about Don. He had a brilliant mind. I will miss working with him."

"They were all screaming and running everywhere, what happened?" the boy asked his mother.

The woman smiled at the boy, then looked right at them through the two-way glass. "I killed a couple of the bastards. At this rate I ought to have everyone in the building killed off by late winter."

"If you aren't a little more cautious, that's just exactly what will happen," Francis told Fritz.

"HELEN, AH..." ROBBY couldn't believe that he was stammering. He'd thought about it all week. "You want to go to the movies?"

Helen smiled at him. "You mean like right now?" she asked, putting away her apron.

"Well...yes." Robby said.

"I'd love to if we could go by my house first so I can change. It's only a couple of blocks away," she said.

Robby just nodded his head like a big dumb idiot and led the way out to his car. They got in and he started towards her apartment, without waiting for her to give him directions.

"So, you never have said. How long do you plan to stay here?" Helen asked. "In town I mean."

Robby shrugged. "I...I don't really know. I've got to hang around till...well, till I get my business done, and then I'll have to leave— probably in a hurry."

Helen laughed. "You make it sound like you're some kind of gangster or something."

Robby laughed then. "I wish. At least that would be profitable."

"What are you doing, then?" she asked.

"I can't say," he said.

She squealed with delight. "I knew it! I knew it! You're an FBI agent and you're checking out those eggheads down at SWTF."

"I can't say," Robby said again.

"They're up to no good, aren't they? A bad bunch. Is it danger-ous, your assignment I mean?" Helen asked in a hushed whisper.

"Helen, I really can't talk about it with you. I wish I could, but I have orders." *They were given to me by a big ole dyke cop, but I still got orders.*

"I'm sorry, it's just so interesting. I always knew they were up to no good. Right bad feelings you get from that whole bunch. This is my apartment."

Robby pulled over and parked.

"You want to come up with me? It will only take me a minute."

Robby nodded and followed her up the outside set of stairs to her second floor apartment. It wasn't a very nice building, but her apartment was clean, and she'd obviously done a lot of work on it.

"Sit wherever you like, I'll just be a minute."

She walked into another room and Robby sat down in the re-cliner and kicked back. His feet were a little tired from standing on them all day, but when all was done and said the dishwashing job was the easiest job he'd ever had.

"Your apartment is nice," Robby said.

"It's a dump, but it's home," she said. "There's some soda in the fridge if you want it."

"No thanks." Robby looked at the pictures scattered around the room. No doubt pictures of her family. It made Robby homesick for his own family. Made him wonder how the kids were doing. "Pictures of your family?"

"Yes. I come from a big family. Catholic—three sisters, three brothers," she said.

"I come from a big family, too. Welfare—three brothers, four sisters. We all have different daddies, and mother's a big time crack whore. I've raised them mostly on my own. I sure do miss them."

Helen walked out then fully dressed. She was brushing her hair over the front of her face and he thought it was the most spectacu-lar thing he had ever seen.

"My family is kind of boring. Mama and Papa have been mar-ried forever. No one in jail, no one on drugs, all married with kids except me. I'm the baby." She stood up then, flipping her hair back over her shoulder. "So, you ready to go then?"

Robby stood up. "You're…you're the most beautiful woman I've ever seen."

Helen blushed. "Thank you, Robby."

"I'm sorry." He looked at his feet and then back at Helen. "I have a confession. I've never been on a date before."

Helen laughed, but not hatefully. She walked over and took both his hands. "Now that doesn't sound like the kind of thing I would expect an FBI agent to say."

"I never said I was FBI," Robby said.

Helen kissed him on the lips, then, and he kissed her back.

"What was that for?" Robby asked, trying to keep the stupid grin off his face.

"Now you don't have to spend the evening wondering if I'm going to let you kiss me good night."

She was with Carrie, and Carrie was with her. Their flesh melding into one being as they made love. She felt that love radiating through her body.

There was a loud noise, and she was in the trench. The sand was blowing— it was always blowing. She heard the whistling sound of an incoming scud.

"Look out!" she screamed and ran. The strength of the explosion sent her flying. Something wet and sticky hit her face. When she looked down at her feet, Carrie's disembodied head was staring up at her. She screamed and kept screaming.

Spider jerked into a sitting position, her breath coming in gasps. She quickly rubbed the tears from her eyes. She was shaking all over and covered in a sickly cold sweat.

"Are you OK?" The boy asked.

"No. I'm not OK. None of us are OK!" She jumped to her feet and started yanking on the chains that held her. The chain was about twice the size that the old one had been, and all she was doing was eating the skin off her hands.

"You bastards!" she screamed into the dark. She flopped onto her ass on the concrete. Sleeping on this shit was enough to give anyone nightmares.

"Go back to sleep, boy."

"You have a nightmare?" he asked.

"Yes, something like that," Spider said.

"My mom...well, the other..."

"She's your mom, kid," Spider said gently. "She gave birth to you, took care of you when you were sick, and changed your shitty diapers. She's your mother. All I did—and not on purpose—was supply an egg. An egg that doesn't get incubated doesn't hatch into a chick, and a chick that doesn't get fed and cared for doesn't grow into a chicken."

The boy laughed, and Spider thought about what she had said. She guessed it did sound pretty silly.

"So. What about your mom?"

"When I have a nightmare my mom has me tell her about my happiest thought. Maybe it would help if you told me your happiest thought."

Spider laughed. "I don't think it would be appropriate for me to tell a nine-year-old boy about my happiest thought."

"Why not?" Mark asked.

"Because my happiest thought has to do with sex."

"Oh," he said in an embarrassed tone. He lay down then and laid his head on her leg. "Spider, are you married?"

Spider thought about that a minute. "Well...kindah."

"You live with your boyfriend?" Mark asked.

"No. I..." She took a deep breath and decided to just tell him. "I'm gay, Mark. I live with another woman. Her name is Carrie."

"I thought so," Mark said matter-of-factly.

Spider shook her head. "Why did you put me on the spot, then? Why didn't you just ask me if I was queer?"

"I was afraid you'd be mad." The boy sighed. "Can we go back to sleep now? I'm tired."

"All right." Spider moved to lay beside the boy. "Mark?"

"Yes."

"When I was a kid about your age my brother Scott used to take me down to the park and we would play catch. One day a bunch of kids from the neighborhood were all going to play baseball. The kids my brother played with didn't want to let me play because I was too little, but Scott said he wasn't playing if I couldn't play, and so they let me play. I hit a home run that day, and our team won the game, and everyone said how great I was. That's my happy thought."

"It's a good happy thought," Mark said sleepily. "Now just keep thinking happy things, and if you go to sleep thinking happy things, you won't have any more nightmares."

It sounded like good, strong logic to Spider.

ROBBY WOKE UP to the sun on his face and a warm female body in his arms. He hugged Helen tight and she woke up.

"Good morning," she cooed. She kissed his chest and then moved to kiss his lips. They kissed for a long time.

"I...I love you," Robby said when they parted.

Helen laughed. "You don't have to say that, Robby..."

"But it's true. I do. I love you, and I want to be with you the rest of my life."

"That's very sweet, Robby, but...Robby, I'm the first woman you've ever dated. The first woman you've ever had sex with. Don't you think..."

Robby kissed her lips gently. "I may be green, but I'm not stupid. I know how I feel, Helen. I know you—what kind of person you are. I know everything about you..."

"Robby, we just met..."

"Believe me, Helen. I know you in a way that no one else ever has or ever will, and I love you."

Helen looked at him. He was dead serious. "Robby, this is a little fast..."

"Not too fast for sex, but too fast to say I love you?" Robby laughed.

He had a point there. She smiled at him. "OK. Sounds good to me." Helen lay down with her head on his chest. She could definitely deal with some attention from a really nice and very good-looking young man after all of the total losers she'd had in her life. Besides which, he was one hell of a lover. He seemed to know what she wanted and how to give it to her. Considering it was his first time that was amazing. Maybe this one was *the one.*

Robby wanted to ask her to marry him. Wanted to stay there with her. But Spider had given up everything to save his ass, and he owed her.

"Helen, you know...You know I have business."

"Oh yes. The strange and mysterious business." She giggled.

"Sooner or later the time will be right and I'll have to make my move. Could be tomorrow, could be next week, could be a month from now. I don't know when, but when it does...I will have to go, and I don't know how long I'll be gone. But I promise you the most righteous promise a man can make, that I will be back. If I'm alive, I will come back."

Now Helen had heard some lines in her life, but she just didn't think Robby was feeding her a line. It just sounded so much like bull shit that it had to be true.

"Can't you tell me what's going on, Robby?" Helen asked. "I'm just beginning to like having you around. I don't want you to leave even for a little while."

"I can tell you this much. The SWTF are bad people. A friend of mine figured out what they were up to and now they're holding her in that building trying to find out where I am. I have to find a way to get her out of there before they kill her. Then, together, we'll have to find a way to stop them, or my friend and I will be running the rest of our lives."

"That place is a fortress, Robby. You can't get in there. Nobody could."

Robby smiled. "I can get in. I just have to wait for a time when I can get in, get my friend out, and have us both live to tell the tale."

THEY HAD LEFT her alone with the boy for two or three days, Spider couldn't be exactly sure how long. The only contact they had with the outside world was the food trays that were slid through a slot in the bottom of the door.

Now Fritz was walking in with six So-what-if guys. One of them she knew from Shea City. If he stayed true to his feelings there, he didn't want to be here now, and he proved his distaste for the proceedings by standing close to the door as if guarding it. Obviously separating himself from what was happening as much as possible.

Then there was the one that Spider had hit so many times with a hatred of Fritz that he now did nothing but snarl at the man. He certainly wouldn't be able to stop someone from killing Fritz.

Mark was smart; he moved close to Spider and stayed there.

"Come here, boy," Fritz ordered.

"Come get me," he said. He knew they were all afraid of Spider Webb and with good reason. If they got close, she could kill every one of them.

"Shoot her," Fritz ordered.

One of the men raised the weapon in his arm.

"No!" Mark screamed.

A white light arched, and Spider hit the floor. While she was convulsing, three men ran in and grabbed the boy. Spider convulsed on the floor a few more seconds, stopped, and got shakily to her feet.

"It's a nice little weapon we like to call the lightning bolt. Effectively, it is a tazer that can be fired from a distance. What do you think of it?" Fritz asked, looking at his nails.

"Don't play this game out, Fritz," Spider warned through chattering teeth. "Let the boy go. Keep this between adults, or at the very least between you and me."

"Tell us who the Fry Guy is," Fritz ordered.

"I *don't know*," Spider spat at him.

They strapped Mark to a chair. "Don't you care about the boy, Spider?

"Goddamn it! I don't know who he is! I told you that!" Spider said.

"Do it," Fritz ordered. They hit Mark with the cattle prod.

Spider slung herself to the floor and started banging her head on the concrete.

Mark screamed and cried because he was hurt and because he knew what Spider was trying to do.

"Stop her, stop her!" Fritz screamed.

They hit her with the lightning gun, but she had already successfully knocked herself out.

Mark watched as a team of scientist started checking her out. It was about ten minutes before one of them, a woman, announced. "She's given herself a fairly bad concussion, that's all. We'll administer an anti-inflammatory, and she should come to in a few minutes, but I can't promise she'll be much good. You know how they are with head injuries."

Fritz nodded, then looked at the boy. He smiled a smile that made Mark want to choke him. "See, boy? Your mother loves you enough to kill herself to protect you. But you tell her this when she wakes up. Tell her you're worthless to us because you have no power. Therefore you are expendable, and there is no reason for us to take chances by putting you back out there with the rest of the world. The only reason you are alive is for her. Tell her that if she dies, you die automatically."

Mark glared at him, a look of utter hatred in his eyes and thought, *Spider's right, you'll screw up, and when you do...*

"Did you hear me, boy?" Fritz asked in a growl.

"Yes," Mark spat back.

"And do you understand?"

"Yes," Mark said.

Fritz turned to one of the SWTF guys. "Leave the little bastard tied up. It will be good for him."

FRITZ AND FRANCIS left, and the SWTF guys started to file out behind them.

The one with the prod hit the boy again, and Mark screamed.

Jason grabbed the guy by the collar and shook him.

"What the hell was that for!" Jason hissed in the man's face.

The man smiled and shrugged. "For the fun of it. It ain't like they're gonna let him live, anyway. He's a fucking freak; he ain't human."

"Don't do it again," Jason ordered. He left the room following the guy with the prod. His palms were sweaty, and he felt sick.

MARK WAS GLAD when he heard the door close. He started to cry. He knew they were watching him, but it wasn't the same as them being in the room.

Another crew of men came in and started putting Spider in a straightjacket.

"Leave her alone!" Mark screamed. "Leave her alone!"

"Shut up, kid!" one of the men screamed at him. "We ain't hurting her, just making it where she can't hurt herself."

Mark kept telling himself that they were going to get away. That they were going to get away and kill all of these assholes. It was the only way he was going to make it through whatever they were going to do to him next.

"WELL, WHAT HAVE you got for me Denisten?" Carrie asked.

Justin looked at the woman. She was not nearly as attractive as he remembered her being. Her eyes had black circles around them and were sunk back in her head. Her skin was gray looking, and she looked like she'd lost a bunch of weight. Obviously, she was getting even less sleep than he was.

"It's not easy. Without drawing attention to the fact that I'm checking out the SWTF it's hard to get to those files. Harder still to do it without leaving any traces. So far I have found a kind of pattern. Seven cities keep cropping up in the files. Shea City, Washington DC, LA, Denver, Phoenix, Las Vegas and Seattle." He walked over and loaded the disk onto Carrie's computer. "If you'll look, you'll see that the numbers go up every five years. I'm assuming that by subjects they mean these hybrids. You can also see that they introduce approximately five new subjects to these areas every five years. Now I don't have a list of names, yet, but we do have dates of birth. If we match the birth dates to the cities…"

"We'll get a list of babies born on that day, and we'll be able to track them down that way."

"Bingo," Justin said. "We have a few problems—most relatively small—but one rather large."

"Problems, we don't need no stinking problems!" George said. Carrie and Justin turned and stared at him, he laughed nervously and shrugged. "Just trying to lighten things up a bit."

"Well, don't," Carrie said. "Go on, Denisten."

"First, I don't know how much the FBI knows. It looks like they started to investigate the SWTF and someone very high up the food chain threw out a red flag and stopped the investigation. The notes I've found with the files would certainly lead me to believe that they had no idea what they were looking at. If the FBI knows exactly what's going on with the SWTF, then they're covering for them. If they are, that means we're dealing with two government agencies, not just one, and the FBI has considerably more manpower than the SWTF.

"Second, all of the agents that did the initial investigation on the SWTF met with unfortunate accidents. All either in the line of duty or under unquestionable, or at least unquestioned, accidental circumstances. No investigations. No arrests. No loose ends.

"And last, the crème de la crème. If you'll look at this list carefully you'll notice that these subjects have all been tested."

"What does that mean?" George asked.

Carrie sighed deeply. "If they know they are being tested, then they know what they are, what they're being tested for, and why. It means at least some of these human weapons may be willing participants in the program. It means they may be working for the SWTF. Which means my whole plan just got scrapped."

Denisten nodded silently, then added after a moment. "So, what now boss?"

JASON WALKED INTO the diner for lunch, although he was almost afraid to eat. He had never been so confused or tormented in his life. He openly admitted that he had done terrible things for the agency before, but torturing a nine-year-old boy was hitting a little too close to home for him.

The girl set the menu in front of him. "Coffee today, Mr. Baker?"

He just nodded and started looking at the menu. The girl came back with the coffee.

"Ready to order?" she asked.

"I'll just have the soup and some crackers, Helen." He forced a smile for her, and she smiled back and hurried off to fill his order.

Robby grabbed Helen in the kitchen and pulled her aside. "That man out there."

"Yes?"

"Give him this napkin," Robby said.

Helen nodded silently and took the napkin. She tried to make her hand stop shaking as she handed Jason his soup and crackers. She put the napkin down by his bowl. "Enjoy your meal." She moved quickly away.

Jason picked up his napkin and started to flip it open. But when he saw the writing, he quickly put it beneath the table and unfolded it over his lap. He looked down and read the note.

If you don't want the boy to die, meet me in the bathroom.

Jason took a couple of bites of soup, then he purposefully spilt a mouthful down the front of his shirt. "Damn!" he cursed and started wiping it off with the napkin. Then he got up, napkin in hand, and headed for the bathroom.

He walked in and heard someone slide the lock closed behind him. When he turned around to look, he found that he wasn't too surprised by who it was.

"So, you're the Fry Guy," Jason said. "I could turn you in and make myself the pride of the agency, get myself a healthy bonus, too."

"We both know you'd never get the chance," Robby said. "I know what's in your mind. What kind of man you are, and what kind of man you wish you were. You want to redeem yourself, and I can help you do that if you help me."

Jason nodded. He threw the note into the toilet and flushed. "OK, buddy. Tell me what you think I can do."

WHEN SPIDER CAME to she was hanging from the ceiling in a straight-jacket again. Not exactly the best position to be in. Mark was still strapped to the chair, and from the wet condition of his pants they had left him there quite awhile.

The door opened, and this time Spider hit the SWTF man on the other side hard.

As Fritz started to walk through the door someone in the control room screamed. "Fritz! We've got a breach and we've got psychic activity!"

About that time the SWTF man grabbed Fritz in a headlock. He was about to break Fritz's neck when one of the other guards hit him with a tazer. The only real plus being that it shocked the shit out of Fritz, too.

They hit Spider with the lightning bolt and hurried in, closing the door behind them. Spider realized that she had shot her wad and blown her one real shot.

"No more stalling," Fritz said rubbing at his throat. "Give us the Fry Guy."

The SWTF guy stood ready to hit the boy with a cattle prod.

Spider swallowed hard. "His name is Fred Brown. Lives on forth and Brooklyn in the projects."

"If you're lying…" Fritz started.

"All that would do is buy me a little more time," she said.

"And you can both stay right where you are till we're sure."

"You'll never take him alive," Spider said. "He'll kill you all before you even get close."

FRED HAD LIVED in the projects all his life and he knew the heat when he saw it.

He crawled out his window and up the fire escape onto the roof, and then he just kept running.

THE SWTF CRASHED the door on apartment sixteen as their man on the street screamed into their comlinks. "He's up the fire escape heading for the roof!"

They went out the window and started after him. Neither one wanted to get too close unless they were sure they could squeeze off a shot first.

Fred heard something ping close to his head as he jumped over the edge of the building and started sliding down the pipe. These bastards were shooting at him without even screaming for him to give himself up! What was more they were using silencers, and the things they were shooting at him looked more like darts than bullets. What kind of heat was this? He took off down the alley, jumping the fence just as two more showed up. Damn! He couldn't remember having to run this hard since those two pigs had tried to chase him down. That Chink had damn near caught him that time.

Fred kept running.

"WHAT DO YOU mean they don't have him!" Fritz screamed into the receiver. "Well get him…Keep looking…It's not that big an area. Where could he have gone?" Fritz hung up he looked at Francis. "We won't know whether she's told us the truth or not if we can't catch the guy, and she knows that." He was mad. He didn't like it when he was played for a fool. The only thing worse was waiting around to have his foolishness confirmed.

"All we can do now is wait," Francis said.

"She's almost too clever," Fritz said, rubbing his throat.

"What do you mean?" Francis asked.

"I mean that if we let her live there is a very real chance that she *will* kill us."

"But we need her for the program. All her previously harvested eggs have been turned into embryos. If we're going to breed her to the Fry Guy…"

"We don't need her, we just need her eggs for the program. If she's dead, we can take all of them and no one will be the wiser."

"Such a waste," Francis said.

"She's served her purpose," Fritz said matter-of-factly. "She's more trouble than she's worth, and nothing we could do would control her."

"WE'VE GOT TO move now," Jason told Robby. They had met in the bathroom at the park. "She's given them some other guy's name, and when they catch him and find out he doesn't have any power they're going to torture and then kill the boy."

Robby nodded. He'd said good-bye to Helen, and he was ready to go—to get it over with one way or the other. "Did you get the stuff?"

"Yeah. Here." He handed a bag to Robby.

Robby pulled out the lab coat and put it on. Then he almost dropped the bag. "Jesus fucking Christ!" Robby said making a face.

"What?" Jason said in disbelief. "You run around frying people's brains and blowing them up, but a disembodied hand in a baggy freaks you out. Give me a big break."

"How is that going to help me get in the building?" Robby asked, making a face.

"The handprint. You're going to need the handprint to get in," Jason said. "You just hold it at the wrist up under your sleeve, and when you get to the door…"

"All right, all right, let's just do it."

Jason helped him put on the fake mustache and sideburns.

"How do I look?" Robby asked.

"You'll pass. Now, come on, let's go."

THE GUYS AT the front gate were easy. They looked in the car, but mostly it was their job to let the car in. If it had the right sticker, they let it in unless they had other orders. The guy at the front door kept staring at Robby; even after his palm print opened the door. He must have noticed some discrepancy in the photo that popped onto the computer as being Dr. Herbert Todd.

Jason was waiting behind Robby, and started bitching. "Christ on a crutch! Am I going to have to stand out here all night? Come on, I'm in a hurry here. I don't come to this dung hole for my health, you know."

The guy let Robby pass, and then passed Jason in.

"Follow me," Jason said and started walking.

They passed a garbage can, and Robby stopped long enough to toss the hand away. The building was a maze of corridors, and at every door—even to get on the elevator—a guard checked their badges.

Robby's insides flinched every time the elevator stopped and the doors opened. His gut was sure that he was going to be facing a wall of armed guards at any moment. Finally, the doors opened on the top floor, their ID's were checked again, and they started down a series of maze-like corridors. There was no way he could have found his way to Spider without Jason's help, and Robby told him so.

"Yeah, I'm a real prince," Jason said. They rounded a corner and Robby was looking at a big steel door covered by four guards.

"She's in there, but don't go in that room. You go in that room and your power is neutralized. I'll stay here and cover your back."

Robby nodded. "Thanks. We'll meet you here."

Jason stayed there at the junction and Robby moved forward. Four guards and a door. He focused on them, and as their sins and transgressions flooded into his brain they started to fry. Sirens went off as the four men fell and Robby hit the door. It blasted open. He saw Spider hanging in the middle of the room.

"What took you so fucking long?" Spider asked him with a smile.

"Sorry." Robby hit her chain and she fell to the floor, landing on her feet.

"Hurry up, kid!" Jason screamed, and then Robby heard him firing. Three guards ran in from a door on the left, and Robby fried them.

"Hurry up, kid!" Jason screamed again.

There was way too much gunfire coming from the end of the hall.

"Go help him. I'll be okay here," Spider said.

Robby nodded and joined Jason at the end of the hall. He killed two of them and the rest went running scared.

"Hang on, kid!" Spider yelled.

She kicked the wooden chair Mark was sitting in and it fell apart, allowing him to get free. Then he quickly undid the strings holding her straightjacket closed and helped her squeeze out of it. They ran out of the room, and as they did so Fritz—who had run out of the observation room—hit her with the lightning bolt. As Spider fell to the floor convulsing, Mark looked up at Fritz and smiled.

"I'm not worthless," he said.

Fritz looked at the boy in amazed fear, and then his brain exploded. Mark helped Spider to her feet.

"Go to Robby; he'll protect you," she gasped out.

He nodded and ran to the end of the hall where Robby and Jason were.

"We've got to hurry," Jason told Robby. "They've got suits to protect themselves from you."

"Spider, hurry!" Robby screamed down the hall.

Spider heard him, but she had things to do. She walked into the control room where six scientists stood huddled in the corner. One held a weapon in his hand, so Spider shot him with the lightning bolt, and as she walked up to the others, she crushed his skull with her foot. Reaching into the group, she grabbed the woman, Francis.

"You come with me. As for the rest of you assholes," she smiled and then pushed as hard as she could. "Kill each other."

As she ran out with the woman they immediately started ripping each other apart.

"Gee! I should thank Fritz for telling me just how strong my mental push was." They were stepping over Fritz's body then. "Oops! Too late! My little boy killed him."

Francis screamed as Spider dragged her along.

Jason looked at her when she came to the end of the hall. "They're not going to let you go because you have a hostage. They'll shoot her just to get her out of their way."

"That isn't why I've got her," Spider said.

She looked at the woman and pushed. "You will stay with us. You will not give up our position."

"We've got to move, Spider. We're on the top floor and Jason says they have suits which will stop me from killing them."

"In that case…" Spider moved to the pile of bodies and picked up every gun she saw. She handed them out, giving Mark the lightning bolt because she had noticed it had no kick.

He shook his head. "I don't know how."

"You just point and pull the trigger, boy," Jason said. "It isn't that hard."

They heard what sounded like a troop of men coming. "Which way to the stairs?" Spider asked.

"This way!" Jason started moving—luckily away from the footsteps.

Spider had a brainstorm.

"Robby?"

"Yes?"

"Blow the hall behind us up."

Robby turned, and while walking backwards did as she asked.

Jason looked back at Spider. "You guys are some scary fucks."

A troop of armed guards wearing suits appeared in front of them, successfully blocking the stairway.

"Give yourselves up!" one screamed. "You can not escape…."

"Open fire!" Spider yelled. They filled the hall with a hail of bullets, and the wall of men fell like rain.

They ran over the bodies and headed for the stairs.

Spider kicked the door open and then jumped to the side. There were no bullets and no darts, so she looked around the edge of the doorframe. "OK! Let's go!"

"You're walking into a trap," Jason said. "They'll have men at every floor. They'll…"

"Never know what hit them. Just keep moving. Robby, keep a hand on that woman. We need her."

Robby nodded.

Spider jumped into the well.

"Spider!" Mark screamed after her.

"What the hell!" Jason started.

"Don't worry. She knows what she's doing," Robby said. He grabbed hold of Francis and started moving slowly, gun in hand.

Spider grabbed onto the rail on the next floor and waited.

Three men pounded through the door, thinking they were making a surprise attack, and instead ran into one.

Spider opened fire, shot all three of them and yelled up, "Come on! Move it! I can't hang here all day!"

She waited till they got there.

"Robby, seal the door."

Robby nodded and started the door on fire. The sprinkler system kicked in almost immediately.

"Your fire isn't going to last long, so move and move fast." She let go and dropped again. She almost missed the rail on the next floor, and while she was trying to get her head back together and her gun out, a team of men jumped out the door and she wasn't ready. So she let go and dropped again.

"Robby! They don't have on suits!" she yelled as she fell.

Robby let go of the woman and practically jumped down the stairs. He focused and fried the guys and then the doorway. The others had caught up with him, so he grabbed the woman again and kept moving fast.

Spider grabbed on and jumped over the rail. She kicked the door, ran into the hall catching the waiting guards unprepared, and started firing. Then she met the others on the other side of the door.

"How many more floors?" Spider asked.

"Three," Jason answered, "and the security is just going to get worse."

She heard a troop running at them from above.

"Robby, take out the staircase."

Above them the staircase erupted, spraying them with concrete and debris and sending two men down the well beside them.

"Let's move!" Spider said and ran into the hallway.

"What are you doing! The stairs are our only way out!" Jason said.

"Which is why they'll catch us if we go that way. We'll have to make another exit."

"The elevator," Robby said.

"Are you nuts? They'll know where you're going when they realize you've left the stairs," Jason said.

"They know where we're going now," Spider said. A troop in suits rounded the corner then, and they took off running. "Get us to the elevator!" Spider fired, a gun in each hand, as she ran backwards.

Several guards fell, and more ran away. The SWTF were only really tough when there was no way they could lose. As soon as you narrowed the odds they were out of there. Their ultimate cowardice in the face of danger was what she was counting on.

The troops guarding the elevator were wearing protective suits and carrying Lexan shields.

"Oops!" Spider said, coming up short. They'd told her that she had telekinetic powers in the days or weeks or however long she'd been locked in that room, and she'd wondered if she really did. "No time like the present to find out," she mumbled. She focused all her rage on the shields, and they went flying out of the hands of the guards with such force that Jason had to dance to the side to keep from getting hit by one. "Cool," Spider said with a smug smile and pulled the weapons out of the guards' hands the same way. She had a brainstorm. "Robby, hit the ceiling."

Robby hit the ceiling above the confused men hard, and it caved in on them. Not waiting for the dust to clear, they crawled over the bodies to the elevator. One of the men looked like he might still be moving, so Spider kicked him in the head hard enough to kill him. She willed yet another gun into her hand and frowned when she realized it had nothing in it but sleeping darts. Still, beggars couldn't be choosers. They dove into the elevator just as a hail of darts rained in around them. The doors closed and they were going down.

"What now?" Jason asked.

"We go down," Spider said.

"You don't have to be a genius to figure out that we're going down," Robby said nervously.

He looked at Mark. "Can't you help me?"

"I don't have anything left!" Mark nearly screamed. He was trying to be tough, but he didn't feel tough.

"He's normal for the project," Jason explained. "You're not. Why the hell do you think they want you so bad? They want to breed you to Spider."

Spider and Robby looked at each other and both made faces.

The elevator stopped between floors.

Spider sighed. "They're holding us here while they get set up."

"What do we do now?" Jason asked again.

Spider took a deep breath and held it for a minute. She really had no idea.

"I can fix the elevator." Robby pried off the control cover and started digging through the wires. "I can do it. I can make it move. What do you want to do?"

"I saw this in a movie once; it just might work in real life," Spider said.

THEY GATHERED AT the bottom of the stairs in their suits and riot gear and waited. The elevator started coming down.

"They've by-passed the system! Prepare yourselves men; they're coming down." The commander had an absolute genius for stating the obvious.

The elevator stopped and they waited. Any minute now they could be staring death straight in the face. The doors opened and nothing happened. There was nothing—no one in sight—no one in the elevator.

"They must have gotten off! Gone back to the stairwell. Spread out! They could be anywhere!"

They started to move out in all directions, afraid to look and afraid not to. Kind of like thinking there was a venomous snake in your bedroom. You wanted it found; you just didn't want to be the one to find it.

Two guards, more intelligent than the others, or just less lucky, went into the elevator to check it out. They lifted the trap door on the top and Spider Webb jumped on top of them. A couple of well placed kicks, and they were down for the count. Jason and Robby jumped off the top of the elevator into it, then helped the boy and the woman down. They entered the now-empty lobby.

"I never would have thought that would work," Jason said.

"Between you and me, neither did I," Spider said.

A troop of men rounded the corner as they made for the front door.

"I can't kill the door guards," Robby told Spider as they ran towards the doors. The two armed guards were standing ready to fire, no doubt with real bullets. "They aren't evil!"

Spider was firing behind them. "An alligator isn't evil, either, but you'd kill it if it was trying to eat you."

"Good point!" Robby fried the guys blocking their way to freedom.

They ran out the door. Robby could see Jason's car just a few feet away.

Jason stopped at the doorway. Spider turned, saw him and ran back. She grabbed his arm.

"Come on, man."

"Can't," he said. "I've got a family."

She nodded. She knew what he meant. "Thank you."

"I'll cover your ass. Just go."

Spider ran to catch up. Robby was already in the car turning the key in the ignition. Spider shoved the boy and the woman in, and then jumped in herself.

As Jason saw the car take off he turned back towards the building. He kept firing, empting one weapon after another, right up till a bullet burned its way through his brain.

"Gates?" Robby asked.

"Break 'em!" Spider wasn't firing now. She was lying back in the seat.

"But…"

"Hit 'em, Robby. You're in command now." Spider reached back, pulled the dart from her butt, and threw it out the window. Then she was out.

"Everybody get down," Robby ordered. He crouched down in his seat, tried to ignore the guards firing real bullets at them this time, and shoved Spider down into the seat beside him as he crashed through the gates. The car made a strange hissing noise and started to lose power. He revved the engine, shifted into a lower gear, and hoped for the best.

He turned and glared at the gate, setting the asphalt driveway on fire. No one would be following them for a while. He saw the boy's hand touch Spiders arm. No worry there. But he kept a half an eye on the woman, not knowing how long whatever Spider had done to her would last. The car barely got them to the park. He loaded Spider into his car. Then he tied the woman's hands and feet up and stuck her in the back seat with the boy. She didn't even seem to notice. Finally, Robby roared off, reminding himself not to drive too fast.

As an after thought, he pulled off the fake beard and mustache and threw them in the floorboards.

"Boy! Help me get this damn lab coat off."

"My name is Mark," the boy said quietly, and helped Robby take the coat off.

"Well, Mark, it looks like we're safe now."

"I don't think we're ever going to be safe," Mark said.

Robby looked around to make sure no other cars were around, then slung the lab coat into the floorboards, too. He had absolutely no idea where to go, so he just drove. As he passed the diner, he looked at it longingly and drove on.

"Don't be so negative, Mark. Put your faith in God and Spider Webb. We've got to beat them; we've just got to because nobody else can."

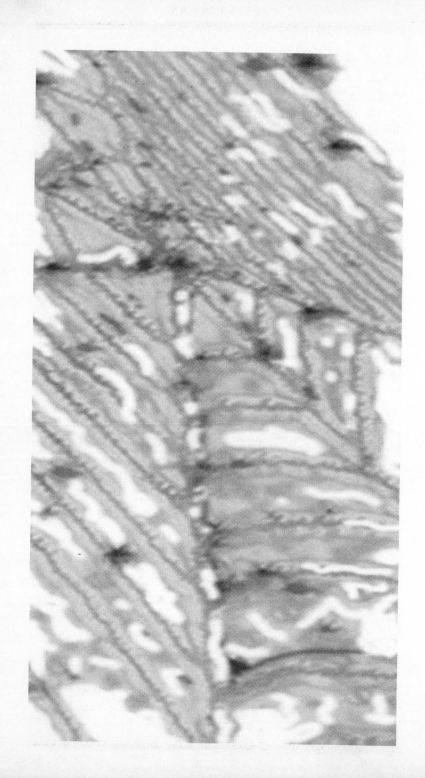

CHAPTER TWENTY

"Because sentence against evil work is not executed speedily, therefore the heart of the sons of men is fully so to do evil." Ecclesiastes 8:11

CARRIE LOOKED AT the data Denisten was sending her on a closed channel. The SWTF's headquarters had been hit and hit hard. Carrie could only hope that she was right about who did it.

"If she got away, if he helped her, we will be inundated with SWTF in the next twenty-four hours," Carrie said. "And the ones we see will be just the tip of the iceberg. If Spider's free, they're going to be waiting to see if she comes to me. I hope she's not that stupid."

"Really?" George asked, looking around the den. Carrie's house had become a pit. Nothing had been cleaned or picked up in weeks. She came to work in clothes that looked as if they'd been slept in, and although so far she seemed to be holding up to her workload, he wondered how long that could last if she didn't get some serious sleep and a decent meal.

"Really," Carrie answered at last. She breathed. "If she comes for me they'll stop her. I'd love to see her, but not dead."

"You have got to quit driving and abusing yourself," George scolded. "You're doing everything it is humanly possible to do. You have got to take time out for yourself, get some rest a real meal."

"Pop tarts are a meal," Carrie said with a smile.

"Carrie…"

"I know, George. I know that you're right. But it's easier said than done," Carrie said with a sigh. She stood up and started pacing. "I try to pretend like nothing is happening. I go to work. I do my job. I go home. I try to eat, and then I remember that Spider usually cooks and I wonder where she is, and what or even if she's eating. I wonder if she's thinking about me. Then I sit down to relax and watch TV, and I remember that Spider doesn't watch very much TV. That she usually reads. Then I begin to wonder if I'm ever again going to walk in and find her sleeping in her chair with a book in her hands. I go to bed and I try to sleep and it's just…so lonely. I can't quit thinking about her." She started to cry.

George walked over and embraced her. He patted her back in an automatic effort to give comfort.

"It's like I'm in this unending nightmare. I keep thinking that if I wake up it will be over. But I wake up every morning, and it's never over."

"This is good news, though, Carrie. She may be free."

Carrie nodded, pushed him away and dried her eyes. "She's not free even if she got away. She may not be confined any more, but these bastards will never leave her alone. And she could also be dead now. I just don't know, and it's the not knowing that's killing me."

DEACON HAD BEEN waiting for over an hour. Of course *he* was the bigwig, and that meant he could make Deacon wait while sitting on hot coals if he liked.

Besides, Deacon was in no hurry to meet with him. The guy made his flesh crawl.

"You may go in now, sir," the secretary announced.

Deacon nodded and stood up. He wiped his sweaty palms on his pants legs, walked over and opened the office door. Before he had a chance to open it all the way, the man inside spoke.

"Come on in, Deacon, make yourself at home."

Deacon came in closing the door behind him. He walked over, sat down, and stared across the desk at the oldest living Nazi war criminal. He tried hard not to allow his features to show how he felt about him.

"Our experiments are going very well," he said conversationally.

Deacon swallowed his *Are you nuts!* retort. "Sir, with all due respect, three of the subjects tore apart this building, killed half of the scientists and over half of the security force, and escaped. Basically without a scratch. God only knows where they are by now, or what they'll do next."

"Which means that *we* have done *our* work, and *you* have *not* done yours." His thick accent broke as he drove his fist into his desk with every word. "We have built the ultimate soldier, and yet you have failed to secure our secrets or our experiments. There are leaks everywhere. One of your own men helped them for no apparent reason."

"Maybe they gave him a mental push."

"Don't try to make excuses or pretend that you understand how they work...everything that we have worked for, that *I* have worked for is unraveling before my eyes. I don't care how you do it, but these two—the woman cop and the black boy..." You could tell it was practically killing the old fuck to admit that the ultimate soldier was not only not necessarily male, but also, in this case, not Aryan. "...must be bred. All we need is sperm from the boy and eggs from the woman. So I don't care if you kill them. I have no emotional attachment to these experiments. Just bring me these things."

"How are we supposed to find them?" Deacon asked.

"That's your job, not mine. I have done my job. Quite excellently well if I may add."

Deacon couldn't help himself. "But you didn't build the Fry Guy. They did it without your work. He's bigger and better than anything you've made, and maybe, just maybe, it's because he's not white."

"Your insubordination will go into the records." He stood up and pounded his fist into his desk. His face went red, and Deacon secretly hoped that this would be the time that the old fuck fell over dead. But, of course, he didn't. "Get out of my office and do as you are told!"

Deacon left. He felt he could die a happy man as long as that old fuck died first.

SPIDER WOKE UP and tried to replay everything that had happened. She stepped out of the car. It was a little cold, especially since she was still wearing nothing but the white pajamas they had put her in, and she still had no shoes. Robby had built a fire, and she huddled up to it.

Robby and Mark looked up at her. The woman who was now tied up just stared at the fire. Robby handed Spider a sandwich. She took it, sat down on a rock next to the fire, and Mark immediately moved to sit by her curling against her legs. Poor little pecker head was wearing the same thing that she was. She looked around quickly to make sure they weren't in some public park somewhere; they weren't. She couldn't even see a road or any lights in the distance.

"I just drove as far into nowhere as I could. I figured you'd have a plan when you woke up."

Spider nodded. "Good thinking, but I hate to disappoint you...see, I don't have any sort of plan."

Spider ate the sandwich and washed it down with the cup of coffee Robby handed her. She felt some better, but her body had been through the mill. Her arms really hurt from jumping down the stairwell and catching herself. Her head where she had slammed it into the floor was pounding. Her legs hurt, her stomach, well, everything, and as neat as the telekinesis had been, it had left her more physically drained than a three-hour training session.

"If it hadn't been for Tommy I never could have done it," she said. "I hope he got out of town OK."

"I'm sure he did," Robby said gently. "How bad was it?"

"Oh, it was bad," Spider said bitterly. She shoved Francis with her free hand. "Wasn't it, bitch? You sick twisted fuck, now you hang in the wind wondering what *I'm* going to do to *you*."

The woman was silent.

"She's dark," Robby said. "Get whatever you're going to get out of her, and let's fry her. Let's not drop to their level."

"Right now we need her, and as long as she behaves she can stay alive," Spider said. Then she added on a sadistic note, "Maybe."

"Why'd Jason..." Robby stared into the fire. "He might as well have shot himself. Why'd he do it when we were damn near home free?"

"He couldn't afford the luxury of living. He never planned to live through the raid. He had a family. He was looking to redeem himself. I think he felt redeemed."

"He was nice, Mom," Mark said. In the sadness of the moment he had forgotten himself.

Robby laughed, and pointed at Spider. "You? Mom? Now that's rich!"

Spider didn't smile. She looked at Robby and shrugged. "Mark *is* my son."

Robby stopped laughing. "But you, you're a...how?"

"Well why don't you just ask Francis the talking asshole about that. I'm going to try to get some real sleep." She stood, took Mark's hand and walked back to the car.

Robby ran ahead of them. "Wait a minute! I've rigged the seats to make a big bed." He hurried and fixed it. "We have pillows, blankets—all the comforts of home."

"Thanks, Robby," she said. She crawled in and the boy crawled in after her, curling up under the blankets with her.

"Now that I know, he does look like he belongs to you," Robby said. "Get some sleep. I'll take care of everything out here."

WHEN LAURA WOKE up Tommy was already gone. No doubt he was out stalking dinner. She got up and started straightening the cabin. When she was done she grabbed a bucket and started down to the creek to get some water.

She had to admit that Tommy was at least partly right. It was certainly peaceful and relaxing here.

It was also boring as hell.

After awhile nature got damn repetitive. Although she was enjoying long walks and talks with Tommy, she missed her job and her friends, her mom and dad. She missed TV and the stereo. She really missed her washer and dryer.

Tommy seemed more than content to play in the woods all day. He had raked most of the camp and re-rocked all the trails. He had managed to put one picnic table together out of all the picnic tables he had found and had rebuilt one of the outside grills. He had even dug up some ground and made a garden, transplanting edible weeds and planting some seeds he brought with them. He watered it daily and spent hours trying to find new weeds to plant in it.

In fact Laura couldn't remember a time when Tommy had seemed so relaxed and happy. While she bitched daily about the outhouse—a solid concrete building with a concrete seat that was sitting on a huge concrete tank—the rationing of toilet paper and hygienic items, the lack of any real variety in their diet, and the dullness of their daily routine, the only thing that seemed to perturb Tommy in his blissful roll of Grizzly Chan was worrying about Spider, which he did every time he sat still for a minute. No doubt this was why he worked so hard at keeping busy.

Laura was mostly curious. How the hell had such seemingly normal people like herself, her husband, and Spider Webb landed in the middle of some secret government conspiracy? A conspiracy that had forced her and Tommy into hiding for an indefinite period of time and made Spider fall off the planet?

After days of worrying, Tommy had snuck into a nearby town. He had parked the car in the woods two miles out of town and walked to the nearest pay phone. After trying to figure out who to call, he finally made a call directly to Carrie. Carrie told him that

Spider had vanished, but that she believed she was still alive. Then she told him not to try calling again, and she hung up. Tommy returned to the camp very depressed with a sack full of garden seed. But by the time he'd dug up and planted his garden he had all but forgotten about Spider's problems.

Laura sat by the creek for a while and watched the water go by. She was in no hurry to get back to the cabin. No schedule here, no place she had to be at any certain time. They got up when they wanted, and went to bed when they wanted. No hassles no worries. It should have been heaven, and it had been while she was recuperating. In fact, feeling like shit those first couple of days, it was nice not to have to worry about anybody dropping in to visit. It was nice not to have to put on a brave face, and she thought the mountain air and clear spring water had helped her to heal faster, too. In fact, health wise she was feeling better than she had in years, which was good because she only had a small amount of insulin if she needed it. Since she didn't normally take insulin but kept her disease in check with diet and exercise she never kept much on hand, and while Tommy had thought to get everything else they would need he hadn't thought to stock up on her prescription, and neither had she. The five pills she'd had in her purse were all she had and of course she had no testing supplies. Luckily, so far she felt fine.

Getting lots of fresh air and exercise, and the fact that they had no other form of entertainment, had also improved their sex life.

But still, when she weighed the pluses against the minuses, she still wished she were home. She could be sleeping on a real bed, cooking in a real kitchen, bathing in a real bathtub and using a toilet that flushed.

Tommy ran up to her then, not even winded. He was swinging some poor animal by the tail. He was a menace to all things that crawled, walked, swam or flew. The man would quite literally eat anything. This time he had a squirrel. It had taken her a couple of days to get over the 'that was a living, breathing animal' thing. Now it was sad, but it was also dinner.

He leaned down and kissed her cheek, then sat down next to her on the rock. He lay the squirrel on the ground beside him away from Laura. "Got something quick today. Think I'm getting better at it."

"Me, too! Scooped that water up first try."

"What's wrong?" Tommy asked.

Laura shrugged.

"Come on," Tommy urged.

"You're really happy here, aren't you?"

Tommy shrugged. "For the first time in my life everything is up to me. I don't have to answer to anyone, except you. When we're hungry we eat; when we're tired we sleep. When I want meat I hunt; when I want fish, I fish. My biggest decision for the day is what do I want to do. The only lives I am responsible for are yours and mine, and our needs are easily filled here. Yes, I am happy here. All my life I have done everything I ever did to please or serve other people. Here I have only to please and serve you and myself. But you're not happy." The last was a statement not a question.

"I didn't think there was anything wrong with our old life," Laura said. "I liked having someplace to go, people depending on me. It gives me a feeling of accomplishment. Here I have no sense of purpose. It's like, what do I do? I live. That's all I do."

Tommy nodded. He knew she was unhappy. "Don't you see, Honey?" he said gently. "Everyone pushes us into believing that we must accomplish something. That each of us has a specific reason for being. Some task we must spend a lifetime discovering and performing. That somehow this something will make us distinct individuals in the world. But the truth is that our only real reason for being is just to be, and very few men change the world enough that they are remembered after they die."

"But we all try. That's what makes us humans," Laura said.

"That's what makes us crazy," Tommy said with a laugh. He stood up, picked up the squirrel and the bucket of water and left.

Laura stared back into the water. Sometimes he made no sense at all.

WHEN SPIDER WOKE up she realized that, although it must be daylight outside, the sun was not streaking in on her. She sat up and looked at the shades pulled down on all the windows. Robby had taken regular window shades, adapted them, and screwed them to the roof of the car. He'd fixed the front seats so that when they laid back they met the back seat, making one large bed. Then he'd taken a piece of foam rubber to shove between the two front seats. He'd apparently counted on them having to live in the car.

She looked around, and when she didn't see the scientist she shook Robby awake.

"Wha...what?" He rubbed his eyes.

"Where's the woman?" Spider asked.

"In the trunk," Robby said sleepily.

Spider laughed and lay back down.

Robby yawned and stretched. He looked at his watch. "It's ten o'clock. I guess we better hit the road."

"Oh, how glorious it is to know what time it is," Spider said stretching herself. "Funny how you can miss such a tiny thing."

"You look like hell," Robby said.

"Well, thank you very much," Spider laughed.

"What are the burn marks from?"

"That damn lightning bolt gun I suppose," Spider said. She looked down at what he was talking about and saw scorched marks on both her pajamas and her skin. She wished he hadn't pointed it out, because now it hurt.

"You can wear some of my clothes for now, but I don't have many. You'll need clothes, and so will the boy. I've still got some of the money you sent me."

Spider nodded. "Good." She got out of the car. She covered Mark up better and then closed the door. Then she walked over to the folding camp table and sat down. For the first time she really noticed the boxes sitting around the camp. They were intriguing.

Robby followed her and started stirring the fire, then he threw on some wood and hit it with some power.

"So, what's all this then?" Spider asked indicating the boxes.

Robby started to tell her. He opened one and showed it to her. "This is my bath box. See, you open it and here's your sink." He pointed to a square pan in one corner. "It has separate partitions for your soap, shampoo, toothpaste, and shaving stuff. Then you have this." He pulled a hose from the box. "The shower." He pulled another hose out the side of the box. "You stick this end into some water, flip this switch here—it's battery operated—and it pumps water up through this hose, and you take a shower."

He closed the box back up and grabbed another. "This one I call the cook box. See, you open it like this. Here's your one-burner Coleman stove. The top is a spice rack, and here's where your pots and pans go."

He closed it up and grabbed another. "This is the food box. It just has different compartments for different food. But see in this corner I have built a small, butane-run refrigerator. One bottle will last about a month. It's perfectly safe and will keep a six-pack of soda and several packets of lunchmeat cool. Vents on the back allow the heat to escape. You just have to be careful you pack it with the vents clear."

He closed it, turned it around, put it down and picked up another box. "This is the light box. So called because it holds…" he opened it and pulled a lantern out "…a light! It's fluid. It keeps it from getting beat up in the back mostly." He closed it and set it down. "I made the table and chair thing, too. It folds down into a box. All of the boxes have been painted in bright, weather resistant colors, and all boxes are completely waterproof. You can stack them together, strap them with these straps, pull out that wheel, and cart it wherever you need to take it, or…This custom-made set fits neatly and completely into the trunk of a Hyundai when there isn't a woman in there." Robby smiled.

Spider laughed. "Hey! I'm sold! You ever think of patenting them? Making them, selling them. There's bound to be a market."

Robby shrugged. "I have lots of ideas. Problem is that it takes money to do things like that, and all my money was always tied up. So was my time. I couldn't justify spending time and money on something that might or might not make us money."

"Well, you're very inventive, Robby. I'm surprised, I mean up till now I just thought you were your typical run of the mill Fry Guy," Spider said.

Robby laughed. "Well shucks, ma'am, you're makin' me blush." He quit laughing then and looked serious. "What do we do now, Spider?"

"We hide until we figure out just what we *can* do."

THE SWTF WERE everywhere. Outside her house. Outside her office. They followed her to work. They followed her to lunch. She wasn't surprised at all when Deacon showed up at her office door.

"Come in and take a load off, Mr. Deacon," Carrie said without looking up. "I see that I have become the object of your attention again."

Deacon sat down, and she finally looked at him.

"You look like hell," he said without any malice.

"Thanks to you and your people I feel like I'm living in hell," she said. "Please make your point and leave. I'm a very busy woman."

"Fine, I'll make this brief. If you see your lover, it would be in everybody's best interest for you to call me immediately."

Carrie looked back down at her papers to disguise the look on her face. Till right then she hadn't been at all sure that Spider was alive, much less free. "I'm not likely to see her, and we all know I wouldn't turn her in if I did. So, if that's all you have to say..."

"It's not." Deacon cleared his throat, so she looked at him again. "This guy she's protecting—the guy that's with her. He's dangerous. He needs to be stopped. You have no idea what this guy can do."

"But you're wrong. I've got a pretty good idea. If you're not going to try to kill or kidnap me, then I suggest you take a hike, because it will be a cold day in hell when I help you."

Deacon got up and started to leave, but he turned in the door. "You have no idea what you are protecting, DA Long. No idea at all."

"And *I* think you have no idea what *you're* protecting."

Robby stayed in the car with the prisoner while Spider and the boy went into Wal-Mart to shop. When Robby protested that the boy was wearing only white pajamas, she ripped the bottom off Francis' black skirt and tied it around his waist.

"There, now if anyone asks, I just picked him up from judo practice," Spider told Robby. Robby laughed and shrugged. He hoped she knew what she was doing.

Spider had put a push on Francis, and she sat in the back seat as if there were no place on earth she would have rather been.

It was taking them longer than it would have taken Robby, and he was getting bored.

"So, Franny," Robby started. "Just what made the government decide to build people?"

"Oh, it wasn't us," Francis said. "*They* started it."

"They, who?"

"The aliens. They found the suitable female candidates and impregnated them. Then there were the Germans..."

"Germans!" Robby shrieked.

"Oh, yes, they were the first ones to have absolute proof that the world was being visited by aliens. You see, the Germans found a downed spacecraft. That's how they found out how to make rockets and how they learned what the aliens had been doing. Then they decided to start their own breeding programs. They found the half-breeds the aliens had made and removed the chips the aliens were using to track them. Then they harvested the eggs and sperm and put the embryos into willing German female volunteers. With technology gleaned from the alien ship, the Germans were able to develop test-tube breeding at least fifty years before anyone else even started to investigate the prospect.

"When the US took over the German bases after WWII, they found hundreds of subjects that the Germans had bred, all blond-haired, blue-eyed, and all carrying alien DNA. That was their 'master race.' Of course, the subjects had been horribly brainwashed from birth, and were so dangerous that they had to be destroyed, but we didn't destroy the data. Once we knew that the aliens existed, and that they really were experimenting on us, it wasn't that hard to find some of their offspring. Using the captured research, and in some instances, the actual German scientists, we started our own breeding program here in the States…"

"But why?" Robby asked. "I don't understand. Why would you want to do that?"

"Because the aliens are out there. They're out there, and why do you think they're experimenting on us?"

"Because they are curious," Robby shrugged. "To them we must be like lab rats."

"Oh, that's what they would like you to believe. But the truth is they want to take over the world. Total global domination. Then they can use us in whatever manner pleases them…"

"Isn't that a little paranoid?" Robby interrupted. "I mean, surely a race that is so technologically advanced could just wipe us out any time they wanted to."

"We're the government. We get paid to be paranoid. Who knows why they haven't made their move? Maybe the fact that we have interrupted their experiment means that we are a little smarter than they thought we were. Our plan is to breed this race of people to their top potential. By leaving them in normal American settings, we hope to avoid making them into the kind of unconscionable killing machines that the German subjects had become. They will grow up with allegiances to home, family and country. If there is an alien invasion, we will have an army of people ready to fight to defend our country."

"If you treat them the way you have treated us, isn't there a very good chance that we may go over to the other side? After all, we are half alien, who's to say where our allegiances may lie?"

"With the people and the families you know. That's just normal psychology."

Robby nodded. That at least made sense. He'd certainly choose his family over a bunch of big-handed aliens.

Spider and Mark came back then with more stuff than he thought they needed. They stacked most of it on Francis. They got in and Robby started the car. He looked over at Spider.

"You're not going to believe what Francis just told me…"

"WHERE THE HELL is he!" Rudy yelled. "I thought this guy was dependable."

Helen looked at him. "Shush!"

"Don't you shush me, girl! Where's your lover boy?"

"Rudy…Robby's in the FBI. No one's supposed to know that he was here on an assignment…"

"Oh, God, Helen! When are you ever going to learn? Some pretty boy comes in here with a line you could hang clothes on, and you're in love," Rudy said sympathetically.

Helen started to get mad at him, but his conclusion was not entirely without justification. Helen did have a history of falling for the wrong kinds of guys. But this time Rudy was wrong.

"Why would he leave the day before payday? He was after those SWTF creeps, and you know something went down over there last night," she whispered.

Rudy laughed. "And you think that had something to do with lover boy? Come on, Helen…"

"OK, OK. Let's just say you're right. But for my sake could you not mention that he's gone when we have customers?" Helen asked. "They might think I know something, and I could be in big trouble. You know how those guys are."

Rudy nodded and sighed. "OK, Helen." He shook his head. "But you gottah know that this guy fed you a load of crap."

"I'll do the dishes till you get someone else, if you just please…"

"I said I'd keep it on the QT, and I will. Rudy Hardly is nothing if not a man of his word."

As the SWTF personnel started filing in, Helen noticed two things. First, many familiar lunchtime regulars were missing, and second, they weren't talking much. The slices of conversation she did catch sounded like they had just been through a war instead of a day's work.

"We're picking up shit," one was whispering. "We lift up this huge piece of the ceiling, and under it there's like four guys—all dead."

"Shush!" the guy he was talking to ordered.

Helen put the menus and water in front of them and smiled. "Be back in a minute." She hurried away to wait on another customer.

Everything she overheard was in the same vein. This one was dead, or that one was dead. This part of the building was totaled. Estimates on times and amounts of money it would take to repair the damage, etc., etc. But the most interesting piece of conversation had come from a couple of scientists sitting at one of the corner booths.

"My point is," the one said to the other, "that the suits can only protect you from their psychic power. It can't protect you from things they can do with it. Like jerking guns out of your hand, starting the hallways on fire or caving the roof in."

Either these guys had all seen the same sci-fi flick, or something really destructive had taken place at SWTF headquarters last night.

Helen drove by the complex on her way home from work. A paving crew was working on the driveway, and another crew was installing new gates.

When Robbie had said goodbye she'd hoped that he really was feeding her a line, and that he would be back later that night. But he hadn't come back, and he hadn't called, and he didn't come in for work. Now something had definitely happened at the SWTF complex.

She wondered if Robby had been able to get his friend out. Wondered if he was still alive. For the thousandth time she wondered what the hell the SWTF really was.

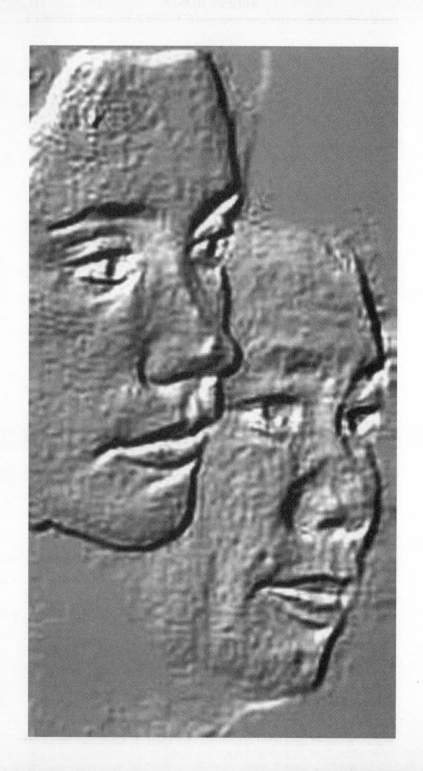

CHAPTER TWENTY-ONE

"Lo, this only have I found, That God has made man upright; but they have sought out many inventions."
Ecclesiastes 7:29

HE KNEW THEY called him the oldest living Nazi war criminal. He didn't really care. It wasn't true, of course. He was a scientist, not a thug. He'd never gotten his hands dirty, not in Germany, and not here in the States. The government asked him to do a job; he did it and did it well. Hans Schultz couldn't help it if everyone else in this organization was an incompetent buffoon.

He moved away from the window and sat down at his desk. They were right about one thing, though. He was old, very old. Shooting himself with alien DNA every few years had slowed down the aging process, but had by no means stopped it. While his mind was still sharp as ever, his body was slowly falling apart.

He knew his remaining time on earth was short, and now at a time when he should have been able to sit back and enjoy the work of his hands, what happens? These idiots jeopardize the entire future of the project.

Every time he turned around they were killing someone else to cover up their incompetence. And every time someone died, more questions got asked and more people got closer to finding out the truth. Therefore, more people had to be killed, causing more questions, getting an army of people ever closer...

It was a vicious cycle. Once it got started, like a tidal wave there was no stopping it until it destroyed everything in it's path. Damn it! They were so close! So close to having the perfect being. The people they made were smarter, faster, stronger, healthier, and the powers of their minds were unfathomable.

But he hadn't bred them to fight an alien invasion. Nor had he bred them to be used in a war as common soldiers. Hans had a theory that mankind had started out smart and wound up stupid. He theorized that the Aryan world had started out as a hybrid, and had become stupider as it became more and more interbred with the ancestors of the mud races.

For this reason he had very carefully allowed only whites in his breeding program. When the computer found an alien hybrid that was of another ethnic origin, he had it destroyed usually before the "parents" could take it home.

Hans had wondered why the aliens bothered to impregnate inferior people, and now he knew why. Apparently, when you crossed the superior intellect of an alien with the inferior intellect of a mud race, the hybrid could inherit all of its genes from the father, the superior genes of the father canceling out the genes of the inferior mother.

Either that, or he was wrong, and there were no inferior people. Which would mean that when you mixed two things that didn't match, you could wind up with just about any combination of the two. Hans shook the insane thought from his head. He was tired, that was all. He needed a nap. He leaned back in his chair and closed his eyes.

"Sir?" a voice at the door said.

"What the hell is it!" Hans said, hammering on his desk with his fist. "Can't you see I need some rest?"

"You sent for Brawn, and he's here, sir," his secretary said after clearing her throat.

"Ah! Good! Send him in." Hans sat up straight in his chair, suddenly feeling revitalized.

The man walked in. He was so huge that he seemed to fill the room. "Sit! Sit, my son," Hans said.

Brawn sat in the chair Hans indicated. "You sent for me, Father?"

"I have a bit of a problem, son," Hans said. "Americans are incompetent. I don't have to tell you that. They are foolish and sentimental. So there are leaks, and I want you to stop them. There are some troublesome people, and I want you to kill them."

Brawn smiled for the first time since he had entered the room. "It will be my pleasure."

TOMMY WAS HOEING in his garden. He was starting to see what he was sure were seedlings, and he pointed them out to Laura.

"Do you see?" he asked pointing.

"No, not really," she said.

"Right there, see?"

Laura shrugged. It looked like dirt to her. "Sorry, Baby."

"Well, it is. I know it is." He continued to hoe the weeds he didn't want out of his garden, carefully preserving the weeds he did want. Mostly, he was trying to loosen up the soil so that it would soak up water better.

"Don't you ever wonder what's going on out there, Tommy? The President could have been assassinated and we wouldn't even know about it."

"Yes we would. We listen to the radio every night for fifteen minutes. We hear the news," Tommy said.

"Don't you miss the people you work with?"

"Most of them are turds. They don't like me, and I don't like them. I miss Spider, but who knows where she is right now?"

"We don't know because we haven't been home…"

"I told you that Carrie said Spider disappeared," Tommy said.

"I wonder what my parents are thinking. I miss my friends at work. I miss Carrie. I miss the toilet. Tommy, I want to go home," Laura said.

Tommy sighed. She did this almost every day now. "Laura, I told you. We can't go back. Not yet. Maybe not ever. Why can't you just enjoy being here and put everything else out of your head?"

"Because there is nothing to occupy my brain, Tommy," Laura said. "I had one book and I've read it six times. Should I count rocks, or take up a hobby collecting strange looking pieces of moss? Come on, Tommy. We can't continue to live like this!"

"I can't believe that you would rather go back there and die than be bored. Besides, it's your own fault that you're bored. I'm not bored, because there are lots of things to do."

"All the things there are to do here are things that I hate to do," Laura said matter-of-factly. "Let's go out there. Change our names. Go to a new town. Start over again. Like the witness protection program, thingy."

"Oh! That would be a lot of fun. I could pump gas for a living, and you could get a lovely job in fast foods. We could live in a fucking trailer court and eat TV dinners. Besides which, where the hell am I going to get the paperwork? I don't have any connections, and you can't do shit any more without ID. Why can't you be reasonable?"

She started crying and ran towards the cabin. He let her go. The first ten times she had done this he had gone to her and apologized.

Now he was tired of it. Why couldn't she just get it through her head that this was the way things had to be—at least for now—and learn to enjoy it?

Something fell into the middle of his garden and rolled up to his feet. He looked down at the baseball for a second, then grabbed his gun and scanned the area. From across the camp Spider grinned back at him, waving a baseball mitt in the air.

"Wanna play catch?" she yelled.

TOMMY RAN, JUMPED his makeshift fence, and raced the full length of the camp. He jumped on Spider and tackled her to the ground. Then he kissed her whole face. He finally got off her and hauled her to her feet.

"Spider, I..." he hugged her.

"Yeah, me, too." She smiled and hugged him again.

Laura heard the commotion and came out of the cabin. When she saw what all the ruckus was about, she ran down to greet Spider as well.

"How the hell did you find us?" Tommy asked.

"You told me about coming here all the time when you were a kid. How secluded it was. I figured you'd come here."

That didn't exactly answer Tommy's question. "But how did you find us?" Tommy asked again.

"The library. Reading Is Fundamental, don't you know," she said. "I knew you grew up in Oxburg. I knew you said it was in the area, so I drew a circle on the map. Then I looked for national forests. Then I looked up old WPA and CCC sites in the area. When I overlaid those, it was easy. Once we found the car all I had to do was use my extra sensory perception to feel you out."

Tommy laughed. Then he stood back and looked at her. She looked bad. A black eye, bloodied lip, skin and bones, and tired. Her eyes lacked their usual gleam. "You look like you've been through hell," he said gently.

She almost smiled. "At least."

"Come on, I'll get you something to eat..."

"I'm not alone," she said.

Tommy's guts rolled. "Someone followed you..."

"No. I brought people with me."

"Carrie?" Laura said hopefully. Tommy had no idea when she had gotten there.

"I wish," Spider said. "Robby, come on in!" she yelled.

Then she said to Tommy. "I was afraid you might shoot first and ask questions later, so I came on in alone."

Tommy watched as three figures walked out of the woods. He recognized the man from one of their interviews. "Him! The garbage man is the Fry Guy?"

"Yes," Spider said.

"You!" Laura screeched. "You knew who the Fry Guy was. You...you brought him up here!"

The man was pushing some kind of wheelbarrow looking thing. There was a boy with him, and a woman who had been handcuffed with one of those cheap jobs you could pick up at a gas station.

It only took them a few minutes to catch up to them. Tommy watched with curiosity as the boy walked immediately up to Spider and took her hand, almost hiding behind her. Either there was some genetic link between Spider, the Fry Guy, and this kid, or he had just landed on the planet of the big-handed people.

"Tommy, you've kind of met Robby. This is Mark, and the woman is a So-what-if fuck and our prisoner."

"Her name is Francis," Robby supplied.

"You have a prisoner!" Tommy said, shaking his head in disbelief. "Why do you have a prisoner?"

"It's a long story, and I've got to sit down," Spider said.

"She isn't feeling very well," Robby said.

Tommy led them over to the picnic table. Spider sat down, and the boy sat beside her. He wouldn't look at Tommy. Robby set the wheelbarrow thing down and sat on a piece of log Tommy had brought into camp. The prisoner sat on the ground where Spider pointed.

Tommy sat down across from Spider, and Laura sat beside him. "Now, can you finally tell me what the hell is going on?"

"Let's see. How to put this?" Spider was thoughtful. "There really are aliens. They do, periodically, abduct humans, do experiments on, and impregnate them. Robby, Mark, and I are all at least half alien. I'll give you a second to digest that, then I'll tell you about the huge government conspiracy that started with the Nazi regime."

It was almost dark when Spider finished talking. They ate a dinner consisting of poke salad, squirrel stew, and some sandwiches from the supplies Robby and Spider had brought. They laid out their bedding in the cabin.

"We can fix one of the others for ourselves tomorrow. You wouldn't believe all that Robby has in his amazing folded, hinged, rolling thing," Spider said with a smile. "It's a good thing too, God only knows how long we'll be holed up here."

"Where am I going to sleep?" Francis asked, noticing that they had only laid out three palettes.

"Someplace else," Spider said. She hauled the woman to her feet and started yanking her out the door.

Tommy and Robby followed her, Robby carrying a flashlight and a blanket. Mark started to go with them.

"No, you stay here, sport," Spider said.

"But..." Mark started.

"But me no buts," Spider said with a smile and rubbed his head. "Go lay down and get some sleep. You can't tell me that hike in didn't wear you out."

He nodded and let her go.

Laura smiled at him and he smiled back. He went to his pallet, moved it closer to Spider's, and then lay down in it. Laura smiled. It had to be driving Spider crazy having this kid hanging all over her. Spider just wasn't the maternal type.

"You can sleep with us if you want," Laura said. "The mattress is quite comfortable, and there's plenty of room."

"No, thank you," he said.

Laura rubbed her arms. "It's a little chilly in here. When Tommy gets back I'll have him light the fire. He has this flint and steel thing I just can not figure out."

"I can do it," Mark said sitting up.

"You don't have to do that."

Mark smiled at her. "It's easy." He looked at the logs and kindling already laying in the fireplace, focused, and the fire started.

"Did you...did you do that?" Laura asked in amazement.

"Uh huh," Mark said. He looked disappointed as he added, "but I don't have very much fire. I can make lots of little fires, or one big one. But after a big one, that's it for while. Robby can just burn and burn and burn things."

"How nice for Robby," Laura said. She remembered the headlines and TV news. She'd seen the reports, knew what the man was capable of, and decided it was definitely better to be his friend than his enemy. "Well, I think that was very impressive. It takes Tommy thirty minutes to get a fire that big going."

"Thanks." He lay back down. "I panicked and I used a big fire on Fritz. If I was smart I would have just put a little fire on him, and then I would have had some left."

Laura lay down and made a face. Here was a little kid who had already witnessed a bloodbath. He couldn't ever be normal again, even if he had been normal to start with. "You know what they say, hindsight is twenty-twenty. I don't think you should dwell on it, Mark. Sounds like that's some awful heavy stuff for a kid to be worrying about."

"But I have to think about it," Mark said in a far away tone. "I heard Robby and Spider talking. They said they're going to have to destroy the SWTF or none of us can ever get our lives back. I'm one of them, and this time I have to help, not just stand there like a lump, too scared to fire the gun Spider gave me."

"Mark…you're just a kid. You have to let us worry about this stuff. Spider's not going to take you back into…" she couldn't think of another word for it, "…combat. Who knows? Maybe we'll just stay here in the woods forever," Laura said.

"Maybe," Mark said he snuggled into his pillow. "Maybe she will take me with her if I can make more fire."

"THIS ONE HAS the most door," Tommy said.

"It'll do," Spider said. They walked inside. "What are we going to chain the bitch to?"

"Wait here." Tommy ran off. He came back several minutes later rolling an old volleyball goal post. It was one of those that was sitting in a tire full of concrete, and the old hooks welded on the side to attach the net would keep her from pulling it off the top. They left one of the cuffs on her wrist, attached the other to the pole, and stood it in one of the back corners. They checked the cabin for anything that could be used as a weapon or tool, threw a blanket at her, and started to leave.

"Wait! You're not just going to leave me here, are you?" Francis gasped. "Alone in the woods! What about bears?"

"They won't come inside," Tommy assured her.

"This is barbaric!" Francis screamed.

"This is a fucking cakewalk," Spider hissed. "I can't believe you have the nerve to bitch about your incarceration to me. How about we hang you from the ceiling in a straightjacket and occasionally drug and/or torture you? I hate your guts, so don't give me any reason to hurt you, because I will. You know I will. Now shut up, lay down, go to sleep, and be happy that I'm not you."

Tommy shut the door, and Robby leaned a log against it.

"What the hell do you have her for?" Tommy asked.

"Because she knows everything about the project, and we still don't," Spider said tiredly.

She stumbled, almost fell, and Tommy caught her. He put his arm around her to steady her. She didn't protest, just leaned against him. She had lost way too much weight.

"They hit me with this weapon they call a lightning bolt gun. They tazed me. They used a cattle prod on me. Drugged me all the time. Just to name a few. I need to think, and my head's so screwed up I can't."

"You got out of there, and you got here. I think you're thinking just fine," Tommy said.

"Robby got us out of there. I figured out where you were, but Robby got us here. Hell, I almost couldn't make the hike in," Spider said.

"We'll get some good food in you. With plenty of rest, fresh air and exercise, you'll be back to your old self in no time," Tommy said.

"I'm worried about Carrie, but I can't figure out if she's safe where she is or not. I feel like I can't think at all any more. Who's going to take care of this mess if I can't think any more?"

"You'll be fine as soon as you heal. In the meantime I'll take care of things," Tommy said.

"I'm tired," she said.

"All you need is some rest," Tommy assured her.

He took Spider to the cabin and helped her lie down on her bedroll. He watched as the boy pulled himself closer to her.

Tommy motioned for Robby to follow him outside, and he did.

"She does seem really out of it," Tommy said in a worried tone. "Her eyes are kind of glassy, and she's not thinking on her feet."

"What she's not telling you is that she attempted suicide by beating her head on a concrete floor. I think she's sustained a pretty serious concussion," Robby said.

Tommy thought about the injuries he had suffered on the dock. The doctor had given him anti-inflammatory drugs to keep his brain from swelling. He might still have some left. Those would probably help Spider. "I think I've got something that might help. Why was she banging her head on the floor?"

"They were going to torture Mark because she wouldn't tell them where I was," Robby said matter-of-factly. "Guess she figured if she was dead they'd leave the boy alone. But then while she was out, they told Mark that the only reason he was alive was because of Spider, and that if she died, he died."

"Sounds like a real fine batch of human beings," Tommy said. He was thoughtful. "Why were they torturing the kid?"

Robby was silent.

"Well, what is it?" Tommy demanded.

"The program has been using Spider for a breeder," Robby answered quietly.

"They've been doing what!" Tommy screeched. Then lowered his voice. "What the hell are you talking about?"

"Spider's one of the women they've been taking eggs from for fertilization and implantation. Mark is Spider's son, one of her children. She's probably got dozens. They chose him because he looked too much like Spider and her brother for her to deny him."

"Wow!" Tommy found a rock and sat down. "You know that she's…"

"Gay. Yes, I know," Robby said.

"It must have been a real shock to learn that she was anybody's mother," Tommy said "No wonder he's hanging all over her. Separated from his…parents…knowing she's his real mother."

"She cares very deeply for him, too," Robby said. "She tries not to, but it's like she just can't help herself."

"She needs him, too," Tommy said thoughtfully.

DENISTEN SAT AT the keyboard. What he had just found was bound to bring the SWTF to their knees. He couldn't wait to show this shit to DA Long. He'd just started a download when he heard a noise behind him and turned. When he saw the big guy he knew he was screwed, but he pulled his gun and tried to fire anyway. His gun slipped out of his hand. He felt like his brain was on fire, and then nothing. Meltdown.

Brawn picked up the body, the gun, and the disk and headed for the door. "Silly man," he said to the body. "If you want information, you have got to come during business hours." He went out the back door and walked over to the car. The trunk was already open, so he tossed the body in, and tossed the disk in on top of it.

The FBI man walked over and held his hand out to Brawn.

"You would sell out your friend for a couple of dollars?" Brawn shook his head in disgust.

"He's not my friend, and he was messing in something subversive."

"He was trying to fight for something he believed in. I can admire that. I don't admire you." He hit the guy with his power, caught him as he fell, and then tossed him in the trunk with the other one.

Brawn wasn't sloppy; he didn't leave *any* loose ends.

CARRIE LOOKED AT her watch and then at the wall clock. Both said ten o'clock.

"He's not coming, Carrie," George said. He was scared. "Maybe he got caught."

"George, listen to me…" Carrie was thoughtful for a moment. She took off her glasses and rubbed her tired eyes. "I want you to take all the information that we have so far." She collected all the disks, put them into an envelope, and then into his hands. "Take them, put them in the box with the evidence from the Dunn's case, and then take it to the evidence locker. Make sure that it goes inside. Do it now."

George nodded and left. Carrie had insisted that security on the evidence locker be beefed up after what had happened to Spider, and now a fart couldn't get out of there without being seen. But she, as the DA, could take it out and put it back with no one being the wiser. If Denisten had been caught, she was going to have to be even more careful.

Carrie walked out of her office and the two cops fell in behind her. They walked her to her car, and then stood guard while she got in and started it. Only then did they get in their car and follow her home. At the house one of them went in first and checked all the rooms as the other one stayed with her. She only entered her own home when she had been given the all clear, and then she did her own check with her hand on her gun.

After everything was locked up, she went to the den and sat down. As usual, the light was flashing on her answering machine, so she walked over and punched the button, expecting to hear a long string of messages from people who had already called her at the office. That's what it was—up to the fifth message.

"Carrie. I just wanted to let you know that I'm all right, and I miss you."

Carrie's heart stopped. She played it over and over before she erased it.

"I miss you, too, alien or not."

THE ANTI-INFLAMMATORY DRUGS hadn't helped her a lot, and neither had fresh air, sunshine, or good, healthy food. Spider didn't know what they had fed them in SWTF HQ, but it had all been gray, and she had eaten very damn little of it—afraid that they were drugging her, and they no doubt were.

Tommy threw the ball, and Spider caught it, but then almost dropped it. She wasn't feeling any better or stronger.

She threw the ball to Robby, who missed it and ran into the woods. He came back waving the ball and threw it to Mark.

Laura watched them play ball as she hung the laundry. Funny, she had complained about being bored one too many times, and now they had found her something to do.

To watch them play, you wouldn't guess that they weren't just a normal group of people on a camping trip. Or for that matter that they had a care in the world.

She still couldn't believe that Spider was a mother.

The prisoner, unhandcuffed and unwatched, was wandering around, seemingly looking at rocks. She knew what these people were capable of, and she wasn't stupid enough to think she had any chance of escape. But to be on the safe side, Spider had put a push on her. Whatever the hell that was. Apparently, it made the woman believe that rocks were absolutely the most entertaining things on earth, because she kept picking them up, spinning them round and round in her hand, and then oo-ing and aw-ing.

Spider jumped up for a catch, caught it, and then lost her balance and fell. She jumped up, took the glove off, slung it to the ground and stomped towards the woods.

"Spider!" Tommy called after her. "It's all right! Come on…" He ran, picked up the ball, threw it to Robby, and then ran after Spider.

Spider stared into the woods. Tommy stood at her shoulder. "What's wrong?"

She didn't turn around. "You know what's wrong, Tommy. I don't have any sense of balance. I'm not getting better; I'm getting worse."

"You're better every day. Just give it some time…"

"Maybe I don't have any time. They're getting desperate. They've got to be. We're free, we have one of their scientists, and they can't find us. Carrie is absolutely the only leverage that they have right now. Worse than that, you gave the disk to her."

"If I hadn't, the whole world would know right now," Tommy defended.

Spider nodded. "And right now I can't tell you whether that would be better or worse. Even if they don't find out about the disk, it's only a matter of time till they decide that we're more of a risk to them loose than kidnapping a prominent big city DA would be—if they haven't already. If they think she knows too much, they might just kill her outright. Up here I don't have a clue what's happening. I need to go get her before they do, but I can't walk, much less think straight."

Tommy took her gently by the shoulders and turned her around to face him. "But I can," Tommy said. "I can think and move just fine. I'll take Robby with me. No one really knows what he looks like, and me…" He pointed at the mustache he was growing. "Slip on some dark glasses, and who would know me? I can get her and get out, and if I do it right, I might even be able to make everyone think the SWTF did it."

Spider seemed to be thinking. Tommy put his hands on her shoulders. "Listen to me, partner, and listen good. We have trusted each other, relied on each other, for fifteen years. Is it really so hard for you to trust me now? I can get her for you. With Robby, who could stop us?"

Spider nodded. There was no choice. She couldn't do it, and she would only get in the way. "Please…"

"I won't let anything happen to her, and I won't come back without her," Tommy promised.

Spider nodded. "Then get the hell out of here already."

CHAPTER TWENTY-TWO

"For to him that is joined to all the living there is
hope: For a living dog is better than a dead lion."
Ecclesiastes 9:4

CARRIE COULD FEEL them putting the squeeze on. Every day there were more of them than there had been the day before. Everywhere she looked there were fucking SWTF. Maybe she was just being paranoid, but she didn't think so. They were either sure that Spider was on her way and were preparing a trap with Carrie as the bait, or they knew what Carrie had been doing and were closing in for the kill.

Either way, it made Carrie feel like she was standing on shaky ground at the edge of a cliff. One wrong move and she would plunge into the abyss.

She ran her hands through her hair, and continued what she was doing. She had to cover as many bases as she could think of to cover. She took the micro disk out of the machine, deposited the other disks in the evidence box, and called her new legal assistant to come and cart it away. Then she stuck the micro disk in a case and stuffed it into her bra. She still didn't know what to do with the information on the disk.

She could make it public. If she did, she exposed the SWTF and all that they were doing. This disk was proof that aliens were a fact, which would no doubt cause worldwide panic and expose Spider and people like her to the worse kind of scrutiny.

Her second choice was to not make it public. But if she didn't, there was nothing to stop the SWTF from continuing to do what they had been doing all along, manipulating and destroying lives. Using people like guinea pigs as if they had no feelings and no souls.

There didn't seem to be any real answer. Even when she selfishly thought only of herself, she realized that exposing the SWTF meant exposing Spider. Spider might be able to run and hide from the SWTF, but how could she ever run from the masses? There would be nowhere that she could go and be safe ever again.

She thought about her favorite bumper sticker of all times and smiled. 'Mean People Suck.' That said it all.

She pressed the button on the intercom. "Agnes, send George in here, please."

"Yes Sir."

A few minutes later George walked in. "Carrie?"

"Sit down, George," Carrie said. She took a deep breath. "Have you noticed..."

"Strange people everywhere? Yes, I have."

"Suddenly this building needs all kinds of work. The road outside my house has suddenly sprung a leak. Don't ask me how that happened, or why it's taking them three days to fix it. I want you...no matter what happens...to forget everything that we have talked about. Forget about everything, do you understand?"

"But, Carrie..."

"Just listen, George. Please. Jackson Harris would make a damn good assistant DA..."

"Carrie, what the hell are you saying?" George said.

"I'm saying I don't know what the hell is going to happen!" she said hotly. She forced herself to calm down. George didn't deserve her wrath. "There is no reason for them to believe that you are part of anything that I have done. None of it can be traced back to you. If I come up missing..."

"Carrie, for God's sake..."

"Please shut up, George. This isn't easy for me. I don't know if it's the right thing to do, but it may be the only thing." She paused and took a deep breath. "If I come up missing, I don't want you to say a word about the SWTF or anything that I've been doing. Play dumb. Say it was one of the homophobes who phone this building daily with threats. If you don't hear from me in," she thought for a minute, "...four weeks—one month, or I turn up dead, then take the disks and give them to the press."

George nodded silently, then said, "Carrie...isn't there something we can do to stop them, to protect you?"

"No. I don't think so." She forced a laugh then. "Who knows? Maybe I'm just being paranoid, and nothing at all will happen."

ROBBY DROVE, AND Tommy rode shotgun. He had to think, and think clearly. Spider was counting on him to bring Carrie back in one piece. Laura was counting on him to come back in one piece. He couldn't afford even one fuck up.

He'd had a chance to talk to Robby on this trip and he now understood—at least in part—why Spider had gone to such lengths to protect him.

Robby talked about the siblings he had raised and the grandmother he had helped to support without any bitterness and with such love. Here was a man who had never had a chance to be a boy, who had never had a chance to get an education or even go on a date, and was currently being hunted like a wild animal. Yet he wasn't bitter. He wasn't even unhappy.

He talked about the girl he had fallen in love with in such glowing terms that you'd think the woman had a gold-plated pussy.

Robby was sharp and friendly. In short, he was the nicest motherfucker Tommy had ever met, and he couldn't think of one reason not to like the guy. Yet he had probably personally killed more men than any other single man in history.

It just really did not compute.

"Is she going to get better?" Robby asked, talking about Spider.

"I hope so," Tommy said. "You've never really seen her at the top of her game. There's no stopping her."

"If she's not operating at the top now, she must be hell on wheels. I've seen her do things…" He told Tommy about her dropping down the stairwell. "She seemed to have her balance then. Maybe it was that last sleeping dart."

Tommy shrugged. "When I got hit in the head the doctor kept talking about something called post concussion syndrome. Laura said it can take days to manifest. Apparently swelling in the brain causes short-term memory loss, loss of balance, and irritability. I'll bet it's nothing a little time and some attention from Carrie can't cure. Pull in here."

Robby pulled into the parking lot of the bar without question.

"Come on. It's show time."

SHERRY AND A woman Tommy didn't know were sitting at the corner table. Sherry wasn't a very big woman. Average height, thin, nice build—a real looker. At first glance, one might dismiss her as an airhead, a lightweight. Tommy knew better. He started making his way across the room, and Robby followed.

"Hey, Sherry," the girl at the table said. "You know some pretty sleazy people. What if I wanted to have someone killed?"

"Linda, I know people who'd ice a guy for a twelve pack and a joint," Sherry said. She looked up at the two strangers as they approached. "Take these two for instance...Can I help you guys, or are you just here for the view?"

"Need to talk to you, Sherry," Tommy said. Linda didn't have to be asked to leave—she just made tracks. Tommy sat down and Robby followed his lead.

"Tommy Chan, is that you?" Sherry asked in a whisper.

Tommy nodded.

"Hell, boy! We thought you were long dead. Word on the street had it you got in trouble with some mob thing."

"The mob I could have handled, but we're talking government. Listen, Sherry, you know that favor you owe me?"

"I knew that was going to come back and bite me on the ass some day." Sherry leaned forward with a sigh and rested her chin on her hands. "Well, get on with it."

"I need you to make a diversion."

"Is that all? I thought you were going to ask me to hand over my first-born or some other goddamn horrible thing. You want a diversion..." She snapped her fingers in a Z. "Sherry can make a diversion."

SHERRY'S GUM POPPING was starting to get on his nerves. "Do you have to do that?" Tommy asked in a whisper.

"What?" Sherry asked with a shrug.

"That popping, smacking shit," Tommy said.

"What are you waiting around for, anyway? Are we just going to sit here all damn night?"

That was a good question. Tommy wondered where the hell Carrie was. She should have been home an hour ago. He hoped he wasn't too damn late. But if he was, why were the damned SWTF guys there? He was sure that was what the road crew was.

Suddenly he saw what he was sure was Carrie's car turn around the corner of the street. "OK, Sherry. Do your thing." He handed her a hundred dollar bill and she looked at him. "For cab fare."

She nodded, stuffed the bill in her bra and got out of the car. She pulled her skirt up as high as it would go and headed for the "construction workers."

"Hey boys!" She sauntered up to them. "Pity to be working on such a nice night." She purposely dropped her purse, and then bent down slowly to retrieve it, flashing her ass for them.

"We ain't looking for no hooker, lady. Just doing our job. Now move along."

Sherry smiled before she stood up. All she had to do was create a diversion, and he had just given her a hell of an opening.

"What the hell did you call me!" she screamed. "I ain't no fucking hooker!"

"I'm sorry…"

"Sorry! Why you pencil-dicked, geek! Why, you couldn't get laid in a monkey whorehouse with a sack full of bananas. I wouldn't fuck you if you had the last dick on earth!"

"Hey, now…" he started to protest.

"Hey now, my ass!" Sherry screamed. "You think you can call me anything you like and get away with it?"

The other three men were obviously very amused by the fourth one's predicament.

"What are you bunch of cackling hens laughing about, there ain't a rooster in the whole damn bunch of ya! If any of you were real men, you wouldn't let him talk to a lady like that…"

CARRIE PULLED INTO her driveway with the police close behind her. They got out and one stood with her while the other went inside to do the regular check of the house.

She heard all the hubbub across the street. Apparently some tramp had mistaken the So-what-if guys for humans. Carrie wished he'd hurry up with his check so she could go inside, throw off her shoes, and sit down.

In a matter of seconds a man jumped out of the bushes, delivered a knock out punch to her guard, grabbed her, and pulled her into the bushes. She started to scream, but there was a hand over her mouth.

"Listen! It's me—Tommy. I'm going to get you out of here."

Carrie nodded and followed as he pulled her around and through the hedges, successfully keeping her out of view of the SWTF guys.

He was leading her towards the hole in the hedge on the west side of the house. She squeezed through and into the car that was parked right beside the hedge.

"Damn! That was way too easy," Tommy said. He was kneeling in the floorboards with Carrie. "OK, Robby. Get us the hell out of here."

There was nothing. "Robby?" Tommy looked slowly up. A big blond guy looked down at him.

"My name is Brawn," he said. "And I'd say I have just about all the leverage I need now to bring a certain lady cop back into the fold."

Tommy saw the size of the man's hands, and knew what he was up against, but it was a sure bet that Brawn didn't know what he was up against. Tommy whipped his right hand up quickly, letting his left shoulder drop to add impact. His palm hit Brawn's nose, and he kept pushing. Then he jumped as far up as the car would allow, and plowed the monster's head into the top of the car hard enough to dent the roof. The man's face caved in around Tommy's hand, and when Tommy pulled his hand back the man fell into the front seat and started to spasm.

"Stay here," Tommy ordered Carrie.

Carrie nodded. She had no intention of even getting out of the floorboards.

Tommy crawled over her and out the door they had crawled in. He opened the front door, dragged the body out, and rolled it into the bushes—not without an effort. Then he started looking for Robby.

"Robby," Tommy whispered. He was ducked down below the hedges. Across the street and around the corner he could hear Sherry still screaming at the SWTF Guys. Then their tone changed. He heard one of them scream over Sherry.

"Something's going down over there!"

A quick look through the hedge showed him that the cop had come out of the house and found Carry gone and his partner down.

"Robby! Damn it, man." He couldn't wait; he had to go. He ran back to the car, jumped in and started the engine.

"Stay down, this could get hairy." He took off.

"Sorry, Robby, but you're on your own," he muttered.

He drove at a normal pace, but they still tagged him.

"Damn! They're following us," Tommy hissed. He tried to lose them without looking too obvious, but they stayed with him, so he wasn't just dreaming it. Suddenly, there was a loud knocking.

"Oh! Just what we fucking need! Car trouble. I wish we had fucking Robby." The knocking got louder, and Tommy realized what it was. He laughed.

"Robby, is that you man?" The knocking got louder and more urgent.

"Carrie, there's a latch in the top of the back seat that flips it down so you can get in the trunk."

Carrie found it and opened it. She could see the man—he had a bucket shaped helmet on his head, and she helped him get it off.

"Tommy! I'm so sorry, man," Robby said.

He was handcuffed, but with Carrie's help he managed to squirm into the back seat. "The fucker snuck up on me, hit me with a fucking lightning bolt, and than slammed that damn thing on my head. I couldn't do shit."

"It's OK, man. Can you do something about our tail?"

Robby looked back. "Which one?"

Tommy checked in his rear view mirror again. Damn! They had picked up another car. "Both of them."

Robby focused on the front car for a second. "It's not working."

Suddenly, a large sedan pulled out in front of them. Tommy swerved and hit the gas. The jig was up; no more pretending. This was a full-scale chase.

"Try again," Tommy begged.

"I am. It's just not working."

"Is it the hand cuffs?" Tommy asked.

"No. It's got to be that damned lightning bolt. My heads still sort of fuzzy. It must have fucked me up."

Cars were coming at them from everywhere. Suddenly SWTF, FBI, and local police—everyone—was in hot pursuit. Tommy swerved in and out of traffic.

He saw Carrie pull a gun out from under her arm. She put her arm out the window and started firing behind them. She didn't appear to be hitting anything, but it seemed to be keeping them back a little.

Just as Tommy was sure they were going to get away, a fucking panel truck turned out into his lane. There was nowhere to go except through the front of a department store.

"Get down and hold on!" Tommy screamed.

He drove through the window, diving into the floorboards with his foot still hard on the accelerator.

The car plowed through the window and most of the way across the store before it stopped against the back wall.

Tommy kicked the door open, opened the back door, grabbed his gun with one hand and Carrie with the other. "Come on! Let's move it!"

Robby piled out behind Carrie and they started running for the down escalator, which went to the basement parking garage.

The cops and SWTF started plowing through the front wall and coming after them. Robby turned, and this time his power was back. As the front three SWTF guys blew up, everyone else hit the floor.

The three of them made it to the escalator and started running down it. As they reached the bottom, five SWTF men rounded the corner beside them. Tommy let go of Carrie, grabbed the rail with one hand, and bounded over the side. He kicked one guy in the neck, then spun and snap kicked another hard enough to drive him to his knees. Another kick to the second guy's head finished him.

As Robby hit the other three, Carrie scooped up two of their fallen guns without being asked, and Tommy suddenly realized just why Spider was so taken with her. He'd always known that Carrie was intelligent, but it had never dawned on him that she might also be street smart, and quick. He had certainly never considered that she could be physically tough if the need arose.

She fired on a troop of SWTF men who were coming down the escalator after them. Two of them fell.

Tommy grabbed her arm and pulled her behind a concrete post. Robby followed them, watching their back.

"Tommy," Carrie said a little excited. "I'm still on-line."

He looked at her, a bit puzzled about her obvious implication that this was somehow important.

"They can track me. But it also means I still have my clearance."

Tommy nodded. He finally knew what she was getting at. He looked at Robby. "If we can get to a cop car—any cop car—Carrie can get us in."

They started to move again, and were spotted again this time by the police. Carrie waved her comlink at them, but they drew down on Robby and Tommy.

"I think we just caught a break," Carrie mumbled to Tommy.

"Put those away! This is agent Chan and this…" she slapped
Robby hard, and pointed at the handcuffs, "is one of the men who
tried to kidnap me. The others are back there. Be careful! They are
armed and dangerous. I need your car, where is it?"

They all pointed in different directions.

"Well, don't just stand there! Go after them." The police ran one
way, and they ran the other.

They located a car, got in and took off. No one followed them.
No one questioned them.

Tommy sighed with relief. "All right. But what now, boss? This
car is linked up, and so are you."

"Let's just get the hell out of town for now. We can get another car in Jones Port or fucking walk for all I care. Right now I
just want as much distance between us and them as we can get. As
for me." She reached in her pocket, pulled out the wand and rubbed
it over her ear. "Now I'm off-line, and with this we can put me
back on-line if we need to."

"Great!"

Robby, now riding alone in the back seat behind the partition,
rattled the handcuffs. Carrie pushed the button to lower the shield,
passed her comlink over the cuffs, and nothing happened. She smiled
at him and shrugged.

"Sorry, must be coded different than mine."

"Hit them with a little heat," Tommy said.

"That only works in the movies. If I get that metal hot enough to
break, it's also going to burn the shit out of my wrists," Robby said.

He looked at Carrie then and smiled. She looked haggard and
rattled, but she was still every bit as pretty as Spider said she was.
"You must be Carrie. I've heard a lot about you."

"And you're the Fry Guy." No hint of surprise in her voice, so
obviously she'd already figured it out. Carrie shook his hand as he
worked at presenting it to her. "You sure did open up a big ole can
of worms, now didn't you?"

He nodded, head down. "I'm sorry."

Carrie shrugged. "It's all water almost under the bridge now."

She looked at Tommy. "So, how is Spider?"

Tommy started to answer.

"The truth, Tommy. If she was in perfect health nothing would
have stopped her from coming with you to get me."

Tommy took a deep breath. "She's in pretty bad shape…they did horrible things to her, Carrie. They beat her up pretty bad. Pumped a lot of drugs into her body. She's lost a lot of weight."

Carrie nodded and looked out the window. "Is she going to be all right?"

"I think so," Tommy said. "In time. I think your being there will help."

THEY LOST THE car and stole another out of a parking lot. Robby explained how to do it, and Tommy followed his directions exactly. They stopped along the way for Carrie to get some suitable clothes. When they stopped to sleep for the night Tommy fiddled with the lock on the handcuffs till they came off.

"I could drive," Carrie said.

"No. For the hundredth time, Carrie, we need some sleep," Tommy said.

Carrie nodded. She knew he was right, but it didn't help her much. She needed to see Spider right then. To see how bad she really was. While Tommy and Robby slept like babies, she didn't sleep a wink. She woke them up three hours later and demanded that they hit the road—which they did.

On the way up to the cabins she kept running ahead of them. Even Tommy's reminders that she didn't know where they were going didn't slow her down.

When she stepped into the clearing ahead of Tommy and Robby, the first thing she saw was Spider sitting on a rock in the sun. Spider's head turned to meet her, no doubt sensing her there. She cringed as she watched Spider struggle to get up, then she ran to meet her. Carrie threw her arms around Spider, and Spider embraced her.

They both had a good cry.

"I thought I'd never see you again," Carrie said.

"I was so worried. I knew you wouldn't be safe for much longer. I trusted that Tommy would come through for us. I'm sorry…I couldn't go after you myself."

Carrie dried her eyes and then she dried Spider's. "Tommy told me. We'll get you well, Baby."

Tommy and Robby caught up to them then. "That damn woman of yours tried to run our legs off," Tommy said with a smile.

"Thank you. Both of you," Spider said. It didn't look like she planned to let Carrie go anytime soon. Or Carrie her for that matter.

"She's a hell of a gal, Spider. A real trooper," Tommy said with real admiration. Then he took Robby by the arm and steered him away.

Mark came running out of the cabin, very excited. Laura walked out behind him, looking more than a little shaken.

Mark ran up to them. "Tommy! Robby! You know what happened? Laura and I were getting water, and there was this snake, and zap! I just fried it." He almost snapped his fingers, but didn't quite succeed. "Just like that. I think I'm ready to go with you guys now."

Laura hugged Tommy. "It was the most horrible thing; it almost bit me."

Tommy looked over Laura's shoulder at where Mark was making a face and shaking his head no.

Laura saw Carrie then, and started to run off to greet her, happy for real female companionship at last.

Tommy grabbed her arm. "Give them some time, Honey." He looked around. "Where's Francis?"

Mark started yanking on Tommy's pants leg. "Come on, I'll show you."

Francis was in a clearing behind the cabins stacking rocks in some weird formation.

"What the hell is she doing?" Tommy asked.

"She told Mom she's calling the aliens. Mom told her she hoped that she did, because then they were going to kick her ass for what they did to us. But she ain't black anymore."

"What do you mean?" Tommy asked in confusion.

Robby answered him.

"She's not dark anymore. We see evil people as a black shadow. We can see all the bad things they've done. See their dark desires. Francis was like that, and now…Well, she's not exactly light, but she's not dark anymore. She's changed." Robby seemed troubled.

"What?" Tommy asked.

"Well, if she could change…What about all those people I fried?"

"I'm not sure she deserved a second chance. Most of the assholes you fried had been given more than a second chance, and they just got worse and worse and worse. If I were you, I wouldn't lose any sleep over those scum."

ROBBY HAD BEEN messing with it for hours.

"Well?" Tommy asked.

Robby shrugged. "I just don't know that much about computers. I'm sorry, but I don't know if I can make it work or not."

"Let me see if I can help. I'm not terribly mechanical, but I do know computers. Between the two of us, maybe we can figure it out," Carrie said.

Spider sat down on the hearth, and Mark immediately sat down beside her, taking her hand.

"Why don't you just tell us what's on the disk?" Spider asked impatiently.

Spider wasn't herself at all. The longer Carrie was here, the more she realized that. She was weak and got winded easily. She was irritable and edgy. Carrie knew who the boy was, but she kept waiting for Spider to introduce them. Kept waiting for Spider to tell her what she'd been through, but so far in the approximately six hours since she'd arrived, Spider hadn't talked much at all. After the initial excitement of seeing her wore off, she had in fact seemed distant—almost cold. Carrie fiddled with some lines on the comlink. There was nothing really compatible about the disk and the comlink; it was a long shot at best.

She didn't want Spider to see how disappointed she was by her reactions. Laura had told her about the head injury and what she knew about the conditions Spider had been kept in. It explained all of her symptoms, and made her behavior tolerable if frustrating and disappointing.

"What's on the disk!" Spider screamed.

When Carrie looked at her, Spider's face was red with anger.

Carrie took a deep breath and reminded herself that she had to be rational, because Spider really couldn't be held accountable. "It's a list of all the hybrids the SWTF have made. I've found fifty of them, twenty males and thirty females…"

"So, now that we're aliens, we're not women and men anymore, we're males and females," Spider said hotly.

It wasn't till then that Carrie realized that not all of Spider's reserved nature was directly related to her injuries or her captivity. Carrie hadn't really had time for the implications of what she had learned to soak in. At least not in relation to Spider. Carrie'd had more pressing matters to worry about than the fact that her lover was half alien—half *not* human.

It didn't really matter to her. Or at least that was what she'd told herself from the moment she'd pieced it all together and figured it out. But she had just said males and females, so maybe in the back of her head she did see them as different. Of course they *were* different, but different was not synonymous with bad.

Carrie was about to explain all that when Tommy said, "That isn't what she meant. You know that's not what she meant. Quit being such a damn moody piece of shit. No one can say anything to you without you getting pissed off."

"It's the cranial injury," Francis chimed from where she sat in the corner polishing rocks on her shirttail.

"I'm sorry, Spider. I've just gone through these files so much, and that's the way the files are labeled." Carrie looked at Spider, and held her gaze. It wasn't easy. She was used to seeing love in Spider's eyes, and it just wasn't there right now. Spider seemed to be running on primal energy, almost more animal than human. Existing at least mentally in a place where everyone was her enemy. Where no one was to be trusted. "Feel me, Spider. Can't you feel that I love you? If you are anything different, you are superior to us. Why would I look down on you? Don't you know I love you?"

"I...I can't feel anything." Spider now sounded more confused than angry, or even afraid. "My power is all but gone. But notice that I'm not part of us anymore."

Carrie thought over what she had just said. She decided to take off the kid gloves, because that obviously wasn't working anyway. "Christ on a crutch, Spider! Would you listen to yourself? We're gay; they're not. That makes them, them—and us, us. Tommy's Asian; we're not. That makes him, them—and us, us. You and Robby and Mark are half alien; we're not. So that makes you, them—and us, us. But we're still all human..."

Spider glared at her through slitted eyes.

"Goddamn it! You know what I mean." Carrie sighed deeply. "Do you really think I would have stuck my neck out for you if I thought you were some freak? If I didn't love you? Look at us! Look at all of us. We've been forced to give up our lives because of the SWTF. We're all in this together, Baby. There's only one enemy here—and it isn't me."

Spider nodded silently and looked at her feet. "I'm sorry. I'm sorry I'm being such a jerk." She started to cry.

Mark frowned and started patting her on the back.

Carrie stood up, walked over and took Spider's hand.

Mark gave her a dirty look. Obviously he blamed Carrie for Spider's tears.

Carrie didn't really care what he thought. "Come on, let's go somewhere and talk." She helped Spider to her feet, and Spider followed her out of the cabin without argument.

Mark started to follow them, and Tommy grabbed his arm.

"Hey!" Mark protested.

"Give them some space, boy," Tommy said. He pulled gently on Mark's arm till he was sitting beside him. "You stay here and help us."

"She looks worse," Robby said to Laura.

"She does not," Mark said harshly.

Tommy glared at Robby, and Robby nodded. "I wasn't talking about Spider. I was talking about...this radio, computer shit...stuff."

"That's the way they do," Francis said matter-of-factly. "They use more of their brain than we do. They do more with their brains, and for this reason they are capable of complete regeneration of brain cells. But to do so they have to shut almost completely down."

"What exactly does that mean?" Robby asked.

Tommy shook his head indicating that he was as confused as Robby was.

"She gave herself a head injury, and she used a power she'd never used before, she drained herself. Her brain has been damaged. When we take a hit to the head, drink, do drugs, just about anything, we kill brain cells. That's a permanent loss, because when our brain cells die, they don't come back, they're gone. Not the hybrids. Their cells are harder to kill, and they are capable of the total regeneration of brain cells. But, in order to do it, their whole metabolism has to slow down. In cases of severe head trauma hybrids have been known to go into a coma. Then they arise from the coma in perfect mental and physical condition."

"Damn! All this time she's been pushing herself trying to get exercise. Making herself stay up. Trying not to just lay around all day sleeping, and instead of helping her it was hurting her. That's why she's getting worse," Laura said thoughtfully. She glared at Francis.

Francis shrugged. "No one asked."

"Maybe someone should go tell Spider and Carrie," Laura suggested.

"I'M SORRY, CARRIE," Spider said looking at her feet.

Carrie squeezed Spider's hand tighter. No reassuring pressure was returned. Spider's hand felt cold and clammy.

"It's all right. I know you've been through hell emotionally and physically..."

"It's not just that..." She seemed to be having trouble breathing. "I need to sit down."

Carrie helped her over to a rock and they sat down. Carrie moved close to Spider without letting go of her hand.

"How bad are you?" Carrie asked carefully. "Tell me the truth. Don't blow smoke up my ass."

Spider laughed.

"What?" Carrie demanded.

"It's just funny to hear my sayings coming out of your mouth. You used to talk so classy."

"I'm still the classy one—don't you forget it. And don't try to change the subject," Carrie demanded

"I don't really know. To tell the truth, I actually feel worse instead of better." Spider looked up at the full moon. "It's all still a little hard to believe. All my life I knew I wasn't like everyone else, but I thought I was just psychic or something. When I first realized there was a connection between Robby and me, I thought about genetic engineering. I never thought...I never dreamed... extraterrestrial! I'm so sorry that I got you into all this shit. Sorry about your job, and your house, and all of the shit with the SWTF. When I met you, all I thought I was doing was tampering with a little evidence in a way that would ensure that I'd never be caught. I never had any idea that we'd end up like this."

Carrie put her hand on Spider's shoulder, and was a little hurt when Spider flinched at her touch. She told herself that Spider didn't find her touch revolting. It was just that she had been tortured, and it would take a while before she could accept that every touch wasn't going to be accompanied by pain.

"How could any of us have known? You don't have to apologize to me for anything. Like you said you had no way of knowing. If this is what I have to go through to be with you, then I'd do it twice."

Spider put her arm around Carrie's shoulder and pulled closer to her. "The boy...Mark...he's..."

Carrie let her off the hook. "I know already, Spider. I knew the minute I saw his picture. Everything I discovered after that just proved what I already knew in my heart. So, what's that like? Having a son, I mean."

"You know, of course, that I probably have a dozen," Spider said.

"From the files I've seen I'd say at least that," Carrie said matter-of-factly.

"I never thought I'd have kids. I never really had parents, so I have no idea how to raise a kid. Besides, I've seen the worst that this world has to offer, and I'm not sure I would want to willingly bring children into it. Even when you and I got together, I never thought kids would be part of our future. We were both too caught up in our jobs."

"We might have taken a break from work to raise kids," Carrie said with a smile. "I can't say I never thought about it, especially since you and I have been together. But, in all seriousness, I always thought that if one of us were going to have kids—it would be me."

"It's weird, because suddenly here's this kid. I didn't give birth to him, didn't nurture him, and didn't raise him. Hell! I didn't even know he existed. Yet I feel this unbelievable closeness to him. If I let myself think about the rest of them, I could become really seriously weirded out. Who knows what's happening to them? Mark had a good family a good life, but who knows about the others? Where they are, or what's happening to them. Those bastards killed Scott, you know. My mother, too."

"He didn't pass the test," Carrie said. "These So-what-if guys are some real heartless bastards. Seems that when the hybrids reach a certain age if they haven't done something that obviously shows their power, then the SWTF tests them. Apparently they hire a bunch of thugs to attack them. They don't do it themselves, because if the subject passes the test all of the thugs wind up dead. If the subject doesn't kill them, he flunks the test, and they kill him. It's that simple. They didn't have to test you because you went into the service, and that was all the test they needed. After all, they bred you to be soldiers. What better testing ground than a real war? But in order to keep you under wraps, every doctor who ever examined or took care of you had to either be one of their own, or be convinced not to tell."

"If they couldn't convince them…"

"They just killed them," Carrie said. She looked up at the moon. "The more I found out, the more scared I got. The SWTF are completely ruthless, single-minded bastards. I had no idea what had happened to you—or Tommy and Laura for that matter. I didn't want to expose them, because in exposing them I would have to expose the entire project, including you. But at the same time I was very quickly running out of options. I'm glad Tommy got me when he did."

"I'm not sure the general public is ready to learn that they aren't alone in the universe, much less that the federal government has been using American citizens as guinea pigs in their experiments. That we are living among them, look like them, and have the power to cook their brains in their head." Spider looked at Carrie. "I think…Carrie, I think I'm dying, and…"

"You're not dying! You can't die." Carrie was insistent. She hadn't given up her life for a corpse.

Tommy walked out of the shadows. He hadn't been eavesdropping; not really, he had just been waiting for a good time to interrupt them.

"You're not dying, Spider. You're regenerating."

CARRIE WAS MORE than a little disappointed. She would have liked to curl up around Spider, but the boy was sleeping between them instead, and she had to be content to hold Spider's hand. Laura tried to convince the boy to stay with her and Tommy, but he freaked out, and Spider insisted that he stay with her. Then, of course, he had to sleep with them—and not just with them, but between them.

No doubt he felt that Carrie represented a threat on his claim to Spider. Spider was all the boy had, and after the shit he'd been through he needed Spider. Needed Spider to be his mother.

When Carrie told Mark that she'd talked to his parents, that they missed him and were worried about him, he didn't even seem to care. He hadn't asked her a single question about them or about his sister. It was weird, because they had been the only family he'd ever known, and yet he didn't seem to be suffering from any separation anxiety. He seemed more than happy to forget them and form a new life with his biological mother.

It was a good thing, too, because God only knew if any of them would ever get their old lives back.

Carrie wondered where she was going to fit into the equation if that happened. If Mark stayed with them, would he accept her as part of Spider's life? Could he grow to love her, and she him? Or were they just going to be in each other's way, each trying to get what they both wanted—Spider's attention.

For now, she was the adult. She realized that a little boy who had been through the trauma Mark had been through needed someone to hold on to. For the time being she could take a back seat, but she was damned if she was going to do it on any sort of permanent basis.

She could just barely make out Spider's face in the moonlight. She had fallen to sleep the minute she lay down, and seemed to be sleeping peacefully. Behind her, sleeping on a cot close to the door was the black man. The Fry Guy. He had killed dozens of people, but then so had Spider Webb. He had an awesome power, but if he had wanted to kill them he could have done it easily, so she wasn't afraid of him.

Spider trusted him, so she trusted him, too. Spider had given up everything, risked all of their lives for him. Therein lay the real rub. He was the cause of all of their problems. If it hadn't been for him, none of this ever would have happened. She and Spider would be home in their own bed, as would Tommy and Laura. Mark would still be with his family with no idea that he wasn't right where he belonged.

Suddenly a chill went up Carrie's spine and she was covered with gooseflesh as somewhere in her mind enlightenment dawned. She was where she was supposed to be. They were all where they were supposed to be. All that had happened to them their whole life had brought them to this place at this time. If only one thing had been different...

Everything she had ever done had pointed her to this moment in time, and given her the strengths she needed to help take down the SWTF.

With this new enlightenment, Robby Strange became not the man who had witlessly ruined their lives, but the purveyor of their destiny.

CHAPTER TWENTY-THREE

"Moreover, land has an advantage for everyone:
he who tills a field is a king." Ecclesiastes 5:9

DEACON LOOKED ACROSS the desk top at the evil, prune-faced man, and wondered just how he was going to break the news that Hans's favorite project was dead.

"Well?" Hans asked after it had been too long. He put an inhaler up to his mouth and took a deep, wheezing breath.

He looked worse than usual, so maybe he already knew.

"Get on with it, Deacon. I'm a busy..." another breath from the inhaler, "...a busy man."

Deacon decided to just spit it out. After all, maybe the old fuck would have a cardiac and die—hopefully in pain.

"Brawn is dead."

The old man's head jerked around and he stared at Deacon with his cold blue eyes. He was a tired, fragile, wizened up old man, but when he looked at Deacon like that, Deacon's blood ran cold and the hair stood up on the back of his neck. This fucker was just plain wicked.

"What!" Hans shouted with a quiver in his voice.

"He's dead," Deacon said matter-of-factly.

"Did you capture the others?" he asked, all emotion now vacant from his voice.

"No, sir, and they got the DA, too." Deacon only kept the smile from his face with an effort. "She'd uncovered a lot. Apparently Denisten was able to access files through the FBI and he down-loaded them to Carrie Long. What they don't already know they can get from Doctor Grant. At this point they no doubt know more than I know about the project."

Hans looked thoughtful. "How did he die? Was it the black one?"

"No, Sir," Deacon couldn't quite keep the smug grin off his face. "He was most probably killed by the Oriental."

Deacon watched the old man's face with bated breath. His super-hybrid son had been killed by a normal human. The old man's face contorted in rage. He glared at Deacon, and Deacon looked down at his own feet.

"So, what are you going to do now, Deacon?" he hissed.

"Excuse me, Sir?" Deacon didn't understand the question.

Hans got slowly out of his chair, and stood up behind his desk. His every movement was a lesson in pain. He put his fists on the desk and turned slowly to face Deacon, and now Deacon had to look at him.

"It's your job to take care of security, Deacon!" His voice shook in anger. "You incompetent fools! We did all the work. All you had to do was take care of security, and you screwed it up. We were so close, and now...The whole project is in jeopardy because of you American idiots."

For some reason Deacon just didn't feel like taking his shit today. "With all due respect, Sir. They killed Brawn. Brawn who was in every way superior to any of us. If Brawn couldn't stop them, what makes you think we could?"

"Get out of my office! Get out!" Hans hissed.

Deacon left. He didn't slam the door, but he did in his mind. His comlink buzzed and he answered it. "Hello, Deacon here."

"Deacon, this is Franklin. Get over to my office right away."

Deacon took a deep breath. Franklin was further up the food chain than Hans. He didn't know what to expect, but he didn't like it.

FRANKLIN'S SECRETARY WAVED him right into the office.

Franklin looked up at him.

Deacon couldn't read his face.

"Just talk to Hans?"

"Yes, sir."

"Sit down, Deacon," Franklin said.

Deacon nodded and sat down.

"How'd the old fuck take it?" Franklin asked.

Deacon shrugged. "He was angry. I think he's basically incapable of any emotion as complex as grief."

"Deacon ole boy, word just came down from the top. We're going to put an end to the project."

HAVING BEEN TOLD what she needed, Spider had gone to bed and stayed there, getting up only to use the bathroom and eat a light meal, the rest of the time she slept a deep, dreamless sleep.

They had given up on trying to get the comlink to work as a computer.

To pass the time, Tommy was teaching Robby and Mark Jujitsu. When they weren't doing that, Robby and Tommy were hunting or working in the garden.

Francis was still gathering rocks and laying them out on the ground in the clearing in a strange formation. When Mark couldn't find anything better to do he helped her.

Laura had started talking and as far as Carrie could tell she hadn't stopped except to sleep or eat since she had arrived. Apparently she had really been starved for female companionship, and hadn't found it in either Spider or the weirdo scientist chick.

Carrie was usually a very attentive listener, but today as she helped Laura hang out some laundry they had beat on rocks down at the creek, her mind was on more important matters. However she did realize that Laura had asked her a question.

"I'm sorry, what?"

"Where the hell were you?" Laura asked with a laugh. "I asked if you ever thought in a million years that you'd be going back to the stone age."

"No, I didn't," Carrie said. She was still far away from thoughts of laundry.

"OK. What is it?" Laura asked.

"I left instructions with George to post the files on the internet if I came up missing for more than a month. It's been a week and a half, already. Spider's still sleeping most of the time, Robby and Tommy are off playing martial arts, and no one's come up with a plan of action yet," Carrie said.

"We're all waiting for Spider, Carrie. After all, Spider's the only one who's ever really done anything like this before."

"You don't understand, Laura. We're running out of time. If George posts the information on the net before we have a chance to do whatever-the-hell it is that we are going to do, then…well, we're running out of time, that's all."

"If the information got out to everyone, then they'd have to stop the SWTF," Laura said. She really didn't understand the problem.

"And what about the hybrids? There are hundreds of them, Laura. What about the general public? Hell, how do we know they won't go nuts and decide to make war with the aliens? As of this date, the aliens haven't shown any signs of being hostile. They're experimenting on us, but then so is our own fucking government. Who knows what kinds of weapons they might have, or if they themselves are weapons?"

"People have wondered for years whether there was extraterrestrial life. Now we know there is. I think people will be happy to know that," Laura assured her.

"Just like the Spaniards were happy to find out there were people living here in the 'New World?' Humans don't have a very good track record, Laura. We have a history of discovering strange and beautiful cultures and destroying them. The masses will hate the aliens, and they'll hate the hybrids all the more because part of them are us. And no one wants to know that there is someone out there who can download every sin they've ever committed." Carrie looked at Laura. "We've got to do something before George puts the information on the web. At the time, I thought it was the perfect stopgap measure. After all, it was what Spider had instructed Tommy to have his friend do with it in the first place. If Tommy hadn't had him give it to me instead…the more I think about it the more I believe that what the SWTF has done will seem like a cakewalk next to what the general public will do. We're talking mass hysteria. At which point we can all kiss any chance we have of going back to anything approaching a normal life goodbye."

Tommy and Robby walked over then. Robby looked right at Carrie. "What's wrong?"

Carrie explained what she had been telling Laura. "I need to make contact with George."

"OK. But let's not bother Spider. We'll drive to Weston. That's about a hundred and fifty miles from here. That should keep them off us. You can call George from there," Tommy said.

"What if they have his phone tapped?" Robby asked.

"They no doubt do." Carrie was thoughtful. "I'll just have to be careful how I word things."

"Who will go?" Laura asked.

"Me and Robby and Carrie," Tommy said.

"What if they find us here?" Laura said. "Spider wouldn't be much help right now."

"Mark…" Robby started.

"He's a boy. You can't expect him to stop an army." It was Carrie who said it.

"They're not going to find this camp," Tommy assured them.

"I don't think we better count on that," Carrie said.

"I could go with Carrie and you could stay here, Tommy," Robby suggested.

Tommy nodded. He didn't like being left behind, but Robby could handle anything they threw at him. Realistically, Tommy knew that he couldn't—especially not their pet hybrids.

"OK. You leave tomorrow morning. After Spider eats her breakfast, she'll go back to bed, and while she's sleeping you guys take off. You should be back long before she wakes up for dinner."

CARRIE HADN'T REMEMBERED the hike being so long, but then all she had been worried about was getting to Spider. They took the trail at a fast jog. Carrie was not in as good shape as Robby was. She was about to pass out, and he wasn't even winded.

"Hold up there, Rob." She stopped and leaned against a tree.

Robby came back up the trail to meet her.

"You OK?" he asked.

"You're trying to kill me!" Carrie panted out. "I've got to take a break." She scooted down the tree and sat on the ground at its base. Then she took her canteen from her shoulder and took a long drink.

"But if we're not back before Spider gets up, she's going to…"

"The rest of you are a lot more worried about her being pissed off than I am. I've incurred her wrath before, and lived. Believe me, its just not all that bad."

"You love her a lot, don't you?" Robby said, leaning on the same tree she was sitting against.

"Yes, I do," Carrie said.

"Even though she's an alien?" Robby said.

Carrie thought about it a moment. "I love Spider. She's a hybrid, so maybe I love her because she's an alien." Carrie shrugged. "Why do you ask?"

"I'm in love with a woman. I hope it won't matter to her, either, but I can't be sure. Of course, who knows whether I'll ever see her again?"

"You will." Carrie got up and patted him on the back. "Come on, let's get going. I'm not really afraid of pissing her off, but I'd rather not worry her if I can keep from it."

GEORGE LOOKED ACROSS his...Carrie's desk at Deacon. It was the third time he'd been there that week.

"Well?" Deacon asked expectantly.

"How many times do I have to tell you, Mr. Deacon? Carrie didn't tell me where she was going. Why, she didn't even tell her parents."

"She met Spider Webb somewhere?"

"I wouldn't know if that was true. As far as I know Carrie had no idea where Spider was. In fact, I got the impression that the only ones with information about her whereabouts were you guys. To tell the truth, most of us think you guys nabbed her, and that you're just asking us where she is to throw the scent off you."

Deacon looked at a spot somewhere behind George. When he looked back at George his expression was hard to read. He may have been angry or worried or just plain tired. "Mr. Parker, if Carrie Long gets in touch with you, will you give her my message?"

"I've got it written down right here," George said. "Although I'm sure she'll find it as cryptic as I do."

Deacon got up. "Just do it, Georgie boy."

George watched him go. He was always glad to see the back of Deacon.

Every day he did this job he respected Carrie a little more. Being DA was a tough job under the best of circumstances. A job, quite frankly, that he had never wanted. He was more than happy to be assistant DA. DA carried with it too much stress and responsibility. Add to that Deacon sticking his head in the door every other day, and it was too damn much. He wondered how the hell Carrie had done it.

The phone rang and he jumped. He answered it quickly. "Acting DA Parker."

"George," Carrie laughed. "You sound like someone just walked over your grave."

"Carrie!" he whispered. "Are you all right?"

"We're all good. Listen carefully. What I told you to do? Don't do it. Understand?"

"Yes, but why?"

"Just don't. I've got to go now…"

"No! Not yet. Deacon has been here; he left a message."

"Quick," Carrie said. They could trace a call immediately now, and she wanted to get as far away from the phone as fast as she could on the off chance that the SWTF had men in Weston.

"He said to tell Spider Webb that they want to make a deal. That she holds all the cards and they're ready to play the game her way."

"I'll give her the message. Be careful, George."

SPIDER STARED DOWN at her squirrel stew. She was still wondering how mad she should be. She was feeling better. In fact, her mind was clear for the first time since the tranq-dart had hit her. She could feel the emotions of those around her again and felt less like a raw nerve.

"What's he mean?" Tommy asked. "What kind of deal does he want to make?"

"That's a good question," Spider said thoughtfully. She drew in a deep breath and it didn't hurt. She wasn't sure, but she thought she was completely healed. It was funny because she hadn't really felt any better when she lay down that morning.

"It's obviously a trap," Carrie said. "A pretty lame one if you ask me."

"Not necessarily," Francis said from her place in the corner. They looked at her expectantly, and she shrugged. "The science corps and the security corps are often at odds were policy is concerned."

"Like we're ever listening to her," Tommy said.

"She's not trying anything," Spider said matter-of-factly. She whispered in Tommy's general direction. "I really wasn't sure what I was doing when I was sick. Apparently I pushed her too much, and something in her brain snapped. She's not capable of lying anymore." She lowered her voice a little more. "She's not all there."

"I heard that," Francis said.

"See? I told you that playing with people's brains would make them snap," Carrie told Spider scoldingly.

Spider looked at her and smiled. Suddenly Carrie looked good. Real good. Spider realized her libido was back—a sure sign that she was healed.

Carrie recognized the look in Spider's eyes and smiled seductively back at her, forgetting all about what they were talking about.

"Let's…ah," Spider got to her feet. "Let's go for a walk."

Carrie nodded excitedly, got up and beat her to the door. Mark got up and ran over.

"Me too," he said.

Spider messed his hair up, and then putting her hand on the top of his head pushed him back. "Not this time, sport. You, ah…have to finish your dinner."

He grumbled as he went back to his seat.

Spider took Carrie's hand and they practically ran out the door.

"It's a miracle! It's a miracle! She's healed!" Tommy said waving his arms in the air like a fire and brimstone Baptist preacher on a Sunday morning.

"I don't see why I couldn't go," Mark grumbled.

"Because they're going diving," Robby laughed.

Laura glared at Robby, and then turned to Mark.

"Just eat your dinner," Laura said.

Mark nodded. "It's hard. I feel sorry for the squirrel," he mumbled as he picked at it.

"Don't think about it," Robby said. Then seeing the expression on Mark's face change, he shoved Mark on the shoulder so hard he almost fell off his chair.

"Don't do that!" Robby ordered him.

"Robby! What the hell was that all about?" Laura protested.

"He's a fucking little perv, that's what." Robby smacked Mark again for good measure.

"Ouch," Mark protested rubbing at his shoulder.

"Quit hitting him," Laura ordered.

"Well, make him stop," Robby ordered her.

"He's not doing anything," Laura said shrugging.

She looked at Tommy, who was laughing like a big idiot. "Tommy?"

"There not going on a walk," Mark said making a face. "They're having sex."

"See? He's a fucking little pervert," Robby said.

"I didn't know what she was doing!" Mark protested.

"What the hell is going on?" Laura demanded. Then, as Mark opened his mouth to speak she held up her hand. "On second thought, I don't want to know. Robby's right. You should stay out of her head. It's a private thing between adults."

Mark nodded silently.

"What about this shit with Deacon?" Robby asked, successfully changing the subject.

Tommy shrugged. "I don't know. We can't trust these guys. At the same time, if we don't do something we're going to be stuck running for the rest of our lives. If we wait too long, they're going to have time to repair all the damage you did. As Spider pointed out at dinner yesterday, we don't want to wait around till they can re-arm and prepare themselves. But what kind of an attack do we make, where do we strike, and at who?"

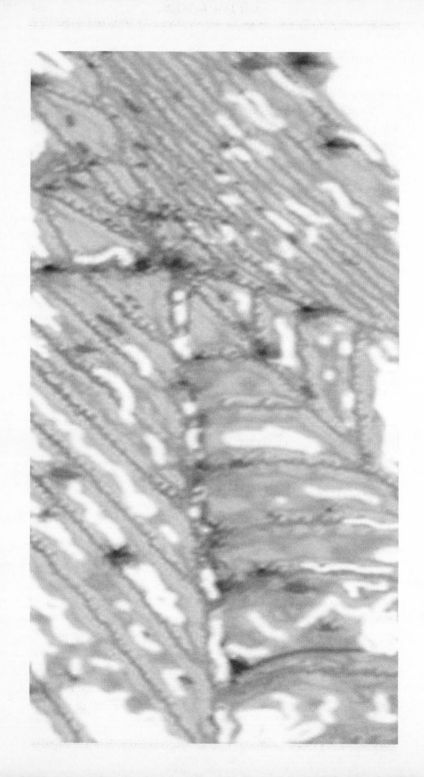

CHAPTER TWENTY-FOUR

"Do not say, How was it that the former days were better than these? for thou does not inquire wisely concerning this." Ecclesiastes 7:10

DEACON STEPPED INTO his apartment. He didn't know who he expected to see when he flipped on the lights—the cat maybe, or the dog. He sure as hell didn't expect to see her.

She sat in his favorite chair with the gun he kept hidden between his mattress and box springs in her left hand. He supposed that she just wanted to make sure he knew she'd picked up all his spare weapons.

"Hands up, Deacon," Spider Webb hissed.

Tommy Chan stepped out of the shadows and started patting him down. Chan found his main piece, the one on his leg, and the one in his pocket. He even found the knife in his belt buckle. Tommy yanked his suit coat off him, then unbuttoned his pants and pulled them down around his ankles.

"Hey!" Deacon protested. He started to pull his pants up, but when he heard a gun cock he stood up slowly, raising his hands again and looking at Spider Webb.

"We're not taking any chances. Ever try to make a break for it with your pants around your ankles?"

"He's clean," Tommy announced unloading the guns. He threw the guns on the floor and pocketed the ammo.

Deacon took a deep breath. They really *weren't* taking any chances.

Chan joined Webb, standing at her shoulder. "Tell us about this deal, Deacon, and don't jack with me. Lying to me is just an exercise in futility, and you know it."

Deacon felt the push in his brain, and then in spite of himself, he was spilling his guts—telling her everything.

When he was done she stood up. She was taller than he remembered. "OK, Deacon. We'll think it over, and then we'll get back to you. Tell your superiors that if they try to fuck us...just tell them not to try."

Deacon nodded. He watched them as they headed for his door. Chan turned as he was leaving and pulled a face. "Pull up your pants, man."

He didn't do it till they were out the door. Then he flopped down in his chair and looked at his trembling hands. He didn't even want to think about what might or might not happen next.

"WELL?" CARRIE ASKED Spider and Tommy as they slid into the car.

"I don't think we can afford to say no," Spider said. She motioned and Carrie put the car in gear and took off.

"So what next?" Robby asked.

"We do what we came here to do," Spider said.

"But I thought you said we were going to take them up on their deal," Robby said.

"This is part of the deal," Spider said.

Robby looked longingly at the diner as they drove by.

"It won't be long now, Robby," Spider promised.

"Or will never be again," Robby said.

Tommy shared Robby's pessimism. When they'd left the camp yesterday he had promised Laura that he would come home in one piece, but it was an idle promise. One that he couldn't be sure he could live up to, and Laura had known it just as well as he did.

The boy had raised hell. Mark didn't see why Carrie was going and he couldn't. What he didn't know was that Carrie had insisted, and the only way they could have left her behind was if they tied her up. She was convinced that she could help if only by driving the 'goddamn car,' and she wouldn't take no for an answer.

The SWTF building loomed before them. Spider looked over the schematic of the building that Francis had made for them.

"How can we trust something Francis drew?" Tommy asked.

"I told you. She's not dark anymore," Robby snapped. Fear was making them all a little edgy.

"That's all fine and good, but the reason why is because Spider all but fried the bitch's brain doing whatever the hell it is that she does," Tommy said.

"It matches up with what Robby and I know about the building, and she still seems to have retained all of her scientific knowledge. She's just become a little eccentric," Spider said.

"I can't believe we're putting our lives in the hands of the SWTF screws and Francis, for God's sake! She plays with rocks all day!" Tommy said. The closer they got to the building the less this sounded like a good, sound plan.

"Well?" Carrie asked, looking at Spider.

Spider looked at the gate—now less than a block in front of them. She looked back at Carrie. No doubt about it, the decision would be a whole lot easier if Carrie wasn't with them. She'd be a lot more willing to take wild chances, and she realized now that was exactly why Carrie had insisted on coming along.

"Let's do it."

The guard at the front gate saw the car coming, but wasn't alarmed until he saw it speed up. He hit his comlink.

"I think we got trou…"

A ball of fire hit the barrier, and the steel gate splintered into pieces. The guard hit the ground and rolled out of the way as the car ran through the now empty gateway.

"Oh God! They're back, man!" the guard screamed into his comlink. "They're fucking back!" He scrambled to his feet and took off running through the empty gateway and down the sidewalk away from the building. No job—no matter how good the pay and bennies were—was worth dying for.

As Carrie slammed the car to a stop in front of the main door, she began to wish she hadn't insisted on coming. The guards at the front door opened fire on them, and she instinctively ducked into the floorboards. The next thing she knew, the guns were silent and the putrid smell of burning human flesh hung heavy in the air. There was no going back now.

"Go! Go!"

She heard Spider scream. Finally, Carrie realized the command was for her—Spider and the others were already out of the car. Carrie took off as ordered, and two SWTF cars came around the back of the building and started in pursuit. She watched in the rear-view mirror as first one and then the other exploded into flames. She would go to the meeting place, wait, and pray. That's all she could do now.

ROBBY STARTED BLOWING up cars. It was almost too easy for him, what with a nice catalyst like gasoline to help him out.

A line of gunmen in protective suits met them just inside the front doors.

"Robby, the guns!" Spider ordered as she and Tommy fired on them.

Robby hit the guns the men held, and they blew up in their hands. The shrapnel ripped into them, burning them and cutting them to pieces.

Spider looked at Robby and made a face. "Yuk!"

Robby just shrugged.

The next wall of men they encountered weren't carrying weapons, so apparently they were capable of learning. There were at least twenty of them running as fast as they could. The three of them turned to run in the other direction and found another troop of suited men. Robby took out the ceiling above them, but that also blocked their exit, and the others were now on top of them.

Tommy kicked one of them in the head and he fell like a rock. He started moving like Bruce Lee on speed. He was a one-man killing machine. As Spider was firing into the crowd of bodies, Robby started to take out the ceiling, and Spider slapped him.

"We've got to have some way out!" Spider screamed.

"Duh!" Robby said, feeling like an idiot. Somebody hit him in the head. It pissed him off, and he found himself automatically using the techniques Tommy had been teaching him. "Hey!" He laughed as he slung one guy into another, successfully knocking them both down. "We're kicking some ass, here!"

HANS WATCHED HIS viewscreen with disgust. "What are they doing here? Why would they come back? There is nothing for them here except…" He looked blank for a moment, and then he got on his comlink.

"Stacey! Get me Franklin. I know what they're after."

Hans waited impatiently for Franklin to appear.

Franklin stomped into his office unannounced and had the nerve to look put out.

"What do you want, Hans?" Franklin asked. "In case you hadn't noticed we're in the middle of a siege here."

"You insubordinate imbecile. I know why the Hybrids came back. I know what they are after."

Franklin smiled at him—a big shit-eating grin. "So do we, and we're going to let them have it."

"What? Are you crazy! We're so close to completion. My life's work…"

"Some people live too damn long, Hans," Franklin said. He pulled his gun out of his jacket and pointed it at the head of the world's oldest living Nazi war criminal.

"What the hell do you think that you are doing, Franklin?" "Making sure you don't get away this time, you fucking creepy old bastard." Franklin emptied the gun into Han's head, enjoying watching the bullets tear through his flesh. Han's secretary ran in and Franklin shot her, too.

He walked out of Hans's office and addressed the small group of SWTF men facing him. "It's time for us to leave this party, men. This whole mess has just become someone else's problem."

THEY WERE QUICKLY running out of adversaries.

"I don't like it," Tommy said. "It's too easy."

"That was the point, Tommy," Spider said. She looked at the schematic of the building. That was the door, all right, but no one was guarding it.

"That's it."

"It's a trap," Tommy said. "A set up."

"Then we open the door prepared, but we still open the door," Spider said. She looked at Robby, and he took a stand in the middle of the hallway looking at the door.

Tommy smiled. With Robby there, he wasn't nearly as worried about ambush.

"All right then, let's see what's behind door number one," Tommy announced. Whatever was behind that door was the main reason for their assault on this building today, but Tommy had no idea what it was.

Spider read the combination off the paper and applied it. The door opened slowly. "Let me check it out first."

Spider stepped in, gun ready, and looked around. Tommy was about to go after her when she stuck her head back out the door.

"All clear!"

Tommy followed her back in. "Holy fuck!" Tommy said looking around. He realized now why Spider hadn't been afraid of ambush. It was a giant freezer. Way too cold for anything living to exist for more than a few minutes with the door closed. There were thousands of little tubes filled with greenish looking shit with little blobs of something…He looked closely, and then jumped back. "What the hell?"

"An unstoppable army," Robby mumbled picking up one of the tubes, and then putting it back when he found it too cold to hold.

Tommy wondered who was watching the hall now. He looked out the door—it looked clear.

"What's he talking about?" Tommy asked.

"They're frozen embryos for implantation into unsuspecting women. So that they can keep doing what they've been doing for three generations now. It's got to stop here."

Robby looked shocked. He stared at her. "But these are people. People like you and me."

"No. They're just like me. Made and contrived by these idiots to be used and exploited. Each one of these embryos represents a woman that would be used and as many as dozens of people that would be killed to keep their secret. They aren't people, Robby, they're embryos, pre-people at best. They were never meant to be, and we have to stop them. The only way to do that is to destroy what these monsters have done. What they would do."

"What's to stop them from starting up all over again?" Tommy asked.

"Lack of this material. This represents decades of work, millions of dollars." She looked at Tommy. "You heard what Deacon said. It's too big a risk. Too many people have figured out what's going on. They've killed too many people trying to cover their asses. They're afraid of full disclosure. This conspiracy goes to the very heart of our government. Who knows who would burn if this ever came to full light?"

She looked at Robby appealingly. "If we leave them here, we're basically saying that what they are doing is all right. If we leave them here, then we're giving them their army, and God alone knows what they will do with it."

Robby nodded. He knew what he had to do. He watched as Spider grabbed Tommy's arm and walked with him out of the freezer. Robby hit the freezer over and over, till the whole interior was on fire.

Spider closed the door.

"What now?" Tommy asked.

"We hope the SWTF keeps their end of the bargain."

CARRIE ORDERED A cup of coffee and a burger. She didn't feel like eating, but didn't want to look too conspicuous. It was late, and the diner was mostly empty. In the distance she could hear the sirens—two or three cop cars and a few ambulances roared past. She tried to ignore them and failed.

Helen had waited on her, and it wasn't hard to see what Robby saw in her. she was a pretty little thing with a quick smile and an open, honest face.

She noticed that Helen was a little preoccupied herself.

"What's going on at the SWTF building? Do you know? Did you go by there?" she asked Carrie.

Carrie shrugged. "I wouldn't know. I'm just coming through town headed for White Springs."

A guy ran in the doors just then. "Something's going down at SWTF again. A bunch of fires and explosions, and I ain't gonna buy that it's some chemical fire this time. It's terrorists I tell you, Terrorists with a capital T." He sat down at the counter. "Gate's blown clean off this time, guys runnin' everywhere, lots of smoke and fire."

Helen screwed up Carrie's order twice. "I'm very sorry."

"It's all right," Carrie said. She would have liked to tell her that she was as nervous as she was. That her fate was also tied up in what was happening at the SWTF building. As the night wore on and her burger got cold she began to fear the worst.

Helen sat down across from her, and filled her coffee cup for the fifth time. "You OK?" she asked.

"Ah, yeah. Don't need any more coffee, though" Carrie said forcing a smile.

"Something wrong with your burger?" Helen asked.

"No it's fine. I'm just not as hungry as I thought I was."

"You waiting for somebody?"

"No. Why do you ask that?" Carrie asked.

"Why else would a classy lady like you, who's 'just going through town,' be hanging out in a dump like this at twelve thirty at night?" Helen asked.

Pretty and smart, too. Carrie smiled and looked down at the sweatshirt and jeans she was wearing, her once perfectly manicured fingernails now chipped and uneven, she could only hazard to guess what her hair must look like. "Me, classy?"

"Class isn't in the clothes someone wears, it's in their attitude. The way they carry themselves. So, who are you waiting for?"

Carrie shook her head and took a deep breath. "Some friends. I'm waiting for some friends."

Helen nodded as if she now knew everything and got up. "That's what I thought," she said and walked away.

Carrie watched the front door for what seemed like an eternity, and then there was Spider. She jumped up, ran to her, and threw her arms around her neck. "I was afraid you were dead," she whispered.

"Nah. Just a little scuffed," Spider said patting her back.

Carrie felt something hard and cylinder shaped under Spider's jacket. She put her hand on it.

"What's that?"

Spider took her hand off it. "I'll tell you later."

Helen looked at the couple and smiled. It was obvious that the newcomer had just been through some kind of battle. Helen was glad the woman's soldier had come home. She knew what it was like to wait, not knowing, and to have someone you loved disappear forever. She dried a tear from her eye, picked up a stack of dishes and headed for the kitchen.

"Helen."

Helen dropped the dishes and turned. Robby was right behind her. He grabbed her before she could grab him. His lip was bloody, his clothes were torn, his eye was bruised, and he was the most beautiful thing she had ever seen. She started kissing his whole face.

"Helen! For God's sake, girl! You're going to cost me a fortune!" Rudy screamed from the back room.

"We have to go," Robby said. "We have to go right now. Will you come with us?"

Helen nodded silently.

"Helen, damn it!" Rudy screamed. He dried his hands on his towel. "Fool girl, going to break every dish in the place. "Helen!" He stomped up to the front, ready to chew her ass out, and found the diner empty.

CHAPTER TWENTY-FIVE
Five years later

*"Behold that which I have seen: it is good and
comely for one to eat and to drink, and to enjoy
the good of all his labour in which he toils under
the sun all the days of his life, which God gives
him: for it is his portion."* Ecclesiastes 5:17

SPIDER SWIVELED IN her fancy leather chair in her huge office
atop the federal building in Shea city. She was nervous. These days
she was always nervous.

Her comlink buzzed, and she jumped. She punched the button.
"Carrie, is everything all right?"

The man on the other end laughed. "This isn't your wife, Chief.
It's Franklin. We got a little trouble with the LA job. Seems our guy
took out the wrong creep. We got another corpse today, same MO."

"Call Sever back in," Spider said. "No harm, no foul. Shame
another innocent citizen had to die, but we'll get two serial killers for
the price of one. Oh, and it looks like we got a stray in New Orleans.
Send Devlon and Thompson to pick him up and bring him in."

"You got it, Chief," Franklin said. "Oh, and Chief?"

"Yes Franklin?"

"Good luck."

"Thanks." She closed the link and the front door buzzed.

"Enter."

Deacon walked in. "Spider, it's Mark."

"Send him in," Spider said.

Mark walked in and flopped down in the chair across from
Spider. "Thpider, you hathf to do thomething," Mark lisped. "Mom
and Dad, they don't underthtand me. They keep making all thethe
thtupid ruleth. They don't underthtand what it'th like to be uth."

Spider laughed. "I don't understand you, either. In more ways
than one. Why on earth would you want to put a damn stud in your
tongue? It's the stupidest thing you've ever done, and that puts it way
up there, boy."

"Ah, they got to you," Mark pouted.

Spider smiled. "Go home, Mark. Take the stud out of your tongue and let it heal. Unlike most kids your age, you don't have to do weird shit to be an individual. And don't pick at it or it will never heal."

"But, Thpider!" Mark whined.

"But me no buts, Son. Now go home—I'm working."

"Thankth a lot," Mark said facetiously and headed for the door. "You thtill going to take me to the conthert on Thaturday?" he asked.

"If at all possible. If I can't, Deacon will take you."

"Call me when…"

"I'll call you first. Now go on."

She smiled as she watched the door close behind him. It wasn't always that easy to stay out of decisions made by his parents. She didn't always agree, but it wasn't really her place to meddle. He was their son; she was just the chicken that laid the egg.

However, she agreed with them a hundred percent on the tongue-piercing thing.

The comlink buzzed and she answered it more professionally this time. "Hello. Chief Webb, SWTF. How can I help you?"

"Spider, this is George…Carrie's water just broke. We're on the way to the hospital."

"ONE MINUTE I'M standing in court giving deliberations, and the next…" Carrie started to cry. "I didn't even know I was in labor, how stupid is that? I thought I had gas from lunch."

"It's all right, Baby," Spider assured her.

"It was embarrassing." Carrie cried harder. With the next contraction she all but broke Spider's hand.

"Breathe, Baby, breathe." Spider prompted, trying to get her hand out of Carrie's death grip.

"I'll breathe you!" Carrie cried. "This was…a bad…idea! This was…a real…ly bad…idea." After the contraction, she looked at Spider. "I've changed my mind. I don't want to have a baby. Especially not your baby. He's going to have a great huge head, and it's going to hurt."

The doctor laughed as she examined her. "It's a little late for that, Carrie. With the next contraction you can push."

"Spider," Carrie whispered.

Spider leaned down, and Carrie grabbed her by the front of her green smock. Then she started shaking her. "Look what you did to me! Look what you did!"

The Doctor had to stop herself from laughing. This was the usual fair when dealing with heterosexual couples, but you didn't expect it with a lesbian couple.

"Honey, it was your idea to have a baby," Spider reminded her gently as she removed Carrie's hands from her gown.

"I know. I know, but...Oh, my God!"

"Push," the Doctor coached. "Push."

TOMMY STOPPED A minute to look out over his ten-acre spread. He would have liked to have more land, but this was the compromise. He got to have his farm as long as Laura could still drive to work. He wiped his brow, looked up at the sun, and then started hoeing his turnips again.

He felt his life had begun on the day he quit the police force and started teaching Jujitsu to the SWTF's "new agents." He worked at the "office" three days a week and had the rest of the time to work on the place. Working with the hybrids, teaching them the disciplines of the old ways, made him feel like his life had purpose. The way he had felt about police work until he had learned that they didn't really want you to make a difference, just keep the status quo. When the agents he trained now collared a criminal they didn't live to become repeat offenders.

Laura should have been home by now. It was a forty-five minute commute one way, but she didn't seem to mind too much. She loved her job, but surprisingly she really enjoyed living in the country. She had been skeptical when Tommy had told her he was tired of police work. She had gone along with his idea of moving and working part time for SWTF, but had really thought that the new would wear off and he would miss the streets. She seemed just as happy when he didn't.

Tommy was sure he knew why Laura was late, and when the phone rang it just confirmed it. He jumped in his car and headed for the hospital.

TOMMY STOOD BESIDE Spider and looked into the plastic box at the baby boy. Spider was rattling a mile a minute. "As soon as they've checked him out he's going back to the room with Carrie."

Tommy looked at the baby's hands and then at Spider. "Spider," he said in a whisper. "This baby is yours! How the hell did that happen?"

Spider looked at him and smiled. "Would you believe I have really potent alien semen filled spit?"

"No, I wouldn't," Tommy said.

Spider shrugged; she obviously wasn't going to tell him.

"What happens when they do their little tests and find out he has alien DNA?" Tommy asked in a nervous whisper.

"That's been taken care of," Spider said

Tommy watched as the doctor came over and took the baby out of the incubator for tests. Her hands dwarfed the tiny baby. Tommy looked at Spider, and Spider smiled and shrugged. "We're everywhere, man."

ROBBY HELD THE phone receiver to his ear with his shoulder as he took a clipboard and signed a paper. He handed it back to Devan.

"I'll bet she did," Robby said. "I'm very happy for you...Just like you...Well, the poor little pecker head...No, we'll come see him when you bring him home...Yeah, I bet...I'll talk to you later."

"Who was that?" Helen asked walking up and taking his hand.

"It was Spider. Carrie had the baby. Eight pounds even, twenty-one inches long."

"Did she have any trouble?" Helen asked.

"No. Baby came natural childbirth. No meds, although Spider said *she* came close to taking a Valium."

"Daddy!" Carlos ran over and begged to be picked up. Robby picked his two-year-old son up and hugged him.

"What's wrong, Carlos?"

Carlos pointed to a man who had just walked into the shop. "Bad man, Daddy. Bad man."

Robby looked at the man and saw the darkness. He made a face and glared at the man. The man, sensing the invasion of his brain looked up at Robby.

"You there! Get out of my shop!" Robby ordered.

"I came about the help wanted ad. This is Strange Camp Furniture, Inc., isn't it?" he asked.

"The position has been filled. Get out of my shop!" Robby put just a little heat in the man's brain. The man all but ran out the door. The boy instantly wanted back down.

Robby looked at Helen. "He has the power." Robby sounded and looked worried.

"You'll show him how to use it, and he will be as good a man as his father," Helen said with a smile. She wasn't worried; and since she wasn't worried, Robby felt less anxious.

He walked over and sounded the whistle. Everyone looked at him like he was crazy. After all, it was an hour early. "Have you all forgotten? Donna's graduating tonight—she's valedictorian." So far, most of the people who worked for him were his siblings, and the ones that weren't knew what came first to Robby. Besides, they didn't mind getting off an hour early.

DONNA LOOKED OUT at the crowd, just a little afraid. Then she saw her family. She saw her brother Robby smiling at her, and she found her courage.

"Today we graduate and go on with our lives. Some of us will go to college, some of us will go to work, and some of us, unfortunately, won't do anything. I could have been one of those do-nothing people, but I'm not. My brothers and sisters could have all become bad statistics, but we didn't. The reason we didn't is my brother, Robby. Robby taught us right from wrong, and Robby gave us love and discipline. If it hadn't been for Robby we would have fallen between the cracks and rotted, but he didn't let that happen. Robby never got to have a childhood because he had to take care of us, but he never made us feel guilty. He picked us up when we fell and gave us pep talks when we needed them. More than that, Robby told me I could be anything I wanted to be. He told me that I could soar with the eagles. I didn't have a mother or a father, but I had Robby. I wish everyone could have someone like Robby. I thank the school and my teachers for helping me out and bringing me this far, but mostly I have to thank him. I love you, Robby."

Robby looked up at her and smiled the biggest smile that he could find for her. He wiped the tears from his eyes with the back of his hand.

Carlos, who sat on his lap leaned up and whispered in his ear, "Donna is very good."

FRANCIS LAID THE rock upon the ground, and then she stood back and looked. She smiled at all that she had done.

"Finally, it's finished."

When she'd asked to be allowed to live in the woods at the camp, they had been more than willing to abandon her there. She kept a garden and fished and lived a simple but pleasant life. Occasionally Spider or the boy brought her extra supplies.

Francis sat on a rock at the edge of the clearing and waited. She didn't know how long she sat there, but it was dark, and she was just about to doze off when a bright light appeared in the sky. She watched as the ship slowly descended. It was much bigger than she had thought it would be, and she had to get up and run further into the woods to keep from being pelted with dust particles. The noise was deafening, and then all was still, and the ship rested in the field. When it was quiet, she walked back over to the ship.

One of the beings materialized right in front of her. It spoke to her in labored English, obviously something it had learned, not something it knew simply 'because.'

"What is it that you want?" the visitor asked.

"I just wanted to apologize for meddling, and to tell you that now everything is going according to your plans."

The End

BIOGRAPHY

Selina Rosen lives in rural Arkansas with her partner, her parrot, Ricky, assorted fish and fowl—both inside and out, several milk goats, an undetermined number of barn cats and her dog, Spud. Besides writing, editing, and taking care of the farm, she's a gardener, carpenter, rock mason, electrician (NOT a plumber), *Torah* scholar and sword fighter. In her spare time she creates water gardens, builds furniture, and adds to her on-going creation of the "Great Wall of Kibler."

Selina's short fiction has appeared in several magazines and anthologies including *Sword and Sorceress 16*, *Such A Pretty Face*, *Distant Journeys*, three of the MZB Fantasy Mags, *Tooth and Claw*, *Turn the Other Chick*, and the new *Anthology At the End of the Universe*, just to name a few. Her critically acclaimed story entitled "Ritual Evolution" appeared in the first of the new *Thieves World* anthologies, *Turning Points*, and her second *TW* story, "Gathering Strength," appeared in the new *TW* anthology, *Enemies of Fortune*. *The Bubba Chronicles* is a collection of her short fiction which features—strangely enough—bubbas.

Her novels include *Queen of Denial*, *Recycled*, *Chains of Freedom*, *Chains of Destruction*, *The Host* trilogy, *Fire & Ice*, *Hammer Town*, *Reruns*, and novellas entitled *The Boatman* and *Material Things*.

Bad Lands, a gonzo-mystery novel co-written with Laura J. Underwood, is due out from Five Star Mysteries in 2007.

In her capacity as owner and editor-in-chief of Yard Dog Press, Ms. Rosen has edited several anthologies, including the award-winning *Bubbas of the Apocalypse*, and *The Four Bubbas of the Apocalypse: Flatulence, Halitosis, Incest and…Ned*, and two collections of "modern" fairy tales—the Stoker-nominated *Stories That Won't Make Your Parents Hurl* and *More Stories That Won't Make Your Parents Hurl*.